RUTH LOGAN HERNE

Yuletide Hearts
&
Mended Hearts

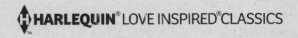
HARLEQUIN® LOVE INSPIRED®CLASSICS

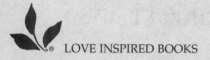 LOVE INSPIRED BOOKS

Recycling programs for this product may not exist in your area.

ISBN-13: 978-0-373-20864-7

Yuletide Hearts & Mended Hearts

Copyright © 2017 by Harlequin Books S.A.

The publisher acknowledges the copyright holder of the individual works as follows:

Yuletide Hearts
Copyright © 2011 by Ruth M. Blodgett

Mended Hearts
Copyright © 2011 by Ruth M. Blodgett

www.Harlequin.com

Printed in U.S.A.

CONTENTS

Multipublished, bestselling author **Ruth Logan Herne** loves God, her country, her family, dogs, chocolate and coffee! Married to a very patient man, she lives in an old farmhouse in upstate New York and thinks possums should leave the cat food alone and snakes should always live outside. There are no exceptions to either rule! Visit Ruth at ruthloganherne.com.

Books by Ruth Logan Herne

Love Inspired

Grace Haven

An Unexpected Groom
Her Unexpected Family
Their Surprise Daddy

Kirkwood Lake

The Lawman's Second Chance
Falling for the Lawman
The Lawman's Holiday Wish
Loving the Lawman
Her Holiday Family
Healing the Lawman's Heart

Men of Allegany County

Small-Town Hearts
Mended Hearts
Yuletide Hearts
A Family to Cherish
His Mistletoe Family

Visit the Author Profile page at Harlequin.com for more titles.

YULETIDE HEARTS

My son, if your heart is wise, then my heart will be glad; my inmost being will rejoice when your lips speak what is right.
—*Proverbs* 23:15–16

This book is dedicated to my mother-in-law, Theresa Elizabeth Blodgett, a woman who has never been afraid to put her hand to any task, large or small. Her strength and devotion are a constant inspiration to me. She's one of those gals who could have settled the West single-handedly and would have coffee waiting for the crew at day's end. Merry Christmas, Mom!

Acknowledgments

Big thanks to Bob Dean of Dean Remodeling in Hilton, New York, known affectionately as "Bob the Builder." Bob's advice on construction and his dedication to a job well done helped lay the foundation for Cobbled Creek. Huge thanks to Karen and Don Ash of the Angelica Sweet Shop and The Black-Eyed Susan Café in Angelica, New York, for getting behind this project. You guys are truly amazing! Hugs and gratitude to Major Tony Giusti and his lovely wife, Debby (my Seekerville sister), for their sage advice on military basics. I'm spoiled to call so many experts "friends."

To Beth for finding silly mistakes…and there were several! To Mandy for being my right-hand gal on road trips and for giving me a namesake. I love both! To Jon, who has taken on stove and refrigerator duty. You rock! To Stacey and Lisa for the spontaneous gifts of coffee; you have no idea how that spurs me to work into the night. Thank you! Hugs and thanks to Kyle and Casey Kenyon. I don't know what I'd do without you guys. And always to Dave, whose work ethic inspires my own: thanks for the sandwiches. And the coffee, dude. And for being there, night and day.

Chapter One

Complete and utter desolation.

Peering through a driving November downpour caused by remnants of Hurricane Karl, Matt Cavanaugh surveyed what might be the biggest mistake he ever made as sheeting water sluiced from unprotected roofs. Wind-driven storm rains pummeled gaping window openings. Expensive, irreplaceable topsoil washed down unprotected berms, each muddy water trail sweeping centuries of rich, organic soil into the watershed.

Basically he was watching a large share of his life savings wash away. What had he been thinking?

"I see merit here, son."

The memory of his grandfather's reassuring voice eased the tension snaking Matt's back, crowding his neck. Simple words from a gentle man, an industrious construction worker unafraid to lift a hand to any task, great or small, including the gift of unconditional love to his bad-boy grandson.

Matt clenched his jaw, then realized that would only fuel headache potential. Surveying the muddy mess he'd just purchased with significant help from the bank, he fought the urge to run hard, fast and long when a banging screen door drew his attention to the left.

A boy raced out of the faded farmhouse facing the neglected subdivision. A dog chased after him, a black-and-white spitfire, his non-pedigreed look perfect for the place and the boy, a pair of mutts enjoying the tempest.

Within seconds they were soaked, the rain blurring their features, but the combined excitement apparent even from this distance.

The boy aimed for the uncompleted subdivision, the dog racing alongside. Too late, Matt realized their intent.

The kid dived through a window opening.

The dog followed.

The kid emerged from a door opening.

So did the mutt.

Then back in another window, a little higher this time, the crazy game of follow the leader probably not the smartest of ideas for a kid and a dog around a construction site. Matt left his truck at the now-unnecessary roadblock and raced downhill. "Hey! Hey, you! Kid. Stop."

Visions of leftover two-by-fours, nails, screws and abandoned tools raced through his head, the innocence of youth unfettered by the hazards of life. As the new owner, Matt didn't have the luxury of relaxation. Construction insurance rates skyrocketed with a claim, and the kid and the dog were a hospital visit waiting to happen. "Kid. Stop! Now!"

The driving rain swallowed his voice and the thickening mud did a similar number on his feet. The dress shoes he put on for the bank closing weren't meant for tromping around construction sites.

He lost visual of the quick-paced pair as he neared the skeletal houses, his descent and the rising rooflines blocking his line of sight. He wasn't sure if the storm made it impossible to hear the kid and the dog or if they were just unusually quiet. Since unusually quiet might mean unconscious, Matt increased his pace. "Kid! You hear me? Come out of there!"

No answer.

Matt continued along the road, mud-slicked shoes slowing his progress. The graveled areas would have been inconsequential in his boots. In worn dress shoes, the rough curves and sharp points of stone reminded him that if new shoes hadn't been on the list before, they'd gain a spot now, and all because some fool didn't have sense enough to keep their kid out of harm's way.

Kind of like his mother.

He refused to flinch at the memory. His mother was no June Cleaver, but he hadn't been a choirboy, either. He had the juvie record to prove his stupidity before Grandpa Gus realigned him with old-fashioned hard work, faith and fishing.

A movement drew his attention left. He darted between two incomplete houses, saw the kid about a house-and-a-half away, yelled again and took off in pursuit. The boy appeared fairly savvy about dodging among the half-built homes, so Matt ducked through a window and raced across the subflooring to the front door of the house, burst through and collared the kid just as he angled toward the house Matt had cut through.

"Hey! Hey! Let go! Let me go!"

"Not until we've had a few words, kid."

"Let me go! Let me go!"

Matt held tight.

The dog raced into the fray, tail wagging, obviously unconcerned about his young owner's welfare.

"Jake? Jake? Where are you?"

The dog's tail flagged faster. He dashed to the front door of the house, barked a welcome, then raced back, his gaze expectant, his angled doggie look wondering what was going on.

Which reflected Matt's feelings to a tee.

A disheveled woman strode through the nonexistent front door, her hair a mess, her shoes not quite as bad as Matt's, her jeans rain-spattered, her fleece pullover soaked.

"In here, Mom! Someone's got me!"

"Someone's got you all right." Matt sent the kid a look meant to quell and refused to relinquish his grasp, despite the fire-breathing mother striding his way. Her purposeful gait seemed militaristic even though she wore somewhat impressive heeled boots, which meant she'd most likely served at some point in time. If that assumption proved true, she should know enough to keep her kid where he belonged. He raised his chin, noted she almost matched him in height with the shoes on, met her glare and stood his ground, refusing to scowl, letting his stance make his point. "This your kid?"

"Let him go."

Matt ignored the command. "Do you have any idea how dangerous it is to have a kid running around a construction site? The things that could happen to him?"

The woman's gaze returned his look, one on one. "I'm well aware, thank you very much, although Jake knows his way around construction sites. Usually." She leveled a tough, knowing look to the kid, shoulders back, feet braced, her posture adding evidence to Matt's guess that she'd been in the military at one time. "Were you supposed to leave the house?"

"N-no."

"And what if something happened to The General?"

The General? Matt frowned, followed her glance to the dog and realized it must be the dog's name.

The boy snorted, a pretty gutsy act for a kid being collared by an absolute stranger while his mother reamed him out from a few feet away. "The General knows all the enemy hideouts. He's trained to sniff out snipers and UXBs."

"UXBs?"

The woman kept her gaze on the boy, her profile taut, worry lines marring a perfect forehead over sea-green eyes. Light brown hair fell to her shoulders, a side clip meant to keep the bulk of it out of her face, but the storm had outmaneuvered the clip's potential. She shoved the errant hair back, obviously irked. "Unexploded bombs. London. The Luftwaffe."

"I get the war reference." Matt switched his gaze from her to the kid as he released the boy's collar. "What I don't get is how *he* gets it. You're what? Seven? Eight?"

"Almost nine."

"Which means eight."

The kid's glare matched his mother's, obviously a genetic trait. "You can't play around these houses. It's off-limits," Matt told him, his voice stern. He turned his attention to the woman, realizing she was probably chilled through, the November day wretchedly wet and cool. "You'll keep him out of here?"

"Yes." Something in her look told Matt she didn't say things lightly. That quality reassured him. She turned and hooked her thumb toward the door. "Jake, let's go. The banker's got better things to do than chase you around where you don't belong."

Her words registered as she neared the door, the kid following, head down, chin thrust out, forehead furrowed. "I'm not a banker." Matt strode forward and yanked down a bill of foreclosure notice attached to the front window. "I'm the new owner."

Her head jerked up. She stared at him, then the house, then him again, utter disappointment painting her features. Wet, bedraggled, rumpled, cold and wickedly disappointed.

Her look grabbed a piece of him, the air of disillusionment needing comfort and joy, but at the moment, confronted with the enormity of what he'd undertaken less than two hours ago, Matt's personal comfort level had nose-dived into incredulity.

"Seek and ye shall find. Knock, and the door will be opened, son."

Gus's wisdom reminded Matt that he wasn't in this alone, that despite Gus's death while Matt served in the desert sands of Iraq, he'd never be alone again, not in spirit anyway.

"You bought this house?"

The reality of the recent transaction tightened his neck, his look. "I bought the subdivision."

"All of it?" The kid's air reflected his mother's again, a shadowed starkness making Matt feel like a crusty headmaster, cold, cruel and crotchety.

The cold part was accurate, his wet clothes and the brisk wind a chilling reminder of what was to come. He met the kid's eyes and nodded. "All of it. Yes."

"But, Mom—"

"Stop, Jake. It's all right."

"But—"

"I said stop."

The kid's baffled look made Matt feel like scum, but why? Why should it matter if…

"You bought Cobbled Creek?"

A new voice entered the fray.

Matt swung around.

Three older men stood at the back door opening, backs straight, heads up, their posture definitely not at ease.

Military men, despite the paunch of one and the silver hair of another.

The man in the middle stepped forward, drew a breath and extended a hand. "I'm Hank Marek."

The name sent a warning bell of empathy. Hank Marek of Marek Home Builders, the now-defunct contractor that started this project over two years ago.

Matt wasn't a sympathetic person by nature. He'd hard-scrabbled his way up the ladder of success despite illegitimate beginnings followed by a fairly miserable upbringing, but coming face to face with the man who lost his dream so that Matt could have his, well…

He hauled in a breath and accepted Hank's hand. "Matt Cavanaugh of Cavanaugh Construction."

The older man's face revealed nothing of what he must be feeling inside, the loss of his work, his livelihood, his well-designed subdivision the victim of overextended loans and the burst of the housing bubble.

The other men stepped forward, concerned.

Hank moved back, nodded and directed a look beyond Matt to the woman and boy. "There's stew just about ready and the temperature's supposed to dip lower tonight before coming back up tomorrow. Jake, can you help me fire up the woodstove?"

The boy scowled Matt's way, scuffed a toe, huffed a

sigh, then trudged past Matt, the dog trailing behind, their mutual postures voicing silent displeasure.

"Callie? I'll see you at home?"

"I'm on my way, Dad." She pivoted, her mud-slicked heel tipping the move.

Matt started to lean forward to stop her fall, but she managed to right herself despite the wet floor and the mud. High, flat, wedged heels marked her departure with a tap, tap, tap as she hung a right turn at the door. She strode up the drive to her car, the soaking rain deepening the pathos of an already melodramatic situation.

Matt watched her go, then headed to the back door opening. The older men and the boy trudged in measured steps across the banked field, faded flag stakes symbolizing the wear and tear of waiting through too many seasons of sun, wind, snow and rain.

Matt watched their progress, his brain working overtime, the reality hitting him.

Hank Marek lived alongside the subdivision he had tried to create in the beautiful hillside setting, the curving road nestling the homes in the ascending crook of the Allegheny foothills.

It was that eye for setting that drew Matt to the initial showing, then the ensuing auction, his appreciation for the timeless, reasonably priced and aesthetically pleasing housing, a plan that not only fit the terrain but added to it, a rarity.

But he had no idea Hank lived in the quaint, small farmhouse on the main road, just steps away from the sign labeling Cobbled Creek a community of fine, affordable homes.

He pinched the bridge of his nose, muttered a prayer that combined a plea for understanding and a silent la-

ment that he might be following the foolish imprint of
the older man's footsteps, and headed to his truck, the
cold, soaking rain a reminder that winter loomed, and
he had an amazing amount of work to do in a very limited time frame.

Which was probably something he should have
thought a little more about before papers were signed
and money exchanged, but the delayed closing was the
bank's fault, not his. Matt understood the time constraints
he faced, but God had guided him this far. Someway,
somehow, they'd get these sweet homes battened down
for the winter.

As he crested the rise to his truck, the woman's car
backed toward the roadway, a wise decision on her part.
Mud-slicked shoulders weren't to be trusted in these conditions, and when she curved the car expertly onto the
road, then proceeded to the farmhouse beyond, he recognized the meaning behind Hank Marek's words.

The woman and the kid probably hated him for who
he was and what he'd done. On top of that, they appeared
to live across the street from where he would take over
Hank's dream because he was lucky enough to be in the
right place at the right time.

The hinted headache surged into full-blown reality,
a niggling condition spawned from a really nasty con-
cussion while fighting in Iraq, a grenade explosion too
close for comfort. But if occasional bad headaches were
his worst complaint after a double tour in the desert, he
really had no complaints at all.

Dad's dream is gone.
Callie steered the car into the drive, angled it between
the catalpa tree and Tom Baldwin's classic Chevy, then

headed inside, determined to put on a happy face despite what just happened. The smell of Dad's stew reminded her of how often her father had been there for her, supportive, honest, caring and nonjudgmental.

Returning that respect was imperative now.

The men trouped in, their footsteps heavy on the back porch. Callie pulled out a loaf of fresh-baked Vienna bread crusted with sesame seeds, placed it on the table and settled a plate of soft butter next to the bread, her mama's custom because cold butter seemed downright unfriendly.

Right now a part of Callie felt unfriendly, but not to Dad and the guys. Or Jake, her beautiful son, her one gift from a sorry attempt at marriage to a fellow soldier.

Hank dropped a hand to her shoulder. She looked up, sheepish, knowing he'd see through her thin attempt at normalcy. "It's okay, Cal. He's young. Looks competent. And he must have the numbers behind him because the bank signed off. Those homes need someone now, not next spring when things might look better for us."

He was right, she knew that; she'd been handling his books for three years, and truth be told she did as well with a nail gun as she had with an M-16 and a computer spreadsheet, but—

"The important thing now is to save the houses. I'm hoping Matt Cavanaugh and his crew can do that."

She nodded, not trusting herself to speak.

Hank had personally planned that subdivision to honor her mother, the name reminiscent of her mother's childhood home along the shores of Lake Ontario, the quaint family cobblestone a salute to artisans of old. Hank had been determined to carry that classic neighborhood warmth throughout Cobbled Creek, his plans lying open on a slant board he'd erected at the back of the family room. He didn't glance their way now, and neither did she, the thoughts of all that time, effort and money gone in the blink of an eye, a slash of a pen.

Hank lifted the stew pot onto the center of the table. Tom and Buck grabbed bowls, napkins and utensils, the old-timers a steady presence at the Marek homestead. Jake put The General on the back porch and shut the door. He ignored the dog's imploring whine and triple tail thump, a sure sign The General would rather be curled up on the braid rug alongside the coming fire, but the smell of wet dog didn't rank high on Callie's list.

An engine noise drew her attention to the north-facing kitchen window.

Matt Cavanaugh's black truck sat poised at the end of Cobbled Creek Lane. Sheeting rain obscured her vision, but something about the truck's stance, strong yet careful, imposing yet restrained, reminded her of the man within, his shoulders-back, jaw-tight stance just rugged enough to say he got things done. His dark brown eyes beneath short, black hair hinted Asian or Latino, maybe both, his look a mix that defied the Celtic last name. She'd faced him almost eye-to-eye in three-inch heels, which put him around five-eleven, not crazy tall, but with shoulders broad enough to handle whatever came his way.

She refused to cry, despite the disappointment welling inside. Stoic to the end, she'd been practicing that routine for years now.

Too long, actually, don't you think?

Callie pushed the internal caution aside. Survivors survived because they manned up, took the shot and stood their ground. Four years in the military taught her how to draw down the mask, put on the face, pretend disinterest as needed.

"Great bread, honey. Thanks for picking it up."

Callie turned, flashed the men a smile, laid a gentle hand on Jake's shoulder and nodded. "You know I'll do anything to keep you boys happy. Any word on when this storm's going to let up?"

Jake took her lead, such a good boy, so much like his grandpa. "Supposed to be nice tomorrow, Mom."

"Perfect." She smiled, ruffled his hair and sank into a seat alongside him. "We've got to finish the front of the house while we can, get it cleaned up so we can decorate for Christmas. We'll save cleaning the gutters—"

"Again?"

Callie sent Jake a "get serious" look and nodded. "Yes, again, they're filled with leaves and maple spinners. You know we can't leave them like that for winter."

"We don't want ice damming that porch roof again," interjected Hank.

Tom took up the thread, his face saying he'd play along, pretend everything was all right. "I remember Callie up on that roof last winter, luggin' that smaller chain saw, cutting through the ice."

"Bad combination of events, all around," agreed Buck. "To get that much snow, then warm up just enough to get a quarter inch of ice. Rough circumstances."

"But nothing we couldn't handle," Callie reminded them all. She'd used the short chain saw to hack through the pileup, pretending she didn't recognize the risk of being on a roof bearing thousands of pounds of unwanted ice, chain saw in hand. The roof's shallow slope helped steady her, but that flattened slope caused the initial problem, the lack of height allowing snow to gather and drift beneath the second-story windows.

"Exactly why we used steeper roof pitches on the subdivision," Hank reminded them. His expression said he was determined to face this new development like he handled life, head-on. "Quick water shed is crucial in a climate like ours."

"It is, Dad."

"Right, Grandpa."

Mouths full, Buck and Tom nodded agreement, pretending all was well, but Hank's old buddies were no fools. Faced with the new realization that Hank's dream was in someone else's hands just beyond the big front window, Callie was pretty sure that nothing would ever be all right again.

Chapter Two

"What do you mean you've got no crew?" Matt asked his roofing subcontractor the next morning. "I can't do a thing until we get these places under cover with good roofs. We've got water-damaged plywood to replace, it's November and I need the crew you promised today. Not next April."

Jim Slaughter, the owner/manager of Slaughter Roofing and Siding, sighed. "I'm tapped out, Matt. Fewer housing starts and reroofs. I'm filing for bankruptcy restructuring and hoping I can keep my house so we're not tossed out on the street. I had to let the guys go."

Matt's marine training didn't allow temper tantrums or bad vibes, even though he was tempted. "Who else might be available?"

Jim went silent, then offered, "You've got the Marek family right there, and Hank is friends with Buck Peters. They've all done roofing."

Ask the guy whose dream got yanked out from under him to finish that dream for someone else? Matt didn't have the callousness to do that.

Did he?

Matt eyed the farmhouse across the way. A ladder leaned up against the front. While he watched, the woman came out of the house with a bucket. She climbed the ladder, the unwieldy bucket listing her to the right until she settled it on the ladder hook. She pulled out a large green scrubbie and began washing the faded paint systematically, until she'd extended as far as she could, then she climbed down, shifted the bucket and the ladder and repeated the process despite the cold day.

A scaffolding would be so much easier. A power washer? Better yet.

He clenched his jaw and shook his head internally. "Another option. Please."

"I've got nothing. Literally. There aren't a lot of roofing contractors close by and making time for your job would be hard with a clear schedule. For anyone with jobs lined up, getting yours in would be next to impossible and a lot of people let their crews go from November to March because of the holidays and the weather. I was hoping to hold out, but the closing took too long."

It had, through no fault of Matt's. Bankers didn't comprehend weather-related restrictions and rushed work meant shoddy work.

Matt didn't do shoddy. Ever. He inhaled, eyed the house across the street and released the breath slowly. "If I get help, can you crew with them?"

"If it means fighting my way out of this financial mess, I'll work night and day," Jim promised.

"Can we use your equipment?"

"Absolutely."

Matt made several futile phone calls, carefully avoiding people who wouldn't give him the time of day for good, if old, reasons. And while plenty of construction workers were laid off, most had left the area, unable to survive on nonexistent funds. Half the remaining sub-contractors were the type Matt wouldn't trust with his hammer, much less his livelihood, and the others were too busy to take on a huge project like Cobbled Creek.

Matt eyed the Marek place again and squared his shoulders, determined to find another way. He took two steps toward his truck, then gave himself a mental slap upside the head.

Jim made two very important points earlier. Was Matt willing to risk his investment on the possibility of bad workmanship?

No. His intent was to implement the appealing de-sign plan that drew him initially. Of course it was less than beautiful now, and that had steered other develop-ers clear. But Matt saw the potential and was determined to watch this pretty neighborhood spring to life under his guidance.

But rot problems would continue if the homes sat un-roofed for another winter, and in the Allegheny foothills, rough weather came with a vengeance. He could com-plete inside work between now and spring, but outside endeavors were dictated by conditions. Lost time meant lost money, an unaffordable scenario to a guy who'd just invested a boatload of his and Grandpa's money into this venture.

He pivoted, then headed across the front field, his gaze trained on the house facing him, uncertainty and deter-mination warring within.

Callie strode into the house after her lunchtime wait-ressing stint and came to an abrupt halt when she saw Matt Cavanaugh seated at their kitchen table, sipping coffee like he was an old friend. A heart-stopping, good-looking old friend.

Except he wasn't.

"Callie, Matt needs some help."

Callie bit back a retort, trying to separate the tough-as-nails guy before her from the situation that wrested her father's dream out of his hands.

Nope. Couldn't do it.

She moved past the table, set a couple of plastic grocery bags on the counter and headed for the stairs. "I'll leave you men to your discussion."

"It's a family decision, Cal."

Callie swallowed a sigh, one hand on the baluster, her feet paused, mid-step, then she shielded her emotions and faced them, albeit slowly. "About?"

"I need a work crew for roofing," Matt explained. His deep voice kept the matter straightforward and almost a hint detached, as if this wasn't about as insulting as life could get because he was talking about roofing *their* homes, *their* dreams, *their* project. "Jim Slaughter's run into bad times, he had to let his crew go and you guys know how crucial it is to get these houses roofed."

Hank nodded. "It broke my heart to see them sitting unprotected. Uncovered."

Callie knew that truth firsthand; she'd lived, breathed and witnessed her father's depression. His Crohn's disease had contributed to the ruination of what could have been a beautiful dream, a feather in his cap. She'd prayed, promised, cajoled and bullied God and this...

She swallowed a sigh, eyeing Matt, trying to look beyond the tough-guy good looks, the steel gaze, the take-charge attitude so necessary in a good contractor.

But right now this man represented their failure

through no fault of his own other than being fiscally sound at the right time. While she couldn't hate him for that, a part of her resented his success in light of her father's failure.

A pessimist sees the difficulty in every opportunity; an optimist sees the opportunity in every difficulty.

Churchill's quote stuck in her craw. She crossed the room, poured a cup of coffee, moved back to the table, sat and eyed the two men. "I'm listening."

"Matt's offered some good money if we can crew alongside Jim Slaughter while his business is restructured."

So Jim's company had succumbed as well, and he had a nice, hardworking wife and two kids. Callie choked down a sigh. "Good money as in?" She turned Matt's way, keeping her affect flat, her gaze calm. Extra money was worth getting excited about for a combination of reasons, but taking it from the victor who now owned the spoils?

That cut. Nevertheless, her twenty-five hours of waitressing offered small monetary respite, not nearly enough to get by on, and she'd crewed for her father and his construction friends for years after leaving the military.

Matt's calm expression went straight to surprise. "You crew?"

And there it was, old feelings rubbed raw, his look reminding her of her ex-husband's disdain, how Dustin found her unfeminine and unappealing. She met his gaze straight on. "Yes."

The bare-bulb wattage of his grin should have come with a warning label. Sparks of awareness flickered beneath her heart, but she'd served in the military for four years and good-looking smiles had been a dime a dozen. But something about his...

"Well, that's an unexpected bonus."

When she frowned, he explained, "Numbers-wise. I knew your father was experienced, and his friend Buck, but to have a third person." He raised his shoulders in a half shrug. "That's clutch in roofing. And Jim Slaughter will help, too, so that makes five of us."

"Six, actually."

Matt turned back toward Hank.

"Tom Baldwin might be on in years, but he's a solid roofer. I know that firsthand."

"Excellent." Matt swept Callie another quick smile, just quick enough to make her want to shift forward.

Therefore she pulled back. "Except I haven't said yes."

"That's true." Matt stood, his shoulders filling the tan T-shirt beneath a frayed brown-plaid hooded flannel, the plain clothes adding to his hard-edged charm. "Here's my number." He handed her a business card, reached across and shook her father's hand, his frank gaze understanding. "Can you let me know by tonight?"

"Of course." Hank stood and walked Matt outside. "Let me talk to Buck and see if he's available. Tom, too."

"And, sir..." Matt hesitated, then turned, his eyes sweeping Hank, then the subdivision across the road. "I know this is difficult," he began.

Hank cut him off. "Things happen for a reason, son. Always did, always will. I can't pretend I wasn't disappointed by my run of bad luck, especially because it affected more than me."

Callie knew he'd shifted his gaze her way, but she kept her eyes down, not ready to rush this decision, although seeing Matt's grin on a regular basis wouldn't be a hardship. No, she'd definitely go to delightful. Maybe even delicious. But seriously off-limits.

Like you're all that much to look at in hoodies and jeans with a tool belt strapped around your waist? Step back into reality, honey. Been there, done that. Bad ending all around.

"But I've wound 'round God's paths all my life," Hank went on, "the ups and downs, the back-and-forths, and we've always come out okay in the end."

"Good philosophy," Matt noted. He moved across the side porch, then down the steps. "I'll look forward to hearing from you."

"I'll call," Hank promised.

Callie stared at her coffee, not wanting it, not wanting to be broke, not wanting to work for the attractive guy across the street who seemed bent on getting them involved in his success while facing their loss.

"It's a good opportunity, Cal." Hank laid a hand on her shoulder, his gentle grip understanding.

"The location's convenient."

"Yes."

She sighed and stared out the window, seeing nothing. "And the money's good."

"And welcome."

"I'll say." She paused, drummed her fingers along the table top, then slanted her eyes to his. "I know we have to say yes, Dad."

He winced, then shrugged, understanding her mixed feelings.

"But I have to recount the reasons why before I do it."

"Like bills to pay?"

"For one." She nodded toward the school bus lumbering down the road. "I spent my Christmas budget on school clothes and supplies for Jake. He grew so much this summer that nothing fit, so I had to totally re-outfit him."

"And my little stash went toward truck engine repairs."

Two relatively minor things had dissolved their meager savings. Callie hated that, but then gave herself an internal smack upside the head.

Jake was strong, healthy and athletic, a good boy who loved traipsing off to a fishing hole, who behaved himself in school and accepted the necessary extra tutoring with little argument. He knew his way around a hammer and saw, a Marek trait tried and true, and wasn't afraid to don a hard hat and be a crew gopher.

Her father's health had returned with his colostomy, and if he continued to do well, they'd be able to reverse the procedure mid-winter. And while his appetite waned occasionally, she couldn't deny that good old-fashioned hard work was the best appetite builder known to man, and that getting back to work was in her father's long-term best interest.

The General dashed off the porch to greet Jake, his fur blending to grays in pursuit, the flash of white tail fringe the kind of welcome any boy would love.

"But the needy will not always be forgotten, nor the hope of the afflicted ever perish."

The words of the ninth Psalm flooded her, their comfort magnified in simplicity.

Callie liked things simple. She loved the feel of crewing on a house, walking scaffolding, climbing ladders, working a rooftop. Her father had affectionately called her his "right-hand man" from the time she was big enough to eye a square alongside him, and they'd laughed at the expression.

But you stopped laughing when Dustin walked out, citing your lack of femininity as a total turnoff.

Jake's dad had tossed her over for the former Livingston County Miss New York entrant, a petite gal who'd promptly given him two daughters in their suburban home in Rhode Island, neither of whom Jake had ever met. Dustin made it abundantly clear that his first family was an anomaly in an otherwise perfect life, therefore best forgotten.

Jake's entrance stopped her maudlin musings. She stood, smiled, grabbed him in a quick hug, then examined the papers he waved her way. "Another hundred on your math test?"

His grin said more than words ever could.

"And a plus on your homework sheets." She ruffled his hair, nodded toward a plate of cookies and the refrigerator. "Grab a snack. There are fresh apples in the crisper. I'm heading out front to get more of that mold washed off."

"Can we work on my science project tonight?"

"Absolutely." Halting her work on their home's western exposure for dinner, dark and homework left her little time to make progress, but Jake's enthusiasm over schoolwork outranked everything. His excitement came after years of grueling practice, nights when he hated her, mornings spent crying, not wanting to get on the bus because school proved too difficult.

"Success is not final, failure is not fatal: it is the courage to continue that counts."

Churchill's words uplifted her, World War II a favorite study topic for Jake, and having served in Iraq, Callie understood war rigors firsthand. While hyped battles might gain more press, small battles, fought daily, wore down the enemy, except when the enemy came from within.

She pushed that thought aside, refusing to revisit old feelings that should have abated long past. Sure, she'd been dumped. Callie was adult enough to handle that. But Dustin dumped Jake, too, and despite prayer and her best efforts, what did she long to do?

Give her ex the quick kick he deserved for abandoning a God-given miracle. The first gift of Christmas. A child.

But Callie refused to dwell on Dustin Burdick's shortcomings, although that proved harder at holiday time. She was home, safe and sound, with a beautiful son, a warm house and good friends. What more could she need?

The sound of a generator drew her gaze across the street. A light winked on in the model home, the only home near completion, and she caught sight of Matt Cavanaugh trekking back and forth from his truck to the pretty Cape Cod house, lugging things inside.

She pulled her attention back to the task at hand and climbed the ladder with her bucket and thick, green scrubbie, determined to get as much done as she could despite the chill, waning light.

Determination. Valor. Perseverance. She had the heart of a lioness and the grit of a soldier, two things vital to soothe the scarred soul of the woman within.

Chapter Three

Matt recognized Hank Marek's name and answered his phone quickly, praying for a "yes."

"We're in, Matt."

Thank you. Matt breathed the thought heavenward, knowing what even a day's delay could mean this time of year. They'd already been hammered by squalls packing hail, wind and rain. Time was of the essence.

"Everything's being delivered tomorrow morning," Matt told him. "I started roof examination today, but my day got chopped by having to order supplies."

"We'll be there at eight," Hank promised. "Callie works the lunch shift in town, but she's got Wednesdays off, so we'll have her all day tomorrow."

"What about Thursday?" Matt asked, assuring himself it was strictly a job-related inquiry.

Yeah, right.

"She'll split things up. She'll crew with us, then the diner, then back here."

Matt knew how abbreviated days curtailed time frames, but did his frustration stem from Callie's prior commitment or...

No.

He refused to go there. Callie would be working for him. Matt didn't mix business with pleasure, no matter how intrigued he was by soft brown hair and gold-green eyes.

"That's her job," Hank continued.

It didn't take good math skills to realize roofing paid more, but Matt liked people that honored their commitments. His mother forgot she had a child when the world discovered he was Neal Brennan's illegitimate son. He was eight years old when life capsized. His mother sought solace in a string of random men, while his stepfather found comfort in a bottle. That left no one around to raise an eight-year-old kid with learning problems. Jake's age, he realized.

"But Buck and Tommy are available whenever. With respect to Tom's age I wouldn't put him on the tallest roofs, but he's sure-handed and has a good eye. And quick."

"He's welcome, then. Anyone else you can think of, Hank?"

A moment's hesitation followed, then Hank offered, "Your um—" indecision lingered in the older man's voice, his tone "—father's in town."

"Stepfather, you mean."

"I guess."

Matt didn't blame Hank for sidestepping the issue. When your biological father turns out to be the wealthy but drug-using, gambling vice-president of a local big business, Walker Electronics, the poor guy who'd been publicly emasculated took a hard hit. Don Cavanaugh became the classic definition of deadbeat dad, but because he *wasn't* Matt's dad, Matt guessed the expression didn't apply.

But it hit hard when the guy you called dad for eight years walked away and never looked back because of biology. That hurt, big time.

"He crewed with me a few times when I really needed help," Hank explained further.

"Then you know he's fairly unreliable on a day-to-day basis."

"When he's drinking, you're right. He's sober right now."

Sobriety was temporary in Don Cavanaugh's life, a hit-and-miss condition Matt would rather miss. "I can't trust him."

"Then I won't mention this when he's around. He'll notice when you change the sign, though."

"How?" Matt's father had no reason to be this far out of town and he hated the cold and snow. He'd race to Florida once the weather turned just like he had years ago, leaving Matt with his drama-queen mother.

Face front, eyes forward. No flashbacks, got it?

"Don comes by for coffee and soup with the other boys from time to time."

Which meant he'd see them working on Matt's new project, and the inevitable face-to-face meeting. "I can't have him over here, especially right now. I've got to get my bearings for this job. Find my comfort zone."

"I understand."

"Thank you, Hank."

"See you in the morning."

Matt disconnected the call and walked outside the house, eyeing the gloaming shadows beneath a waning gibbous moon.

A noise drew his attention to the Marek place. In the almost dark he saw Callie's silhouette, captured by the porch light. She clambered down the ladder, a bucket in hand, its weight making the descent awkward. At the bottom she splashed water onto the street, then headed for the side porch, humming.

Pride and strength embraced her maverick beauty. The idea of working for him obviously bothered her, but if she was as experienced as Hank made out, he was glad for the help.

Lights blinked on in the front of their house and he caught a glimpse of Callie and the boy, heads bent, eyeing something, a family moment that resurrected all he'd missed as a child. A father's love. A mother's touch.

He headed into the nearly complete model home, studied the mattress and box spring on the floor, the small generator outside giving him power for minimal light and heat. He'd surrendered his apartment in Nunda because the commute would eat up too much time. And saving nearly seven hundred dollars a month was nothing to take lightly. Wear and tear on the truck, his equipment? That took a toll over time.

No, better to headquarter himself here, on the job site, guarding his investment.

The house wasn't certified for dwelling, so Matt would have to sequester his sleeping arrangements when the inspector came by, at least until he could get a certificate of occupancy on the model. He'd complete that once the roofs were in place on the other houses, his first-things-first mentality key to this situation. Then he'd set up properly upstairs, but for the moment, this would do. He set his alarm clock early to take a shot at bookkeeping, not one of his strongholds, and burrowed under the covers, burying dreams of heat. And a woman with gold-green eyes.

"He's staying over there." Callie jerked her head west, her hands plunged into soapy dishwater the next morning.

"Makes sense," Hank replied as he gathered their tool belts and supplies. "Why pay rent when you've got a nearly finished house?"

"Because Finch McGee will be all over that if he finds out," Callie replied. She wiped her hands, waved goodbye to Jake as the bus approached, then headed to the table.

"Finch is a little power-hungry," Hank admitted.

"A little?"

Hank shrugged. "He's got a job to do, Cal. You know that. He just does it with more zeal than most."

"Maybe Matt will be lucky and Colby will be his inspector." Colby Dennis had taken the job as Finch's assistant two years before, and he was a decent guy on all levels. Finch?

Callie'd been privy to more than one run-in with the divorced building inspector, and she knew a jerk when she saw one. She'd kept him at arm's length, but he'd taken to coming into the diner at lunchtime lately, when he'd always eaten at the Texas Hot before. And it wasn't a fluke that put him in her section, day after day, any more than it was coincidence that she traded tables with the other servers, keeping him at bay.

"Finch won't let the new kid on the block oversee this." Hank shifted his gaze to Cobbled Creek as they headed down the stone drive. "And while his inspections are all right, he doesn't have a lick of common sense when it comes to balancing economics."

"Ready, guys?" Buck grinned at them, crumpled his coffee cup and set it inside his truck cab.

"I am," declared Tommy, a knit hat drawn over his bald head, a thick flannel layered over a turtleneck.

"You expectin' a blizzard, Tom?" Hank teased.

"I'm expecting it's cold now and warmin' up later," shot back the older man, "and I've crewed with you often enough to know that cold and number of hours don't mean all that much."

"I knew I liked you." Matt smiled as he approached the group. "Supplies are due to arrive in three hours and Jim Slaughter should be here anytime with his equipment. Hank, can you get these guys together on inspecting the roofs, marking any part that needs to be redone while I finish a few phone calls?"

"I'm on it."

They spent the first hour setting up ladders and scaffolding, then split into two groups, checking for damage.

"We've got a problem here," Callie called out midmorning as Matt passed by below. He clambered up the ladder, saw what she'd uncovered and grimaced. "We'll have to take this section back down to the rafters."

"I'm on it."

She'd been amazing and quick, working hard and long beside the men without a break, and in her hooded sweatshirt and loose-fit blue jeans, no one would even know she was a girl.

So why couldn't Matt get it off his mind? *Focus, dude.* "You really have to go to the restaurant tomorrow? No chance of getting someone to cover you?"

Callie looked up. Had he tempted her? Heaven knows he tried. She shook her head. "Sorry, can't be helped. But I'll see if one of the girls wants to pick up my shifts next week because working here pays better than waiting on the lunch crowd at the Olympus."

"If you can do that, lunch is on me every day next week."

"For all of us or just the pretty girl?" Tommy wondered out loud.

"Everyone." Matt shot Tommy a quick grin of appreciation as he jerked a thumb in Callie's direction. "Although she's easier on the eyes than the rest of you lugs." He headed back toward the ladder, the crew's work ethic easing his concerns. "I've got a friend who works at the Tops deli in Wellsville. She can hook us up with some pretty good eats."

Tommy exchanged a grin with Buck. "I had a few of those friends back in the day."

Matt laughed and discovered it felt good to laugh with a crew like this, as unlikely as they appeared. A gray truck turned into Cobbled Creek Lane, the town emblem emblazoned on the cab doors. Matt swung onto the ladder, his features relaxed.

Callie stepped toward the roof's edge, then squatted alongside him as though checking something. "It's Finch, the building inspector."

Matt paused his descent and nodded, wondering how the scent of fresh-sawn wood could smell so agreeably new and different to a longtime contractor like himself. Or was it her strawberry-scented shampoo?

"You're not from around here, but he's a little high on himself."

Relief tweaked Matt. She obviously didn't know he'd grown up here a long time ago. He chalked it up to their four or five year age difference. The old Matt Cavanaugh was best left forgotten, although that wouldn't be completely possible. He'd messed up big time back then. Now?

Now it was his turn to make things right. Make Grandpa proud. His newfound peace with his half brother and half sister, Jeff and Meredith Brennan, was a good start. Glancing down, he swept the gray truck a quick look. "Overzealous?"

"Bingo. And you can't let him see you have stuff in the model, that you're staying here."

"How did you…? Never mind," Matt continued.

Of course she'd notice, she lived across the street. His truck had been there all night and his lights were on before 5:00 a.m. "I'll steer him clear."

"Five-hundred-dollar fine," she muttered under her breath. "No contractor wants to waste a cool five hundred."

She was right. He'd traded off the apartment to save money, not throw it away. He climbed down the ladder, nodded his approval at the scaffolding Matt rigged in front of house number seventeen and stuck out a hand to the inspector. "Matt Cavanaugh. Nice to meet you."

"Finch McGee." The guy looked around amiably enough, but Matt hadn't tap-danced his way through the marines. Friendly snakes were still snakes, and Hank's daughter had this one nailed. That only made him wonder why, but he'd ferret that out later.

"I examined the initial plan when it came before the zoning commission." Finch surveyed the half-done houses with a thin-eyed gaze, then rocked back on his heels. "I wanted to give myself an up-to-date visual. You've got the copy of town code my assistant gave you?"

The demeaning way he said "assistant" tightened Matt's skin, but he tamped that down and sent McGee a comfortable look of assent. "Yes. How much leeway do I need with your office to set up inspections?"

"Forty-eight hours should do it. We're not slammed right now."

Not slammed? Talk about an understatement. The town had been literally asleep for the past eighteen months. But Matt heeded Callie's warning and gave in easily. "Forty-eight hours it is."

"You've got Hank Marek helping you?" Finch turned Matt's way. His approving expression insinuated that having Hank working on this project was some kind of power-hungry badge of glory. "Gutsy."

"Necessary." Matt clipped the word, needing to get back to work. "Hank knows this project inside and out. Who better to have on board?"

Finch shrugged. "Just seems funny, but no worse than hanging out in that farmhouse watching this place get ruined."

"Well, it's in good hands now," Matt told him, ready to cut this conversation short. "Mine and Hank's." He wasn't sure why he included the older man in the statement, but realized its truth right off. Despite hard times, Hank Marek was unafraid to put his hand to the task, a guy like Grandpa, tried and true. That kind of integrity meant a great deal to Matt.

"Nice outfit, Callie."

Matt turned in time to see the wince she hid from McGee as Callie came down the ladder.

McGee's words pained her, but why would a pretty girl like Callie Marek be hurt by a little teasing? Two thoughts came to mind. Either Callie'd been hurt before or McGee's words came with a personal tang.

"She's working for you?"

Matt turned, not liking the heightened interest in Mc-Gee's tone but not willing to make an enemy out of the building inspector who would be signing his certificate of occupancy documents. "Yes, they're a talented family."

McGee acknowledged that with a nod as he headed out. "They are. I'll stop around now and again, see how things are coming along."

Translation: I'll stop around now and again to see Callie and maybe find you cutting code.

The latter insinuation didn't bother Matt. He refused to shirk and never used slip-shod methods in building. That had kept his reputation and business growing heartily in the northern part of the county. Now back home in the southern edge of Allegany County, where teenage bad choices dogged him, he'd be choirboy good to erase those dark stains on his character.

But realizing McGee would be stopping by to check Callie out?

That scorched.

And while Matt knew Callie was off-limits, the way his neck hairs rose in protest when Finch McGee eyed her said his heart was playing games with his head. The way she'd faced the decision of crewing with him, up-front and honest, the way her hair touched her cheek, the brown waves having just the right sheen, like newly applied satin-finish paint…

Words weren't his forte, but feelings…those he got, and since he was fresh out of a relationship with a woman who'd wanted to change every single thing about him, he wasn't ready to charge head-first into another one, especially in a place where everyone knew his name and all the baggage that went along with it. With an employee. Nope. Wasn't going to happen for a host of good reasons.

"If you can trust yourself when all men doubt you, but make allowance for their doubting, too..."

Kipling's famous poem soothed the angst McGee stirred up, the poem a gift from Grandpa back in the day. Matt had to trust himself. He couldn't afford mistakes or missteps. He'd already made his share.

"Matt, you wanna cut those sections we removed or have me do it?"

Matt turned, grateful for Buck's interruption. "Have at it, Buck."

Buck nodded and swung down the ladder. "Be right back."

Matt climbed back up, inspecting each seam before they added the underlayment and the shingles. A mistake now would cost time and money later, every builder's nightmare.

Do it once; do it right.

By the time Matt glanced at his watch again, it was nearly one o'clock. "Hey, guys, lunch."

Hank waved a sandwich from the roof across the street. "Got mine right here, boss."

Tom did the same thing.

Buck straightened and rolled his shoulders to ease muscle strain. "I'll bring mine up so we can keep going here. You want something, Matt?"

Their dedication touched Matt's heart. He'd worked with a lot of crews over the years, good and bad, and from both ends of the spectrum as low man on the totem pole and supervisor, but this...

He cleared his throat and nodded to Buck. "I've got a sandwich inside the truck. And some of those snowball cupcakes."

"I love them," Buck declared.

"Bring the box. We'll share. And see if the other guys want some."

"Hank won't. Coconut bothers him since he got the Crohn's, but Tom will dig in. So will Callie. She loves chocolate. Thanks, Matt."

"You're welcome."

Callie headed across the roof just then, a soldier's satisfaction marking her gaze, her walk.

A really good-looking soldier.

With great hair and pearl-soft skin.

Stop. Now.

He couldn't afford to mess up this job. He'd seen the careful way Hank handled his daughter, although this woman didn't seem to need protecting.

The image of her quick wince revisited him, the way she'd cringed at McGee's teasing, and that brought back another Grandpa Gus-ism. "If you respect women, you'll respect life."

Maybe Callie Marek *did* need protecting and was good at hiding it, but either way, she was off-limits. Her warm voice reenforced that notion a short while later. "Jake's home."

A yellow bus rolled toward them, lights flashing. Jake climbed down the steps, let the dog off the porch, then hurried their way with The General racing alongside. "You guys got a lot done today!"

Matt grinned as the pair drew closer, their enthusiasm contagious. "We did, but it's easy with a great crew."

"I can help." The boy's excitement made it tough for Matt to say no, but—

"We'd love your help," Callie told him, staving Matt's refusal with a sidelong glance. "First, get changed. Put on proper gear including your boots and hard hat, then head over here. There won't be much time, but you can work on cleanup."

"Okay."

The kid dashed across the open lot at a run, the dog streaming alongside, his pace pretty solid for an eight-year-old. Matt turned Callie's way, disapproving. "I—"

She held up a hand to thwart his argument. "I know what you're going to say, but trust me on this. Jake understands construction sites. He's been working side-by-side with us for years with no harm, no foul. He's great on cleanup duty and this is a much better choice than television or computer games, right?"

"Yes, but…" Matt met her gaze, decided that was dangerous because her eyes made him remember how lovely she was, even in roofing gear, and he didn't want to go there. No woman in her right mind would find his teenage police record a good thing to have around an impressionable kid like Jake. A *good* kid, Matt reminded himself. "Doesn't he have homework?"

"Yes." Callie nodded, chin down, focusing on her work, talking easily. "But he's got some processing problems so school doesn't come easily. We'll do it together, step by step, after supper."

That's what they'd been doing last night, Matt realized. "After working here all day, you'll do homework duty at night?"

She gave a brisk nod. "Of course."

He'd have given anything to have a mother like that. He'd tackled educational difficulties on his own and failed miserably. "That's amazing, Callie."

She turned, surprised. Their eyes met.

She went still, her eyes on his, her mouth slightly open, the parted lips looking very approachable.

And she read his gaze, his thoughts. It was there in her slight intake of breath, the way she blinked, the quick flex of fingers as realization struck.

Amanda Slaughter created a welcome diversion by pulling into the tract with promised coffee.

Matt was pretty sure he didn't want to be diverted.

Callie turned toward the ladder, breaking the connection. That was good, right? Neither of them had the time or energy to put into that quick flash of recognition. Obviously they'd be smart to ignore it.

But he caught her shifting a surreptitious glance his way moments later, and that confirmed what he'd been struggling with all day.

Working side by side with Callie Marek meant he couldn't ignore her. And the over-the-shoulder look said she wasn't oblivious to the spark of attraction.

But a kid like Jake deserved to be surrounded by the best examples possible. Matt had been anything *but* a good example for a long time. Sooner or later Callie would discover his past. No self-respecting woman wanted a guy with a record setting an example for her kid, and Matt understood that. Respected it, even. He needed to remember he was in the southern sector of the county for two things only: to make amends to those he'd hurt and help Cobbled Creek become what Hank Marek meant it to be.

And although he was thrilled by the skill level and dedication shown by Hank and his crew, no way, no how was he looking for anything else. Especially where Callie Marek was concerned.

Chapter Four

McGee's truck reappeared while the crew grabbed coffee from Jim's wife. He braked quick, scattering stone, then climbed out, strode their way and met Matt's gaze head-on, his expression taut. "You living here, Cavanaugh?"

Matt's face showed surprise, not a good thing, but Hank's quick reaction spared a clash. "Of course he is, Finch. Wouldn't make sense to travel back and forth to Nunda while daylight hours are scarce, winter's closing in and every penny he's got is invested in Cobbled Creek."

"You don't have a C of O," Finch barked, his typical attitude more evident this afternoon. "There's reasons we've got regulations, Cavanaugh, although you were never real good at following rules, were you?"

Matt's flinch surprised Callie, but then Hank sighed and frowned as if wondering what the clamor was about. "Finch, I don't know any rule that says Matt can't live with us while he gets the model done and inspected. It makes good sense, all in all." Hank kept his voice easy and his surprise genuine, as if taken aback by Finch's intrusion.

Callie swallowed a lump in her throat the size of a small two-by-four. Live with them? Was her father kidding?

"He's staying at your place?" Finch swept Callie a look, then drew his gaze back to the two men.

Hank shrugged, sidestepping the truth. "We have extra room. Matt needs to be on site. It works out for everyone."

Everyone but me, Callie wanted to shout. She was having a hard enough time keeping her distance from Matt in the short time they'd been working together, but to have him staying at their place?

"A perfect solution," Matt added, as if everything was suddenly hunky-dory. "And just so you know, I'm ordering us a fresh turkey for Thanksgiving."

Finch scowled.

Hank grinned.

Tom covered a laugh with a cough.

Callie decided more coffee would only tax her already-twining gut and headed back to the roof, trying to untwist the coiled emotions inside.

Yes, she was attracted.

No, she shouldn't be.

And having him under their roof, sharing their home, their food?

Way too much proximity and she had too much to lose, but Hank had extended the invitation and Hank Marek carved his word in stone. He kept a General Patton quote framed on his dresser: "no good decision was ever made from a swivel chair."

Great. Just great.

Finch would be annoyed, which meant he'd annoy others. She'd have Matt underfoot, which would entail having her guard up 24/7. And the guys were clearly delighted with the prospect of having Matt around, his friendly grin and storytelling a welcome addition to their circle, a perfect match.

But she'd found out the hard way there were no perfect matches. Not for women who strike a different path, a career that includes tool belts weighted with claw hammers and tape measures. Nails and utility knives. Unfeminine suspenders to distribute the tool weight appropriately.

Some lessons a girl never forgot.

Matt's footsteps followed her. He crouched by her side, pretending to work, his gaze down. "Hey, if it bothers you that much, I'll just get a place in town. Or stay at my brother's house in Wellsville. That way I'm not breaking the rules and McGee won't have anything to complain about."

Finch would dog Matt's steps, Callie knew. He wasn't above pestering contractors he didn't like, and he'd had his eye on Callie for the last several months. She'd kept it cool and friendly at the diner, but Finch added another component in an already-complex puzzle. She didn't want Matt targeted by the zealous building inspector, but she didn't want him living with them either.

Nevertheless, the invitation had been extended, and Hank wasn't a man to go back on his word, a quality she shared.

She bit her lip and swallowed a sigh. "It's fine. It just came as a surprise."

"I'll do my own laundry."

His earnest words almost made her smile. "You bet you will."

"And I can cook."

"Excellent."

"How big a turkey shall I get?"

"You weren't kidding about that?" She turned to face him and felt the draw of those deep, brown eyes, tiny hints of gold sparking warmth and laughter. "I got a couple of frozen turkeys at Tops while they were on sale. That's a lot of good eating at a bargain price. Fresh birds are expensive."

"Have you ever tasted one?"

She brushed that off and turned back to the task at hand. "Turkey's turkey."

He grinned and moved a step away. "It's not, but I'll let you discover that next week. And now—" he shifted his attention back to the nail gun "—we need to get back to work. Can you help your dad and Buck get started on number twenty-three?"

Across the street and two houses up. Just enough distance to calm things down. Smooth them over.

"Sure."

"And Callie?"

She turned at the ladder and arched a brow, waiting for him to say more.

He eyed her a moment and shifted his jaw. "You do good work."

His awkwardness told her he meant to add something else but thought better of it. Just as well. Too much fun and teasing could be misconstrued. She headed down to ground level, crossed the street, moved up the block and joined her father on the elongated roof covering the well-designed ranch house. Hank noted her presence with a welcome smile and nod.

"Ready?"

Ready for roofing?

Yes.

For having Matt's teasing smile, his easy manner, his firm jaw around every day?

No way.

But Callie had withstood basic training and a deployment in Iraq. She could handle this.

She adopted a noncommittal look and started handing her father shingles, pushing thoughts of Matt aside, but with the steady pop of his nail gun keeping time with his whistling, she was mostly unsuccessful. Luckily no one knew that but her.

He'd be moving in tomorrow.

Ignoring Matt's light proved impossible as Callie helped Jake recognize consonant–vowel patterns for his language arts class. Her chair faced the front window, overlooking Cobbled Creek and the unshaded reminder of Matt's existence.

Change chairs, her conscience scolded.

She could, she supposed, warm yellow light pouring from the uncurtained windows of the model home. But…

"Mom, can I help Matt this weekend?" Jake asked, pulling her attention away from cute guys and broken dreams, definitely in everyone's best interest.

"We'll all be working this weekend, as long as the weather holds," Hank told him. "Your mom has a couple of shifts at the diner—"

"I switched them up with Gina," Callie cut in.

Hank eyed her, speculative.

"I make more crewing and we have no guarantee on the weather this late in the game," she explained to Hank, then turned her attention back to Jake's word list. "Yup, short *I* words here, long *I* there. Perfect."

Jake beamed. "Mrs. Carmichael told me to picture them like puzzle pieces, looking for clues."

God bless Mrs. Carmichael, Callie breathed silently. Between Hannah Moore's tutoring and Jake's teachers, he'd come a long way academically, and since his ADD prognosis, his continued progress thrilled Callie. She knew strong middle school academics required a solid foundation now, and she'd worked extra hours to pay for his tutoring, his book club, his interactive educational games, anything it took to surround him with learning opportunities.

So far, so good.

She smiled, ruffled his hair, tried not to glance out the window and failed, then said, "Yes, you can help, but The General can't be over there all the time, okay? We can't have someone's attention diverted when they're on a rooftop."

"Okay."

"And I want to get those Christmas lights strung this weekend. Thanksgiving's next week and I'd rather do it before we get big snows than after."

"That's a good idea," Hank agreed. "If we use both ladders we can do it together and get it done in half the time."

"True." The ladders were about the only thing not seized when Hank's business bellied up. The bank had considered them household use instead of business inventory. "I want to finish scrubbing that side, too. Get rid of the mold."

"Not much sense if we don't have time or the right temperature to paint," Hank told her.

"It looks better when it's clean." Callie didn't elaborate, but something about coming home to that worn facade weighed on her. Painting could wait until spring, but decorating for the holidays with the front of the house looking tired and worn…

That didn't sit right.

"When can we get our Christmas tree?" Jake's eagerness refused to be contained.

Callie laughed and stood. She stretched and fought a yawn. "Let's tackle Thanksgiving first, okay? And decorating the front of the house."

"Can we put up Shadow Jesus?"

Hank exchanged a grin with Callie. He'd created a plywood Holy Family years ago, the images of Jesus, Mary and Joseph done in silhouette, then painted black. Two spotlights tucked into the grass bathed the cutouts in light at night, making their shadowed presence appear on the white house. The simple, stark visual was an eye-catcher for sure.

Jake had referred to the infant in the manger as "Shadow Jesus" from the time he could talk, a sweet memory and a good focus on the true meaning of the upcoming holy season. "Next weekend," Hank promised. "It doesn't take long, but let's get the outside lights up first."

Jake nodded, satisfied. "Okay. Good night, Grandpa."

"'Night, Jake."

He was such a good boy, Callie thought as Jake headed upstairs to bed. She would never understand Dustin's cool disregard for his beautiful son, but then she hadn't understood Dustin for a very long time.

Maybe ever.

"He's doing fine, Callie." Hank drew her attention with a nod toward the stairs. "Don't borrow trouble."

"I know. It's just rough at holiday time, when most kids get presents from their dads. Visits. Cards."

"He's happy enough."

"But he wonders, Dad." When Hank went to speak, she held up a hand to pause him. "I know he's content, but it weighs on his mind from time to time. His birthday. Christmas. When they do father-son events at school and church. And those are the times when I could wring Dustin's neck for brushing him off."

"And brushing you off."

She shrugged. "Not so much. We married young, we were both in the service, we thought we could conquer the world and when that didn't work, we grew apart."

Hank's snort said more than words ever could. "In my day skirt-chasing was called just that, and it didn't involve growing apart. It involved breaking vows, going back on your word. A good soldier never goes back on his or her word."

His righteous indignation struck a chord with Callie. "You're right, Dad, but it's in the past and I've moved on. We all have."

"And the future is ripe with possibilities," Hank reminded her. "Seek and ye shall find. Knock and the door will be opened unto you."

Callie leaned forward and planted a kiss on Hank's bushy cheek. "Are you letting your beard grow to keep your face warm on those rooftops?"

"Yes, I am." Hank scrubbed a hand across the three-day stubble and grinned again. "One of the advantages of age and gender. I can grow my own ski mask."

Callie shook her head, laughing. "And I'm just as thankful I can't." She headed for the stairs. "I'm turning in early so I can work on the front of the house before first light. I'll turn on the small spotlights to help me see. Another few hours of washing should do it."

"If we had a power washer…"

Hank's quiet aside made her shrug. "We don't want to disturb the paint too much anyway. It's pretty loose in spots and a power washer might peel it off. Hand washing is fine for this year."

Hank hugged her shoulders and planted a kiss on her cheek. "You make me proud. You know that, don't you?"

She did. And she appreciated Hank's common sense take on Dustin's behavior, but the image in the mirror once she climbed the stairs showed a strong, rugged woman, a laborer. And while her father's approval was a lovely thing, and Callie took pride in her work, her dexterity, her intrinsic knowledge of building, some days it would be nice to look in the mirror and have downright beautiful looking back at her, the gracious swan that evolved from the misunderstood fictional duckling.

But that wasn't about to happen.

Startled awake, Callie stared at the clock, rubbed her eyes and peered again.

She'd overslept the alarm. Not only would she not be scrubbing clapboard that morning, but she'd be lucky if she got lunches made before the bus pulled up for Jake. And what on earth was that noise?

Her father sent her an amused smirk as she ran down the stairs in her robe. "Tired?"

Grr.

Hank held up Jake's lunch bag. "We're good to go."

"Thank you." She gave him a half hug as she kissed his cheek on her way to the coffeepot. "I have no memory of turning the radio off or hitting the snooze bar. I must have zonked. And what is going on out there?" She jerked a thumb toward the subdivision.

Hank shook his head. "Not there." He pointed toward the street side of the house. "Here."

Here?

Callie followed the direction of his finger, pulled back the curtain and stared.

Matt Cavanaugh had brought over a small power washer. Using care, he splayed the jet of water against the siding in a slow and steady back-and-forth sweep, his attention locked on the task at hand.

"Pretty nice of him." Hank's words drew her gaze around.

"Very."

"Must have seen you working out there."

Callie was pretty sure the flush started somewhere around her toes and worked its way up. "Probably just wants to make sure we can use daylight hours on the subdivision."

"Most likely."

"Dad, I—"

She stopped as Jake clamored down the stairs, his expression a mix of surprise and delight. "Matt's washing the front of the house!"

"He is, yes."

"Then we can put up the Christmas lights this weekend!" He raced for the door and barreled across the porch, then down the steps and around the front. Callie watched from inside, pretty sure Matt couldn't hear a word Jake was saying.

It didn't matter. Matt's grin said he understood a little boy's excitement. He nodded and sent Jake a quick thumbs-up as he guided the spray around the windows. He spotted Callie watching and for a quick beat he forgot to move the water wand.

Oops. His look of chagrin said he'd peeled a bit of paint.

He swept her one more quick look, barely noticeable except for the wink. And the smile, just crooked enough to be endearing.

Callie rolled her eyes, shook a finger at him and tried not to smile. She couldn't feed this flirtation and she had plenty on her plate dealing with Jake and Dad, but...

She let the curtain fall into place as Jake raced back in to grab a bagel and his lunch. "It looks great out there, Mom." He switched his look to Hank and raised both brows. "So we can decorate this weekend? Right?"

"When we're not working," Hank promised.

"Perfect." Jake gave Callie a quick hug and pointed toward the clock. "Matt says you've got fifteen minutes before you have to be at work and that you might want to get your coffee to go."

"Oh, he did, did he?"

Jake grinned and headed outside. "He's funny."

Funny. Right. She shooed Jake on. "Have a good day."

"I will." She heard him hail Matt as he headed for the road, The General at his heels, his voice upbeat. "See you later, Matt!"

She refused to check out Matt's reply, to see if he heard the boy's call.

She never overslept. Ever.

Her father poured a fresh cup of coffee into a thermal cup and swept her and the clock a look. "Twelve minutes and counting."

Laughter bubbled up from somewhere far away, a different kind of laughter. Sweet. Girlish. Kind of silly, actually.

But nice.

She hustled up the stairs, donned her layers and refused to think about the nice thing Matt was doing, saving her work, saving her time, precious commodities these days. And the joy in Jake's step…

That thought nipped the gladness. She didn't want Jake hurt. He'd taken a shine to Matt, but Matt was only temporary. If Jake grew too close…

Are you worried about Jake or you?

Both. Callie tugged her hoodie into place, grabbed a pair of fingerless gloves and headed back downstairs.

Matt's grin was the first thing she saw as she rounded the bottom step, his shirt cuffs damp from the sprayer, his hands wound tight around a mug of coffee. He flicked a gaze toward the clock, then back to her. "Right on time."

She faced him, tongue-tied. Despite her efforts, she couldn't get beyond that smile to create a quick comeback. And he saw that. Recognized the reaction. Probably because girls fell at his feet on a regular basis. His grin widened, lighting his eyes.

Not me, not now.

Callie grabbed her insulated coffee mug, not ready to play this game. Maybe she'd never be ready, and that might be okay. She headed out the door with Matt following, but as she passed the front corner of the house, she couldn't ignore what he'd done. She turned back and caught him studying her, his gaze curious. Maybe a little concerned. "Thank you." She waved toward the front and a hint of his smile returned.

"You're welcome."

"It looks much better."

He nodded, quiet, still watching her, one eye narrowed as if wondering something.

She pointed over his shoulder and slightly left. "Except where you peeled the paint above the window."

His smile deepened. Softened. He shrugged. "Distracted."

Talk about smooth.

Again the flush rose from somewhere deep and low, the pleasure of having a man flirt with her awakening sweet memories.

Memories that crashed and burned, honey. This guy's way cute, but he's here today, gone tomorrow. Let's not forget that.

She headed across the road, chin down, knowing he followed a pace behind, not hurrying to catch up. Was he waiting for her to come back? Match her pace to his?

Or just enjoying a walk with his coffee?

"House looks good, Matt." Buck smiled and nodded appreciation toward the Marek place as they drew alongside. "And that means we can rig up Shadow Jesus soon, I expect."

"And the lights," Hank added. "Jake sure is excited."

"I got that." Matt grinned, took a sip of coffee and settled an easy look Callie's way. "He's a good kid."

"Thanks. Same assignments as yesterday, boss?"

A muscle clench in his chin said he recognized the marker drawn. "Sure." He headed right while she moved to join her father and Buck on the roof they'd begun the previous day, but his light whistle followed her, the tune young. Bright. Carefree. It called to her, but she'd put carefree aside a lot of years ago and it would take more than clean clapboards and perfect teeth to bring it back. Most days she was pretty sure it was gone for good.

* * *

So much for maintaining a distance, Matt thought as Callie headed across his roof on steady feet a few hours later. "Tom said you needed a hand over here."

Matt nodded, brisk, pretending immunity. "I do, thanks. The pharmacy called to say his wife's prescription was ready."

"And he didn't want her waiting." Callie adjusted her gloves, flexed her fingers and squatted beside him, close enough to notice how her lashes curled up on their own with no help from mascara. "That's Tom, all right. And since Dad and Buck are capping twenty-three, I was the logical choice. Looks good, Jim," she noted, raising her voice so Jim could hear. "And it's almost straight."

Jim made a face at her. "Ha, ha. Do I have to remind you that I've put on more roofs than anyone else in Allegheny County?"

Callie laughed. "Since there's no one here to argue the point, I'll let you stake your claim. In the meantime," she turned her gaze toward Matt.

"Do you want to feed or nail?" he asked.

"I'll nail. Then we can switch so neither one of us ends up with a backache later."

"And you didn't leave for the diner today. How about tomorrow?"

Callie shook her head, eyes down, working the nail gun as they edged right. "Nope."

Matt fought off the quick glimmer of appreciation her answer inspired. *Focus on your work. Remember that you're on a rooftop and concentration might be in everyone's best interest.* But he'd be lying to say that Callie wasn't a pretty nice distraction, totally against the norm of women he'd known.

"I switched with Gina," she continued, working as she talked. "She's a single mom, too, and she can use the extra shifts. She'll do doubles, which will help her out at this time of year."

"Christmas."

"Christmas and winter clothes," she told him as she shifted her angle to give him more room. "With kids you go right from back-to-school clothes to winter clothes and then Christmas. There's no such thing as saving a dime in the fall. Not with children."

Tom's truck pulled back in a few minutes later. He climbed out, surveyed their progress and whistled, appreciative. "Nice work."

Matt grinned, showed a thumbs-up and jerked his head toward Hank and Buck. "Can you finish up with Hank and Buck?"

"And let you have the pretty girl all to yourself?" Tom drawled. He tipped his wool hat toward Callie, ever the gentleman. "Good thing I'm a happily married man. I might be giving you a run for your money."

Matt shook his head, pretending indifference, but when he glanced Callie's way, twin spots of color brightened her cheeks.

The wind, he decided.

"Ready here."

He started feeding her shingles again, her speed and concentration commendable when it was all he could do not to notice how she moved, the way she handled the nail gun as though born to it, her manner decisive, her gaze intent, her lower lip drawn between her teeth as she squared up each section.

She didn't talk, she worked, and Matt appreciated that. Talking slowed things down, and they were already racing the clock. Callie understood the time line and stayed focused on the job at hand while Matt had a hard time focusing on anything but her.

A car pulled up. Amanda climbed out, toting a drink tray of fresh coffees from the convenience store at the crossroads.

"She's a lifesaver," Callie muttered from behind Matt.

Matt met her gaze and smiled. "I'll say. Now if she only thought to bring doughnuts…"

Amanda set the tray of large coffees down on the saw table tucked inside the garage of number seventeen, then headed back to the car and pulled out a big box of doughnuts.

"No wonder he loves her."

Callie laughed out loud, Matt's easy humor a comfortable draw. "And times aren't easy for them."

"Exactly." Matt nodded her way, before tilting his gaze toward Amanda. "But they go the distance. That's why I contracted Jim initially, but the closing took weeks longer than expected and he was already treading water."

"Tough business climate for builders," Callie noted as she climbed down the ladder ahead of him, pretending not to notice how nice he looked from behind in his jeans, his movements sure and steady. A guy who looked that good in denim ought to be doing TV commercials.

This is a work relationship. It's money in the bank, Callie. It's a chance to get through this winter in the black, instead of the red. You can't afford to let anything mess this up.

She knew that, but couldn't deny the pull. She'd been a soldier for years. A good soldier learned to assess and acclimate, then decide.

She'd assessed Matt, all right, and she was tempted

to get a little more acclimated, but when it came to the decision-making part of things, she had one job first and foremost: to take care of Jake and her father.

She couldn't afford to tip this job into negative territory, and romance gone bad could do just that.

Nope, she'd be friendly, work hard and hope Matt kept them on as he proceeded to finish the homes her father had started.

Matt turned and handed her a coffee. Their eyes met. He stood, holding the coffee, her hand skimming his, their gazes locked, electrifying the moment.

"Cream?" He half choked the word, then rolled his eyes, smiled and leaned forward, his voice soft. "I don't think my voice has broken like that in nearly twenty years, and I was talking to a pretty girl that time, too."

Callie accepted the coffee, slanted him a wry glance and reached for two little creamers. "Twenty years between girls? That's so not normal. You get that, right?"

He grinned and added sugar to his coffee before sidling her a look. "Maybe it depends on the girl."

"Makes men choke." Callie nodded, stirred her coffee, put the lid back on to help ward off the cold and turned his way. "I'll put that on my list of attributes if I decide to go on one of those internet dating sites."

"Or you could spare yourself the trouble and just go out with me." The look he sent her said he was only half-teasing.

An offer she'd love under different circumstances. She'd figured that out when she'd found him sitting at their kitchen table, firm but at ease, decisive, but kind when pushed to ask for their help. Matt's warmth and self-confidence spelled "good guy" in bold letters, but this good guy was also her boss.

"I never date the boss," she told him, keeping her tone easy but her answer firm. "If things go bad it makes for a rough work environment."

His look said he agreed but wished he didn't. He handed her the open box of doughnuts and indicated them with a glance down. "May I offer you first choice in doughnuts at least?"

She grinned, wishing she could have said yes to going out, but glad he recognized the dangers, too. "That's quite chivalrous of you."

"The least I can do, ma'am." He tugged his wool hat slightly, the maneuver endearing, but Callie couldn't risk endearment.

Could she?

Not when he controlled the paycheck.

Chapter Five

Callie walked into the familiar setting of the Jamison Farmers' Free Library for the weekly fundraising meeting that evening. In partnership with Walker Electronics, the towns were raising funds to upgrade and expand the tiny library tucked in the vintage village. Callie loved being on hand to help raise money for the good cause because Hannah Moore, the former librarian, had tutored Jake the last two years, inspiring him, laughing with him.

And now Hannah was engaged to Matt Cavanaugh's brother, Jeff Brennan, her cochair on the library committee. Which meant Callie couldn't stop thinking of Matt while seeing Jeff and Hannah.

But she was having a hard time not thinking of Matt without Jeff and Hannah around, so tonight wasn't much different than every other night this past week.

"Callie." Hannah sent her a quick grin of acknowledgment and handed off meeting minutes from the previous week. "Do you mind setting these around for me?"

"Glad to." Callie laid a copy on each chair while Hannah finished measuring coffee.

"Done."

"Me, too." Hannah crossed the room and grasped her hands. "Hey, I wanted to say I'm sorry about your father's subdivision. It's got to be hard, watching it being developed right across the street from you."

"Actually..."

"We all know how hard you worked on it..."

Callie grasped her friend's hand to shush her. "Hannah. Pause. Breathe. Dad and I are still working on it."

Hannah frowned. "Huh?"

"Matt hired us to crew with him."

Hannah's frown turned into surprise. "Gutsy move. Not like that should surprise me." She sent a wizened look toward the door as Jeff walked in, looking confident and happy to see his future bride. "They are brothers." She refocused her attention on Callie as Jeff paused to talk to Melissa, the young woman taking over Hannah's job at the library. "Are you okay with all this?"

Callie's hesitation outed her.

"Oh, honey." Hannah made a face of concern. "You don't have to work for him, you know. Not if it's that hard."

Hannah had clearly misunderstood her pause in conversation. As Jeff moved into their area, Callie hedged. "It's fine, really. Matt's amazing and we're already making great progress on the houses. And that's good for Dad, mentally and physically."

"Glad to hear it." Jeff slipped an arm around Hannah, planted a soft kiss to her hair, but kept his attention on Callie. "And I told Matt he could stay with me, but he said he was going to finagle a spot onsite because he can't afford to lose time with the short days now."

"And that's a fact." Callie didn't mention that Matt had moved into their extra room, and that his burly presence added a whole new dimension to their home. That his laugh shook the rafters and his smile...

Oh, that smile...

Luckily other committee members began trouping in, saving her from making a complete fool of herself. Jeff moved off to greet people, but Hannah stayed put. She swept Callie an up-and-down look before nodding. "Hmm."

Callie frowned. "Hmm?"

"Hmm."

Hannah tossed Callie a knowing look over her shoulder as she set pens around the table. Callie shook her head, firm. Resolute. "No hmms. Strictly business."

"I know exactly what you mean." Hannah jerked a thumb toward Jeff in the crowd of new arrivals. "A few months ago I was fighting tooth and nail to get off this committee. Now I'm marrying my cochair. Oh, I get it, Cal."

"I barely know the guy," Callie protested.

Hannah leaned closer, grinning. "I think that must be one of their special gifts, honey. And I can't say I'm a bit sorry. But because they are aggravating, industrious, somewhat know-it-all men..."

"With a great sense of humor."

Hannah acknowledged that with a brisk nod. "Call me if you need me. Or if you just want girlfriend time."

"Aren't you busy planning a wedding?"

Hannah laughed and lowered her voice as others approached. "Dana took over."

Callie grinned. Jeff's mother was well-known throughout town, a pillar of the community, a stalwart, God-loving woman unafraid to get dirty or put her hand to any task.

"Leaving me free to teach science." Hannah tipped another smile Callie's way. "And see my fiancé."

"Perfect."

"It is." Hannah gave Callie's hand a light squeeze. "And Matt, well…" Her smile deepened. "Dana raves about him, and I'd trust her opinion on anything. I'm just getting to know him myself, but he seems like one special guy."

Callie didn't need that reminder. Still, it was nice to see the approval and appreciation in Hannah's eyes because Matt was sharing their home, their food, their table. She faltered, then dropped her gaze to Hannah's hands, Hannah's soft skin tweaking her. "Do manicures help?"

"Help?"

Heat rumbled up from somewhere deep inside Callie. Not that she cared about what her hands looked like, but soft skin, pretty nails…

"My hands take a beating," she confessed. As committee members started to settle into seats, she held up her hands. "Construction work is tough and this cold, dry weather isn't exactly friendly to the skin."

Hannah tilted her head, smiled and winked. "You need a little Meredith time."

Callie frowned. "Jeff's sister?"

"Jeff's sister ran a posh spa in Maryland until a month or two ago. Let me set up an appointment for you."

Callie shook her head. No way could she justify spending money on a frivolity like that when cash was so tight.

"And don't worry about the money," Hannah added as if reading her mind. "Meredith's a sweetheart and she'll do it just to help her brother's friend. We can do it at Dana's place. Or mine."

"Um…"

Hannah's laugh said she realized she'd railroaded Callie and didn't care. Callie had never met Meredith Brennan, but she knew Hannah. Trusted her. She had a hard time imagining people spending hard-earned money on fancy nails, a true skeptic when it came to anything construed as froufrou.

Except a great pair of heels. Those she understood.

The press of committee members pushed her back into meeting mode, a good thing when talking about Matt just made it easier to think about Matt. Better for both of them to keep him out of sight, out of mind.

And definitely better from a paycheck perspective.

"I think the rain will shut down roofing tomorrow," Matt announced the next evening. He set two bags of groceries on the counter and laughed when Jake zeroed in on the Christmas tree snack cakes.

"I love these!" Jake exclaimed, eyes wide. "Mom, can I—"

"First, no, it's too close to supper. And second, they're Matt's, not ours."

"Rule number one," Matt said. "Any food I buy is up for grabs."

"Sweet." Jake mimicked Matt's grin and Matt high-fived him like they'd put one over on her.

"Still, not before dinner. Either of you."

Matt sent her a look across the room, a look that said more than words. He gripped Jake's shoulder and nodded toward the homework table. "If you've got homework, I'd be glad to help."

"Sure."

"He's been here two days and already he's replacing me?" Callie asked Jake, a hand to her heart, feigning hurt.

"That way you can have some downtime after supper," Matt advised. "Maybe we can play Yahtzee. Or UNO." He scanned the game shelf. "But watch out if you take me on in war." He pumped up his chest and drew his shoulders back. "Me being a soldier and all."

"Mom was a soldier, too," Jake chattered as he pulled his agenda and binder out of his book bag and laid them on the window table. "So was my dad."

Callie kept her wince hidden, but something about Matt's analytical gaze said he saw too much. He carried the discerning air of a marine, and while that should be a comfort, Callie didn't need anyone discerning too much. Not now, not ever.

She lifted the soup pot lid and breathed deep before spearing a carrot. "Almost done, so you guys have about fifteen minutes. Because I've been replaced, that is."

"Only temporarily." Matt flashed her a teasing grin, but his words reminded her this was a short-lived setup, not a permanent convenience.

She'd tried ignoring him for the first twenty-four hours he lived there.

Fat chance.

Then she tried treating him like a brother.

That didn't even come close to working.

Friends, she decided that morning. Good friends.

They'd worked side-by-side all day and now had only two houses left to roof. With Thanksgiving approaching, the guys would need time to be with their families.

The weather forecast didn't look great, and each day meant the odds against them were growing. They needed two solid days, maybe three of decent weather.

God, please, asking you to govern the weather seems

a little bossy with all you've got going, but please... Help us get these last two homes covered.

"If it's raining we can install windows."

Matt nodded, pointed out a problem to Jake and turned her way. "Exactly what I was thinking. That way we don't lose time and prevent further damage. And the Tyvek wrap will help keep external walls from getting damaged over the winter if we can't side them right away."

Not getting them sided would disappoint him. He'd laid out his plans the first night in their house, showing the time line to Hank and Callie after Jake had gone to bed.

Hank had eyed the plans and made a skeptical face. "It works if everything goes perfectly."

"Exactly."

"So if it doesn't," Hank continued, turning a frank look Matt's way, "We prioritize. Roofing. Tyvek. Windows. Get them sealed as best we can. Then interior work over the winter won't suffer damage."

"And with a four-month window to get the Tyvek covered," Matt observed, "we can apply siding when the weather starts to ease."

"Yes." Matt's respect for the manufacturer's guidelines earned him Hank's approval. "Warranties remain in effect and the town doesn't cite us for not following code." Hank's expression changed as he realized what he'd said. "You, I mean. Not us."

Matt had offered him a straight look. "I wouldn't be here if it wasn't for you, Hank. Your vision. Your plans. Your project. Having you on board makes my life a whole lot easier right now. I'd be foolish not to realize that, and I finished being foolish a long time ago."

Matt's words eased her father's strained expression,

and Callie blessed him for guarding the older man's ego. Hank's self-esteem had taken a beating these last two years, first from a debilitating and somewhat embarrassing illness that left him wearing a colostomy pouch, followed by losing the business he'd spent thirty years building. And because Callie had worked for Hank's company, the double loss of income spelled near disaster.

Matt's investment in Cobbled Creek changed all that.

His presence in their home was changing more than her business perspective, but she'd made a firm decision to keep her distance. Her father and son had been through enough, and adding romantic drama to an already-tense life would be foolhardy. Hadn't Matt just mentioned how he'd stopped doing foolish long ago?

Well, so had she, about the time Dustin walked out leaving her with an eight-month-old baby and little money.

Matt's engaging laugh drew her attention to the man and boy profiled in the window, heads bent as Jake worked out a word problem. Matt fist-pumped when Jake got the answer right, and Jake's answering grin reaffirmed what Callie had shared with her father the week before. Jake didn't know his dad enough to miss him, but he missed *having* a dad. That was evident in the shine he took to Matt, the way he tried to emulate Matt's moves on a house. If she wasn't careful, Jake would fall in love with the square-shouldered, sturdy builder and have his heart broken once Cobbled Creek was complete.

She couldn't let that happen, but she couldn't deny Jake the chance to hang with Matt, talk with him. Chat with him. Matt's positive influence was good for Jake. She recognized that. And while life handed out good and bad, some rough turns could be character-building.

A boy didn't grow to be a man without scraping a few knees, and Jake was no exception.

"Done." Matt grinned at the boy, satisfaction lighting his face.

"Done." Jake echoed, exuberant. He glanced at the clock. "And we did it quicker than Mom does. She talks a lot."

"I do not."

Matt held his hands up in surrender, his eyes bright with humor. "I didn't say it." He jerked a thumb Jake's way. "He did."

"'Cause it's true," Jake added as he put his notebook away.

"She's mighty quiet on those rooftops," Matt noted as he withdrew plates and bowls for the table. "Hard to imagine her a chatterbox here."

Callie sent him a faux-withering look. "I talk as needed."

"And then some," offered the boy.

"Jake."

He laughed and dashed off to the living room to call Hank and Buck.

Callie eyed their study table and shifted her gaze to Matt as she piled biscuits into a napkin-lined basket. "He might be right. I tend to go overboard, always explaining. Showing him the whys and wherefores."

"That's not a bad thing." Matt took the basket from her, lifted it to his nose and breathed deep, appreciation brightening his dark eyes. "These smell wonderful."

She grinned. "Good change of subject."

"I do what I can, ma'am."

Callie paused, one hand reaching for the soup kettle,

Matt's words and tone sparking a memory of life in the service. Soldierly reparté.

"You okay?" Matt gazed at her, puzzled, a brow thrust up.

"Fine." Callie shrugged, grabbed the soup with both hands and shook her head. "Just a déjà vu moment."

Matt set out spoons and butter knives like he'd been setting tables all his life, but the look he sent her was only half-teasing and not at all unappreciated. "Cal, trust me on this. If we'd met before, I'd have remembered."

She felt the blush rise from her chest, staining her face and neck, and despite her best military ways, she couldn't tamp it down. "Artful flattery, marine."

"Yes, ma'am." He smiled across the table as the older men lumbered through from the living room. "Two tours in Iraq taught me to plan for the future but live in the moment."

"Good advice, son." Hank nodded approval as he sank into the chair, breathing deep. "Cal, this smells wonderful."

"It does," Buck chimed in. "And I grabbed some ice cream this morning. It's in the freezer on the porch. I thought someone might like a sundae tonight." He targeted Jake with a grin of appreciation. "There's fudge sauce in the cupboard 'longside the sink. And whipped cream in the fridge."

Jake beamed. "Thanks, Buck. I thought you forgot."

"No, sir, I did not." Buck ladled his bowl of soup, set it down and passed the ladle on to Hank. "When this old soldier makes a promise, he keeps it and you worked hard to make that honor roll."

"He sure did." Hank smiled approval at the boy. "Hard work pays off. Got your homework done already?"

Jake waved toward Matt. "Matt helped me while Mom finished supper."

"Ah."

Her father's partial word said a lot, maybe too much, but Matt took it in stride. "The smell of this soup prevailed on me, sir. A good marine does what he must to facilitate great food."

"Amen to that," added Buck. "And speakin' of amens, if you'd bless this food, Hank, we could commence to eatin' and I for one am mighty hungry after workin' rooftops all day."

Hank offered his typical short, clipped blessing and Callie sent him an "Are you kidding me?" look.

He grinned and dipped his spoon into his soup. "No need to look at me like that, daughter, I spent my day praying on that rooftop. God understands short and sweet as well as he does long and drawn out."

"Can't have the biscuits cooling off," Matt chimed in reasonably.

"Would be a cryin' shame," added Buck as he slathered butter across his. "Though Callie's biscuits are fine hot or cold."

"A good selling point," Matt noted, grinning.

"Yet totally unnecessary when nothing's on the market." Callie kept her tone light but directed a pointed gaze at Matt.

"Duly noted."

"Good."

"Did they come and switch up those shingles for number thirty-one?" Hank asked Matt, shifting the subject to Cobbled Creek, a change Callie welcomed.

"First thing in the morning. I'm glad you caught the

mistake, Hank." Matt shook his head. "I can't believe I almost missed it."

"The three and the eight in the code looked mighty similar, but gray shingles in the midst of all these other homes?" Hank made a face. "That would have been bad. This way they're here in time and we don't waste a day. If the rain holds off."

"And I can be here only Monday and Tuesday next week," Buck explained, his tone reluctant. "We're headin' down to the daughter's place for Thanksgiving and won't be back until Saturday. Mother's got to have her shopping day with Jeannine while Bob and I hang out with the kids on Friday."

"Family time's important." Callie smiled at Buck, then shoulder nudged him lightly. "And you know you love wrestling with those boys."

"Though they're too big for that now," Buck admitted. "Tim's in sixth grade, and Tyler's a freshman in high school this year. Seems funny to have them that grown."

"Family is meant to be enjoyed," Hank assured him as he went back to the soup pot for seconds. "The good Lord wouldn't have it any other way."

Hank's choice of expression struck Matt.

Nothing in his family had been enjoyable. Hank's words shone a new perspective on his parents' choices. Neither one held any belief system holy or sacred, neither one invested time in anything but themselves. Matt hadn't known the warmth of a candlelit church service until Gus took charge of him, and it took the rough stint in juvie to put him back on track.

But he'd done it. Finally. With help from his beloved grandfather.

He felt Hank's gaze on him, measuring. Assessing. That single look said Hank knew his past and understood his present, and Hank wouldn't have invited him to live under their roof if he didn't trust him, right?

But Hank knew Matt's stepfather, which meant he knew the clutch of drama surrounding Matt's parents. The two fathers left a legacy of drinking, gambling and womanizing. It wouldn't be a big leap to wonder if Matt carried either man's hard-hitting characteristics. Half the town knew Matt had been headed full-bore in that direction as a young man.

He'd stopped that train of self-destruction, but folks had long memories. His past would intrude on the present, which meant he had to make the here and now as pristine as possible, no hassles, no hurries, no mistakes.

And sitting at the Marek table, Matt never wanted anything more.

"Uh-oh."

Callie peered at Hank as she shimmed a window from the inside while Hank and Buck adjusted the outside the following afternoon. "What?"

Hank jutted his chin toward their house, visible through the back opening. "Don's here."

Callie followed his gaze. "And that's bad because?"

Her father made a face, then pushed out a breath that sounded long overdue. "He's Matt's father."

"He's…" Callie paused, squinted toward the window, then faced Hank. "He's what?"

"Matt's father. Stepfather, actually. In a convoluted weird kind of way."

"You either are or you aren't," Callie corrected him. "It's a legal term. So, is he or isn't he?"

"Is he or isn't he what?"

Perfect. Just perfect.

Callie turned toward Matt's voice, mad at herself for talking about him when he wasn't there. Except he *was* there.

"Don's at the house." Hank pointed toward the road. "I was just explaining to Callie..."

"No sense explaining what can't be understood." Matt rubbed his hands against his jeans, two wet stripes darkening the denim. "I lived it and I still don't get it."

"I'll go talk to him," Hank said. He made a move toward the door and Matt caught his arm.

"I'll do it."

"But you said—"

"I know." Matt studied the view beyond the window, the older man climbing out of his truck, heading toward the house. "But there's no time like the present to have this said."

"You sure?"

Matt shook his head and made a face. "Not by half, but I'll do it anyway."

He strode out the door, climbed into his truck and drove the quarter mile, wind-whipped rain beating on his truck, the wipers slapping up and down in furious fashion. Callie turned toward her father. "I don't get it."

"Neither do I," Hank admitted. He turned his attention back to work. "But it's Matt's story to tell. I just happened to know some of it."

She sent her father an incredulous look. "You're not going to explain this?"

"Nope. Sorry. Gotta ask him."

That wasn't about to happen. She'd managed to keep personal conversations to a minimum so far and...

So far? You're on day five. Not exactly world record pace.

Oh, she got that. But it *was* significant because she'd fought off the inclination to share sweet banter with Matt, knowing he could get under her skin.

Worse, he recognized the ploy. She saw it in his gaze. The set of his chin. The tilt of his head, the tiny muscle that twanged now and again in his jaw.

Knowing his marine background and his patient demeanor, she'd sidestepped anything that might be of import conversationally.

But now, seeing him climb out of his truck and mount their side steps, she kind of wished she knew what was going on.

"I've got the rest of the windows unpackaged." Buck's voice interrupted her wandering thoughts. "Callie, you need help?"

"I'm good, thanks."

Buck stared out the window and then met Hank's gaze. "Uh-oh."

"I said the same."

Callie swept the pair a look of disbelief. "You both know what's going on?"

"Before your time, I expect." Buck helped Hank balance the living room picture window as they lifted it into place from outside. "Cal, can you give us a hand here?"

Callie helped leverage the lower edge of the window into the expertly cut opening. "Nice job, Dad."

"Thank you. And I'm still not telling you. A man's got a right to privacy."

"She could ask him herself," Buck supposed.

Like Callie needed to hear *that* again. "Or not."

"Suit yourself." Buck nodded approval of the window

fit as Callie leveled it from inside. "Kind of nice to have an uncurious woman around. Refreshing, you might say."

Uncurious?

No way.

But she refused to feed the gossip mills at anyone's expense. The thought that Don and Matt were related shouldn't be a surprise with the same last name, but lots of Irish had settled into the lower counties of New York State. Cavanaugh wasn't exactly rare.

But she'd noticed the pained look that crossed Matt's face before he hardened his jaw. That flash of emotion said the past colored the present, and Callie understood that reality tenfold.

Chapter Six

"Matt." The older man's face paled when Matt strode into the Marek kitchen, giving Don an unhealthy hue. Not that Matt cared.

"Don." Matt kept his voice calm, his effect flat, and refused to use the term *Dad*. That title had been forever tainted in his mind by both men, but he was beyond letting their callousness affect the boy who lingered within. Most days. "No one's here right now."

"What are you doing here?"

"Working." Matt jerked a thumb west. "I bought Cobbled Creek from the bank. Hank and his buddies are helping me get things winterized."

Don lifted his chin, surprised. "You own Cobbled Creek?"

"Yes."

Don passed an aging hand across the nape of his neck. It didn't tremble. A good sign, Matt supposed. "Hank was hoping to buy it back himself."

Matt stayed quiet, his silence punctuating the obvious.

"You need help over there?"

A part of Matt's gut seized. Another part froze. Did

the guy who walked out on an eight-year-old boy who'd known him as dad just ask for a job?

Matt conquered his instincts and shook his head, wondering if he could locate a punching bag nearby. "Got it covered, thanks. Hank's invited me to stay here." He waved a hand, indicating the house. "Until I get the model certified."

Don's expression hinted at the sorrowed man within. But Matt had endured more sorrow than a kid should ever have to, so Don could just take his angst and—

"...forgive us our trespasses as we forgive those who trespass against us..."

The sweet words of The Lord's Prayer proved wickedly hard to follow right now. Matt would discuss that with God later, but for the moment... "I've got to get back to work."

"Oh. Sure." Don hauled his wet hat back onto his balding head with two hands. "I'll get on, then."

He'd put on weight. And lost hair. And his teeth could use work. Matt saw all that and tried to equate it with the guy who played catch with him in the backyard. Who took him to Little League games to cheer on the home team. Who promised him the world until the day he realized he had no legal responsibility for Matt and walked out the door, never to be seen again.

Old anger resurged, too sharp to be considered controlled.

But Matt managed it. As he led the way out, he waved toward the subdivision again. "I expect this will take a while."

"I see."

Don's expression said he understood what Matt didn't

say. *Keep your distance until I'm out of here*. He nodded. "Good luck on your project."

Matt refused to acknowledge that. He didn't need luck; he had faith. He didn't need handouts; he needed workers. And God himself knew that Matt didn't need a pretend father hovering on the outskirts of his life, one who should have been holed up in Florida collecting unemployment checks until spring.

If I was a father...

Whoa. Matt put the brakes on that train of thought in whipcord fashion. He carried enough bad genes to ruin a dining room table full of kids, so the idea of procreating?

Wasn't gonna happen.

Nope, he'd stop the craziness of passing on Neal's and his mother's self-absorbed genes right here. He had his work. His company. His service buddies. And a host of construction people in the northern section of Allegheny County admired him for his pledge of excellence and work ethic.

His brother, Jeff, and his new fiancée, Hannah, could produce the next generation of Brennan blood.

Guilt speared him as he approached 17 Cobbled Creek Lane. His grandfather had loved his Latino heritage. And he'd married an Asian woman who taught at a local preschool until her untimely death from ovarian cancer. Matt only knew her in pictures, but Grandpa's praise painted a rosy picture.

And his mother had been beautiful. But looks only go so deep, and if he had to hunt two generations back to find goodness in his family tree, that was too far. Being upfront about that saved a whole lot of wasted time and emotion.

He parked the truck, climbed out and ducked inside the house, damp chilled air surrounding him.

Comfort later. Work now.

That's how he got through the Corps. And through the early days of forging his own company. And through the lean times of project start-ups. He should be used to it by now.

"Need help over here?"

A new warmth stole over Matt. He turned.

Callie stood inside the door. She indicated the house across the street with a nod. "Dad and Buck have that one just about done and I figure we've got a couple of good hours of daylight left, even with the rain."

"Did you have lunch?" Matt didn't remember seeing her leave or eat, so…

"Work first," she told him, moving inside. "Plenty of time to eat once it gets dark and you stay warmer if you keep moving."

A part of Matt respected her stance. Another part wanted to bundle her in a blanket by a cozy fire and make sure she was warm. Fed. Comfortable.

Red alert. You've entered a "no cozy fire" zone. Proceed at your own risk.

"You're right." He headed outside as she moved into the great room area. "Let's see if we can get this done before Jake gets home."

Callie laughed. "He's spending the night at Cole's house, so I'd hope so. I figured that worked out well because we can't put the Christmas lights up in this rain. But maybe tomorrow."

Matt wanted to help with that. He wanted to see Christmas through Jake's eyes, the eyes of a beloved child.

"We'll make sure they go up tomorrow, one way or another," he promised. "I'm not afraid to get wet. As we're about to witness."

"Thanks, Matt." She smiled his way and the warmth that flickered when she walked in the door intensified. "I can manage the lights, but it's easier with two people."

"Yup. Hank and me. You can make supper, or something."

She sent him a "get serious" look as she unpackaged a window. "Keep the little woman in the house? Are you kidding me?" She flashed a glance around them. "You get what I do, right? Climbing a ladder to hang Christmas lights is no biggie."

"Even so." Matt double checked the window dimensions, snapped his tape shut and raised one shoulder. "It wouldn't hurt for you to be warm one day out of seven."

A spark of pleasure brightened her eyes, but she quenched it pretty quick. Not quick enough, though, and Matt wondered how long it had been since anyone had taken care of Callie. Treated her like a woman. Treasured her.

Seeing Don must have lit some emotional fire within him, a flicker of flame that better get squelched quick. He needed the Mareks to make his dream happen. They needed him and his paychecks to survive their current situation. No one on either side could afford to muck this up. So he wouldn't, plain and simple.

Although catching her gaze through the rough-cut window opening made him want to rethink his position.

Time to change the subject. "I figured church first thing. Then a few hours over here. Then Christmas lights and football."

Callie laughed out loud. "After the week you've put in, I'd call football well-deserved entertainment."

He winked in agreement. "Monday's weather looks clear. We can resume roofing then. And if we get this house enclosed by tomorrow night, we're better than halfway done."

"And making sweet time."

"Which brings me back to tomorrow's schedule."

Callie helped stabilize the window as he lifted it into position from outside. "Yes?"

"You in an apron."

She blushed, shook her head and slid thin wooden shims beneath the frame, eyeing her carpenter's level.

"With some kind of great Sunday afternoon meal going," he continued, raising his voice to be heard through the window and over the rain.

"An apron?"

He widened his grin and flicked her outfit a glance. "Saves wear and tear on your flannel shirts."

She didn't answer right away, and when he balanced the window and glanced down, she wasn't smiling.

"Hey, I was kidding. You can get your flannel shirts dirty if you want to. They're washable."

Something flashed in her face, the pain he thought he'd seen the week before, as if…

He had no idea, but he felt bad. And stupid. "Hey, Cal, you don't have to cook." Was her lower lip trembling?

No. She wouldn't do that, would she? Get girly on him?

"Actually, I'll cook," he added hurriedly, anything to put off the possibility of a woman's tears. Nothing in the corps taught him how to deal with those, and that seemed downright wrong and maybe dangerous because he didn't know a male soldier that muscled up to a crying woman. "And put up the Christmas lights. And finish the windows. Just don't cry, okay?"

She scowled, blinked and shrugged, eyes down. "I don't cry."

Right. Matt refused to argue the whole shaking-lip thing. He knew what he saw, but God had also given him a working brain and arguing with an emotional woman? Not smart. "Well, good. So I'll cook…"

"I'll be glad to cook." She finished the shims, assessed the level, then whacked the excess shim board away with more energy than required. Like double that. "I like cooking. Occasionally."

Something wasn't adding up. "Then why the long face?"

"No long face." She straightened and sent him a reassuring look. "See?"

Oh, he saw all right. He saw a soldier that knew how to draw down the shield, a gallant woman who'd learned to quell emotion. And normally he'd praise that talent, a skill not easily attained, but here? Now?

He wanted to help. He longed to ease the flash of hurt and insecurity. Inspire her laughter. But seeing Don face to face left him fresh out of funny things to say.

Cut him some slack, Callie's inner voice advised. *That meeting with Don couldn't have been the easiest thing in the world.* And something she'd like to know more about at some point in time. But not now, when she'd already gone girly and emotional over an innocent comment about her work clothes that should have been funny.

But it wasn't.

Callie moved to the next window, then drew up short. "Oh, I forgot."

Matt checked the frame size before he looked up. "Forgot what?"

"You got a call on the house phone."

"Oh. From?"

"Reenie."

He sent her a puzzled look, one that almost looked sincere, and it wasn't as if Callie cared who called him. Or what they looked like. How they dressed. Really.

"What did she want?"

"Does secretarial pay come with the job?"

He grinned, which meant she let too much emotion creep into her voice, a trend that occurred regularly around Matt Cavanaugh. "Under 'hazard pay' in the fine print. Better read your contract more carefully next time." He held the window in place while Callie leveled it. "So?"

Silent, she winged a brow through the glass.

Matt heaved an overdone sigh, playing along. "Did Reenie leave a message?"

Callie was tempted to pretend she hadn't, except because she had no vested interest in Matt Cavanaugh, why would she even consider such a thing? "That she's fine with next week and your cell phone was out of service."

He pulled out the phone, scanned his bars and made a face. "Signals get choppy down here."

"Sometimes. That's why we kept the landline. Something to think about when you get your C of O on the model." She bent low, then made a quick sure cut, her home-building confidence intrinsic.

Her self-confidence?

Whole other kettle of fish, but she wasn't going to get

into that with Matt. Hopefully he'd chalk it up to bad timing or whatever. And she could care less who Reenie was.

Liar, liar, pants on fire...

She stood back as he positioned the next window, shushed the inner voice, then nodded approval. "I've always loved these house plans. Each one distinct despite the neighborhood similarities."

"That's what drew me to Cobbled Creek." Matt sent her a frank glance of approval. "Your dad has a great eye for manipulating design just enough to maintain a neighborhood feel but leave each house unique. And the hillside setting, leaving established trees in place." Matt's appreciation for the aesthetics raised Callie's confidence a notch. "A perfect draw."

Callie slanted up a knowing smile. "He had help."

Matt read her inference and grinned. "You?"

She nodded. "I love that kind of thing. Setting. Blending. Coordinating."

"Interior stuff, too?"

She shook her head. "Decorating's not my forte. But home design. Placement. Light filtration. And kitchen setup. That stuff I get."

"That's a gift, Callie."

"I know." She moved to remove the casing from the dining bay windows. "And Dad was never afraid to let me use it. I love that about him."

"So you do that with Jake."

"Is it obvious?"

He nodded. "Definitely. You draw the best out of him, but don't smother him. You let him find his way. That takes guts."

She shrugged, not wanting to explain too much, but grateful for Matt's compliment. "I want him to feel independent. It's hard for kids who need extra help in school. It gets embarrassing."

"It sure does."

His wry note drew her closer. "Don't tell me you struggled in school, marine."

"Ha." He moved to the east side of the house and measured, then remeasured before grunting satisfaction. "School came hard. That's why I think it's cool how you help Jake. Teach him. Coach him."

Callie heard what he didn't say, that no one had bothered to do that with him. Her heart pinched at the thought of his little boy struggles, how challenging it must have been. And yet he'd conquered those dragons. He must have, or he wouldn't be standing here today. "Somewhere along the way you caught up."

He winced. "Took too long. Wouldn't wish that on anyone, so you just keep doing what you're doing. Jake's a great kid."

The unspoken part of that comment said he hadn't been a great kid, and that quiet admission nicked Callie's work-hardened reserve a little more. "Thanks, Matt."

He didn't reply, just angled a look toward the far side of the window. "Can you catch this when I slide it into place?"

"Sure."

They inset and leveled the five tall, slim windows framing the dining space. When he finished setting nails in the last one, he grunted approval. "It looks good and it's getting dark. Done."

"I love the look."

She gathered tools and left the mound of wrapping. "We'll stow it all once we're finished with windows." They headed down the walk, then the stone drive. As they hit the road, Callie turned. "It's starting to look like something, Matt."

"It is." Matt's approving tone made her feel good, which was silly, really, and yet…

"Which one is your favorite?"

She didn't need to consider the question as they moved into the street. "The model, of course. That's why it's the model. It's the one I pictured living in. Hearth and home, classic Cape styling, paned windows, stone front." She turned and waved a hand to the rest of the street. "These are all good designs, but when I tweaked the model I tried to incorporate everything I'd love in a home, starting with the feel. The emotional response it creates in people."

"Women, mostly."

She laughed and bumped shoulders with him. "Probably, yes. But is that bad? What man doesn't want his wife to be happy? Or what woman wants to scrimp on the home she's worked for years to get?"

"But you kept it affordable." Matt paused and turned her way as they reached the Marek driveway. "That's a rare talent, Callie."

She started to shake her head, but he paused the action with a hand to her shoulder. "Don't shake me off. It's true. Especially now, with mortgage lending tight and housing needs tanking. You managed to make these homes something that invites investment, promotes families and is affordable. That took knowledge and a keen eye for placement. Thank you for that."

His words rang sweet because she'd adjusted the original plans for all his listed reasons, but gazing up into his eyes, those deep, dark pools of chocolate, his grateful expression put a hold on her heart. And her tongue. For the life of her, she couldn't wrap her brain around anything to say, not when he held her gaze and her shoulder, the strength of his grip something to lean into. Rely on.

"Callie…" His attention slipped from her eyes to her mouth, his expression wondering. Maybe hoping.

Callie took a firm step back, unwilling to wonder, not daring to hope, refusing to play in waters that nearly drowned her before.

Matt stood strong and silent, watching. Waiting. Giving her a chance to move toward him or step away, and despite how badly she'd like to take that first step in his direction, she moved back and quieted a sigh. "We had an agreement, remember?"

"I was hoping you'd forgotten."

"No, you weren't." Callie pulled her flannel closer and swept the subdivision a look. "We both need this done. You need to guard your investment, I need a paycheck. Dad, too. And muddying the waters would be ill-advised. Besides, the guys all kind of look out for me."

"Because your husband left you alone to raise Jake while he traipsed around with another woman?"

She smacked his upper arm and refused to feel bad when he cringed in pretend pain. "Leave it alone. Please. And have you noticed that while I've guarded your privacy like an MP at the gate, you've managed to dig up half my life history? Level the playing field or change the subject."

"First, that's some left jab you've got there." He sent a look of overdone admiration to her left arm as they climbed the stairs to the side porch and rubbed his arm, pretending she'd really hurt him. As if. His corded upper arms were steel bands and locked mighty good in a T-shirt. Not that she noticed.

"And second," Matt continued, "I think it was the

guys' way of issuing warnings. Letting me know they stand to protect you from other stupid men who don't appreciate how wonderful you are."

"I don't need protection." She made that pronouncement as they approached the door. Matt paused her with a hand to her arm again.

"What *do* you need, Callie?"

Need? Want? The list was too long to articulate, but she'd trained herself to keep things to a minimum. She leaned forward, just enough to let him think she was reconsidering the glance he'd sent to her mouth, then tapped him on the nose when he drew close. "A paycheck. And peace on Earth would be nice, too."

She stepped back, gave his knit cap a gentle tug and headed inside, leaving him to follow.

As she shed her outer layer of work clothes, the memory of that near kiss played with her heart. Her head. But she knew better than most what fickle things men were, so she'd keep herself focused on the task at hand. Home-building. Roofing. And while a little flirting might not be a bad thing, she couldn't risk upsetting this apple cart of opportunity.

"I'll start a load of heavy stuff."

She turned straight into one of those dull brown T-shirts he favored, muscled marine chest and shoulders straining the worn seams, the soft cotton fabric needing a good washing at the end of the day.

And he was still appealing.

She didn't need an air raid siren or blackout curtains to remind her she was in grave danger, but she couldn't quite remember the last time danger felt this refreshingly good.

Obviously she was food-deprived.

Hank saved the day by walking in with an extra-large

pizza. Callie headed for the kitchen while Matt started the washer, the mingled scents of pepperoni, sausage and cheese replacing cotton knit.

But even after skipping lunch, there was no way Callie could fool herself into thinking the pizza smelled better than the well-worn shirt, and that spelled trouble.

Chapter Seven

Matt studied the five church choices facing the park green, a sweet template despite the bone-chilling rain. And from the steady stream of cars rounding the circle and pulling into backyard parking lots, Jamison folk weren't about to be deterred by the seasonal drizzle.

What's your goal?

To pray.

Soldiers didn't need a church for prayer, but Matt wouldn't confuse Jake by staying home on a Sunday morning. He also wasn't about to go to Good Shepherd with the Mareks, not when so many people from his past were members.

He wasn't after confrontation, just peace and quiet. Solace.

He slid the truck into a parking space along Main Street, climbed out and approached the White Church at the Bend, second-guessing himself.

Maybe he should have headed north. Route 19 went straight to Houghton, a sweet college town with several churches, but that extra twenty minutes meant productive time wasted.

It also ensured privacy. Matt was less likely to meet his past on the streets of Houghton. Jamison and Wellsville?

The past met the present at every corner.

Man up, marine.

Matt entered the small church, found an innocuous seat on the far left and sat, eyes forward, determined to pay attention to nothing but the service.

The sound of dripping water thwarted his vow. A spreading damp spot encroached the plastered ceiling over the altar. The budding smell of mildew shouted wet basement.

And was that a taped-up electrical connection on the left?

The old place had seen better days. Flaking paint above the congregation meant damp wood. The floor was older than dirt and looked it.

The little church needed help, and a construction guy like Matt knew how quickly things went from bad to worse if left too long.

"Gettin' worn around the edges, ain't it?"

Matt turned toward the outside aisle. A small woman with a cane stood alongside his pew. Matt moved in to make room, and when she had trouble wrestling her cane into submission, he helped hook it on the pew's back.

She breathed a sigh of gratitude as she sank into the seat. "Thank you."

"You're welcome."

She nodded forward, then leaned back against the cream-colored pew. "You're in for a treat this mornin'."

"Am I?" Matt settled back and smiled. "Good."

"Katie's playin' for us."

"Ah." He nodded politely, ever the gentleman.

"Her father don't like that she comes here, but Katie

ain't never been one to listen to his harping on this, that or the other thing."

Matt twitched inside. He'd come to pray, not catch up on local news, and he was just about to sidle right when a young woman entered the sanctuary area from the left.

Katie Bascomb.

Guilt power-washed his heart.

A C-clamp seized his lungs, the turning screw tightening with each breath.

His fingers went numb, the adrenaline rush pouring pins-and-needles energy into his extremities.

She looked lovely, and that beat the way she'd looked the last time he saw her. Broken. Bloodied. Bruised.

Memories blindsided him, images streaming like a bad video feed, showcasing what he'd done.

But mostly what he'd failed to do.

He started to leave, feeling certain he had no right to be here, invading Katie's life. Her time. Her peace.

The old lady leaned closer. "Do you mind helpin' me out when service is over?" She skimmed the cane and the rain a cryptic look. "I'm not as steady as I used to be. I live a few doors down Main Street. If it's not too much trouble," she added, as if asking for help pained her.

He wanted out, big time.

But he couldn't deny this grandmother's petition. "I'd be glad to, ma'am."

Her smile soothed a little. Or maybe it was God. Or memories of Grandpa Gus hugging his shoulder and saying, "We all make mistakes. Then we learn from them and go on. Or not." He'd nod and grip Matt just a little tighter. "The choice is ours."

Katie positioned herself in front of a stool. Two clips

held her long, blond hair back from her face, a face that seemed too serene for what she'd suffered because of him.

A long, flowing skirt rippled its way to the floor in some crinkled material, a blend of bright fall colors vying for attention. An earthy necklace hung against a pale sweater, its chunky beads accenting the colors below.

She looked beautiful. And mature. And peaceful, a violin grasped in one hand, a bow in her other. She quickly glanced at the small but growing congregation as if teasing them, as if guarding some fun-loving secret from her vantage point at the altar.

Shame wrenched his gut because he knew that under the placid beauty lay a broken woman.

His fault. All his fault.

He had to leave.

A young couple with two small children edged into his pew from the right.

Blocked.

Unless he *wanted* to be noticed and he could guarantee that was the last thing on his to-do list that morning. Why hadn't Katie stayed at Good Shepherd, where her parents had gone forever?

Sweet notes sang from the front, single haunting notes inviting prayer.

Right until they jumped into quick succession, the small congregation grinning as if in on the secret. Katie's hands flashed the bow across the instrument. As one, the congregation stood, keeping time, heads bobbing, wide smiles matching hers. Clapping.

Obviously Matt had landed in a place that *looked* like Jamison but became some sort of "sixties"-style Celtic fair once you walked through the double oak doors of the White Church at the Bend.

The old woman jutted his arm. "Ain't she somethin'? And our new pastor, well, he's got people comin' in to do all kinds of things now. Nothin' slow or easy 'bout his way of doin' things and I say good for him!" She punctuated her approval with a firm nod that looked almost grim. "'Bout time we had someone rile up this old church. Best we've been doin' lately is diggin' holes, settin' one after another to rest. Now we've got young families comin' in. Bringin' their babies." She grinned across him to where two preschoolers eagerly awaited whatever was going to happen next. "New life."

And that's what he wanted, wasn't it? Why he'd come back to Jamison? To atone for the old and make way for the new.

A young man wearing a black-and-gold football jersey and wide grin strolled onto the small altar as Katie picked out a foot-tapping arrangement of "When the Saints Go Marching In."

The small crowd erupted, singing and clapping, welcoming the man despite his presence in the heart of Buffalo football fans. Matt grinned in spite of himself.

It took a gutsy guy to claim his team in enemy territory, but the young pastor's face said he'd handle whatever came his way. Matt liked him immediately, an uncommon occurrence for a marine.

By the time the atypical service concluded, Matt was sure of two things.

Katie was doing okay.

And Jamison had changed.

"Loretta, you've found yourself a new beau," the young pastor exclaimed as Matt assisted the aged woman out the back door once the life-affirming service had concluded. "And you're new here." The pastor clasped Matt's hand, grinning an amused welcome.

Matt swept the town a glance. "I grew up here."

"You did?" The old lady shot him a look of shrewd interest.

"Then you know how wonderful it is firsthand." The pastor pumped Matt's hand with an easy vigor. "A great place to settle down. Raise a family. Or come home to. Right, Loretta?"

"Yessir."

Because Matt wasn't inclined to do any of the above, he hedged. "Nice to have you here, Reverend."

"Si," the other man corrected. "Simon MacDaniel, but everyone calls me Si."

"But you *are* a reverend, right?"

Si grinned. "Got me a nice diploma from one of those mail-order places to prove it."

"Oh, you!" Loretta's grin lit up her face, easing the chronic line of worry.

Matt grinned despite himself. "Then I should expect reggae next week?"

"I'll get Katie right on it," the pastor affirmed as he turned to greet the next person. Matt hoped Si turned quick enough to miss his reaction. As he headed down the front walk, commotion across the leaf-strewn park said his timing had gone awry.

The doors of Good Shepherd swung open opposite them. Either Reverend Hannity cut his sermon short or Si had waxed on. Matt glanced at his watch and made a face.

Si's fault, which made him a good preacher in Matt's book, but that proved small comfort as streams of people headed toward vehicles parked creatively here, there and the other place. While the five churches created a postcard-like ambiance to onlookers, the Sunday morning reality became a logistical nightmare, guided by a sheriff's deputy in rain gear, allowing traffic into and out of the circle.

Only in Jamison, Matt thought, but as confusing as the moment appeared, he found himself longing to belong. A huge part of his life had been lived in this town, like those unfinished houses he now tended.

He'd been rough-cut. Unpolished. Not plumbed to fit anywhere, so he'd made up his own rules and crashed and burned, taking Katie and two of his buddies with him.

The guys had walked away with barely a scratch.

Katie hadn't walked away at all. Not for a long time, and then it took a prosthetic and loads of therapy. She'd been doing physical therapy while he did time, but in the end, he gained his release and walked free.

Katie was still missing a leg.

He longed to move quickly, berating himself mentally for not going to Houghton, but the aged woman's pace urged caution.

Jake ran their way, oblivious to the rain, a wide grin lighting his face. "Matt! Did you see this?" Waving Matt forward, Jake stopped in front of a large sign. "They're doing Christmas lights in the park! And sleigh rides! In the dark!"

Jake's voice spiked the exclamation points to new highs, his enthusiasm contagious.

"Looks fun, bud."

"A little pricey," Loretta noted.

Matt eyed the ticket cost and saw Jake's expression dim, but the boy didn't wallow or pout. He manned up with a stout smile and said, "It is kinda pricey and who wants to go see old lights anyway?" He turned a bright gaze up toward Matt, his earnest expression pulling Matt in. Brave. Stoic. Sturdy. What a kid. "And we're putting our lights up today, right, Matt?"

"Right. But let me get this nice lady out of the rain, Jake, and I'll see you at home."

He raised his gaze and saw Callie watching from the edge of the park green. A hint of winsome softened her smile, as if wishing...wondering...

Hoping?

Back off, dude. Would that pretty lady be looking at you that way if she realized what you had done? Who you were?

No way.

You there, God? I thought this was a good idea. I thought I'd come down here, make amends, fix things and move on. But maybe I'm being selfish. Maybe my presence will hurt more than it heals.

Matt passed a hand across Jake's head, escorted the old woman to her door, then headed back to his truck, eyes down, pretending oblivion.

"Cavanaugh."

Most civilians didn't realize how dangerous it could be to sneak up on a marine. Matt stopped himself from putting a hold on the middle-aged man, but just barely. "Mr. Bascomb."

"What are you doing here?"

Since Katie's father served on the town council, he knew why Matt was in town. Howard Bascomb had tried to nix Matt's zoning approvals for Cobbled Creek but couldn't, and that bit deep with the older man. Because Matt was responsible for what happened to Katie two decades back, he couldn't say he blamed him. Still... "Going to church."

"Katie's church."

Matt raised two hands, palms out, in surrender. "I didn't know that until she stepped onto the altar."

"Stay away from her." Howard took a step forward, his gaze menacing, but Maude McGinnity must have sensed something was up. She bustled through the door of the Quiltin' Bee, her sewing and quilt shop that pulled in tourists from all over. "Howard, good morning. And Matt." Maude reached out and gave him a hug, an obvious move meant to quell Howard's angst. "So good to see you. I hear you're doing some fine work up there on Dunnymeade Hill. We'll all be happy to see Cobbled Creek finished, Hank Marek most of all."

"Yes, ma'am."

She grinned and tugged him inside, leaving Howard in the rain. "May I show you something?"

"Yes." Matt elongated the word, reading her ploy. "And thank you," he added as Howard trudged in the opposite direction.

"You're welcome." She kept drawing him forward and Matt paused, puzzled.

"You really have something to show me?"

She frowned. "Yes."

"That wasn't just a maneuver to break up the drama on your front step?"

Her knowing smile confirmed his guess. "That, too." She led him into a room where racks of hand-sewn quilts were displayed away from the south-facing windows.

"Wow." Matt eyed the walled display, then the racks. He arched a brow and angled Maude a look of admiration. "Amazing work."

"My Amish women." She nodded, brisk, and moved

several poled quilts aside. "But this is the one I wanted you to see."

He stepped forward as she singled out a beautiful coverlet arrayed in a mix of quilted and embroidered flowers. "Mama's Flower Garden," she told him, a fond smile crinkling her face.

The blanket was a virtual backyard of color, tone and warmth, the three-dimensional feel of some of the blossoms a salute to warm, sunny days. The vibrant mix of hues heralded spring, and in the dank, gray days of November, spring seemed a long time off.

"It's lovely." He fingered the quilt again, then turned, puzzled. "But why are you showing me?"

"Hank Marek commissioned this for Callie before everything tanked. It was a Christmas present for her, but then he couldn't afford it, so I put it out here."

Matt flipped over the price tag and winced. "The most expensive one of the bunch, of course."

"Let's call it creative financing." Maude grinned at his hiked brow. "I didn't want anyone else to buy it, so I discouraged the purchase. Think half what you see and it's yours."

"Mine?"

"If you're interested, that is." Her facial expression read "all business," but the gleam in her eye said "yenta."

Matt took a broad step back. "Hank might want to get it himself."

"Possibly." Maude's look said she wouldn't push, but it also said she didn't think it likely that Hank could put together over five hundred dollars for a blanket.

Matt started to turn away, but reached out for one more touch. "He really commissioned this for her?"

Maude regarded the quilt, then Matt. "He said when

Callie came back from Iraq, she was different. More subdued."

Matt could understand that. War could change people, but because women weren't allowed in combat, he didn't think the effect held true for them. Maybe he'd been a little simplistic in his assumptions.

"And that she missed color most of all."

That statement hit a note as well. The flat, dull tones of desert duty held none of the warmth and drama of Allegheny County, its beauty ever-changing in the dance of seasons. "That's true."

"Callie's mother loved to garden. She had a knack, that's for sure. That's why Hank picked this design." Maude flicked the quilt a quick, dismissive touch. "Well, you know it's here. That's really all I meant to do."

"And break up the confrontation with Howard."

She mulled that as she walked him out front. "Howard's not a bad person, but he's unforgiving. And Katie had a rebel streak in her that he tried to squelch six ways to Sunday."

"But—"

"No buts." Maude turned a firm gaze his way. "I've known that girl since she was in the cradle. And Howard's as responsible as any for her wild years. He knows that, which is why he needs to blame you. Howard Bascomb isn't about to shoulder that responsibility himself."

"I was sixteen, driving the car and drunk." Matt laid out the facts with no defensive strategy. "I'm going with my fault."

"Huh." She sighed and looked aggrieved. "You're such a leatherneck."

Her use of the marine term made him smile. "Guilty."

"And two tours in Iraq."

"Didn't give Katie her leg back." He reached for the door handle, then turned back toward Maude. "I appreciate what you're trying to do."

"But you're too dad-gum stubborn to see it yourself," she shot back. "And that's the one thing you are guilty of, Matt Cavanaugh." She reached out a hand to shake his, her grip firm and direct. "I married a marine. Smartest move I ever made, so forgive an old lady for doing some matchmaking as opportunity arises."

"Yes, ma'am." He grinned, tipped his chin down and headed back into the rain, the bustle of people gone, the park round empty. He realized he'd half hoped Callie would still be here, which was downright silly because he'd see her back at the house in just a few minutes, right?

"Hey, marine."

He turned as her car rolled up alongside him, unable to fight back the smile of welcome. "Hey, yourself. You folks going the wrong way?"

Callie shook her head. "Just wanted to make sure everything was okay. I saw your truck parked here once I dragged Jake away from his buddies and…" She shrugged, pretending unconcern. "I didn't want you stuck or anything."

Add compassionate to her growing list of attributes, as if Matt needed more reasons to be attracted. He bent down, leaned in and grinned, pleased that she checked on him, staunchly refusing to examine why such a little thing felt so good.

Why did his smile make her heart feel stronger? Prettier? More desireable? Why did mere seconds in his company make her long for more?

You don't get it? Really?

Callie hushed the inner admonition. She *couldn't* get it, plain and simple. And since Matt understood the rules, they should do fine, right? "Then I'll see you at home and we can get started on the next group of windows, right?"

"Meaning you'll make food in the nice warm house while the rest of us install windows."

"And don't forget—" Jake began, excitement coloring his words.

"Christmas lights." Matt interrupted Jake with a grin and a wink. "And there's a great four o'clock game today." He gave his watch a pointed look.

"Reason enough for living right there," Callie drawled. "See you at home."

Her innocent phrase sparked something in Matt's eyes, a hint of longing that gave him a lost puppy look. The cool, crisp marine facade took over quickly, but Callie knew what she'd seen.

While not all soldiers bore physical wounds, all soldiers bore effects of service, good and bad. Life extracted nothing else.

But behind the wide smile, the patient hands, the warm embracing gaze, Matt's expression sought something. Yearning. Searching. Much like the face she saw in the mirror when no one was looking.

Pulling away, she refused to look back. Couldn't look back. Jake helped her out by pointing to the large sign at the front of the green. "Do you know how expensive those sleigh rides are, Mom?"

Callie shook her head.

"Way too pricey," Jake told her firmly. "And why would anybody need to go see Christmas lights when we can put up our own?"

Callie recognized the tactic and loved him for it.

"You're right, of course. And we always take a drive to the neighborhoods and check out the lights, right?"

"For free."

A part of her wished that lack of money didn't govern every turn. Another part respected how Jake cared enough to accept certain things without haggle. "Free's a good thing these days. For a lot of people."

"And Shadow Jesus?"

She grinned, his innocence wiping away old thoughts of bad times. "After the lights. If not today, then one day this week after school."

"Good." They drove another minute forward before Jake twisted. A quick glance his way showed his concern. "Who was that guy yelling at Matt?"

Callie sighed. She'd hoped he'd missed that little confrontation on their first pass through town, but the kid was too smart for his own good. "That was Mr. Bascomb. I don't think he was yelling, honey. They were just talking."

Jake snorted. "He was mad, Mom. At Matt."

Conceding, she met him halfway. "He did look irritated."

"Ticked off." Jake shook his head. "I don't know why anybody would get mad at Matt. He's the best."

"He is." It wasn't bad to admit that, was it? Here in the privacy of their car, just her and Jake? "And if you want to help today, I'll have you work on window shims with us. The guys are coming by for a few hours to see if we can finish up."

"Cool." Jake swung open his door and turned Callie's way as they hurried toward the house. "And you don't have to pay me, Mom."

"Jake, people work to get paid. It's the norm. Blame our capitalistic society."

He grinned, held the door for her, then shrugged out of his jacket once they were on the porch. "I don't need money. You and Grandpa do. Really." He gazed up at her with earnest eyes, his expression firm. "I don't want you to pay me. I just want to help you and Grandpa."

Tears pricked her eyes.

"Aw, geez."

"You're such a good boy."

"Mom, get over it already." He ducked his head, shrugged under her arm and through the kitchen door, but sent her a teasing look over his shoulder, a look that reminded her of how Matt joked with her. Laughed with her.

"I'm getting changed for work."

Callie pegged her coat and headed upstairs behind him. "Me, too. And it looks like Grandpa's beat us over there with Buck and Jim, so we can get a quick start."

"I'm here, too." Tom's voice hailed her from down the stairs. "I'll meet you guys across the way. There's doughnuts on the table."

"Doughnuts! Thanks, Tom!"

Callie smiled, warmth seeking into her bones despite the cold rain.

Two weeks ago the future looked dim, Cobbled Creek looming like a dark abyss of failure.

Now?

She woke up excited each morning. To crew alongside the guys, watching these homes go together step by step… The entire process brightened her day, lightened her step.

She loved building. Creating. Operating power tools.

Eyeing a square and a level, getting things just right. And not one of these men made her feel less feminine for her aptitude with a power hammer. So why had Dustin's rejection stung that much? That deep? Had she even loved him, or was their spontaneous marriage just a young lark gone bad?

She pulled on snug clothes, attached her tool belt to the air-channeled suspenders and headed across the street with Jake, humming a tune, then realized she was humming the tune Matt whistled all the time.

His truck pulled up alongside them. "I thought you were cooking today? Staying warm?"

His gruff tone revealed more than the cautionary words. She tapped her watch and continued toward the subdivision. "I've got two hours before I have to start the chili and the bread. I can do a lot in two hours, marine."

She didn't wait to hear his response, but knew she'd pleased him and refused to question herself on why that felt particularly good.

"See ya over there, Matt!"

"I'll be right behind you, bud."

Callie wasn't sure what jack-hammered her heart out of its easy rhythm—his voice or choice of words. But the smile on Jake's face showcased Matt's dual effect.

And when he's gone, her conscience niggled. *What then?*

Callie shoved that aside. Homes weren't constructed overnight, and if Phase One of Cobbled Creek sold in quick fashion, Matt might expand his efforts into Phase Two, a second grouping of homes moving up the slope. In the meantime she intended to enjoy doing what she loved most. Working side by side with family and friends, making dreams come true.

Chapter Eight

"I've got this covered," Matt called down to Callie from the upper reaches of Hank's ladder late that afternoon, raising his voice above the rain. "It's not rocket science."

"Goes faster with two, especially in these conditions." Callie thumped the second ladder up against the house with military ease.

"Then send Buck out," Matt chastised, striving for patience. Wasn't this the day he wanted her to rest up? Stay warm and dry? She'd been working or cooking since they got home from church. Not exactly the R & R he'd envisioned.

"I would, but he's sound asleep in the recliner." She adjusted her ladder, drove in a couple of quick stakes to maintain the position and headed up the rungs, Christmas lights suspended from her shoulders.

"Nice necklace."

The rain blocked her grin, but he pictured her wide smile. Her reply only deepened the vision. "I wore it for you."

"And the boots?"

She laughed, and the bright sound eased the steady

torment of being perpetually wet for nearly seventy-two hours. "Bloomingdale's. Like 'em?"

She waggled her foot off the edge of the ladder and he had a sudden urge to save and scold.

He quelled both. "Bloomingdale's carries army surplus? Sweet."

She began unwinding the lights from her neck, slipping the cord through the permanently affixed light hangers along the roofline, the long extension cord flagging in the wind and rain.

Matt worked her way until he had to shift his ladder. He climbed down, made his adjustment, then realized how close they were to being done as he headed back up. "I didn't realize this would go so fast."

"Dad put in the hangers years ago. And it takes exactly two strings minus eight inches, so when I get to the middle, we should meet up and be perfect."

Matt knew he should resist, but an opening like that was made to be used. "Nothing I haven't been saying right along, Cal."

"Ha, ha." She reached out, hooked a light, scrambled down the ladder way too quickly for his peace of mind and the wet conditions, moved it three feet toward center, applied her stakes and headed back up.

"You're quick," he observed, noting how much closer she was now. Touchable, actually.

"What I am is soaked," she shot back, deftly stringing the green wire through the last of the turned brackets. "And cold. Hence the speed."

"I'd feel sorry for you if you hadn't totally ignored instructions." Matt reached left as she finished the length of her light string and grabbed her hand as well as the cord.

"I could have done this. I was already wet. And I wanted you to have one day to be comfortable. Warm. Dry."

"Well." She slanted him a smiling look, then swept their linked hands a glance. "This way I got you to hold my hand."

"Honey, you didn't need to climb a ladder in the rain for that. I'd have obliged under much more hospitable conditions."

She winked, wiggled her hand free, then watched him connect the two ends. "Someday when you're not my boss, we'll talk."

"Back to that." He climbed down the ladder as she did, stepped off and reached out, tugging her closer, her look of surprise and wonder saying more than words ever could. He held her gaze and her hand, the rain soaking through their hats, their neck warmers, their hoodies. "I can't even fire you for my own selfish purposes because you're too good at what you do, Callie."

A smile stole across her face, a look of pleasure that hinted more than humor. "Thank you for saying that."

He grinned, dropped her hand but wished he didn't have to, removed his ladder stakes and hers, then shooed her toward the house in a no-nonsense voice. "I only speak the truth, ma'am. Go inside. Sit by the fire. Get warm. I'll put the ladders away."

She looked about to argue, but then that hinted contentment invaded her features again, as if having someone watch over her was the most magnificent thing in the world. And that only made Matt want to do it more.

Except he couldn't. At least not right now.

Not ever, soldier. You think she'd be all doe-eyed and sweet-talkin' when she hears how you passed your teen years? Detoxing in a detention center after wrecking people's lives?

And yet, Katie hadn't looked wrecked that morning. She'd looked…wonderful. Content. Peaceful. And her spark of humor that earned them more than one scolding in junior high was evident in the grin she flashed the congregation as she challenged them with her fiddle.

What had Staff Sergeant Weckford told him years ago? "Never let a memory become stronger than a dream."

Matt thought he understood the inference, but relocating to Jamison and Wellsville, seeing old haunts, old friends, new faces… His head accepted the practicality of moving on.

His heart longed for a do-over.

"Fire's nice and toasty," Hank greeted him as he came in. The warmth enveloped Matt, a comfort that came from more than the woodstove fire, although he wouldn't deny the welcome the DutchWest offered.

There was Jake, sprawled in front of the game, a bowl of popcorn to the side, maneuvering a team of soldiers through dense jungles of Pacific islands. Buck, head back, sound asleep in Hank's recliner, looking utterly content. And as Hank grabbed Matt's soaked hoodie and hung it near the fire to dry, Callie hustled down the stairs, a pair of fitted jeans replacing her loose working variety, while an aqua knit turtleneck hugged her like a second skin, the ribbed knit looking comfy-cozy while it showcased curves her work gear camouflaged.

If Matt had a hard time getting her off his mind in flannels and hoodies, he'd jump straight to impossible now, the soft blue-green knit complementing her green eyes.

She looked absolutely beautiful and if Hank hadn't

clapped him on the back as the home team scored on their opening drive, he probably would have stood and stared for who knows how long. Forever, maybe?

His family didn't do forever, not since Grandpa's time, but seeing Callie here, in the worn but genteel home setting, Matt began to realize that no one charted his destiny but him. Sure, he had a past.

Who didn't?

But maybe, just maybe, he'd be able to have a future, too. At that moment it seemed almost doable.

Jake spotted him and jumped up, a welcome interruption. "Are the lights hooked up?"

Appreciation for the boy's eagerness turned his serious thoughts to more youthful pastimes. "Yes. Once it gets dark, all you have to do is plug them in, bud."

"And it's getting dark earlier and earlier," Jake noted.

"Ah, to be the age when that was a joyous thing," Callie muttered to Matt. "And then tomorrow we'll put up the Holy Family."

"Not tonight?" A hint of whining drew Callie's gaze around.

"No. And no arguing. Everybody's been working hard all week. Tonight is rest time."

"Although I might be talked into a reenactment of our Aussie mates holding off a blitzkrieg on the carpet," Matt told him. "Once I get cleaned up."

Jake's brows shot up. "Really?"

"Jacob Henry."

Jake shot a quick glance to his mother. "If you're too tired, Matt, it's okay."

"Let me take care of this wet stuff." Matt made a face that had both Callie and Hank nodding agreement. "And then some of your mother's amazing chili."

"And her fresh bread," shot in Buck, awake just in time to publicly laud Callie's achievements.

"And that, of course." Matt let his eyes twinkle into Callie's, his thoughts only partially on food. "And then I'm yours, bud."

Callie moved closer, but kept her voice low. "You wanted to watch the game. It's okay to tell him 'no.' He'll survive. Promise."

Matt matched his voice to hers. "My way means I score points with the kid *and* his mother while Rodgers puts the offense over the top. Everybody wins."

The hint of color inspired by his banter made him long to touch her cheek. Feel the heat there. Maybe steal a kiss.

But a gentleman didn't toy with a lady's affections, especially a lady who'd been raked over the coals by someone not smart enough to realize how wonderful she was.

Exactly why he *couldn't* step out and act on his feelings. She didn't need more hurt or heartache, he was pretty sure of that. What she did need was money to cover basic things like food and shelter. One mess-up wouldn't only cost him great laborers, but it would also cost her the simple basics of life. Home. Heat. Groceries.

He'd cling to common sense. Help out quietly because he was living there. And try to think of a way to keep his distance, but seeing Callie in her everyday, nonconstruction clothes?

That image added a whole new level of difficulty to his task.

He noticed.
He noticed not.
He noticed...

Callie bit back a growl the next day, seriously disgruntled with herself, men in general, Matt in particular.

A convent would be so much easier.

"Callie, your level's off."

She jerked straight and eyed her bubble, chagrined. "Sorry, boss."

"No big deal. You feeling all right?"

Ignore the concern in his voice and the look on his face that says you matter. Trust me, you don't, except as a means to an end, which is getting these roofs in place now that the rain has passed. "Fine. Just thinking."

"Stop that, okay?"

Eyes down, she nodded, knowing he was joking but unable to reciprocate. "Won't happen again."

He stopped nailing and whistling, the sudden silence making them seem like the only two people on Earth, but that was silly because her father, Jim and Buck were on the opposite side of the street installing underlayment over the plywood roofing on the last house.

"Hey." He moved closer and bent low. "You okay, Cal?"

"Yes, thanks for asking."

He didn't tease her back, didn't chuck her on the shoulder, didn't take the bait. "You sure?"

"Quite. And busy. How 'bout you?"

He touched a hand to her shoulder, a simple gesture of friendship, so why did it feel as if he was ready to lay down his jacket over the puddles in her life?

Too many puddles, not enough Carhartt.

Finch McGee's van pulled in, followed by Amanda Slaughter. Matt paused at the ladder and caught her eye. "It's almost worth not having coffee to avoid him."

"Tell me something I don't know." She waited one

beat, then two, eyeing the ladder. "Are you waiting for me to go first?"

Matt shook his head, his gaze thoughtful, then inclined his gaze toward Finch's truck. "Does he ever bother you, Cal? I mean, *really* bother you?"

She hid the part of her that longed to bask in his concern because Callie knew what Matt meant by "bother." "Matt, I might have been army to your marine credentials, but I can usually take care of myself. I am trained in mortal combat, remember?"

"And I'd welcome a personal demonstration sometime," he quipped back, but the hand to her shoulder returned. "If anyone ever pesters you, I've got your back, okay?"

"It's not like they're lining up on the street, marine." She stepped onto the ladder in front of him and shot him a disbelieving look.

"A situation I haven't been able to figure out," he told her as he climbed down after her. "Guys down here aren't the sharpest tools in the shed."

"And here's a rope to prove it," Callie muttered as Finch approached. She beelined for the coffee, successfully side-stepping Finch, leaving Matt to deal with him.

Cowardly?

No.

Self-preservation at its finest. For some reason Finch McGee had set his sights on Callie either because she was in financial constraints and possibly an easy target, or he wanted to make a full one-eighty away from his blonde, petite ex-wife.

Either way, she wasn't interested, but he wasn't an easily discouraged guy.

She loved that about Matt.

It annoyed her with Finch.

"Things are really coming along." Amanda noted as she handed Callie an insulated cup. "You guys have done a great job and Jim said he's never worked with a better crew."

"Back at ya." Callie raised her cup, sniffed and smiled. "I love that you buy me girly coffee with flavored creamers. That makes my day. You know that, right?"

Amanda leaned alongside the truck and watched as Jim joined Matt and the building inspector. "We girls have to stick together. And protect our men from snakes in the grass."

Callie didn't have to follow her look to know it embraced McGee. "Except I don't have a man, so we'll join forces to protect yours."

Eyes forward, Amanda sipped her coffee and grinned. "You keep telling yourself that, honey. According to my husband, aka Mr. Obtuse, Matt Cavanaugh can't keep his eyes off you."

Callie stretched out her flannel covered arm. Worn, faded flannel at that. She swept her working attire a disparaging look. "Are ya kiddin' me?"

"Good men see beyond what we wear."

Callie made a face. "That sounds so wrong."

Amanda laughed. "It did, kind of, but you know what I mean. They see our heart. Our soul."

"You're watching that *Tender November* romance series on PBS, aren't you?"

Amanda didn't confess, but she did sigh. "Brontes. Austen. Alcott."

"No wonder you're twitterpated." Callie dipped her chin as the men headed their way. "Let's ix-nay the omance-ray, okay?"

"If you insist."

"Oh, I do." Callie straightened as Matt reached across for the coffee bearing his initials.

"Thanks, Amanda."

"You're welcome. Finch, I'm sorry, I'd have grabbed you a coffee if I'd known you were going to be here."

"Just had one, thanks." Finch's expression and tone eased up as he answered Amanda, then hardened again as he indicated his reason for stopping by. The one that *didn't* include checking out Callie. "I wanted to make sure those berms were re-covered with tarp and straw. Topsoil doesn't grow on trees."

"No, it doesn't," Amanda agreed.

Amanda's straight face only strengthened Callie's urge to laugh. Jake's school bus rumbled down the road, its caution lights flashing, a perfect diversion. "I'll be right back," she said to Matt with a wave toward Jake. "And I'll bring Jake over for cleanup."

She wasn't quite quick enough because Finch managed to fall into step beside her as she headed for the road. Figuring she'd lose him at his truck, a shot of dismay hit her when he didn't open the door and get in. No, he stayed alongside her, giving him ample opportunity to talk when the last thing she wanted to do was listen.

"I miss seeing you at the diner."

Face first, eyes forward. "I love what I'm doing here, though. If this could last forever, I'd be a happy girl."

"Lots of ways to find happiness, Callie."

Just when she thought she'd have to turn around and slug him in the solar plexus, Matt appeared alongside them. "Those notes for number seventeen are still on Hank's desk, right?"

Thank you, God. And thank you, Matt. "They are, yes.

Would you like me to get them?" *Please say no. Please say you'll get them yourself and walk me to the house.*

"I'll grab them. I'm going to have the plumbing and electricity inspected before we apply the drywall, and I want to familiarize myself with the layout changes your dad made."

"Like the built-in bookshelves in each bedroom?"

"Exactly that. So, Mr. McGee? Is Wednesday good for you?"

Matt stopped along the road, his presence an obvious wrench in the other man's works.

Finch stopped, faltered, then nodded. "And you know I'm a stickler for code, right, Cavanaugh?"

The way Finch used Matt's last name, coupled with his caustic tone, made Callie want to give him a good, swift kick.

But nothing got inhabited without Finch's signature. Ticking off the building inspector who was also a zoning agent wouldn't be in anyone's best interest. He'd already shown disrespect for Matt, and that tweaked Callie's protective instincts because Finch had no cause. The people who moved into these sweet homes wouldn't have to worry that the builder cut corners. So why was Finch nailing Matt with a glare? Because of her?

Ridiculous.

"And I appreciate that, Mr. McGee." Matt kept his tone level, but there was no mistaking granite for anything else. He'd be polite because they were professionals, but his voice and stance said he didn't back down. Ever.

Finch drew a hint closer, just a smidge, as if trying to intimidate Matt. Not much intimidated a marine. Callie loved that.

"Mom!"

"Go get changed, Jake." Callie called across the two-lane road. "We're coming."

"Wednesday, Cavanaugh."

Matt nodded as if Finch weren't acting like a first-class bully, then headed toward the street with Callie.

"He was a jerk to you."

Matt glanced both ways before heading across. "Who cares?"

"I do."

"Aw." He slowed his step and shoulder-nudged her, an easy grin erasing the whispered pain she'd seen with Finch's tone. His words. But nothing bothered Matt, right?

"I knew you cared, Cal. Thanks for admitting it."

"I care about seeing a friend get rudely dismissed by a guy who shouldn't be washing your bootstraps."

"As I have done for others, so you should do." Matt settled a gentle look on her. "Christ washed the apostles' feet and told them to humble themselves. Humility isn't a bad thing."

"I don't think he was talking about Finch McGee."

Matt caught her arm just outside the door. "Sure he was. To a point." He shifted his gaze to Cobbled Creek Lane where Finch waited for a car to pass before heading back toward Jamison. "His words can't hurt me, Callie. His actions can. And in the interest of time and funding, I'll let his rudeness slide. If we get this section done and sold and go on to Phase Two of the subdivision, then I'll ask to have Colby Dennis oversee our work."

He said "our work" like it was a given. Callie choked back a surge of anticipation because nothing was a given these days in home-building. Matt had taken a big risk by buying Cobbled Creek. She prayed daily that all would go well, although that hadn't come close to working in her father's case.

Oh, honey, I think the answer to your prayers is about eight inches from you, front and center.

Callie hushed her inner voice, but not before heat climbed to her face as they headed inside.

"You blushing, Cal?"

"Exertion."

A knowing grin set the laugh lines around Matt's gorgeous brown eyes a little deeper. "Coffee drinking is hard work." He took in her cup and her heated cheeks with a swift look of amusement. "So." He glanced around, the sound of Jake getting ready punctuated by things hitting the floor above them. "What did you come over here for?"

"To avoid Finch."

He burst out laughing and grabbed her in a hug, a spontaneous and wonderful two-arms-wrapped-around-you kind of hug that couldn't have been more perfect if he'd tried.

Until his laughter paused. His arms tightened, the grip different. Wonderfully different.

Should she look up at him?

Yes.

No.

But she did because there was no way she *couldn't* look up. Gaze into those coffee-no-cream eyes. See the look of gentle awareness there, the strength of a good man, a man who talked of washing feet and building homes, a man who walked with God and fellow soldiers.

"Callie…"

He whispered her name about the same time he feathered a kiss across her lips, the feel of strong, gentle and muscled arms tumbling her into a world of possibilities she hadn't dreamed feasible in a long time.

"Mom! Do you know where my thick socks are?"

Callie stepped back, joy and chagrin vying for emotional space. "Try the laundry basket in the hall."

"Got 'em!"

"Good."

"Very good." Matt whispered agreement and stroked one finger across the intensified heat in her cheeks. "I'd apologize, ma'am, but I'm not a bit sorry."

"No?"

"Oh, no." He stepped back as Jake's racing footfall announced his eager approach. "I had to know."

Know?

Oh, man.

"Ready, guys. I've got my stuff." Jake patted his waist where a smaller version of their belts held a boy-size set of tools, his hard hat clutched tight in the other hand.

"You know you're on cleanup, right?" Callie sent his tool belt a hiked-brow look. "You probably won't need those today."

Jake's face fell. His lower lip hinted a quiver. "At all?"

"Not today, bud, but how about you work with me on Thanksgiving while Mom cooks?"

"Who said I'm cooking?" Callie drew herself up to her full height and met Matt's gaze straight on. "Why is it the girl gets elected to cook while the guys play with power tools?"

Matt's look of surprise said she got him. "I just thought—"

"You thought wrong." Callie waved a hand toward the kitchen behind them and figured they might as well get this straight. "I cook because I have to. I build because I can't *not* build. There's a difference, Matt."

"There is." He contemplated her, made a face and ran a hand across the back of his head. "But it *is* Thanksgiving, so someone has to cook, right? Maybe we can break it down? Do different jobs?"

She smiled, nodded and whacked his arm. "Now you're talkin', marine. And if we order pies from the bakery, that's one more thing I don't have to do."

Matt wasn't about to say that the very thought of homemade pies brought him to his knees. It had been a lot of years since he'd shared a holiday meal with anyone, so the anticipation of joining hands for Thanksgiving around the Marek table had painted a slightly different picture in his head.

Obviously the wrong one. Therefore… "I'm picking up the turkey tomorrow." He followed Callie and Jake out the door and down the porch stairs, The General loping alongside them, his shaggy ears keeping time. "We can pick up the pies Thursday morning."

"And make stuffing and sweet potatoes Wednesday night."

Now things were looking up. "Squash?"

Callie made a face.

"Okay, no squash. Jello?"

"I love Jello!" Jake fist-pumped that idea.

"One yes takes the prize on that one. Rolls?"

"Same bakery we get the pies from."

"Gravy?"

"Dad makes the best gravy known to humankind."

Matt ran the list through his head and nodded, surprised. "So we can actually all work on Thursday morning."

"Now you're getting it." Callie grinned up at him, her friendly smile ignoring the sweet kiss they'd just shared while his heart was counting the possible moments until they might share kiss number two.

His phone rang. McGee's number flashed in the display box, reminding Matt of why he couldn't pursue this delightful road with Callie while he let the call go to voice mail. Reason number one jogged ahead of them, the dog keeping pace.

Callie thought she knew him. She knew the improved version. No way would a strong, forthright woman like Callie want the old version around her kid. Her home. Her life.

Hank knew. Matt understood that.

But Callie didn't have a clue. That was evident in her easy manner. The calm, admiring looks she'd shift his way as the houses began to come together.

No doubt Hank was waiting for Matt to tell her. And he'd do that soon. Better to have this out in the open than let worry fritter away his heart, his soul. He had enough of that after seeing Katie, knowing he had to face her, another confrontation he needed to schedule.

Once the roofs were on and the windows in, he'd face his past with both women. Not wanting to do a job didn't get a man out of that job. Not a marine, anyway.

The houses should be sealed by the first Sunday of Advent. Then he'd switch gears and concentrate on completing the model, starting with the kitchen cabinets he hoped to put in on Thursday and Friday when they'd be low on help. By Saturday, Jim would be back to work, and Tom, too.

"Lost you, marine."

He sent her a quick look of apology. "Planning. Strategizing."

She nodded, having no clue that his plans might very well disrupt their working relationship. Once Callie realized the guy flirting with her had been a teenaged con, a whole lot of things would most likely change. The thoughts of that kiss, of seeking a different bond that went beyond work?

That would probably tank as well, but he'd be unfair to take this further without Callie's awareness, and Matt had vowed to never be unfair again.

Chapter Nine

"This is the coolest thing I've ever seen, bud." Matt finished positioning stakes meant to tether the wood-sculpted Holy Family into place on Wednesday night, then motioned Jake left. "Shall we turn on the spotlights, see what we've got?"

"Just make sure they're centered, or Mom will move 'em."

"Got it. See if anybody else wants to watch the lighting ceremony."

Jake dashed up the porch steps, calling for Hank and Callie while Matt stepped back, eyeing left, then right.

Centered.

Then he examined the spotlight positions, knowing that could slant the image.

Also centered.

He smiled. Callie liked things focused. Symmetrical. So did he.

She loved building. Climbing ladders. Working rooftops.

Ditto.

As Callie and Hank crossed the yard with Jake, Matt

wondered what it would be like to be part of this family, a plan he'd never allowed himself. But at this moment, with these people, the vision seemed attainable.

Because you're living a lie.

Seeing Jake's grin and Callie's smile, he wouldn't think about that. Hank clapped him on the back as Jake flipped the switch, the colorful roofline lights adding nighttime wonder to the simply shadowed nativity scene below.

Matt's heart clenched, the reality of Bethlehem rubbing raw. They'd hobbled into town to find no room. No shelter, other than a cavelike barn. And a manger lined with coarse straw on a cold winter's night. Little Jesus had been born there, in crude, meager conditions. Truly a child of the poor.

Like him.

"Hey." Callie moved alongside him, looking up as if he were the most wonderful thing in the world, all because he'd taken time to set up Jake's favorite Christmas decoration. "It's perfect."

"Centered properly?"

She laughed and hugged his arm. "Yes. Jake ratted me out, huh?"

"Nothing wrong with wanting things done correctly," Matt supposed. "And it saves a lot of work to do it right the first time."

Gazing forward, Hank's easy tone pondered Matt's pragmatic words. "But if we *do* mess up, God usually gives us chances to make amends. Embrace new ways."

His words targeted Matt. They both knew it. Matt breathed deep and shrugged, the thought of a baby born in less-than-perfect circumstances hitting home. One big difference pierced his heart like a three-penny nail.

Christ lived his life sacrificially; Matt had messed up repeatedly. "Not everything's fixable, Hank."

"True enough," Hank replied. "But I try to never second guess God's vantage point. Ours is limited. Omniscience gives God the advantage to see all. Heal all."

How Matt wished that were true. But he'd seen the horror on Katie's face, the shock, the realization that she was damaged beyond repair. A look he put there through careless, callous misdeeds.

"Thanks, Matt!" Jake launched himself at Matt, hugging him, his excitement over the decorations innocent and contagious. Matt could do nothing less than haul the boy into his arms, wondering again what kind of moron ignored a great kid like Jake.

"You're welcome, bud. Hey, it's getting cold out here. Shall we head inside? Start those sweet potatoes?"

"Got 'em done while you boys were doing this," Hank announced as they moved toward the steps. "The cookin' part anyway. I'll do the glaze in the morning, then all we have to do is heat 'em up to go with the turkey."

"And I cut up all the bread for the stuffing," Jake added as they pegged their jackets inside the door. "While Mom did the onions and celery."

"Teamwork." The idea of a family working together to produce a holiday meal was both alien and fun. Mostly fun. "Do I smell…?" Matt followed his nose toward the kitchen, then turned to see Callie watching him, waiting for his reaction. "You made pies?"

"I did. Not because I had to, mind you." She sent him a warning look and wagged her finger like The General wagged his ears. "Because I *wanted* to after you looked like a lost little boy when I said we'd buy them."

He pretended to scowl. "You weren't supposed to see that."

"Army training. And great peripheral vision. Anyway, what do you think?"

At that moment he thought she was the most remarkable, wonderful creature on Earth, but he couldn't say that out loud for a host of reasons. He cleared his throat and grabbed a fork from the table. "There's only one way to know for sure."

"Which will wait until tomorrow," she scolded, grabbing the fork. "But they smell great."

"Perfect."

She turned and met his smile, but the look on her face said she realized he was talking about more than the pies.

"Thanks, Callie."

"Well, you gave me plenty of time between the nativity scene and your book work."

"I hate keeping books," he admitted as he tugged off his shoes and set them by the fire. "And it's not even hard math, it's just tedious."

"Callie kept my books for me." Hank brought a plate of ham-melt sandwiches to the table, the quick supper a salute to Thursday's feast prep time. "And I can't say she didn't warn me we were skating thin ice a number of times."

"Everybody takes chances, Hank." Matt met his gaze candidly. "There are no givens. If you'd gotten this done before the housing bubble burst, you'd have been called a hero. But getting sick on top of rough financial circumstances." Matt shook his head. "Tough all around." He sat next to Jake, his attention on Callie. "But I'd be glad to pay you to take over my bookkeeping. Not much, of course," he added with a grin. "Are you familiar with QuickBooks?"

"I used it for Dad's records." She brought the coffee pot to the table and filled Hank's cup and his before topping off her own. "Which meant the bank could see there was no wrongdoing when things went bad. Just horrible timing."

"And overextending." Hank grimaced, then sighed. "But I've got to say, Matt, that having you here, working with you, seeing those houses take shape at last." Hank nodded his relief. "My dream is coming true, thanks to you."

"Thanks to us," Matt corrected smoothly. "And I've never worked with a better crew, including you, bud." He chucked Jake in the upper arm, making the boy grin. "So things worked out all around."

"And tomorrow…" Jake waved toward the front window, his mouth full, not waiting to swallow before reminding Matt of his promise.

Matt angled him a patient look. "Let's say grace. And yes, I remember. We're putting the kitchen in the model tomorrow and you're helping."

"Me, too," piped in Callie.

"Count me in," added Hank.

Matt waited as they joined hands, then lobbed a look around the table. "The whole family's rushing to get this kitchen done and the C of O signed?" He winked toward Jake. "Must be wearing out my welcome around here."

Callie squeezed his hand, her touch inciting sparks against his skin. "Oh, you're not so hard to take, marine. Kind of nice, actually. And you'll only be across the street. Easy visiting."

"Until the model sells," he added.

Her face shadowed.

Hank did his customary quick grace, and Callie let go of Matt's hand once done, but he had pretty good peripheral vision, too.

Was that a glimpse of misgiving because she'd put her heart and soul into that model?

Or because he'd move to town once the model sold?

But like it or not, he needed to get a couple of these houses contracted. And holiday time was the worst for selling homes. Most people avoided the time-consuming task of directing a building project until after New Year's. Which meant if the model caught someone's eye, he'd have to sell it and finish another home to occupy until spring.

"Wait on the Lord. Be of good courage and he shall strengthen thine heart. Wait, I say, on the Lord." The Psalm's sage advice had been his mainstay for a long time.

Patience. Perseverance. Persistence. Matt embraced these qualities as a marine, then again as a contractor, but with Cobbled Creek, a part of him longed to fast forward toward completion and the reason for that unusual impatience sat four short feet away, explaining why she'd chosen Golden Wheat stained maple for the Cape Cod's kitchen.

They'd passed the initial inspection today. Within a week or two the model should be deemed ready for occupancy. He'd listed the homes with local Realtor Mary Kay Hammond, but they both knew the score. December was a dead month in real estate sales.

And he should be fine financially as long as they contracted two of the houses before spring, then doubled that by summer.

"I'll have the turkey ready to go in at ten." Callie looked up from the list she was making. "So if we eat at four or so, that works out well, right?"

Matt propped his elbows on the table and leaned forward. "We could always take the day off like normal people do."

Three sets of eyes rounded on him like he'd sprouted an extra head.

"Why would we do that?" Callie asked.

"Yeah, why?" Jake echoed.

"I can't think of a thing to be more thankful for than seeing those houses cared for," added Hank. "If you're worried we'd rather have a day off, then you're sitting at the wrong table, son."

Their earnest desire eased Matt's conscience. "I can't imagine sitting at a finer table, sir."

Hank grinned. "Well, I do make a mean ham melt."

"And the coffee couldn't be better." Matt raised his cup toward Callie.

She ignored his grin and went back to her list. "Turkey at ten, potatoes and sweet potato casserole at three, rolls go in once the gravy's started."

"That way we catch the late game on TV," Jake added.

"With pie."

"And the day just keeps getting better and better." Matt hoisted his mug in salute. "To teamwork. And a beautiful Thanksgiving."

The house phone rang, interrupting the toast. Hank stood, picked it up, sent a quick glance Matt's way, then headed toward the back of the kitchen, his voice low.

"Who was that, Grandpa?" Jake asked when Hank returned to the table.

"Don."

"Is he coming tomorrow?"

The boy's innocent words caused a momentary discomfort. "Not this year."

"But—"

"He's busy, Jake."

"He's going somewhere else for supper?"

Hank was obviously no good at lying. "Well…"

"Jake, he's—"

Sensing the truth, Matt cleared his throat. "Hey, guys, it's fine if he comes. You know that, don't you?"

Hank exchanged a quiet look with Callie. "We'll leave things the way they are for now, I think."

"No, really, I…"

Callie shook her head and sent a swift cautionary look toward Jake. "Don's got plans already and it's not like we're going to be sitting around all afternoon chitchatting, right?"

That made sense to Jake, but Matt felt like a first-class heel. "Listen, if…"

Hank interrupted him, obviously not wanting to say too much with little ears around. "Plenty of time for Don to stop by over the winter. He's staying in town this year, so it's not like it usually is, Jake."

"Oh." Jake nodded as if they were finally making sense. He turned Matt's way. "Don always has Thanksgiving dinner with us before he goes to Florida. He's known Grandpa a long time."

"He's staying here this year?" Matt directed the question to Hank, but Callie answered.

"Yes. He figured it was best all around. Going to Florida isn't cheap and there's no guarantee of work once you get there."

Did Matt sense a hint of something else in her words?

He thought so, and the quiet look she exchanged with her father confirmed his gut instinct. And Don needed work. He'd mentioned that.

But Matt had plenty of help right now. More than enough. He pushed his chair back and stood, the perfect holiday now shaded with guilt.

His father needed help. Except he wasn't *really* his father. And he'd abandoned him long ago. And he had a drinking problem.

Matt didn't do drinking problems. He didn't do family. He didn't embrace the American dream that had emotionally thrashed him as a kid. Thinking of Don brought up thoughts of Neal Brennan and his mother's duplicity, the lies, the scandal, the family breakdown that left him pretty much on his own from age eight.

"When my father and mother forsake me, then the Lord shall take me up."

God had done that in the form of Grandpa Gus, but not before Matt realized that bad apples produce like fruit and the idea of love, marriage and sweet, dimpled babies should be someone else's dream.

His dream?

To love God, love his work and build beautiful, affordable homes that withstood the test of time.

And that's it? Home to an empty apartment every night? A cold stove?

Yes. Less risk for everyone.

Matt met Hank's troubled gaze. "I'm going to turn in early. Get a jump on tomorrow. If you hear me head over before dawn, don't feel like you have to rush. We've got all day."

"Sure, Matt!"

Jake's grin showed oblivion to the rising concern surrounding the table, and just as well. Little boys didn't need to be surrounded by old drama.

Whereas big boys didn't have much of a choice.

"Hey, bud, good job."

Callie and Hank exchanged a smile as Matt advised Jake the next afternoon, the boy's rapt attention the best kind of hero worship.

"Like this, Matt?"

"Exactly like that."

Matt let him read the level and Callie couldn't miss the delight in the boy's eye as he bent slightly. "Perfect."

"I couldn't have done better," Matt assured him. "And I'm real particular about installing cabinets. Finishing kitchens."

"Why?"

Callie suspected he slid a look her way, but pretended oblivion. "Kitchens make women happy. They like their kitchens just so, no matter how much they cook. Or don't cook, as the case may be."

Yup. Definitely targeting her. Such a guy thing to do. Teasing by innuendo. Kind of enchanting, actually.

"And a kitchen's called the heart of the home," Matt went on, abutting the next cabinet group to the first set they'd installed. "People are drawn to the kitchen. It brings back memories for lots of folks." Matt snapped his tape shut, and waved a hand around. "Your mom did a great job planning this one."

"She did." Hank agreed as he and Callie finished the lower bank of cabinets on the inside wall. "Pantry space, work space, and she picked out appliances that weren't top end but would last."

"Top end being ridiculously expensive," Callie added.

"Unless you're a Food Network chef or planning a humongous family, a nice four-burner stove with a convection oven does everything I need it to do."

"Because you don't live to cook," Matt teased from across the room.

"You're a quick study, marine." She slanted him a look of approval as she and Hank marked space for the upper cabinets. "Eating is essential. Cooking isn't. Hence the impressive frozen food sections in today's grocery stores. And a fresh apple." She held up her half-eaten one as an example and grinned. "Lunch on the run."

"Because I've found myself inundated with crew members who tend to elongate their lunch hours rather than shorten them, let me just say I appreciate the difference more than most. The Marek family is amazing."

"Can't disagree." Hank stood, checked his watch and headed for the door. "I'm going across the street to check on the turkey and start the other stuff. No, General, you stay here." He waved the dog back into the front room. "I'll get the potatoes peeled and the table set. Then you guys come on over in an hour or so."

Another hour gave them time to finish those upper cabinets while Jake applied rustic-styled hardware to the lower ones. Callie nodded, balancing with one foot on the ladder, the other on the untopped cabinet unit below to get the best angle for drilling. "Sounds like a plan. Thanks, Dad."

Hank sent her a fond grin. "You're welcome."

"Like this, Matt?" Jake held out a burnished handle and lined it up with the holes Matt had drilled in the honey-toned maple doors.

"Yes." Matt crouched alongside the boy, looking like a proud father. Strong. Determined. Gentle. Stoic. "Now start the first screw just enough to hold things in place, then do the same with the second…" Matt paused while Jake followed instructions, his face a study in concentration while Matt looked on, smiling.

"You've got it."

"I did." Jake sent a grin Matt's way and high-fived him. "You can help Mom now. I've got this."

Callie bit back a laugh.

Matt straightened, patted Jake's shoulder and turned her way, his quiet look saying what they didn't dare say out loud.

The kid was outrageously cute, but at eight years old the last thing a sturdy boy like Jake wanted to hear was "cute."

Strong, yes. Tough? Most assuredly.

But cute?

Not so much.

Matt adjusted the cabinet jack below the first upper cabinet while Callie read the level. "We're good."

He handed her the drill and she did her best to ignore his proximity as she installed the holding screws, but that worked for all of two seconds.

Oops. Serious trouble. *When all else fails adopt a code of silence or go to inane conversation.*

Option two. It *was* a holiday. Silence seemed rude.

"You like this color for the cabinetry?"

Matt swept the kitchen a quick look. "It's great."

"I kept it light because even with south-facing windows, winter nights are long."

Matt nodded, agreeable. Maybe too agreeable. Which meant she might not want to talk about long winter nights. Cozy fires. Deer browsing for food beneath snow-swept hillsides.

"And I did the wall board in here myself," she continued as she settled the last screw into place on cabinet one.

"Lovely," he replied, but it only took one look to see the grin that said he wasn't just thinking about plaster board.

Maybe silence *was* a better choice.

"I like that you allowed space for built-in wall shelves flanking the fireplace in the living room," he told her.

"Dad's idea." Callie angled the drill until she felt the screw bite into the stud. "He said Mom begged for more storage space. Cupboards. Closets. Shelves. And of course, like the shoemaker's wife goes barefoot, she was still waiting for those extra cupboards when she died."

"Sorry." He sent her a look of sympathy that made her feel like what she said mattered. "When did she pass away?"

"I was ten." She made a face as she sidestepped to the next cabinet. "It was rough, but she was a great woman. And Dad loved her so much, the kind of love everyone wants to find, you know?"

"Reason enough to write fiction, I guess."

"Ooh. Cynical." She sent him an over-the-shoulder frown. "Nothing wrong with happily ever afters, is there?"

"If they existed, no."

"And on that note…" She sent him a "let's change the subject" look and quipped, "About the weather we're having lately…"

"Safe topic."

"Weather is what it is. Human relationships?" Callie flashed him a grin and shrugged. "Whole other box of tools."

The General stood, paced to the door and whined. "Jake, can you take The General out, please?"

"Okay."

Once Jake had pulled on his thick hoodie and dashed outside with the dog, Callie nudged Matt for his attention.

"Hmm?" He looked up, a pencil held tight in his teeth, his square positioned to mark the outside of the last wall cabinet on that side.

Callie jerked her head toward the door. "You did a great job working with him."

Matt shook it off. "No big deal."

Callie hesitated, then waded in. "It *was* a big deal to Jake. He loves learning the trade. Trying his hand at things. And when we were working steady two years ago, he was too small to be much help but he longed to learn." She settled a warm look on the work-in-progress kitchen. "This is what he's been waiting for. A chance to try his hand at things. Be the apprentice. I just wanted to say thank you when he wasn't around."

Her heartfelt words made Matt suck in a breath, and her sweet expression loosened a rusty internal clamp left over from his painful childhood. He glanced away, wondering how much to say, then shrugged, wondering where the shot of pain came from after all this time. He'd thought it erased, two decades of good negating one of bad.

Obviously it didn't work that way.

"My grandfather taught me a lot of what I know," he told her but didn't meet her gaze. "He was a lot like your dad. Strong. Kind. Straight-shooting. And he loved God, heart and soul."

"You miss him."

"Oh, yeah." Matt hauled in a breath, then swept the well-apportioned house a look of appreciation. "But mostly I want him proud. I want him watching me from heaven, knowing I stayed on the straight and narrow. Knowing I didn't stray. That I listened to everything he said and carried it with me."

"He knows."

"You think?" Matt faced her, hands out.

Callie smiled down at him, her look endearing. Engaging. "Oh, yes. I believe that utterly. When I've messed up, I can almost feel my mother's arm around me, saying, 'Well, then. Fix it.'"

Matt smiled. "Exactly." He hesitated, then waded into last night's dinner dilemma. "You know that Don's my stepfather."

Callie nodded as she applied the next screw. "Dad said as much. But that's all he said. And I couldn't wrestle information out of Buck either, so that's all I know."

"Neal Brennan was my father."

Callie stopped working and turned full about. "Jeff's father?"

"And Meredith's. Yes."

"Meredith was a year ahead of me in school," Callie mused. "Beautiful. Polished. Cheerleader. I didn't know her, but a part of me would have loved to be just like her."

"Kids hide a lot under an illusion of success."

"Did you?"

He snorted. "Not hardly. I went the other way."

Her expression said "Tell me more," but he wasn't about to spill everything here and now, when Jake would rejoin them at any moment.

"So Don married your mother..."

"If only it was that easy." Matt finished leveling the

last cabinets, face forward. "My mother cheated on Don. She was a waitress, Neal was a customer. A rich customer. I was the result. No one knew until Neal made it public knowledge when I was eight years old. Don walked out, started drinking, and I never heard from him again. My mother began entertaining guy after guy, never happy. Never content. She died during my first tour in Iraq."

"Oh, Matt." Callie touched his arm, sympathetic. "I'm so sorry."

"Yeah, well." He shrugged one shoulder, and changed the subject, feeling like he'd shared enough darkness to shadow a blessed holiday. "We're good here."

Jake burst back through the door, scrubbing his hands together, the dog trotting alongside. "It got cold out there."

Matt knew that. And working in a house all day with no heat wasn't exactly comfortable, even with their layers. "One more cabinet and we'll call it a day. I've got to grab a few things at the lumberyard in the morning, so I'll head over first thing. They open at six."

"It's Black Friday," Callie reminded him.

He'd forgotten that.

"Most of the craziness will be at the big stores and the shopping areas in Olean, but—" she let her voice taper and shifted a brow up "—the lumberyard had an ad in today's paper, so they'll be busy."

He should have made the run yesterday, but he didn't and he hated standing in line.

"Shop-a-phobic?"

He grunted. "Not when there's a point to it. But Black Friday?"

"Want me to go instead?" she asked as she applied the last two mounting screws.

Matt shook his head as he and Jake gathered tools. "No. My bad. And if they have a quick lane open, I'll still be able to get in and out."

Callie's doubtful look said that wasn't going to happen, but Matt could hope, right?

"This is amazing, Hank." Matt walked into the dining area a short while later and swallowed a lumber-size lump in his throat, the laden table set for four. "What can I do to help?"

Hank beamed. "Have a seat. We're all set except for mashing the potatoes and saying grace. Only thing is, Callie doesn't let me get away with quick grace on Thanksgiving, so I might hold off and do the potatoes after we pray."

"Funny, Dad."

Hank grinned her way, his pride and affection for Callie and Jake obvious, and as they finished drying their hands and settled in at the festive table, one of Matt's heart clamps loosened a little bit more.

He fit at this table. With this family.

He didn't dare make too much of that. He comprehended the darkness of past sins.

But it felt good to be here. Real good. And Matt hadn't sat at a family table to have a holiday dinner in fifteen years, so this...

Oh, this was nice.

They joined hands, heads bowed as Hank said the blessing, and while slightly longer than his usual, it wasn't overdone to the point of cold potatoes.

"You were right." Callie sent Matt a look of unsurpassed happiness a few minutes later. "This turkey is magnificent."

He grinned. "Told you so."

"Son, I haven't had a bird taste this good in a long time," Hank confessed. "We always buy the frozen ones they sell cheap in November. This—" he speared a piece of white meat and held it aloft "—reminds me of turkeys we had when I was a boy, when my parents would go to the farm and pick theirs out."

"Free range. Some mighty good eating right there."

"And even though I'm eating a feast," Callie confessed, "I'm already envisioning turkey sandwiches with cranberry sauce. Turkey and biscuits. Turkey and rice."

"And pie," Matt added with enthusiasm.

His tone of appreciation made her flush. "Now the pressure's on. What if they're not good?"

"They'll be wonderful."

"You used your mama's crust recipe, and crust makes the pie," Hank declared. "Now, Jake, if you'll hand me that dish of sweet potatoes, I think I've cleared a corner on this plate of mine."

Jake laughed and passed the bowl left, his eagerness for food warding off the urge to converse, unusual for Jake. But Matt understood the boy's attentiveness to a meal like this, and couldn't deny he felt the same way.

Warm. Fed. A place to belong.

Guilt niggled him out of nowhere.

Where was Don tonight? Did he catch Thanksgiving dinner with a friend? Or had this been his only option and Matt ruined it by being there?

Sizing up the amount of food they had, the twinge of guilt grew. There'd have been plenty of food for Don and leftovers.

Did he want his former stepfather hanging around? No.

But that gut feeling went against the grain of faith.

Matt knew better. And if his original reason to work in southern Allegheny County was to mend old fences, he could have started with Don.

"Matt, you okay?" Jake asked when he'd been quiet too long.

"I'm fine, bud. Just thinking of how wonderful this is. How blessed I am to be here."

Hank met his look across the table. Read his mind. Matt saw it in a tiny flash of satisfaction that crinkled Hank's gaze.

He'd messed up by leaving Don out of this equation. But because Don was staying in town for the winter, Matt could find some way to fix it.

Add it to the list, his conscience scoffed. *And that list is getting a little long, don't you think?*

It was, but Thanksgiving night was a time for rejoicing. Eating pie. Watching football and the first Christmas specials.

"More stuffing, Matt?"

Callie offered the green-glazed bowl full of the most delicious stuffing he'd ever tasted, the bowl's color contrasting with the lighter green of her eyes. "Yes, please. It's the best I've ever had, Callie."

Gladness brightened her features, but she angled him a warning look, sassy and spritely, total Callie. "Don't get used to it. I'd rather build, remember?"

"I won't likely forget. Nor would you let me."

But right then the thought of building together, eating together, grabbing frozen food together...

That seemed too good to be true, but for tonight, this night, he'd relax and enjoy the moment.

Chapter Ten

"Cavanaugh."

Matt cringed inside the next morning. Outwardly, he showed no emotion as Finch McGee sauntered his way, the lumberyard registers doing a brisk Black Friday business. "Mr. McGee. Did you have a nice Thanksgiving?"

McGee's glare contradicted his positive reply. "Fine." He scanned the box of hardware Matt held, the bite in his look unbecoming. "Not taking time off?"

"Time is money."

"It is." McGee drew closer. Too close. Matt resisted the urge to step back, the people behind him too close to allow room, and not wanting to give Finch the satisfaction of knowing he crowded him. But he also didn't want to pick a fight with the building inspector.

"And you know I'm watching you, right?"

Matt fought a sigh. McGee's attitude was growing tedious. And unless he missed his guess, the faint scent of hops meant Finch hadn't gone to bed sober last night. Great. "Any advice I get on finishing those homes is welcome."

"Oh, I'm not advising you." Finch leaned in closer, the

rising volume of his voice drawing glances from nearby shoppers, strains of Christmas music blotted out by the building inspector's mounting tirade. "I'm hounding you. Watching. Waiting. Wondering when you're going to screw up again because I know you will. Your kind always does."

Should he set the hardware down and leave quietly, avoiding a scene?

The combined attention of the cashiers flanking them and the people in line said it was too late for that.

Change of subject?

One look at Finch's bloodshot eyes negated that option. He'd punt the ball, figuratively. "Mr. McGee, what do you think of Councilman Gilroody's suggestion requiring all new housing to have metal roofs?"

McGee stepped back, confused.

Perfect.

"The one-time expense drives initial prices up," Matt continued as he moved closer to checking out and a much-needed escape, "but the home's value stays steady and gives banks less reason to refuse a mortgage, so the long-run offering is substantial."

"Gilroody's a good man."

Matt knew that. And the quick change of subject had gotten him to the cash register, so mission complete. "And the extended life warranty on those roofs is attractive."

Finch gathered his thoughts just long enough for the young woman to ring up Matt's purchases. He smiled at her, accepted the bag of hardware needed to finish off the kitchen in the Cape, then turned toward the door.

"Remember, Cavanaugh."

Matt headed out, saying nothing, unwilling to feed the other man's hungover angst.

Maybe Finch had a drinking problem. From the look of him, he shouldn't have been driving, and Matt could attest that he shouldn't have been talking either, his posture and words drawing attention from a crowd.

It was foolish behavior for a town official, but in Matt's experience, even a little power could turn a man's head. But Finch was in a position to cost Matt two things he couldn't afford to waste: money and time.

He needed Phase One complete before he requested Colby as his inspector. That good faith initiative went far in town government, and Matt was determined to make the grade, but Finch's attitude said this was far from over, and that didn't bode well.

He paused as he backed up the truck. He could return to Cobbled Creek and think about offering Don a job or he could man up and do it.

The clock told him it was early, but construction crews weren't much for sleeping in and Matt had looked up Don's address the night before. He had an apartment in Wellsville, five minutes from the lumber store.

Jesus had seized every opportunity to bring his lambs home. He'd gone hungry and thirsty to teach. He'd supped with sinners regularly, pressing the message that all were welcome at God's table.

Doing less felt wrong because it *was* wrong. Matt shoved the truck into drive and headed into Wellsville, hoping Don was awake. And sober.

"Matt?" Don scrubbed a hand to a lightly whiskered face and squinted at him in the doorway. "What are you doing here?"

"May I come in?"

"Sure." Don pushed the door open wider and let Matt

into a threadbare apartment that smelled like coffee. "Want some coffee?"

"Please."

Don led him into the galley kitchen and filled two chipped mugs. "Got milk here."

"Black's fine."

"Sugar?"

Matt shook his head and figured they'd pretty much exhausted small talk. "You said you needed a job."

Don flushed, tentative. "I'm doing fine, actually. I've got some things lined up in Florida..."

"Except you're not going to Florida."

Don frowned. "Hank told you, huh?"

"Look, Don." Matt sat down in one of the two available chairs and pretended to be at ease. "I need a good drywall seamer. Hank says you're the best around."

"He's right."

"You've got to have steady hands to run seam."

"That's your way of saying no drinking." Don paused, glanced around, then met Matt's gaze. "I don't drink anymore, although there are days I want to. And the more I sit around, the harder that seems, but I don't want a job out of pity." He shifted forward, his gaze intent. "I did you wrong, Matt. I got mad at your mother for living a lie and I walked out, thinking biology made a man a father."

Matt gripped his coffee cup, unwilling to interrupt.

"I tossed eight years of loving you, being your dad, being so proud I could bust, into the trash over a cheating woman. It was a shameful thing to do. Between your mother and me, we did a lousy number on you and you ended up hanging with the wrong crowd, getting into all kinds of trouble. Considering that—" Don hunched forward, his eyes clear, his expression guarded "—why would you offer me a job?"

"Because it's the right thing to do." Matt leaned forward as well, but not as far.

Regret shadowed Don's his features.

"I messed up big time," Matt continued. "But that was my fault as much as anybody's. I didn't hang with the wrong crowd, Don. I *was* the wrong crowd." He took one last long swig of coffee and stood. "I'm not good at all this talking stuff."

"Me neither."

"I need a seamer. I'd like us to get along. I can't have drinking around me, but if you're comfortable with that, I'd like to have you on board while the others work on sealing the remaining houses before the weather gets worse."

"Snow's forecast for next week."

"Which gives me just enough time if all goes well."

Don stretched out a hand, not a tremor in sight. "I'm in. And thank you, Matt."

A simple handshake between two construction guys. Why did it feel like so much more? "Head over once you're ready. I'll be in the model."

"Callie's house."

Don's easy remark made the words more real. The model reflected Callie in so many ways. Strong. Beautiful. Attentive to detail.

The idea of selling it made Matt feel guilty, but that was silly. She and Hank had designed the house with no intention of living there. Why should he feel bad?

He climbed into the truck and stared at his phone, knowing Sunday loomed two days away. And Sunday meant church. And Katie, if he went to the White Church at the Bend again.

So he wouldn't. Why would he intentionally encroach on her life? So what that he felt at home the minute he walked in the door. That he'd eyed the structural problems of the old building, wondering what he could do to help.

He took Route 19 North and hung a right toward Jamison, taking the shortcut back to Cobbled Creek. As he followed the Park Round curve, Simon MacDaniel waved from the driveway of the church.

Matt slowed the truck and rolled down the window. "Hey, Si. What's up?"

Si pulled a worn but thick hoodie closer and grimaced. "I can't believe I'm hoping for snow, but this rain is wreaking havoc with our roof."

Matt thrust his chin toward the church and nodded. "I noticed that. And your interior damage will spread if it doesn't get fixed."

"And money's nonexistent with so many of the congregation heading south this time of year," Si told him. "We've gotten a couple of decent bequests and memoriam donations, but roofing is crazy expensive. We were hoping to hold off until next summer, but I don't think we can."

"I agree. But maybe we can patch the bad spot. Want me to have a look?"

Si stared at him. "You do roofing?"

Matt shrugged. "I own a construction company."

Happiness brightened Si's face. "Providence, right?"

Matt pulled into the drive, climbed out and met the other man's gaze. "You didn't know? Really?"

"Scout's honor," Si promised. "I was just out there,

wondering what to do, praying and staring up while re-alizing I know nothing about constructing buildings..."

"But a fair piece about mending souls," Matt cut in.

"As nice as that sounds," Si replied, "it won't keep us dry when spring blasts us with torrential rains."

"True enough. You got a ladder, Si?"

"Back here."

They set the ladder against the lowest part of the church roof. Matt started up, then paused, looking back. "Thank you for not picking a church with a towering cathedral. Right now small and country seems a whole lot friendlier."

Hinted sadness darkened Si's eyes, passing almost quick enough for Matt to doubt his eyesight. But not quite. "I couldn't agree more." He ascended the ladder behind Matt and hung there while Matt surveyed the roof.

"You're frowning."

"Yup."

"In my experience, frowns equate expensive."

"Yeah. But the good news is, I think I can patch it," Matt told him. "Monday and Tuesday are both supposed to be clear. If I bring a couple of guys by, can we jump up here and get it done for you?"

"I'd be forever in your debt," Si declared.

Matt smiled as he climbed down. "No, you won't, but I wouldn't mind some extra prayers if you've got a mind to. They'd come in handy these next few weeks."

Si clamped a firm hand on his shoulder, his bright blue eyes meeting Matt's. "Consider it done, my friend."

Matt nodded, grateful, then pivoted to climb into the truck, only to stop dead.

Katie approached the two men, and there was no mistaking her look of surprise as she recognized Matt. "Matt, you're back."

He squirmed inside and out. "Katie."

"You're back and you haven't called," she corrected herself, her expression tart.

"I…um…"

"In nearly twenty years," she went on, moving closer, her stride smooth even with the driveway's upgrade. To see her move, he'd never suspect she was handicapped.

"You two know each other." Si offered the interpretation as though heading off trouble, but he needn't have bothered. The look on Katie's face said "storm front coming."

"I thought we did," Katie told Si, her voice signaling otherwise. "But friends don't desert each other when the chips are down. Friends don't abandon one another when things go wrong. Friends—"

"I get it." Matt faced her, feeling unprepared, but wasn't this what he came back for? To have it out with each and every person he'd wronged? Obviously it was Katie's turn.

"So that's it? You stumble across me here, shrug your shoulders and move on?"

He wouldn't do that. Couldn't do that. If God provided this unexpected opportunity, there was obviously a reason. "I have to get back to work right now, but I'd like to talk to you. See you."

Simon shifted beside him, as if wondering about Matt's intent.

"How about tonight?" he continued. "We could meet at that little coffee shop." He jutted his chin toward the café across the green, the artistic sign proclaiming great music, espresso and food beneath a bright yellow flower. "If you're free, that is."

She stared at him with little emotion, but her eyes...

Oh, those eyes said so much. Two decades of anger and disappointment deepened the pale gray to steel. But she nodded and took a broad step away from the truck. "Seven-thirty."

"All right." He turned back toward Simon. "And I'll be sure to come by either Monday or Tuesday with the guys. We'll get that patched up for you."

Simon didn't look quite as happy now, but Matt had enough on his plate. He climbed into the truck, eased it into reverse, and rolled down the driveway, carefully not looking left or right. He didn't need to see Katie's face to read the disappointment there, or Si's to acknowledge the look of question.

He gave up the idea of stopping for coffee, his gut advising him to wait, and headed toward the outskirts of town and Dunnymeade Hill, wondering why he hadn't taken the long way around in the first place.

He knew he had to talk to Katie. Apologize. Set things straight.

But he'd envisioned a more controlled approach. With considerable distance. A phone call, perhaps, or better yet, an email. That's how he'd imagined his first contact with Katie, just enough to give them both time to think. Ponder. Pray.

As he headed into Cobbled Creek, lights in the model told him the Mareks were already at work. The realization calmed him. He'd get through today, then face tonight. Either way, it would be over and done before his head hit a pillow, and he wasn't sure if that was a good thing or bad.

But he'd find out soon enough.

* * *

"Morning, boss," Callie called as Matt came through the side entrance of the model. His look appraised the work she'd gotten done. He whistled appreciation, the clean white primer pulling the kitchen's look together.

"You got here early, Cal."

She nodded, concentrating on cutting in along a cabinet's edge. "Couldn't sleep and I wanted this done before the countertop guys come on Monday. Then we can install the sink." She ducked low to do the baseboard, then asked, "What's your time frame on wallboard seaming?"

"Today."

"Want a suggestion?" She looked up at him, unsure of his reaction.

"Maybe."

Callie grinned. "Don's the best seamer around when he's sober and he's been sober for nearly a year."

He stared outside, then sighed. "I've already asked him. He's on his way."

"Really?"

He directed his gaze down to her.

"No argument, no convincing, no appealing to your sensibilities?"

"Yesterday did that."

"Perfect."

"Even when I'm not sure why I should feel guilty about anything concerning Don."

"Wanna talk some more?"

He pulled hardware out of the box and headed toward the living room. "No."

Okay, then.

He popped his head around a few seconds later.

"Sorry. Didn't mean to be short with you. None of this is your fault, and—"

"It's okay, Matt. Really."

He looked relieved by her reaction. Sympathy rose from within, a whisper of the little boy lost showing in his eyes.

Gorgeous brown velvet eyes. Deep. Soulful.

"Besides, the walls have ears around here," Matt added.

That was certainly true. "We could grab coffee later," Callie mused.

His look of chagrin said he was busy. Worse, that she'd caught him out. "Another time might be better, huh?" Callie asked, her mind going back to the message from Reenie.

Her voice must have said more than her words because Matt poked his head around the corner again. "I'm not dating anyone, Cal. And if you've got something to ask, darlin', just spit it out." He flashed that smile again, the one that said he'd read her hesitation and countered it. "And just to straighten things out, Reenie is the gal who does doll-up for me. She sweeps, mops, wipes things down, makes sure everything's pristine before buyers walk in the front door. She's in her fifties, married and has four grandchildren. Although her macadamia brownies *are* a temptation."

Callie sent him a scathing look, but he'd already ducked back to his side of the half wall. Just as well. She had work to do and conversation might pull her off-task.

"But I'd like to grab coffee with you," he called back, sounding more serious this time, "Talk about things. But not tonight. I, um…"

"Have plans." Callie filled in the blank without looking up.

"Yes."

The guy was entitled to a life, right? And what business was it of hers what he did on a cold, wet Friday night? "Let me know when. As long as Jake's taken care of, we're good."

"Thanks, Cal." Relief colored his tone, which meant he didn't realize she was quietly stewing on the other side of the wall, a ridiculous fact because they both understood the boundaries they'd established.

Maybe she'd be better off returning to the diner. Working for Matt paid better, but dealing with these rising emotions put her at risk.

Why? Her conscience prodded. *You're here to do a job. You need money. And Matt's okay with the parameters, except when he's kissing you.*

That kiss. That one sweet, gentle kiss, a glimpse of what could be.

"Mom! I'm here!"

Reality pushed her wandering thoughts aside. Jake was her certainty. Matt understood and respected that. He'd said so. And God had blessed her in so many ways already. Even now, with losing the subdivision, they'd gained a friend and good employer in Matt Cavanaugh. Bad had turned into good. Callie was smart enough to recognize that.

"Hey, bud, can you keep going on those cabinet doors for me?" Matt called.

"Sure, Matt! Is it okay if The General comes in?"

"Jake. Wet dog." Callie scooted back and frowned. "Really?"

Matt's cell phone rang, a straightforward sound, no

fancy ring tones or songs. Callie liked that. He scanned
the phone, frowned and headed to the garage, his look
saying he wasn't getting a signal in the house, and the
garage was a quieter choice as Hank and Jim's arrival
added to the noise of doggie feet and Jake's excitement.

Besides, a guy was entitled to a little privacy. Callie
refocused her attention on the walls, ignoring pinpricks
of jealousy. She had a life. So did he. End of story.

Matt picked up the call in the garage and sighed relief when Mary Kay Hammond's voice came through
loud and clear. "Mary Kay, good morning. You're working today?"

The Realtor laughed. "Make money when you can,
I say. And while this never happens on a major holiday
weekend, I got a call this morning from someone interested in Cobbled Creek. They're in town for the weekend,
and they're coming by my office later to look at plans.
They'd like to stop by tomorrow and see the model."

"They know it's not done, right?"

"They don't care. They're moving here from down-
state and Cobbled Creek reminded them of the Catskills.
They're enamored."

Matt laughed. "Enamored is good. What time tomorrow?"

"Ten-thirty. We're looking at a couple of existing
homes as well, but these folks seem to prefer a new
build."

Matt understood the difference. Some people cher-
ished the feel of old wood, past times. Others? Nothing
but new would do. And those were the ones he hoped to
court with Cobbled Creek. "See you then. And they know
we can upgrade any way they want, right?"

Mary Kay laughed. "I've got it covered, Matt. You build. I'll sell. And I won't promise them anything you can't deliver, okay? And we'll adjust the pricing accordingly."

"Excellent." Mary Kay's promise sounded light, but Matt had worked with salespeople who didn't have a clue what upgrades meant to the contractor's bottom line. Mary Kay? She got it, which is why she still had a business when others bellied-up with the housing downfall.

"I'll see you tomorrow, then."

"We'll be there."

Matt headed back inside, whistling softly. Callie looked up at him and smiled. "You look happier."

He shrugged, sheepish. "A prospective buyer coming tomorrow."

"Really?" Callie grinned, no hint of envy or remorse shading her features. "Matt, that's wonderful."

"It sure is," cut in Hank as he rounded the corner from the family room. "On a holiday weekend. And this time of year. I figured we wouldn't see anybody until February."

Matt had thought the same thing. He'd hoped for earlier, but knew it was unlikely.

"They interested in the model?" Hank asked.

Matt shook his head. "I don't know." He wanted to sneak a peek at Callie to see if that bothered her, but he'd already figured out that Callie was adept at painting on a game face as needed. "They're exploring their options."

"It would be wonderful to lock in a contract," Callie said from the floor. She stretched to finish the last corner, and Matt thought how nice it was to have her there, keeping the bottom line in sight. Callie's pragmatism about getting a job done kept things focused. Balanced.

"I'll do a really good job on the doors," Jake promised.

Matt rubbed Jake's head as he went by. "Thanks, bud. Oh, and here's Don," he added as the aging car pulled into the drive. "He's going to start seaming today."

Hank slowed Matt's progress with a hand to his arm. The older man didn't say a word, but the approval in his eyes told Matt he'd done well.

But because flashes of the unresolved scene with Katie were fresh in his mind, Matt could only hope Hank was right.

Hank tipped his head toward the driveway. "This will be good for him. He's having a rough go right now."

"Due to?" Matt scrutinized Hank's calm look, then thought back. Don's pallor. His words. "He's sick?"

"I can't say more, but it's treatable. Still, a hard road when you're alone."

"Cancer."

Hank confirmed nothing, but Matt read his face. "Is he healthy enough to do this?"

"Best thing in the world for him. Purpose. Focus. He's never been much of one for leaning on God no matter how much I yammer at him."

Matt had no trouble envisioning that. "Thanks, Hank."

Hank sent him a cautionary look as he moved toward the stairs. "Between us, okay?"

"I hear ya."

Don pushed through the side entry and paused, inspecting what they'd done. "Nice." He turned and saw Matt there, and the tentative smile punched another little hole into the hard core of Matt's heart. "This is beautiful, Matt."

"Thanks. Hank's upstairs." He jerked a thumb toward the stairway. "He can get you started."

Don headed up, looking more confident with a box of tools in his hand. What had Hank said? Purpose. Focus.

Matt hadn't realized what wonderful gifts they were, but seeing the quick difference in Don's gait? His expression?

That combination made Matt glad he'd manned up and stopped by Don's place. Now if only things went well with Katie.

But recalling the look on her face that morning, that didn't fall into the realm of likely.

Chapter Eleven

"You goin' out, Matt?" Jake asked as Matt descended the stairs that evening.

Matt shrugged into his jacket and nodded. "For a little while."

"Oh." The boy's chin dropped.

"What's up, bud?"

"Nothing." Jake shook his head and Callie wasn't sure whether to chastise him or kiss him for making Matt feel guilty. She'd decide that later. For right now she folded laundry while the dishwasher hummed and Jake gazed up at Matt with hero-worship eyes and a quivering jaw. "See ya."

Matt hesitated, torn.

Callie caved. "Jake, Matt spends lots of time with you. It's not nice to make him feel guilty for going out."

"Sorry, Matt."

Matt stooped low. "I'll be here tomorrow, bud. And we can wage war along the Pacific Rim if you want."

"I have to go to a birthday party tomorrow." Jake droned the words as if attendance was a fate worse than death.

Matt moved back, surprised. "Birthday parties rock. Ice cream. Cake. Games."

"For a girl."

"Oh."

"Yeah." Jake looked up, woebegone. "Mom said I have to go."

"Well…" Matt wavered, then nodded. "We've got to be polite."

"To girls?"

"Especially to girls."

"Jake, we've had this discussion." Callie cut in. "You're going, you will be polite, and Matt's going to be late for whatever it is he's doing tonight." And looking wonderful, Callie added silently, but then, this was Matt. He looked great no matter what, but tonight he was freshly shaved and had on a classy black leather bomber jacket.

Gorgeous.

"Be good tonight, okay?" Matt ruffled Jake's hair as he stood.

"I will."

"Good." He shifted his attention to Callie. "I don't know how long I'll be…"

"Grown-ups don't have curfews," Callie assured him, hoping her smile wasn't stretched too tight. "You have a life, Matt. It's okay to lead it."

He faced her across the table, his hands fisted.

She couldn't decipher the tense look in his eyes, or read the clench of his jaw, but instinct told her he might need help. She moved around the table slowly, holding his gaze, needing to reassure him. She stopped just short of him and reached up a hand to cup his cheek, his jaw. "If God is with us, who can be against us?"

His eyes softened. He leaned his cheek into her hand, just enough to send a message of gratitude, the feel of his skin warm beneath her palm. He smelled of pricey aftershave and clean leather, and when he smiled at her it was all she could do not to melt.

"Thanks, Cal."

"See ya."

He nodded, sent her mouth a look that said he wished they were alone, then moved toward the door.

He wasn't whistling. And she recognized the haunted look in his eyes, the stolid set of his face. She went to the door and gazed out, Matt's taillights growing smaller as he headed toward town. "God, bless him. Whatever this is, keep him safe. Sound. Peaceful. Help him bridge this gap, dear Lord. He's such a good, gentle man."

"Mom, can we start decorating inside tonight?"

Callie sighed and shook her head. "No, kid. I'm beat. But tomorrow, yes. However," she added, seeing his look of disappointment, "we can get the stuff out tonight and then we're ready for tomorrow. We can probably get a bunch of things done before the birthday party."

His smile uplifted her. Such a little thing to decorate for the holidays. And Jake's smile?

Totally a gift from God.

Matt paced the sidewalk in front of the café, half wishing Katie would stand him up.

She didn't. She headed his way from across the street, the village quiet, even on Black Friday. He stepped forward, not sure where to begin. Hello seemed appropriate. "Hey. Thanks for coming."

She studied his face as if looking for something, then shrugged. "I didn't want to."

"I know."

"But I had to," she went on as though he hadn't spoken. "Because *I* don't want to be the person who walks away and never looks back."

Matt felt the direct shot. He jerked his head toward the door. "Let's go in. If we're at a back table, we won't get overheard by too many."

A tiny smile flashed momentarily. "This is Jamison. All it takes is one."

True, but Matt wondered if that was such a bad thing. If a person chose honor and goodness, would they care what was said about them? Of course not.

Which meant small towns were fine as long as you behaved yourself. He glanced around once they were seated in the Green Room, surprised by the flurry of customers. "I thought it would be quiet."

"Not on weekend nights. People come in for the music—" she trailed a look to a pair of guitar players settling in near the fireplace "—and the food. And the coffee is marvelous."

"Katie, hey." The taller guitarist moved their way, comfortable in the close-knit setting. "Did you bring your fiddle?"

She laughed. "It's at home, Cedric. It's not my night to play."

"Impromptu becomes you, Katie girl."

Katie leaned forward and gestured toward Matt. "Cedric MacDaniel, this is Matt Cavanaugh."

The man turned his way and extended his hand. "The builder."

"Yes."

"I'm Simon's brother. He told me you were coming by to patch his roof."

Matt nodded. "Hopefully we can get it taken care of this week."

"I roofed my way through college," Cedric told him. "If you need help, I'm available on weekends."

"Thanks."

Katie turned as Cedric headed back across the room. "He and Simon are fraternal twins."

"They're not from here."

"No." Katie shook her head, gave the waiter her order, paused while Matt did the same, then continued, "Simon took over the White Church ministry, then Cedric followed. Their parents were killed in the attack on the World Trade Center."

"Seriously?"

"Yeah." Katie nodded, rimmed her water glass with one finger, then sighed. "Simon was an associate pastor in Connecticut. Cedric was working in the financial district, but several blocks up."

"So he was right there." Matt couldn't fathom it, to be on hand and know your parents worked in the towers that came crashing down. "That's rough."

Katie turned her attention full back to him. "Rough stuff happens, Matt. To most of us. Then we pick up the pieces and move on, which you've obviously done."

Her tone didn't make it sound like a compliment. "I hope so." He paused, drew a breath and waded in. "I came back to apologize, Katie."

"And build houses."

Her cryptic tone said she wasn't buying his apology theory.

"That, too, but the reason I bought Cobbled Creek was to help make amends. To make something pretty out of threatened property."

"And make money."

"Let's hope." He met her gaze. "You don't stay in business if you don't make money."

"Or maybe," she said, leaning forward, her eyes locked on his, "you came back to show everyone how successful you are. How industrious. The bad boy returns and waves his success in the face of the people who wronged him."

"No one wronged me," he corrected her. "I was the one who messed up. I ruined a lot of things in my day, but the worst..." He shifted his attention away, then brought it back, reluctant. "The worst was what I did to you."

"Not calling me? Not coming to see me? Not writing?" She sat back, letting one rhythmic finger tap against the table top.

"Hurting you." He waved toward her leg. "Causing your injuries. Driving drunk and stupid."

"So seeing me is your reparation?"

Matt frowned. "Katie, it's..."

"Because, for your information, Matt Cavanaugh, totally ignoring me after the accident was way more painful than losing a limb ever thought of being."

"Katie—"

"Do you know how long I was in that hospital? In rehab? How I longed for a friendly face?"

"Your father wouldn't let anyone near you, Katie. You know that."

"Then you should have tried harder, Matt."

He scowled, wishing she was wrong.

"You let shame and guilt rule you. And you didn't even help the public defender when your court case came up. You could have pleaded down, you could have told the judge about your life, you could have helped yourself and maybe lessened your sentence..."

"I didn't deserve a lesser sentence. If anything, I should have served longer."

"Shut up."

He sat back, amazed.

"You." She half stood and shook a finger at him, her expression tough and tart. "You acted like a sacrificial lamb, like the whole thing was your fault, like Pete, Joe and I didn't have options. We had choices, Matt. We were stupid drunk just like you, and it was only by chance you were driving. The accident happened because four of us were stupid. Not one. And it was more hurtful to lose your friendship than to lose my leg, and if you think I'm not one-hundred-percent serious about that, then you don't know me."

Her words hit home, but was she right or sugar-coating a horrible circumstance? "I was driving."

"Only because Joe got sick," she reminded him. "Matt, listen." She edged forward again.

Matt leaned back. "Are you going to hit me?"

The tiny smile he glimpsed outside returned. "I'm tempted, but no. We were young. Stupid. We stole that car and went drinking and driving late at night, but each of us made a conscious choice to be there. We were just as wrong as you. But you…" She reached out and smoothed a hand to his face. "You took it on the chin for us."

"Katie, you lost your leg," he reminded her, hating that she felt sorry for him when he'd cost her so much. "I maimed you because I was reckless. I can't forgive myself for that."

"Well, then you're still stupid," she told him, but her voice was softer. Gentler. "Because I forgave you a long time ago. And I forgave my father for being so tough and critical," she added, wrinkling her nose, an expression he remembered as though it was yesterday. "Although I try to avoid him as much as possible, and that's tough in a small town, but Matt—" she bent farther forward, her tone strong but sincere "—our families were a piece of work for different reasons. God doesn't hold that against us. He knows kids make mistakes and need forgiveness. It's what we do as adults that counts. And did you ever stop to think the accident happened for a reason? That it might have been the wake-up call we needed?" She accepted her latte from the waiter and paused as Matt took his coffee.

"We were on the road to early graves," she continued. "That accident put the brakes on. Made us grow up. Now we've all got successful careers. Pete's got two beautiful kids and is a grocery manager at Tops. Joe's a mechanic at a big car dealership in Olean, and loves it."

"He always loved tinkering under a hood," Matt mused.

"And you've done well, Matt," she reminded him. "You've served your country, you've built a business, you're honest and upright."

"How do you know all this?"

She scoffed a laugh. "The web. I've watched you along the way, just checking to see if you were okay."

"I am." Saying the words out loud, Matt almost believed them. "I was nervous about meeting you."

"Me, too. But mostly mad," Katie added, grinning.

"I saw that, which might have been the source of my fear," Matt admitted. "You look wonderful."

"You, too. And I love that you've taken over Cobbled Creek," she added. "Not because I didn't want the Mareks successful," she hastened to add. "But just because they looked so sad that the whole thing fell apart. Callie is about one of the toughest, strongest gals I know..."

"She's incredible. I don't know what I'd do without her," Matt agreed. Something in his tone deepened Katie's smile.

"She is. And she works so hard at everything she does, and her little boy?" Katie lifted her shoulders. "He's wonderful even though his father walked out on him when he was a baby."

"A feeling I can relate to," Matt noted. "But Jake seems fine."

"He does," Katie agreed, "but it's got to bother him. Look back at you and me when we were young. There was a lot we didn't let show."

She was right. They'd hidden their emotional wounds, but things surfaced when they acted out as young teens. "I can't believe the dumb things we did."

"Me neither. And if I'm ever a mom," Katie continued, "I want to be a great one. With a wonderful husband who's committed to God and his family. And a good dog."

"You always loved dogs."

"Still do." Wistfulness softened her expression. "But I can't have one in my apartment in Wellsville and I'm never there anyway. I work as a nurse at Jones Memorial, play violin for the church and teach skiing on winter weekends."

Skiing? Matt didn't shield the surprise on his face quick enough and her finger waved again. "Don't make assumptions about what my life is like, Matt. You see me as broken, but I prefer to think of it as just another challenge. An extra mogul in the downhill slopes of life."

"You're incredible."

"Well." She patted her leg as the waiter brought a serving of spinach and artichoke dip with a side of pita chips. "Computerized prosthetics are a wonder these days. And they're using me to test new apparatus that responds to the brain."

"Your brain tells the leg what to do?"

"And the leg does it." She grinned and grabbed a chip. "Not quite as perfect as the real deal, but amazing, nonetheless. So yeah, I ski, I bike, I run, I play, I work." She reached out and held his hand, her fingers soft and warm. "I decided that I needed to work harder, better and longer to conquer those early demons. So I did. Same as you."

He gripped her hand, grateful for her forgiveness. Her friendship. "I'm proud of you, Katie."

"You, too." She lifted her chin and smiled as the first notes of Cedric's guitar sounded. "And being here with you on a Thanksgiving weekend? Laying all the old drama to rest?" She leaned forward and kissed his cheek. "Thank you, Matt. God bless you."

God had blessed him, Matt realized. In so many ways. He smiled and raised her fingers for a kiss. "You, too, Katie."

Jill Calhoun's Facebook pic shouldn't have hurt so much, but it did, and that only meant Callie'd been careless.

But the picture, sent from Jill's cell phone, showing Katie Bascomb kissing Matt, looking sweet, blonde and beautiful made Callie recognize her vulnerability. Obviously she'd misinterpreted Matt's looks, his words, that soul-searching kiss, but was that his fault or hers?

His, she decided. Men shouldn't toy with a woman's affections, and a single mom to boot? Shameful.

Her phone rang a short while later, Jill's number in

the display. When she didn't pick up, a text appeared. "Is this the hunk working with you? No wonder you gave up your shifts at the diner! When opportunity knocks…" Jill had inserted a smiley face. "A smart girl's gotta be around to open the door."

Not so smart when the guy's off kissing someone else, Callie mused. She headed to bed, not wanting to be awake when Matt came home.

This isn't his home, her conscience stabbed. *It's a convenient place to stay. And that's it.*

The internal warning was just what Callie needed, a reminder to step back. Maintain distance. Being independent worked for her. She'd be foolish to forget that. Relationships meant risk, and her responsibility to Jake curtailed those opportunities. And because Matt was also her boss, and Dad's boss, well…

Time to revert back to what she'd known all along: don't date the boss. Or flirt with him. Or daydream about forever afters in sweet stone-faced Capes with twinkle lights welcoming you home at Christmas.

She fell asleep with a headache. One that was her fault for letting herself get silly. She knew better, and she'd apply the brakes now. That was best all around.

Knowing that didn't help the headache, though.

Chapter Twelve

The smell of fresh coffee roused her early the next morning. She yawned, stretched, then remembered.

Katie and Matt. Kissing.

The headache re-erupted, full-blown.

Ibuprofen for breakfast in that case. She got dressed and headed downstairs, quiet.

"Hey." Matt's quick smile and pleased salute strengthened the headache's hold. Why had she let herself be so stupid?

"Morning." She crossed the room, poured coffee and fixed it in the kitchen, looking anywhere but at Matt.

"You okay, Cal?" His evident concern only strengthened the steel rod along her backbone.

"A little headache. Nothing major."

"Are you getting sick?" He stood and came her way, his closeness offsetting her planned evasive maneuvers.

A plan she was losing because he smelled marvelous. She took a broad step back. "I'm fine. Probably just slept funny."

"Do you want me to rub your shoulders? Your neck? Is your pillow too soft?"

Like she was about to discuss her pillow with Matt Cavanaugh. She shrugged him off, grabbed her lined flannel and headed for the door. "It'll work itself out. And I want to get the model cleared up before those buyers arrive. I'll see you over there."

His gaze followed her out the door, a marine's battlefield assessment. By the time he joined her in the model, she'd applied a finishing coat to the kitchen walls and was ready to hang kitchen lighting fixtures.

"Looks good."

Two words. That's all he said as he walked through, heading into the family room to apply trim. And his tone said they were words he'd have said to any worker, anytime, a casual compliment with nothing else implied, which was exactly what she wanted. So why did it feel so bad?

"Nice kitchen." Don came through the side door next. He examined the kitchen's layout and faced Callie. He smiled his appreciation. "You did a great job with this, Callie."

"Thanks, Don. Most of it was already in the plans."

He harrumphed. "I saw the original layout, remember? And the way you added the plate rack above, the spindles along the far edge, the double pantry…?" He took a contemplative sip of coffee. "Your mother would have loved this."

His words smoothed her prickled feelings, like extrafine sandpaper on wild-grained oak. "You think?"

"Oh, yeah. All this cupboard space, so neat and pretty? She'd have had a ball in a kitchen like this."

"Good." Callie finished the last strip along the upper edge and turned to step back onto the ladder. Her toe caught the lip of the cupboard fascia. She held a wet paintbrush in one hand and a can of paint in the other. No way was she about to spill paint on these new cupboards with people coming in two hours.

She tipped, knowing the fall was inevitable, wishing she'd stayed focused.

"I've got you."

Matt's strong arms braced her, holding her steady, his welcome words emotionally painful. He held on while she unhooked her foot, then asked, "Don, can you take the paint?"

"Sure."

Callie set the can in Don's hand, then the brush. She stepped back onto the ladder, feeling Matt's hand at her waist, wondering if he'd been this nice to Katie last night, wishing Jill never sent the photo.

But a part of her thanked God for the wake-up call. She'd promised herself no more missteps with men and romance. Falling for Matt?

Big mistake?

"Are you okay?"

Strong, rugged hands gripped her shoulders. And she thought she heard a slight tremor in his voice. *Don't look up.*

Too late. He released one shoulder and tipped her chin, scrutinizing her. "Did you pull anything? Sprain anything?"

"Besides my pride? No."

A soft smile brightened his worried features. "Pride goeth before the fall," he quipped.

She tried to ease back.

He didn't let go. And Don had disappeared upstairs, leaving them alone. "You scared me."

Yeah, well… "Glad you happened by, marine."

He studied her like he had before she left the house, then shrugged. "I'm confused. You're mad at me and I don't know why. We haven't seen each other since last night and you were fine when I left to meet Katie."

She flinched. An "aha" moment widened his eyes. "You're mad because I met Katie for coffee?"

She pulled back, harder this time. "Matt, it's like I told Jake last night. You have a life. You need to lead it. Living with us is a convenience, I get that, and we don't want to make you uncomfortable. Do what you've got to do and it will all work out."

She might have pulled back firmly, but her strength didn't come close to matching his, which made her gesture futile. "You're jealous."

"No."

He had the audacity to smile and that nearly got him taken out at the knees. "Yes, but I don't get why," he mused, not letting her go, almost enjoying this. One quick look at his face said there was no "almost" about it. "First Reenie. Now Katie. You got trust issues going on, Cal?"

She did, thanks to a cheating husband and a lousy self-image, but that was none of his concern. "I trust you for a paycheck, Matt. Nothing more. Got it?"

"Got it." He released her then, but the twinkle in his eye said more. Way more. "And I forgot how quickly information travels around here, so the next time I meet an old friend, I'll employ full disclosure up front, okay?"

"No need." She slapped the top on the paint can with more vigor than needed, droplets of paint spattering the subfloor. She growled, chagrined.

He leaned down, close. Very close. "You're awful cute when you're mad. You know that?"

Hank and Jake's arrival warded off her reply, and she

spent the next two hours wiping, polishing, vacuuming and sweeping. When Mary Kay pulled in with the prospective buyers, the crew slipped out the back door. They aimed for the Marek house to give the Realtor time to show the people around. Matt hung back to meet the buyers, but he managed to catch Callie's arm as she left. She bit her lower lip, determined to say nothing. Silence seemed best at the moment.

Matt gestured to the cleaned-up model, his gaze teasing. He leaned in, dropped her a wink and drawled, "Reenie couldn't have done it better, Cal. Thank you."

"You're not funny."

"Oh, I am." He softened his grip on her arm and sent her mouth a wistful look. "But I'm sorry you misunderstood about Katie. I'll explain it soon, okay?" He glanced around the work space and shrugged. "I keep meaning to but we've been busy." He shifted his attention to the guys heading toward the Marek house. "And we're never alone."

That was certainly true.

"Soon. Promise." He smiled at her, his eyes sending a message her heart longed to hear, but was it the longing or the message that ruled the moment? Callie couldn't be sure, and until she was, she was safer maintaining distance.

The chatter of voices redirected her attention. "I'll head home. Make fresh coffee. Go schmooze these people with your charm and expertise."

"Expertise will get me further," Matt replied.

Not necessarily. He might be a first-class builder. She'd witnessed that. But his charm?

Off the charts. And that's what worried her most.

She gave the house one last look as the voices grew

louder, hoping they'd love it, praying they'd see merit in her changes and upgrades, while a part of her hated to see it go. "Good luck."

"Thanks." Matt squeezed her arm and straightened his shoulders, heading back in. "I'll be over shortly."

"Or call if this takes longer than you expected. I'll fix you a cup and bring it over."

"Thanks, Callie."

She told herself she was just being nice, that she'd hope for anyone's success the same way, but the Marek–Cavanaugh building connection had her personally invested. Good or bad, they'd put heart and soul into this venture, and today's viewing could signal success or failure. She sent him a confident nod and turned toward home, wondering what they'd gotten themselves into. "Anytime, boss."

She doesn't want to sell the model.

The realization struck him as he closed the family room door.

Callie's personal investment in this house showed throughout, even though it wasn't quite done, and her quick look of longing?

That gripped his heart, but they'd built the model to sell, right? So why was this so hard?

"Matt, you're here." Mary Kay's warm greeting inspired his smile as she came through the garage entrance followed by a thirty-something couple. They looked nice. Normal. And as they stepped in, the woman grabbed her husband's arm, delighted. "Look at these maple cabinets, Ben. Aren't they gorgeous?"

"Very nice." He stuck out a hand to Matt. "Ben Wiseman. And this is my wife, Chloe, the woman who ignored my instructions about not showing how much you like the house because it drives the price up."

Matt laughed, shook his hand, and then Chloe's. "I've wired the walls to record conversation, actually. That way I can access every exclamation and adjust the price upward accordingly."

"Clever technology."

Matt grinned. "We do what we can."

Mary Kay linked her arm through his. "Matt is a marine. He did multiple tours overseas and when he got home he worked night and day to build this business. And by buying Cobbled Creek from the Marek family…"

The couple nodded, obviously up-to-date on the subdivision's history.

"Matt's been working *with* the Mareks to stay true to the original design and specifications."

"Isn't that tough?" Ben asked Matt. "Working with the family that lost this?"

Matt shook his head. "I'd have thought so, too, but no. It's been wonderful. And they live across the road, so they'll be your neighbors if you decide to live here. And you couldn't ask for better ones anywhere."

"Kids?" Chloe asked.

"A boy. Eight years old. His name's Jake."

"The same age as our Jordan." Chloe surveyed the kitchen. "And I love the ratio of cupboard and pantry space to work space in this kitchen."

"That's Callie Marek's doing," Matt told them. "She's got a great eye."

"We loved the layout of the neighborhood," Ben confessed. "And I probably shouldn't tell you that, but the minute we saw it, it reminded us of the vacation spot Chloe's parents had in the Catskills."

"The way you've nestled the homes into the hillside drew us," added Chloe.

Matt would have to thank Hank and Callie for their hard work. Sure, he'd come in at the last moment to pull things together, but money and timing couldn't fix poor initial planning, and the welcoming look of Cobbled Creek attested to that.

But now it was time to let Mary Kay do her job. Matt shook hands again and headed for the door, cell phone in hand. "If you need me, call, but I want to get out of your way so you feel free to examine things fully."

"Thanks, Matt." Mary Kay's nod said his timing was perfect, making him wish he could do that in all facets of his life.

Hah.

He headed toward the Marek house, his gaze drawn to the plywood Holy Family staked in the lawn. Simple. Austere. Poignant.

Callie and Hank didn't have much, but faith and love shined in everything they did. They took care of each other, the way a family should. Callie'd grown up with one parent. Jake was doing the same. Matt had been left virtually parentless at a young age, and for just a moment he wondered if the American dream of Mom, Dad and kids living together was an illusion. A shadow of reality, an old truth.

It doesn't have to be, son.

Grandpa's sage words washed over him.

It's all about choices. Good and bad. Every step of the way.

Grandpa was right. Eyeing the Marek house, Matt recognized the growing feeling inside himself. The way his heart had stopped beating when Callie nearly fell. The way it ramped up pace when she smiled at him. How she managed to capture his heart by cupping his cheek.

He wanted to be her helper, her protector. Her knight in shining armor.

But that meant he had to set the record straight, and people would talk after seeing him with Katie last night. They'd reminisce and wonder out loud. Which meant he had to tell Callie first.

"Did they like the house, Matt?" Jake spouted the question the moment Matt stepped through the door.

Matt picked him up, tossed him into a fireman's hold and noogied the boy's head while Jake laughed in glee. "They seemed to, bud. But I had to get out of there and let Mary Kay do her job."

"What's that mean?"

"Schmooze 'em," explained Hank.

Jake frowned, confused.

"Mary Kay's job is to point out the good things about a house so people want to buy it."

"Although nothing about Cobbled Creek needs glossing over," declared Don.

"Absolutely not," exclaimed Buck, who must have joined the group after they'd walked to the Mareks'.

"It's beautiful just the way it is," threw in Jim roundly, adding his support.

"You sound like a bunch of pom-pom wavin' cheerleaders," Hank grumped, but his grin of appreciation showed his true feelings. "Matt, Buck brought bagels." He waved a hand toward the counter.

"Sounds good. Thanks, Buck." He turned toward Callie. "Weren't you and Jake going to start decorating?"

She nodded. "I figured now is the perfect time so

those people can wander at will with Mary Kay, then I can work on the model this afternoon while Jake's at the birthday party."

"Good. I'll grab a couple of these," he took two bagels from the counter and wrapped them in a double paper towel, "and we can head back. Get some stuff done on number twenty-three."

Did he just glance wistfully at the stack of boxes? Like a little boy lost, gazing in a Christmas window?

No.

He headed toward the door, bagels in hand, almost hurrying, as if he couldn't wait to leave. *Or because he badly longed to stay.*

"Matt, can you help us?" Callie's voice stretched high, nerves showing.

"Really?" He turned, caught off guard, as if making sure he heard correctly.

"Sure, Matt!"

"I mean, if you're too busy…" Callie went on, offering him a way out. If he wanted one, that is.

"He's not, are you, Matt?" Jake implored. "Because you can work this afternoon when I'm at the party, right?"

"I can," Matt told him, his voice deep and easy. "Happy to do that, bud."

"Matt loved helping with Christmas when he was little," Don added.

A shot of pain darkened Matt's gaze, but Callie drew him forward, ready to fix old wrongs. Now was a time for hope. Happiness. Health. "Good, then you're experienced." She grinned at him and directed him to a spot on the couch. "You sit here and open these." She slid a pile of boxes to his left as the guys grabbed hats and gloves.

"The guys and I will start getting those plumbing lines

laid in number twenty-three, Matt," Hank said smoothly, "because we can't finish those last two roofs until the weather clears. And then Don can head back to seaming the model once it's clear of people."

"I love plumbing," Buck announced. He headed for the door. "You sure it won't bother the folks looking around?"

Matt shook his head. "They know we have to work. And they've had more than a half hour already."

"And time's money," added Hank, but he winked Matt's way, "although we wouldn't mind nailing down that first contract."

"That would be wonderful," Matt agreed.

Chapter Thirteen

As the aging but earnest military crew trooped out, Matt turned, catching Callie's look. "A little obvious?"

Callie smiled. "Blatantly, but sweet."

Matt snorted as Jake dragged a box closer. "What soldier wants to be called sweet?" he asked, making a face.

Too late he realized his mistake as he caught Callie's look. "Present company excluded, of course."

"Uh-huh."

"So what's first?" He surveyed the boxes and let Callie take the lead.

"The manger scene goes on the painted chest alongside the fireplace."

"This box." Jake pulled a smaller one front and center. "And this one," he added, shifting another one forward.

"Great. Let me just grab a—"

"Gotcha covered, marine." Callie slipped alongside Matt and handed off a cup of coffee, fragrant and steaming hot, her thoughtfulness curling around his heart, the scent of coffee, Callie and a hint of wood smoke feeling like he'd come home to a greeting card Christmas. He leaned forward and bumped foreheads with her, ever so gently. "Thank you."

Her smile said so much. Too much? He hoped not. Prayed not. "You're welcome."

"So." He sat on the floor, balanced his coffee on a side table and opened the first box. "I'll unpack while you guys direct. Is that okay?"

"It's great, Matt!" Jake grinned in wide enthusiasm, his bright blue eyes different from his mother's jade green, but his gentle joy at grasping life? That was Callie all the way.

Matt reached into the first box and withdrew a rugged barnlike structure. "The stable."

"Which might have been a cave," Jake explained solemnly. "People aren't really sure, but we know they kept animals there."

"History lesson noted." Matt smiled up at him and handed him an unwrapped camel.

"These guys go over here," Jake continued, intent on detail. He moved the camel off to the side. "The wise men didn't get to see Jesus for a while, but we like to remember their visit at Christmas so we include them."

Matt angled a glance up to Callie. "Does he get his love of history from you?"

She sent him a dubious look. "Dad's been teaching him history since birth. And Jake eats it up. I'm lucky I remember breakfast."

"I get it." He unwrapped more figures and smiled as Jake set them carefully around the rough, wooden stable, frequently stepping back to see if they were placed just right. "The fussiness he gets from you," Matt observed, grinning, a few minutes later.

"I prefer to call it attention to detail," Callie shot back

as she attempted to unravel a tangled set of twinkle lights. "Which is why that model kitchen might just sell a house for you."

"For us," Matt corrected.

She looked embarrassed but pleased to be included.

"I mean it, Cal. I couldn't have gotten this done without a great crew and having your family on hand. And the guys." Matt winked at Jake as he handed off a statue of Joseph. "Made all the difference in the world."

"We could just all work together forever," Jake announced, serious and cute. "That way we can build houses and everyone has a job."

"Jake."

"Great idea." Matt handed Jake a slightly chipped gray donkey and sent a lazy smile Callie's way. "We'll have to see how things go, okay?"

"Okay!" He grinned as Matt continued helping, the easy act of unwrapping history binding in its simplicity.

Callie finished unraveling the lights, plugged them in, then groaned.

Matt hid a chuckle behind a cough. "Might want to test 'em first the next time."

When she turned to scowl at him he tugged her down beside him, pointing to the second box. "Let's do these together. Then the lights. Is there garland for the mantel?"

"Yes."

"Lovely."

"And Mom always puts Christmas cards up there, and candles," Jake explained. "It's real pretty."

"Like your mom."

Jake turned, suspicious. "Are you guys getting mushy?"

"No," Callie said.

"Well…" Matt grinned at her, tweaked her nose, then handed Jake the next figure. She blushed, and in that heightened color Matt read the possibility of a future he'd denied himself, the thought of working with the Mareks, coming home to this family, a gift like no other. He watched Callie hand up a lamb to Jake, then asked, "How about if you and I do some shopping tonight?"

"Can I come?" Jake asked instantly.

"May I," Callie corrected. She shook her head, chin down, and continued to unwrap figures. "We probably shouldn't."

"Sure we should." Matt stretched across her and tugged the box of lights closer. "Jake can stay with Hank and you and I can get our Christmas shopping done."

"I'll be good," Jake wheedled.

"You'll be in bed," Matt corrected him mildly. He gave a lock of Callie's hair a tug. "What do you think? Good idea?"

Instinct had told her to say no after seeing Matt and Katie canoodling at a cozy table in the acoustic café. Shopping with Matt might possibly be the *worst* idea she'd ever heard, so why did she say yes?

Because you're a sucker for the little boy you see behind the rugged marine.

Either way, here they were at the mall later that night, the sweet glow of Christmas lights framing windows and doors, their bright presence climbing columns and archways. "This must look like fairyland to a kid like Jake," Matt mused as they walked through the food court surrounded by mouth-watering smells. Soft notes of Christmas music floated from a keyboard player centered amid the tables.

"You never came to the mall at Christmas when you were a kid?" Callie asked. One look at his face answered that. "Then I'm glad to be with you this time," she told him and hugged his arm.

"You think Jake's mad at us because we wouldn't let him come?"

Honesty was the best policy. *Most times.* "I think Jake has a wicked case of hero worship and thinks you're the best thing since sliced bread."

"No argument there." Matt grinned at her. "The boy's smart. So what are we shopping for?"

"Not much." She paused and faced him, determined to be up front, although admitting her limits made them seem more constraining. "My budget is small. Think miniscule. So is Dad's. Jake needs a new bike, so that's it. And some new socks and art supplies for school. Crayons, markers, cool pencils, tablets, et cetera."

Matt accepted what she said easily. "So if I got him some miniature cars and trucks, would that be okay?"

"He'd love that."

"And maybe his first power drill?"

"Matt—"

"And I could build him a workbench."

"Stop!" She put two fingers against his mouth to shush him, and tried unsuccessfully to ignore the feel of his face, his mouth against her skin. Right then she wished she had soft, feminine fingers, uncalloused, unworn, the silky-soft skin she saw advertised everywhere. And despite her attempts to heal the roughened skin with creams, her fingers showed the effects of working in cold, dry conditions on a steady basis.

Matt caught her hand, kissed it, smiled and said, "Okay, I'm a little excited. I've never shopped for a kid before. Maybe I should do the tool thing for him instead of cars."

"He does have some cars already." Callie agreed, trying to ignore the feel of her hand clasped in his and failing. "And we couldn't afford to get him a real tool kit of his own once everything went bad. He's got a few, but…"

"Tools it is," Matt decided. "And I'd like to get something for Jeff and Hannah. Besides what I'm getting for their wedding," he added. "And something for Dana Brennan and Helen Walker. Helen's always been good to me, and Dana, well…" He paused as though choosing his words, then said, "Dana has treated me kindly through thick and thin. She's one special lady."

"She is." Callie squeezed his hand. "And I'm delighted that Jeff and Hannah are having a New Year's wedding."

Matt bumped her arm. "That we're both attending."

"I—"

"I'll take that as a yes." He grinned, then tugged her along. "Already this is a productive night. I've got a Christmas plan *and* a date for the wedding."

"I didn't say yes," she retorted, shrugging her purse up her other arm. "And you didn't ask. You assumed."

"Will you go with me? Save me from a night of food, romance and music all alone?"

Callie flashed him a once-over. "I don't think you'd be all that lonely."

"Your presence ensures it." He paused outside the cookie and coffee shop. "Want a quick coffee? My treat."

"I'd love one." The piano notes paused as Matt ordered their coffees, then began again, different this time, as though…

Callie jumped as a voice rang out right next to her.

Another voice joined in from across the way, followed by two, harmonizing, about eight tables back.

The piano danced along, the flow of voices joined by others as random people stood and sang around the center court.

"A flash mob," Callie breathed, gripping Matt's arm. He shook his head, not understanding.

"Choral groups and dance troupes put these together and then randomly perform," Callie whispered. She squeezed his arm tighter. "I've always wanted to see one."

"Well, here you go." He smiled down at her as the far-flung choir offered a rousing Christmas medley, their voices blending harmony and praise. As the medley wound down, a lone man mounted a chair in the middle, his haggard appearance making him look cast-out. Wondering. Wandering. Slowly, note by note, he began singing "Joseph's Song," the poignant hymn expressing the awesome wonder and responsibility of guiding God's Son through life.

The lone man was singing to him. *Of him*, Matt decided as emotions grabbed hold and refused to let go.

The words filled Matt's heart, easing more of the angst. Simple piano notes balanced the strong tenor of the prayerful man, seeking God's will, a father's advice, wondering where a common man like him fit into such a wondrous plan.

The words, meant for Christ's earthly father, fit any man guiding a child not his own. A part of Matt wished Don had felt this way, that he'd been strong enough to ask God's help and be part of Matt's life.

Another part envisioned Jake, another man's son, a

child so sweet, so invested in life that Matt wondered if his presence would bless the boy's life. Could it?

Joseph was a simple carpenter.

Like Matt.

He accepted a child not his own.

A boy, like Jake, to father. Guide. Love. And Joseph embraced his wife despite questionable circumstances. He latched on to faith and clung to an angel's direction.

Could Matt be that strong? Could he embrace Callie and Jake, and be a father in the image of Joseph?

A tiny tear slipped down Callie's cheek, the spiritual words working womanly magic. Matt caught the tear and tugged her closer, holding her. Cherishing her. Wondering what he'd done to have this family put in his path, how this perfect timing had come about. No matter. She was here, and unless he messed up big time, her feelings for him reflected his for her.

Just right.

The song came to a whispered close, the soft chain of notes like a puff of wind.

"Here." Matt handed her a napkin, rolled his eyes and smiled. "Women. Always mushy."

"Like that didn't affect you?" she asked. She poked him with her elbow. "Seriously?"

"Oh, it did." He didn't dare tell her how much. "But the coffee's getting cold and the mall's open only three more hours."

"Then it's good we've got a short list," she told him.

He smiled and sipped his coffee, thinking the list might grow, whispers of promises and forever afters niggling his brain. But for now, they'd shop. Figure things out. Take this blessed night for what it was: a time to be together. Get to know one another away from the clatter and chatter that surrounded them at work. Tonight they were just a pair of shoppers, out to have a little fun.

He couldn't have asked for more.

Chapter Fourteen

Callie lifted her gaze to survey number thirty-seven's new roofline on Tuesday afternoon and put an arm around her father's waist. "It's beautiful, Dad."

"It is." Hank regarded the black architect shingles, then twisted to eye the homes leading up to this last one. "The neighborhood looks great."

"You do good work for an old soldier," she told him, basking in the gentle day, a rarity for early December. Snow was forecast for tomorrow, so getting these roofs complete, windows in, doors hung was imperative.

The gift of hard work, focus and God's hand with Mother Nature.

"Are you coming to work on the church roof?" Hank asked, rolling his shoulders to ease two straight days of shingling.

Callie shook her head. "You need only a few people. And Jake's bus will be here before the roof's done, so I'm going to finish painting the family room in the model. And the upstairs should be ready for paint soon, leaving us flooring and bathroom tiling to complete things."

"The countertop looks good, Callie," Hank told her as they walked toward Matt's truck. "It has a rich look to it."

"Thanks." She waved toward the model as they drew closer. "The lighter cabinets let me go a little wild with the counter top. You don't think it's too dark?"

Matt came up alongside them, pulling off his hat and gloves. "The lighting offsets the dark tone," he assured her, smiling. "And I think we've had this conversation before."

Callie made a face. "I'm just wondering if that's why those people haven't made an offer, if maybe I messed up the balance and that put them off."

"They said they wanted time to consider their options and pray about it. Stop borrowing trouble." He bumped shoulders with her, then laughed at her scowl. "If they do move in, they'll probably be good neighbors. And with a kid Jake's age, that would be nice. A few days of waiting is worth it to get good neighbors."

"So it's not about the countertop?"

Matt raised his eyes heavenward and climbed into the truck. Hank took his place on the passenger side. "We've got just enough time to get this patched before dark, I think."

Matt nodded agreement, then waved as he backed the truck out of the driveway, the crunch of stones beneath the wheels a temporary sound. By spring Phase One would be complete, the road and driveways paved. Streetlights would brighten the nights, a torch-lit uphill path complementing the curving road.

They'd have a charming view out the front window, Callie mused as she entered the model. She adjusted the thermostat and smiled, the warmth of the new furnace a welcome presence. Painting a heated family room or working a crisp rooftop? She grinned and shed her gloves, knowing she'd gotten the easy end of this deal.

The front door opened as she rolled paint on the back wall. "Dad? Matt? That you?"

"It's me," said Finch as he strolled through the model, looking left and right, his gaze pinched.

"Hey, Finch." Callie nodded his way and continued working. "Matt's not here, but—"

"I know. That's the reason I came now. To see you."

Callie groaned inside, but kept her face affable. "Really? Why?"

"You and I need to talk." Finch declared. He stood still, folded his arms and braced his legs, battle ready. "It's time you knew a few things about your boss."

Cassie frowned, silent, deliberately obtuse. Rule one of battle: let the enemy state their position.

"You look around here—" Finch waved a hand, exasperated "—and you see Matt Cavanaugh as a knight in shining armor. Well, he's not. Not even close."

Callie kept working but flicked a mild look over her shoulder. "Matt took an opportunity that came his way, then stepped in graciously. He's been nothing but a gentleman and a fine contractor. He doesn't cut corners, he doesn't do shoddy and he's generous to a fault."

"Fault is exactly what I'm talking about." Finch encroached on her space, determined and angry. "This guy waltzes into town and you follow him around like a love-struck puppy when you know nothing about him. Who he is, what he's done."

"First of all." Callie set the roller down, pivoted and met Finch's glare with one of her own. "Don't demean me. I'm perfectly capable of making my own decisions in all matters, so I don't need you to save me from myself.

I have bills to pay and a child to raise, and working for Matt is a sensible way to do both affordably. Anything else is none of your business. Now if you're not here on town business, please leave."

"I make it town business when I'm keeping my eye on an ex-con."

Her face must have showed a reaction because Finch smirked and came forward again. "You didn't know that, did you? That the guy living in your house, teaching things to your little boy, is an ex-con with a record as long as my arm." He edged closer and tsk-tsked her. "You really should pay better attention to who comes through your front door, but then you've always been too trusting."

The best defense is a great offense. Callie strode forward and poked a finger into Finch's very surprised chest. "What is the matter with you, McGee? Why would you come in here trying to stir up trouble? You think I don't know Matt had problems?" She raised her voice and stood tall, straight and taut, a soldier's stance.

"When I was a child, I talked as a child," she summarized the wise verse from Corinthians. "And when I became a man I gave up childish ways." She leaned in, refusing to give ground, determined to have this out with Finch once and for all, hoping it wouldn't affect Matt's certificates of occupancy. "Everybody makes mistakes when they're kids, Finch, and sometimes when they're not kids. But grown-ups move forward and fix things. Do the right thing. So Matt made mistakes. Well, me, too. And I don't think that mirror you face every morning shows a man without scars, so how about we turn this around and figure out why you've been a jerk for two years."

Finch paled, but didn't back down.

"Your marriage failed. And I don't know anything about it, but I bet there's plenty of blame to go around. And you're mad at the world. That two-by-four chip on your shoulder's gotta feel pretty heavy by the end of the day, so why don't you wise up, take your troubles to God, go to church and make things right," Callie halved the narrow distance between them and tightened her gaze, "because I don't want you showing up here angry anymore unless there's something on site to be angry about. If you lay into Matt again about his work methods, or malign him in any way, I'll go to the town board myself and cite personal issues to have them put Colby in your place."

"You wouldn't."

"Would."

"But—"

"There are no buts," Callie told him. She squared her shoulders. "Stop living in the past, stop making trouble and do your job. I don't care what Matt Cavanaugh did before, what I care about is the future. And right now, Matt's work is the cornerstone of success for Cobbled Creek, and if you continue to try and thwart that, I'll…"

"I get it."

"Good." She nailed him with a glare, then sighed. "Finch, I don't pretend to understand what's going on with you, but you didn't used to be like this. Get a grip. Stop drinking, stop whining and move on."

Finch stared beyond her for a long moment, then shifted his attention back. "I've tried. Or thought I did. First it was Katie, way back when, but she didn't have eyes for anyone but Matt. Even after he crashed that car and crippled her, she longed for him. Talked about him.

Wanted to help him, when all I wanted was a piece of him for being so stupid."

Matt had been driving the car the night of Katie's accident. Callie sighed inside, understanding how old wrongs could burn a hole deep into your soul. But only if you allowed it to happen. She swallowed hard, recognizing her own struggles, and couldn't help but wonder if two people with so many doubts could possibly be good for one another. But for now, she needed to set things straight with Finch.

"So this is about a two-decades-old romance gone bad?" Callie folded her arms and sighed. "Get over it already."

"And then there was you," Finch went on. "You knew I was interested."

"But I wasn't," Callie declared because her more subtle clues hadn't worked.

"I got that when I saw you get all goofy about Cavanaugh the first time I came by," Finch told her. "But then I saw him out with Katie and I wanted to punch someone."

"But you didn't." Callie sent him a look of sympathy. "That was good."

He growled and scrubbed a toe against the subflooring. "I miss my wife. I messed up big time. Not being home, being on time, helping with things, going to kid stuff. I got careless and she walked." He lifted his gaze to Callie's. "And now she's in Arizona with my kids, dating a land developer, and then Cavanaugh shows up here, playing the hero..."

Callie recognized the parallel. "You had a lot of buttons being pushed, Finch, but that wasn't Matt's fault."

"Katie's missing leg is Matt's fault," Finch declared,

brows drawn. Then he sighed and acknowledged, "But that was twenty years ago."

"And she's obviously forgiven him," Callie added, remembering the picture.

"She never blamed him."

Callie could understand that. Katie's gentle nature reached out to others, nothing like her hypercritical father. "Katie's a sweetheart."

"She is."

"But Finch," Callie went on, determined to make her point. "You've got to stop spinning your wheels thinking you can determine the next steps. Let go and let God."

He grunted.

"I'm serious," Callie continued. "You said your marriage failed because you stopped paying attention to little things. I disagree. It failed because you missed the boat on one big thing: faith. If you'd grounded yourself in God's love, you wouldn't have messed up in the first place."

"You sound like my mother."

Callie grinned. "Your mother is a smart woman. Finch, you can fix this." She reached out a hand to his arm. "But there are no shortcuts, no quick inroads. And you shouldn't be concerning yourself with romance until you're on solid ground again. Restructure your priorities. God. Family. Country. Friends. And no more beer."

He hauled in a deep breath and exhaled slowly. "Is there a charge for this therapy session?"

Callie smiled and chucked him on the arm. "There will be if the paint on my roller gets tacky and I have to change it. That baby cost two-nineteen in the contractor's pack."

Finch flashed a sheepish grin as Callie picked up the roller. "Nothing but the best."

"Exactly." Callie tested the nubby surface and nodded, satisfied. "I'm glad you stopped by, Finch."

He made a face of disbelief. Callie caught it and smiled. "I mean it. It's better to clear the air than go on dodging bullets. And if you need help…"

"More therapy?"

"Exactly." She nodded, empathetic. "I've gone down your road. I had a husband walk out on me, so I know it's a tough go, but faith and family can get you through anything. But I'd be glad to talk to you more. As friends," she added, sending him a pointed look of amusement over her shoulder.

"Got it." He started to leave, then turned back. "Thanks, Callie. I hope Cavanaugh knows how lucky he is."

"He does," said Matt as he entered from the garage, his eyes sweeping the scene, his expression battlefield ready.

"Everything looks good," Finch told him, waving a hand.

Matt paused, weighing the words. "No problems?"

Finch sent a look of gratitude toward Callie. "None we haven't solved. Thanks again, Callie. I'll be back to check the electric and plumbing lines on the other houses whenever they're ready, Matt."

"I'll call."

"And don't worry about that two-day stuff either."

"You don't need quite that much time?" Matt asked. Callie kept working, but felt his gaze sweep her and Finch again.

"Work's slow," Finch admitted in a tone of voice that

sounded like the guy she'd known years before. "Call anytime. I might even be able to come right out."

Matt smiled. "Thanks. Time's tight now with the weather and all."

"And time's money," Finch added. He nodded and headed for the door. "See you Sunday, Callie. If not before."

She smiled, satisfied. "Looking forward to it, Finch."

Matt was pretty certain he'd walked into an alternate universe.

Callie frowned up at him as she refilled her roller. "Why aren't you roofing at the church?"

"Buck, Jim and your dad have it under control, so I thought I'd come back here and help you." He moved closer and nodded approval, the new paint brightening the south-facing room. "This is beautiful, Cal."

"Isn't it?" She flashed him a smile that brightened the room even more. "I thought it might be too yellow, but it's not. It's just soft enough to reflect the light and keep things warm. Appealing."

"I agree," he said, but he aimed his look at her, not the wall.

"Matt."

"Callie." He moved forward and took the roller out of her hands, wondering when the smell of new paint became so wonderfully enticing. Or maybe it was the smudge on her cheek, the tiny roller spatters across her nose? He rubbed a gentle finger to make them disappear, and sighed, the feel of being close to her a new experience, sweet and good. Inviting. "You smell good."

She grinned and daubed a tiny bit of paint to his face with her finger. "I smell like paint."

He gave her a lazy smile and tightened his grip. "Then I must really like paint, because…" He let his kiss fill in the blank, the combination of Callie, fresh-sawn wood and new paint bringing all the factors of his world together in one pleasurable experience. He had no idea how long the kiss lasted, and really didn't care because he'd like for it to never end, but the rumble of the school bus engine interrupted way too soon. "Jake's home."

"Uh-huh."

He grinned down at her, glad he had a few inches on her in her work shoes, a height advantage that disappeared when she wore heels.

He didn't care. Tall, short, thin, wide, messy or dressed up, to him she was just Callie, the most delightful creature God could have put in his path. As the bus brakes squealed to a stop, he drew her forward. "Let's go meet the kid. I've got a surprise for us."

"A surprise?"

He smiled, set her roller down, then ushered her out the door.

The quick drop in temperature made the forecasted snow seem more real. Callie tugged her flannel tighter as she and Matt waited. Jake raced to see them, excitement showing in every step. "Hey, I got another A on my math paper, Mom!"

"Wonderful!" Callie high-fived him, then stepped back inside the warm house. "Seriously, Matt? It's freezing out there."

Matt and Jake followed her inside and Matt shut the door. "I know, it started dropping about the time we got on that roof."

"So we're patching it just in time," Callie noted.

"Yes." Matt ruffled Jake's hair and added, "Looks like snow tomorrow. And from then on, who knows?"

"I love snow!"

"Most kids do," Matt told him. He reached into his back pocket and held up a flat rectangular piece of card stock. "And once it snows, we're taking a sleigh ride. If that's okay?" he asked Callie, raising his gaze to her as Jake attacked his legs.

"Matt, you shouldn't have..."

"Sure he should," Jake told her, astonished. "Because he knew I wanted to go and it's cheaper if three go, right? Because then we can each pay a third."

"Well, that's a mighty generous offer, bud," Matt drawled, making sure graciousness hid the laughter in his tone. "But I've got this one covered. Kind of a thank-you to you and your mom for all the hard work you do over here."

"But isn't that why you pay us?" Jake wondered out loud. "That's what Mom says anyway. You work hard and get paid for the work you do. She didn't say anything about a sleigh ride in the park with the lights."

"That's a fringe benefit, Jake," Matt explained, exchanging smiles with Callie. "When you work really hard, sometimes extra benefits go with the job."

His words drove up the heat in Callie's cheeks, and that delighted him.

"Then I like those fringe benefit things," Jake declared.

Matt sent a teasing look to Jake's mother. "Me, too."

"And on that note..." Callie headed back to the family room. "I need to get this finished. And our fire is probably out at home, so can you guys start one? And let The General out for a run?"

"Will do."

Jake headed out, but Matt lingered. "So, Finch's visit…" He trailed the words, an eyebrow arched.

"Something we'll talk about without little ears around," Callie told him.

Matt weighed the words and her expression. "He told you about my past."

"Yes. And I reminded him—" Callie kept her voice even as she rolled the wall "—that everybody makes mistakes. And nothing's unfixable."

Matt clenched his hands, wishing that was true.

"Even Katie's leg," Callie went on. She met his gaze across the room and noted his hands with a glance. "We move on. We try harder. Stay strong. Everyone has a past, Matt."

"Even you?"

Her flush said yes. Her eyes said it wasn't a topic she was ready to explore, which meant she'd buried the hurt, just like him. That only made him more determined to fix it. "Don't you have a fire to start?"

"I'm on it."

"Good. And Matt?"

He turned, the sound of her voice a sweeter draw than wood fire flames on a dark December night. "Yes?"

"Thank you."

"For?" He frowned, not understanding, then nodded and raised the ticket. "Oh. Of course. You're welcome."

Callie shook her head and met his look across the room, then waved a hand indicating the house, the road, the subdivision. Herself. "For all of it. Thank you."

He loved her. He knew it fully and truly, standing there, seeing her decked out in spattered work clothes, a day's labor behind her and still ready to do whatever it took to be a good mother. A fine daughter. And maybe, just maybe, something more.

He sighed, smiled and nodded, wishing he could kick his heels in the air like Jake and the pooch. "You're welcome, Cal."

He headed across the field, whistling the "Marine's Hymn," keeping pace with the rhythm and the beat, his soul blessed, his heart... Well, full was the best way to describe that, and while it was an unfamiliar feeling, Matt decided he liked it. A lot.

He eyed the Quiltin' Bee as he passed through Jamison a couple of hours later, then parked the truck and headed inside, determined to make sure Callie had a great Christmas. He waited while Maude finished up with a customer, then frowned when she reached beneath the counter and withdrew a festively wrapped box topped by a big red bow.

"This is?"

"Callie's quilt." She handed him a bill and added, "And if you don't have the money now, I'll wait."

"I've got it," Matt told her as he withdrew his wallet. "What I'm wondering is how you knew I'd be back."

She sent him a wizened grin. "At my age, there's less I don't know than I do. One look at you and Callie on the park round, well..." She softened the smile and shrugged. "Things just seemed to fit."

Matt couldn't disagree. He handed her his debit card, signed his name, then tucked the box carefully behind the seat of his truck, feeling like he was truly getting ready for the old-fashioned Christmas he'd dreamed of as a kid.

Chapter Fifteen

Callie watched Matt tuck the lap robe snug around Jake's legs a few nights later and tumbled right back into the danger zone she'd pledged to avoid. Matt's grin and Jake's answering broad smile made it seem less dangerous and more charming.

Matt climbed into the sleigh, slipped an arm around her shoulders and dropped a kiss to her hair.

If she hadn't tilted head over heels before, she did then, the feel of a strong, rugged marine taking charge, leading in ways of goodness and grace, here with her and Jake, fulfilling a little boy's dream. And maybe a big boy's as well, if the look on his face was any indication. She leaned closer. "I'm not sure which one of you is smiling more," she noted as they passed beneath a lighted arch made of naturally entwined tree branches and thousands of tiny twinkle lights.

"This is amazing."

"It is." Jake grinned up at Matt, his joy palpable. He wriggled beneath the blanket as they came upon an action scene of animatronic elves in Santa's workshop. "Mom, look! They're building a tool bench!"

Callie laughed out loud. "Those are my kind of elves, Jake. And see what Mrs. Santa's doing?" She pointed toward the left of the scene, where Mrs. Santa and a couple of girl elves fashioned baby dolls. "So sweet."

Jake snorted. "They're dolls."

Matt gave Callie's arm a gentle squeeze. "Did you like playing with dolls when you were little or were you always a tomboy?"

"Both," she told him, smiling. "I was never afraid to get dirty or run with the boys and play sports, but—" she slanted him a teasing look "—even then I cleaned up well."

He hugged her shoulder tighter, laughing. "Some things never change. Hey, do you see those reindeer?"

"A real Santa scene," breathed Jake as they drew closer, the horse hooves clip-clopping along the curved road. A well-dressed robust Santa groomed a small herd of reindeer, on loan from a local organic farm, and the picture added a dose of reality to the fantasyland surrounding them.

"Nice," Matt observed, his gaze roaming as if hungering for the next sight, the coming scene. They passed through a tree-lined path bathed in white twinkle lights, a Currier and Ives setting with the sleigh, the horse, the driver, the trees. A photographer snapped their photo as they emerged from the boughs, and Callie wondered if the photo would capture how perfect the moment felt.

Lighted scenes peppered the woods on both sides until they turned a corner that led them into the midst of a living nativity, spot-lit from all angles. Mary and Joseph hovered over a hay-filled manger, concern painting their features, while shepherds gathered in awe, chatting and exclaiming.

Sheep wandered the area, their thick woolly coats

dusted with snow. A donkey stood to the right, placidly munching hay. Two well-dressed angels watched over the scene from above, their raised platforms hidden by dark draperies, while two more knelt below, paying homage to a newborn king, a child of the poor.

"Oh, Matt." Jake clenched Matt's arm and the sincerity in his young voice had Callie fighting tears. "They did it just right," Jake continued, awestruck. "The wise men aren't here, but the angels are gathering around. And the shepherds came back to see if the angels were right. And they were."

"Of course they were," Matt assured him.

Did his voice break a little? Callie peeked up, and the loving expression on his face made suppressing an overload of emotions impossible.

"Whenever I think of what Jesus did for us, I regret every time I whine or crab about anything. Born in a manger, hung on a cross." Matt shook his head and sighed. "And when I feel the most unworthy, I remember He did it for the least of us. And then I feel better."

Jake reached over Callie and hugged Matt. "I love you, Matt."

Fear and hope mixed like concrete and stone in Callie's gut. The thought of how bad this could be began to rise up, but then Jake leaned back and stared up into Matt's face. "If I had a dad, I'd want him to be like you. You're nice to kids like me and that's a good thing for a dad to do."

The look of love Matt settled on the boy was enhanced by the big, broad hand he laid against Jake's cheek. "You're right, bud. That's exactly what dads should do."

Jake matched and met Matt's smile, then sat back. "This is the most beautiful night I ever had."

* * *

Matt heard the boy's words and glimpsed Callie's tear-streaked face and realized he was in for the long haul. Only a rotter would back out now, and Matt had no intention of backing away from this family.

Callie fumbled for a tissue, wiped her eyes and blew her nose, then mock-scowled at him for sending a laughing glance her way. "It's cold out here."

"Uh-huh." He leaned closer, his mouth to her ear. "I think you're a sap, soldier. But pretty enough to be kissed." And he did that, right there, a sweet, gentle kiss feathering over her face, her mouth, not caring if Jake saw because Matt had every intention of establishing his very own family in Cobbled Creek.

If she'd have him, of course. But from the look on her face Matt was pretty sure nothing could get in their way.

"Hey, Matt. What's up?" Jeff Brennan pulled up next to Matt's car at a Wellsville gas station the next afternoon. "I keep meaning to get over to Cobbled Creek, but the factory's crazy busy. How are things going? Okay?"

Matt turned and shot a smile toward his half brother. *Brother*, he corrected himself, determined to mend every relationship he could, regardless of legality.

He nodded. "Amazing, actually. And you were right when you told me the Mareks are wonderful people. And I've got my stepdad doing drywall for me."

He hesitated saying that last bit, pretty sure Jeff would think it weird. As if their convoluted relationships could get any stranger than they already were.

"Awkward." Jeff sent Matt a look of understanding. "But because that describes our family to a tee, it's a good place to start over."

"He's sick, too."

"Yeah?" Jeff's sympathetic expression said he empathized. "What's his prognosis?"

"Good. Just a road to travel. A rough go, alone."

"So it's nice he has you."

"I guess." At this moment Matt wasn't too sure what purpose he served anywhere, except with a hammer in his hands. Give him a toolbox and suddenly everything made sense. "Everybody's gotta have someone, right? How are the wedding plans coming?"

Jeff grinned. "Hannah and I put them in Mom's capable hands. She's happy, she's got Meredith to help her, and we're delighted to let things happen around us."

"Your mother's great," Matt told him. Jeff's mother had been the only person other than Grandpa Gus to visit Matt in juvie, and that was after Dana Brennan had her private life gossiped about in every home when the world discovered Matt was her husband's illegitimate son.

"She is. And you're coming over for Christmas, right?"

"Well…"

"Like you've got a better offer?" Jeff's teasing tone said he doubted that.

"I…um…"

"You *do* have a better offer," Jeff mused. His left eyebrow shifted up. "Which means the Marek family, because you've been holed up in Cobbled Creek for weeks."

"I might be spending it with them. Yes."

"With Callie, you mean."

Matt was hoping for that very thing, but… "Keep a spot at the table open for me. Just in case."

Jeff gave him a brotherly arm punch. "Will do. Although Mom likes nothing more than planning special events. So she'd be glad to jump in and help with any-thing you might need. You know that, don't you?"

Maybe he'd said too much. Or at least too soon. Matt leaned down. "Hey, about Christmas and the Mareks, don't say anything, okay?"

Jeff's grin spread wide. "You'll owe me."

Maybe having a brother wasn't such a great thing after all. "For?"

"Buying my silence."

Matt thought of how convoluted his life had just be-come and didn't hold back his sigh. "This one time, it will be worth it."

Jeff laughed and drove off, leaving Matt feeling like life was racing forward at break-neck speed and he'd for-gotten how to apply the brakes. Except he didn't want to, not really. And he was surprised at how good that felt.

She should stay home, Callie decided, eyeing the storm and the clock on Saturday afternoon.

She moved toward the phone, then paused and studied her hands, strong and blunt. Weathered. Tough.

She should be working. Helping. The guys had been at it all day, with her at their side, until she took Jake to Cole's house to play.

And that was the difference, she realized. Jake was a little boy. Playtime was important for his growth and development. Hers?

Not so much.

She reached for the phone, but paused again, wonder-ing. Was it so bad to take a little time for herself? Do something frivolous?

Not to mention pricey. With money scarce, why would

she even consider seeing Matt's sister about something as useless as a manicure?

Hannah's arrival nixed the cancellation call. She grinned as Callie climbed in the passenger seat, then laughed at the look Callie shot her.

"Cal, seriously, it's not a firing squad. It's a manicure. And it's Meredith. We'll have a great time."

Callie indicated Cobbled Creek with a thrust of her jaw. "Do you know how many things I should be doing right now?"

Hannah laid a hand atop Callie's. "Listen, Martha..."

Callie smiled and groaned, the biblical analogy clear. Martha was the energetic, hardworking, get-'er-done sister of Lazarus. Mary was the quiet listener at God's feet.

"Every now and again, it's okay to take a little time off. Have some fun. And there's nothing wrong with taking care of yourself."

They pulled up to Dana Brennan's beautiful home, sprawling on a double village lot, a detached carriage house-style garage around the back. Callie sighed. "This is gorgeous."

"Isn't it?" Hannah headed for the side entrance. She pushed open the door, waved hello and turned back. "Callie, you remember Meredith, don't you?"

"I do."

One look at Meredith's flawless beauty, her stylish outfit, and Callie wished she'd opted out.

"Although high school was a long time ago." Callie reached out a hand, trying not to bumble, wondering if she should make a run for the door. "I was a year behind you."

"Callie." Meredith grabbed Callie's hands and drew her in, her smile infectious. "I'm so glad you came over.

Hannah said Matt's been working you night and day, and you need a little pampering."

"No, oh, no." Callie shook her head in quick denial. She darted a troubled look at Hannah. "Matt wouldn't think of such a thing, I mean, he's always after me to slow down. Take time off. Relax a little."

Meredith shot Hannah a quick, knowing glance. "Whoa, spot-on. She's got it bad."

"Told ya."

"Hey." Callie frowned Hannah's way, but Hannah moved across the spacious kitchen, ignoring her.

"Come in here." Meredith tugged her forward, laughing, a feminine version of Matt's laugh. Warm. Enticing. Vibrant. "I was only kidding, but you totally took the bait, so there's no denying the spark going on between you and my brother."

"We work together," Callie insisted.

"Oh, we get it, honey." Hannah set out a box of fresh brownies. "I got these in case we needed to bribe you to talk, but as you can see—" she waved a hand toward Callie but eyed Meredith "—totally unnecessary."

"Which means we can probe her for further information about Matt."

"All the good stuff." Hannah withdrew a brownie, grinning.

"Every little detail." Meredith half sang the words in anticipation.

Callie burst out laughing. "Stop. Both of you. I'm not saying a thing. He'd be mortified to think we're talking about him like this."

"More like complimented beyond belief." Meredith argued in sister-like fashion. "But we'll shelve that for later." She took a seat alongside Callie and seized her hands, her fingers and eyes examining Callie's roughed-up skin. Seeing her hands against Meredith's more feminine version made Callie want to shrink back. Maybe run for her life, but then Meredith met Callie's eyes. "You wondered if I could help you, right?"

Self-conscious, Callie fidgeted. "Yes."

"Oh, honey." Meredith squeezed Callie's hands but leaned in, smiling. "I can work wonders on the skin and the nails, but what you've got here—" she raised Callie's hands slightly "—are the hands of a woman unafraid to get the job done. And no matter what you might think up here," Meredith tapped her head with one tapered, manicured finger, "God has blessed you with beautiful hands to match a wonderful heart. I can create pretty-looking skin." She met Callie's look with a bright, knowing smile. "But only God can create amazing hands like yours."

"I—" Callie sat back, touched, pleased and not a little embarrassed.

"Having said that—" Meredith grinned, stood, crossed the room and wheeled back a manicure tray "—let's have a little fun, shall we, girls?" She bent and plugged in a cord, then immersed Callie's hands in the small sink.

Jets of warm water soothed Callie's skin. Her hand muscles. Her fingertips, alternately chilled and dried by nature and job conditions. And as Meredith went through her usual routine of soaking, massaging, oiling and waxing, Callie's heart began to relax along with her skin. By the time Meredith put a finishing coat of clear polish on Callie's French manicure, Callie's hands felt nurtured. Cared for. Pampered.

Not that she'd be able to grow accustomed to this, but for once, to feel soft, feminine hands? Smooth-as-silk skin?

Delightful.

And by the time Meredith finished pampering her, Callie felt like she'd known the other woman forever. Meredith wasn't anything like Callie remembered from high school, but then, neither was she.

"Thank you." She reached out and gave Meredith a hug while Hannah gathered their scarves and gloves. "They feel wonderful."

"Aw, you're welcome." And when Callie tried to hand Meredith money, the other woman waved it off, smiling. "Family gets free perks."

"But I'm not family."

Meredith and Hannah exchanged smiles. "A simple matter of timing, honey." Meredith grinned at Callie's bemused expression and high-fived Hannah. "And having another girl around…"

"One who knows how to get things done," Hannah interjected.

"And puts a smile on Matt's face," Meredith added. "That's like the best Christmas present ever, right there."

Callie fought down the blush Meredith's words inspired, but felt the truth of them in her heart. Her soul.

Matt did like being with her. And seeing his sisters' joint approval?

That just made a season of miracles seem more possible than she'd ever considered before.

Five o'clock.

He was late and in danger of missing Jake's part in the Christmas Salute to Veterans concert at the elementary school, Matt realized as darkness fell that evening.

He finalized the wallboard contract for the remaining houses, rushed back to the Mareks' and jumped into uniform, wishing he'd had someone else swing south to pick up Don. Matt headed down Route 19 and turned west toward Don's apartment, impatient. He parked in the only available spot half-a-block down and dashed for Don's house, wishing he'd paid closer attention to the time.

Don's porch light clicked on. He pulled open the inner door, pivoted to shut it, then turned and stopped, staring at Matt as though he'd never seen him before.

The uniform, Matt realized.

"Ready?"

Don nodded. His gaze flicked up and down, then up again. "You look great."

"Well, thanks." Matt wore the formal uniform with pride, but he hadn't pulled it out since a funeral the previous year. He'd forgotten the reaction it drew from people. Don's was classic. "Sorry I'm late. Think we'll make it in time?"

Don put a hand to his arm, his expression tight. "I'm proud of you, Matt."

Part of Matt's heart churned. He'd have loved to hear those words twenty-five years ago. Now? Discomfort crept up his spine.

Now he just needed to get to Jake's concert in time to see the boy sing. He shrugged, embarrassed. "Let's go."

The overflowing parking lot said they'd gotten there far too late to find Callie and Hank in the uniform-studded audience.

She found them instead, and that made Matt feel special. Beloved. Her waving hand beckoned from down front. He let Don precede him and followed, drawn by a sweet force that linked him to her. "Hey." He flashed a quick smile, grateful. "You saved us seats?"

"Yes."

"Thanks, Cal."

"You're looking good, marine."

He duffed the collar of her desert camo. "You, too."

She made a little face of disbelief, but Matt tucked a finger beneath her chin until she met his gaze. "You're absolutely beautiful, Cal. No matter what you're wearing."

Her eyes searched his, questioning. Wondering. He hoped his sincerity and intent showed in his answering look. Something must have telegraphed through because she ducked, blushing.

The blush. The smile. The averted gaze...

They had it bad, Matt realized anew. And he'd never imagined that having it bad could be so wonderfully good. But it was, right down to planning a future he'd refused to ponder, but being with Callie? Loving her? Anything seemed possible.

He sat beside her, her soft fingers clasped in his, ready to lay old doubts at God's feet, determined to grasp the life God offered, sweet and fulfilling. A life he didn't think he deserved, but he was finally learning not to question God's judgment.

Or Callie's embracing smile.

Maybe, just maybe, he could have it all.

Chapter Sixteen

Callie saw the message light flashing on the home phone as she made coffee for the crew on Monday afternoon, sweet memories of Jake's concert, Matt's presence and Christmas brightening the day. She listened to Mary Kay's excited news, then left the coffee to drip while she drove over to the subdivision. She burst into number seventeen, skirted an electrician running wire and cornered Matt in the great room. "They put an offer in on number twenty-three!"

Matt's brows shot up. "Really? How do you know this?"

"Your cell must be down. Mary Kay left a message on the home phone."

Matt grabbed her, spun her around and then just held her, the steady beat of his heart like music to her ears. "This is wonderful," he whispered.

"Yes." Oh, it was. To be held like this? Respected? Beyond wonderful.

"Good news?" Hank asked from above.

Matt fist pumped the air with one hand. "We've got our first sale."

Hank grinned and let his gaze linger on them. "Among other things."

Callie sidestepped Matt's arm. "Just celebrating success, Dad."

"We should do a special dinner tonight," Matt announced.

"As in?"

"We'll go to The Edge. Celebrate. The whole crew." The Edge was the area's acclaimed fine-dining experience.

Hank leaned over the roughed-in stairway. "Well, that gets mighty pricey. Let's save that meal for when we've got all nine sold. How 'bout for tonight we just throw some good steaks on the grill? It's snowing, but I don't mind cookin' in the snow."

"And we'll make baked potatoes," Callie offered.

"And cauliflower with cheese sauce," added Tom from a room away. "And rolls from the bakery."

"Then we need to shop." Callie glanced at her watch and frowned. Jake's bus would be along soon, but she hated to miss work time for errands.

"I've got to grab some things in town once I'm finished here," Matt told them. "I'll pick up the steaks, cauliflower and rolls."

"Excellent."

His grin reflected her feelings. It was good to have that first house sold, a done deal, long-awaited. "I ran over here to tell you before the coffee finished up, so when I'm back at the house I'm doing two things," Callie told him. "I'm calling to order the steaks because they might not have enough nice ones in the case this late in the day."

"Good idea."

"And I'm ordering a landline phone for the model,"

Callie continued. "And setting up a spare coffeepot there. It's silly to run across the road for coffee now."

"Go for it." He sent her a smile that made her heart feel like they were a team. "And don't bring coffee back for me. I'm going to finish this piece and get the errands done so we don't eat too late for Jake to enjoy it."

"As long as it includes ice cream, Jake'll love it," Hank told him. The smile of satisfaction lighting his face made Callie realize she hadn't seen her father look this at ease in years.

Darkness had descended by the time they'd washed up and gathered at the Marek house. Callie and Jake filled a big bowl with bright red punch, and as each man lumbered into the kitchen, Jake served him a fancy tiny-handled cup of the special concoction.

And not one of those big, burly guys laughed at the prissy glass cup they held.

Matt gave a short, sharp whistle. Conversation stopped as everyone turned his way. He raised his punch cup and surveyed the room, the glimmer of Christmas lights back-lighting him. "Since none of us want those steaks to burn, I just want to thank all of you. To Hank and Callie—" he met Hank's smile and matched it "—for your initial vision and hard work. And letting me bunk here. That proximity means the world to me." He smiled again and Callie hoped he meant proximity to more than the half-built houses.

"Buck, Tom, Jim and Amanda." He nodded to that group. "None of this would have been possible without you guys. You know that, don't you?"

They hemmed and hawed, embarrassed.

"And to Don." Matt turned to his stepfather deliberately and lofted the cup a little higher. "I've never seen better workmanship in drywall and that perfect finishing touch polishes the entire effect. Thank you. It's nice having family on board."

Don's face paled. His hand shook. He opened his mouth to say something, then paused, overcome, unable to speak. Amanda swiped a quick hand to her face when Matt and Don exchanged looks of understanding.

Matt veered his attention to Jake. "And to you, my young friend. I don't think there's ever been a better apprentice in this business and I mean that. Good job, bud."

Jake manned his glass cup of punch with all the seriousness an eight-year-old could muster. "Thanks, Matt."

"To us." Matt raised his cup higher. "To our continued good work and success. And let's not forget to thank God for that stretch of good weather, because—" Matt deadpanned a look outdoors "—I think it was slated to be our last."

They sipped in unison, and Callie marveled at how quickly things had turned around. Six weeks before they'd been watching Cobbled Creek fade before their eyes. The view from her front window now embraced a lovely neighborhood, the hopes and dreams of two families coming together.

Matt gave Jake a quick hug and settled on the floor with him to play a quick round of checkers before dinner. Amanda came into the kitchen to help Callie. She swept Matt and Jake a smiling look. "Pretty nice scene, Cal."

"It is."

"The kind a girl could get used to." Amanda added.

"If the girl were one of those romance-loving gals who believed in happily ever afters," Callie replied, although when she was around Matt Cavanaugh it was easier to dream. Hope. Believe.

"And that's the nice thing about life." Amanda trailed

the words, her eyes laughing at Callie's attempt to maintain distance. "Things have a way of changing up when you least expect it."

"Steaks are done," Hank called out as he came back inside.

"Great." Matt stood, pulled Jake up beside him and surveyed the laden table, gratitude marking his expression. "Thanks for doing this, Callie, because you prefer a hammer to a stovetop."

"You know I make exceptions now and again." She sent him a smile across the table, and hoped he read the pride she felt. Working for him, seeing the homes progress, watching this plan come together at long last.

"I'm glad," Matt told her. His tone said he read her expression correctly.

Jake sat at a card table they set up in the living room with the two Slaughter kids. Once Amanda had them settled, the crew gathered around the table, the mixed scents of rich meat, tangy cheese and fresh-baked rolls teasing the senses. "God, you've blessed us with Matt Cavanaugh," Hank intoned as they clasped hands around the table. "You brought him to us and gathered us together. We thank you for that, and this food. Amen."

"Amen."

"Short and sweet." Buck nodded, affable. "Good job."

"Can't let the meat get cold," said Hank. "And I don't want this to go to Matt's head. All this thankin' business."

"Wouldn't want that." Matt grinned at him, and took a bite of steak. "And right now I can tell you that no one on this planet cooks a better steak than you, Hank."

"Timing." Hank smiled as he savored his own first bite, but he let his eyes twinkle Matt's way. "It's all in the timing, son."

* * *

Matt read Hank's look and recognized the truth in the words. He turned toward Don. "Did I hear you say you've got a doctor's appointment tomorrow afternoon?"

"Yes."

"I'll go along."

Don started to shake his head, obviously uncomfortable, but Matt put him off. "No sense arguing. I know it's at the cancer clinic and that these guys all know about it, so we'll stop work around two and head over there, okay?"

Don's nod said he didn't trust himself to speak.

"And Matt," Buck cut in, jutting his chin toward the subdivision, "I'm putting the plow on my truck tomorrow so I'll keep the roadway into the houses cleaned out for us, okay?"

"Buck, that would be awesome. Thank you."

Buck shrugged that off. "Not too many weeks ago this was stretching to be a long, bad winter." He sipped from his tiny, glass cup and grinned at the looks the other guys shot him. "But now? Well, now—" he raised his cup high in salute to Matt, the Mareks and Cobbled Creek "—things are looking up."

Hank had thanked God for him, Matt mused as he and Don headed toward the clinic in Wellsville the following afternoon. The idea that anyone placed stock in him both pleased and scared Matt, but with the Marek family? He'd go with mostly pleased.

He pulled up to the clinic's door, dropped Don off and proceeded to an open parking space at the back of the snowy lot. As he pushed through the entrance door, he spotted Don being led to a treatment room down a back corridor. Matt settled into an empty seat, picked up a sports magazine and started rifling the pages.

"Burdick? Joyce Burdick?"

"Here." An older woman stood slowly, a haze of pain creasing her features.

"Lean on me, Mom."

The older woman sent her son a fond look. "It's nice to have you home this weekend, Dustin."

"It's good to be here."

Dustin Burdick. Callie's ex-husband. Jake's dad. He was in town, but hadn't told Callie or asked to see his son.

Matt felt like he'd been punched in the gut. He had to hold himself back from having it out with the guy then and there.

"The treatment will take about an hour once we get her settled in," explained the nurse as an orderly helped Dustin's mother into a wheelchair. "So if you want to come back in about ninety minutes, that would be fine."

"Thanks." Dustin bent and kissed his mother's cheek, then headed for the door. "I'll get that Christmas stuff for you, Mom."

"Thanks, honey."

Honey?

The sweet endearment might mean something coming from Dustin Burdick's mother, but Matt found the irony too much to bear. He followed Dustin outside and called his name. Dustin turned, surprise and caution vying for his features. "Yes?"

"You're in town for the weekend?"

Dustin shifted left. "Do I know you?"

"No." Matt braced his feet and folded his arms, keeping his voice and expression taut. "But I know your ex-wife. And your son. And I'm just wondering what kind of guy walks out on a great kid like Jake and never calls. Never sends cards or gifts. Never visits his own flesh and blood. What kind of soldier were you when you can treat your own family like that?"

"Who are you? And what business is it of yours?" Dustin growled the words, his displeasure apparent.

"Callie works for me." *Lame, Cavanaugh, when Callie was so much more than an employee.* Still, he wasn't about to share their relationship with Dustin Burdick, a cheating spouse and deadbeat father. Matt had enough of that to last a lifetime. "And you didn't answer the question. How can you walk out on a kid like that? Just turn your back and go?"

Matt didn't try to fool himself that cornering Dustin in a public parking lot was the smartest thing he'd ever done, but good marines seize opportunities God sends their way. And today God put Dustin square in Matt's path.

Dustin sent him a cool look of appraisal. "I don't know who you are or what it matters to you, but I don't have to answer to anyone. I have a life. Callie has a life. We've both moved on. I suggest you do the same."

"You moved on while you were married to her." Matt kept his voice intentionally soft on purpose. More threatening that way. "You cheated on her, then walked out on your wife and infant son. You discredit the uniform."

Dustin took a step forward and hooked a thumb toward himself. "I hated the uniform. The rules. The time. The drills. The waiting around in hundred-and-ten-degree weather, half hoping something would happen. And there was Callie, kind of cute, working on the base. I'd known her in high school, so when we met up in Iraq..." He shrugged, nonchalant. "It gave me something to do."

Anger put a chokehold on Matt. Dustin married Callie for something to do?

The temptation to beat the stuffing out of this guy forced Matt back. He held up a hand. "You're not interested in being Jake's father? His dad?"

Dustin scowled. "I've got two kids. I'm lucky I can afford them. And don't have Callie try to garnish my wages again either. You can't take blood from a stone and she'll get nothing."

Matt appraised Dustin's leather coat and upscale jeans. "You hide your income so you don't have to support Jake."

Dustin's face said "Yes" as he shook his head. "I've got no income. Fresh out."

A flash of inspiration hit Matt, a possible way to emerge a winner from a bad confrontation. "Will you give up your rights to Jake?"

Dustin's scowl deepened. "Where do I sign?"

Matt really wanted to punch this guy. His fingers ached for wanting. But more than that, he wanted to be free to make Jake his own. If Callie would have him, that is. "If I have the papers sent to you, will you sign off as Jake's dad?"

"I don't have to worry about anybody coming after me for money ever again?"

No, dirtbag. Matt kept that feeling to himself, but it took effort. What he said out loud was, "Exactly. You'll be free and clear and I can adopt Jake."

A light sparked in Dustin's eyes. "This might be worth something to you, then?"

Matt took great pleasure in the spin move that put the other man's face up against the wall. "Don't even think about it, Burdick. Nobody—" he gave Dustin's collar a slightly tightened shake to make his point stronger "—plays around with the value of a child like that, not in my presence. Got it?"

Dustin hadn't spent the last eight years staying in top form.

Matt had.

Whatever Dustin had been doing for money didn't pump up his triceps and biceps. His abs.

Building houses, hauling lumber, lifting windows and cabinets into place kept Matt on an Olympic-training regimen weekly. The reality of that knowledge shone in Dustin's nervous expression. He gave a quick nod, definitely in his best interest.

Good.

"And you'll sign the papers when you get them, and give them back to the courier who will then deliver them back here to Callie. Right?" He tightened Dustin's collar a smidge more, hoping he made his point.

Dustin nodded again. "Yes."

"Excellent." Matt loosened his hold but didn't back off. "I love that kid. And I love his mother. And I didn't spend eight years in the marines *pretending* to be a man, so when those papers come, you open the envelope, sign where noted and send them back. Got it?"

"I said yes."

Matt angled his head slightly as Dustin faced him. "I heard you. I'm just making sure we understand each other."

Dustin blew out a breath. "If it gets me out of any more of her stupid court filings, we're good."

Matt had to take another step back. And nail his hands to his sides. And haul in a big breath. It had been a long time since the urge to pummel someone loomed with such ripe potential, but he pushed to keep his eye on the goal: making Jake his own. If Dustin signed off, Matt would be free to adopt Jake, if Callie gave her blessing.

Matt went back inside as Dustin strode off. He sat down, waiting for Don, his gut twisting. He couldn't make sense of walking out on a kid, maybe because it had happened to him. He'd lived the experience and suffered the fallout.

Why would God let that happen? Who watched out for little ones these days? Kids nudged aside by adult drama?

The strong words from the book of Joshua came back to him. "Then choose for yourselves this day who you shall serve...as for me and my house? We will serve the Lord."

That's what he wanted with Callie. The piece that had been missing from his growing years. Not just a home. Or a family. He longed for a family of faith, hope and love. God-abiding. Together. A tiny light flickered within as Matt realized how Dustin had used Callie for his own amusement. He'd never intended to stay, to be the husband Callie deserved and the father Jake needed.

Matt had every intention of doing just that.

And as Don turned the corner from the corridor leading to the treatment rooms, Matt comprehended something else. Life had sideswiped Don, just as it had him. Sure, Don was the adult. He should have and could have reacted better. Maybe with faith, he would have, but Don had been taken out at the knees when he learned he was living a lie, that his wife had cheated on him and passed off someone else's child as his.

He came toward Matt, his face tired. Worn. Matt moved down the hall and braced him with a soldier's arm.

"I'm okay." Don tried to shrug him off, but Matt held tight.

"Hey, can't a kid help his old man now and again?"

Don's feet shuffled to a stop. He turned. Met Matt's gaze. "I—"

"Do you need a wheelchair to the car?"

Don shook his head. "No. Just a little tired."

"Then lean on me. Dad. It's not that far."

Don looked up at him. His light-eyed gaze grew moist. Matt had to choke back a lump in his own throat, a knot of regret for so much time wasted.

But that was over. He braced the older man and started forward. "I know where there's a pot of stew waiting. Should be just about done. And some fresh, homemade biscuits."

"It sounds good," Don admitted.

"Then let's go. You need to make another appointment?"

Don shook his head. "Not for a while."

"Good, because we got a boatload of plasterboard delivered today, and you need to rest up. We're going to have one busy winter."

Don's shoulders straightened. His chin came up. His step seemed just a little bit stronger. More invigorated. He gave a quick swipe to his eyes and nodded back at Matt. "I'm looking forward to it, son."

An old smile crept up on Matt, the kind of smile he used to share with his father, back in the day. He squeezed Don's arm as he led the way to the snow-filled parking lot, pretty sure his personal life paths had been freshly plowed, and glad of it. "Me, too."

Chapter Seventeen

"What's this?" Matt studied the envelope he received the next afternoon and quizzed the courier standing on the doorstep of the Cape Cod model. "Is this a summons?"

"I need your signature, sir."

Foreboding made Matt hesitate, then he clenched his jaw, signed the form and waited as the courier separated a copy for Matt's records.

He stepped into the quiet and nearly complete home, tore open the envelope and pulled out a sheaf of legal-looking documents. He scanned the information, got the gist of the contents, then sat down hard on the second step to read more carefully.

"...because the rules of due process were not followed in Mr. Marek's case, and because his ownership rights may have been revoked without due cause and/or proper documentation, Wellingtown General Bank will pay you a sum as decided by the appraisal firm of Littinger and Littinger in Olean, New York, as reparation. Amount due will include but will not be limited to wages paid, materials secured and monies invested to buy the afore-named subdivision 'Cobbled Creek.'

"Wellington General regrets any and all difficulties this transaction may cause and sincerely extends its apologies while accepting no blame for the mistaken foreclosure involved."

Mistaken foreclosure?

Reparation?

Had he just lost Cobbled Creek?

Matt stared at the paper and swallowed hard.

They were taking Cobbled Creek away from him. Could they do that?

"No," said his lawyer firmly a few minutes later when Matt got through to him on the newly installed landline. "They can't just send you a letter that says, 'Oops, we goofed, sorry. Let's have a do-over.' This is their first step in trying to rectify a big mistake. They're hoping you'll give in gracefully so they don't look bad or careless, which is exactly what they were in this case and many others, using people to robo-sign documents."

"Robo-sign?"

The lawyer sighed. "Instead of having bank professionals read each document the way they're supposed to, some banks hired new graduates to handle the influx of foreclosure documentation the past couple of years. Their job was to count the pages, make sure they were all there, then sign off as the bank's representative."

"You're kidding."

"I wish I was. And none of this was obvious last month when we closed. Then the scandal broke and banks started scrambling to put their houses in order."

"So I don't lose Cobbled Creek? Is that what you're saying?"

"We have to fight it, but yes, you will be able to keep the subdivision because it's their fault. Not yours. And then it's up to them to pay Hank Marek some sort of compensation for taking it over illegally. And making restitution for his loss of income."

"And his daughter's loss of income for those two years? Do they cover that?"

"No, that would be an indirect consequence unless she's listed as co-owner, but that wasn't the case."

How could he grasp this? Make sense of it? Half an hour ago he had his life mapped out before him, and it looked good. Sweet. Inviting.

Now?

One piece of mail and a bank's overeagerness to seize property put it all in jeopardy. "I need time to think, Jon. To figure this all out."

"There's no hurry," Jon told him, "but Hank Marek has most likely been notified at the same time you were. Just so you're prepared. He may pay you a visit."

"I'm living with him."

"You're what?"

It sounded weird considering this turn of events. "They let me stay in an extra room in their home because it adjoins the subdivision. And they've been working for me from the beginning."

"That's not a good situation to be in right now," the lawyer explained in a no-nonsense voice. "It's a conflict of interest at best and being professionally involved with a family you may bring litigation against could color your judgment."

"I thought it would be against the bank." Matt gripped the phone tighter. "You mean I might have to sue Hank?"

"Depending on how this plays out, yes. It's a numbers

game, Matt. And a power play. But we've got the power because we have ownership."

"Illegally."

"Not on our end," the lawyer said roundly. "We had no information that led us to believe any of this had occurred. This is the bank's error. Not ours. They're just hoping you bow out gracefully."

Bow out gracefully? How about run screaming? "I've got to go, Jon. Think this through. Pray."

"Don't think too long. Wellington General is no slouch in the money department, and they'll cough up a nice piece of change, but we need to respond quickly."

A nice piece of change.

Is that what his hopes and dreams came down to? His attempt to come back home and make amends? Was he here to gain a "nice piece of change" at Hank's expense? At Callie's expense?

Callie.

His gut clenched as realization hit.

What would people think if he courted Callie now? If Hank regained ownership of Cobbled Creek? They would assume he was looking out for number one. People would see it as a ploy to maintain a Cavanaugh Construction interest in a lucrative business venture.

What should he do? What could he do? Sue the bank? That meant suing Hank's interest in Cobbled Creek as well.

What would Grandpa Gus do?

He'd pray, Matt realized. He'd pray hard, then man up and do the right thing, an upright man in all regards.

Matt climbed into his truck and drove north, away from the dream that just evaporated around him, knowing if he fought Hank on this, the entire lower half of the county would see what they'd come to believe twenty years before. A guy who put himself first, all the time.

He found a small church open in the college town of Houghton. He crept in the back door and found a quiet corner, a place to talk to God. Examine his options. And by the time he stood to leave a long while later, he knew exactly what he had to do, but didn't pretend acceptance. He'd be giving up his dream of a home with Callie. Of adopting Jake. Of being the father he'd never had, an upright man in all regards.

Keeping Cobbled Creek when Hank had been grievously wronged could never be considered right.

And the swirl of malicious gossip that would circle around Callie and Jake if he stayed in the picture was the very world he'd come back to fix. Not reinstigate. He wasn't a gold digger. Or a user. But marrying Callie would look that way, and Matt knew firsthand how tongues would wag, mostly because he was involved and he hadn't been in town long enough to prove his worth.

Lousy timing, all told, not unlike what happened to Hank Marek a few years before.

He headed back toward Jamison and the life he thought he'd have, now gone, and couldn't act as if the journey didn't break his heart.

"You worked late, Dad," Callie observed as her father pushed through the side door that evening. "I'll start the burgers when Matt pulls in," she added, then nodded Jake's way. "And this guy's teacher says he's doing great, he's hardworking and focused and she's pleased with his progress. So we'll celebrate that with cupcakes later." She pulled a broiler pan from the lower cupboard, then turned toward her father more fully. His expression said something had gone wrong. Very wrong. "What's happened?"

Face set, Hank settled into a chair.

"Are you okay?"

He scowled and thumped the table with his fist. "Matt's gone."

"Matt's..." Callie worked her brain around her father's appearance, his accelerated breathing, his heightened color and...

Nope. Couldn't do it. She sat next to him and was surprised to see a sheen of moisture in his eyes. Army men didn't cry. Ever. "Dad, you're scaring me." She leaned closer, keeping her voice low. "What do you mean 'Matt's gone'?"

"He left. This afternoon. Packed up his stuff, signed Cobbled Creek back over to me and took off."

None of this was making any sense. "He signed Cobbled Creek over to you? What does that mean?"

Her father withdrew a bundle of papers from inside his jacket. "The bank messed up. They seized Cobbled Creek illegally. And now they want to fix things, which means they'll pay Matt to give it up."

"Illegally? How?"

"Not following procedures. So they notified Matt and me today and Matt got it in his head that he'd be better off bowing out and letting me take it back."

"But—"

"I know." Hank lifted his gaze to Callie's. "He *belongs* here. I felt it. You felt it. For pity's sake, *he* felt it, but then this." Hank grabbed the papers and lofted them into the air. "This happens and everything gets messed up."

"He left."

"Yes."

Without saying goodbye. Because that was the story of her life, it shouldn't come as any big surprise.

Callie stood, her legs wooden, her jaw tight. Suddenly the act of flipping burgers seemed like too much work.

But there was Jake to think of. What would he think when he found out Matt had left? How would he react?

She moved back to the kitchen, her head spinning, trying to make sense of things and failing, but she knew one thing. She'd stepped out of her comfort zone and trusted a man whose heart seemed to match hers. Kind. Caring. Loving to build, to see beautiful things rise from the ground, take shape against a God-given sky.

She'd been stupid. Again.

Old doubts consumed her. How needy was she that Matt's bright smile and sweet compliments won her over so quickly? Hadn't she wondered from the beginning?

Yes.

But she'd let foolish hopes and dreams color her judgment, pull her off task. Make her think Matt really cared about her. About Jake.

Jake.

He'd be brokenhearted, and it was all her fault.

Regret warred with anger and sadness, a sorry threesome. Simple math filled in the rest. Matt would get bank money for Cobbled Creek and her father would have his business back. For a win-win situation, this felt like a total loss.

She swallowed tears around a lump the size of a stair runner and slapped ground beef together with way more power than necessary, but better to take her anger out on meat than on her father. Or her son. Or...

No, that's right, Matt wouldn't be around anymore. At all. Ever. And just like that her hopes and dreams disappeared in the blink of an eye. Just as well, really. Better to count on herself. She knew that. And she'd be fine. Just fine.

"Can we play Christmas music, Mom?" Jake poked his head up from an internet site about the battle at Midway. "And did Grandpa forget to turn on the Christmas lights?"

"I did." Hank pushed to his feet, looking anything but festive. "I'll see to it right now."

"When's Matt coming?" Jake continued. "I'm starved."

Callie ignored the first question by zeroing in on the second. "I'll make the burgers. They can always be warmed up later."

"Okay."

She wanted to shout that Matt wasn't coming back. That he'd moved out. Moved on. He had his money and he'd taken the quickest path north. But she couldn't say any of that, couldn't even think it without wanting to bawl her eyes out. Except soldiers don't do that. They keep on keepin' on.

By the time Jake went to bed, Callie felt numb. Numb from pretending, numb from fielding questions, from avoiding the looks of concern her father shot her.

Mind-bending numb, but nothing an all-night crying jag wouldn't cure. And she was headed that way when her father stopped her. "So, what are you going to do?"

"Do?" She raised her shoulders, dropped them and shook her head. "About?"

"Matt."

"Matt's gone, Dad. End of story."

Hank stared at her, then swiped a hand across his face. "You're not getting this, are you?"

"That Matt needs distance, he's got his money and he

booked out of here like a race car driver? I'm getting it just fine, Dad."

"No." Hank settled his hands on her shoulders and met her anger with compassion. "He didn't leave because he didn't want to be with you. With us."

"Um, right." Callie sent him a look of disbelief and when he smiled, she had to remember why it was wrong to fight with your father.

"He left because he thinks it's the *right* thing to do."

"That makes no sense."

"It makes perfect sense," Hank countered. "Matt came here and helped our dream come true, but when that letter came today he realized we'd been wronged. That the bank acted too quickly. And that wasn't fair."

"So he left without saying goodbye to me or Jake? Right. Thanks for the pep talk, Dad."

She moved to step away, but Hank wouldn't let her. "He loves you."

Callie snorted. Very unfeminine, but then that was the story of her life. Unloved. Unfeminine. Uncherished.

"He does," her father insisted, "but think about this from his perspective. Either he loses Cobbled Creek or he fights us for it. Matt cares for us and doesn't want to hurt us."

"Very altruistic of him. But he still fled for places unknown without saying goodbye, therefore final chapter. End of story."

"It's nothing of the sort, and you've got your mother's stubbornness," Hank replied. "How will it look to people if Matt starts showing interest in you after he's had to relinquish the subdivision?"

"I—"

"Like he's a gold digger. Like he's trying to hang on. People talk, Callie."

"I don't care what people say," she told him, but a sheen of reality started to seep through. "Why would Matt?"

"Because Matt was talked about for years," her father reminded her. "And he came back here to fix things, not stir them up. He'd never want you and Jake to be targeted by gossip."

"You mean…"

"People might think he was after you to maintain his interest in Cobbled Creek."

"But that's ridiculous."

Hank's arched brow said it wasn't ridiculous. It was quite possible, actually, the way some small-town tongues wagged. "You're sure, Dad? Because I'm not a big risk-taker anymore."

Hank leaned closer. "I'm one-hundred-percent sure. I asked Maude to make a blanket for you a bunch of years back. A quilt that reminded me of your mother. All flowery and pretty, like spring."

Callie nodded, unsure where this was going.

"Then things went bad and I couldn't pay for the blanket. Maude hung on to it, and I went into town the other day to buy it."

"What's this got to do with—"

"It was gone," Hank continued as if she hadn't spoken. "Matt bought it for you. Maude said she wrapped it up real pretty. Said she knew he was smitten weeks ago and told him about the quilt, and he told her he was going to make sure Callie had the best Christmas ever."

Tears pricked her eyes, but they were different tears.

Tears of anticipation and hope, not anger. "He bought it for me?"

"Yes, but probably has no clue how to fix this whole mess because of a stupid bank mistake. Do you love him?" Hank's direct question put it all on the line.

"Yes." Callie met her father's gaze. "Oh, yes."

"Then show him."

Callie's mind spun with this new assortment of facts, but she recognized one thing: her father was right. If this was going to get fixed, Callie needed to be the one to do it because while Matt might be handy with tools, he was a proud marine, first and last. And a marine would never shackle those he loved with rumor and speculation. It was up to her to show him the way to the family he never had. If the guy wasn't too proud and stubborn to see what God had laid before him, that is. "I will, Dad, but I'll need your help. Can you call him? Get him to come back here tomorrow evening? And meet you at the model home?"

Hank grinned. "Will do. And Callie?"

She turned from the stairs and met his gaze.

"I'm proud of you, honey."

And she felt it, right to her toes. She met his smile and returned it. "Thank you, Dad."

Chapter Eighteen

Matt saw Hank's caller ID and hated to answer the phone, but he did. "Hello."

"Matt?"

"Yes, Hank. What's up?"

A slight pause tempted Matt to ask about Callie. About Jake. How things were going. It had been one whole day, after all.

Pathetic, Cavanaugh.

"Can you meet me at the model house later today?"

The house Callie loved? "How about we meet in town instead? I'm staying at my brother's place in Wellsville while we get things resituated."

"I'm tied up all day." Apology laced Hank's tone. "And I need to go over a few things with you about the model and the house that's sold. I'd do it here, but…"

Matt understood. Callie would be there. So would Jake. And he wasn't in any shape to see them right now, to witness his sacrifice firsthand.

You don't have to give up anything, son.

Grandpa Gus's wisdom poked him from within.

God's offered you a wonderful chance, the chance to love. Grab it. Run with it. Embrace it.

Right. And have the whole town think he was scrambling to hang on to Cobbled Creek through Callie? Honor first, and that meant Callie first, in this instance. Subjecting Jake and Callie to the gossip mill he'd lived with all his life? Wasn't gonna happen. Not on his watch.

Pride and dismay clenched his gut as he angled the truck down Cobbled Creek Lane that evening. He didn't look toward the Marek house to see their tree winking softly in the side window, or the string of lights he'd helped Callie hang in the rain. Or Shadow Jesus.

The memory of Jake's upturned face C-clamped Matt's heart, his earnest explanations about Bethlehem. Mary and Joseph and a child born to the poor. The little guy paid such close attention to detail, a rare trait, Matt thought; but then, Jake was no ordinary child. He was Callie's son.

The clamp tightened its screw hold on Matt's heart as he approached the model home, the pretty walkway welcoming him.

Should he ring the bell? Walk in?

Swallowing frustration, he pushed open the door and called Hank's name.

"Dad's not here."

Callie.

His heart jumped, then sank. "He was supposed to meet me."

She came forward, looking absolutely wonderful, but then he felt that way when she donned triple layers and flannels to work side by side with him. But tonight the one-shoulder top over fitted jeans left no doubt that Callie Marek was in good shape.

And breathtakingly beautiful.

Matt scrubbed a hand to his neck and looked around. Her presence made his determination to stay away seem somewhat dumb. And maybe impossible. But he was doing it for her, he reminded himself as she drew closer.

"You left."

He nodded, holding himself arm's length away when what he longed to do was reach out and touch her. Slide that curl tickling her cheek back behind her ear.

"It seemed best."

"For whom?"

He waved a hand. "Everyone."

She encroached a little more. "Really?"

"Yes." He thought so at the time anyway, but right now, with Callie so near, smelling Christmas-cookie sweet, he wasn't so sure. Which meant he should take a step back. He did.

Callie followed.

"Cal, listen…"

"No, you listen, marine." She closed the distance between them and gave him a very unromantic thwack on the arm. "What on earth are you doing, Matt Cavanaugh?"

"Trying to find your father and settle our affairs."

She sighed out loud. "Not with him. With me." She waved a hand between them. "Us. Because here's how I see things, and let me just add, it's pretty obvious that you and my father need a woman around and you should be thanking God I'm available."

Available as in…

"First of all—" he didn't think it was possible for her to move closer, and yet she did, wagging her pointer finger in the air "—you love me."

Honor, integrity and honesty disallowed a lie. "Yes."

Callie rolled her eyes. "You could try to sound a little happier about it."

"Callie—"

"Ah." She put two sweet-smelling fingers to his mouth to shush him, the feel and scent reminding him of those shared kisses. The hopes and dreams he'd thought possible the past weeks. "Still my turn. And you love Jake."

"Who couldn't?"

She smiled up at him, and he realized she wasn't wearing heels. She was, in fact, just wearing socks, looking way too cozy and at home, but then, this house fit her as if...

"Here's my proposal," she went on as if sealing a business deal. "You get all this nonsense about what people will think, about giving up your dream and handing over Cobbled Creek to my dad out of your head."

"But—"

"In lieu of that we form a partnership of sorts."

Her slanted smile released the clamp on Matt's heart a bit more. "Are you suggesting a merger?"

Her smile deepened. She poked him in the chest. "Exactly that." She couldn't get any closer without touching him, so she did, letting her hair riffle against his chin, his neck. Then she squared her shoulders. "Of course there are terms to negotiate."

"I'm a great negotiator."

"I don't doubt it for a minute," she agreed amicably, as if they weren't discussing very serious things like weddings. Babies.

Unless he misunderstood her.

One look into those pretty green eyes nixed that. "You know I was no choirboy, Cal." Despite the lure, the attraction, the love, he didn't want Callie blindsided ever again. About anything. "My past might trip us up from time to time."

She met his gaze straight on. "It could, but I'm going to trust God to get us through whatever happens. Once I get it through that thick head of yours that it's okay to love us." She reached up and feathered a soft kiss to his jaw.

"Stop." He put up a hand and stepped back. Confusion swam in her eyes until he dropped to one knee and grasped her hand. "If we're going to do this, we're going to do it right."

Her mouth formed a perfect O, and then she smiled, delighted. "Please do."

He squeezed her fingers and held her gaze, wishing she could see his heart. His soul. "Callie, you are the most incredible and beautiful woman I've ever known. You have a heart of gold and you're really good with power tools."

A bubble of laughter mixed with the sheen of tears in her eyes.

"Will you marry me? Share your life and son with me? Grow old with me, building houses?"

"Homes," she corrected, and drew him up. "Not houses, Matt. Homes. And yes, I'll marry you. Have your babies. And work beside you all my days."

Matt lost himself in the feel of Callie's arms, her kiss, her presence, feeling like he'd come back to a home he'd never really had.

Lights burst on around them. Twinkle lights. They lined the windows of the first floor, and a tree, a real Christmas tree, lit up the soft yellow great room at the back of the house. Matt hugged Callie and grinned as

Hank and the guys tried unsuccessfully to slip quietly out the back.

"Jake."

The boy broke ranks with the older men and raced back into the house. He barreled into Callie and Matt and Matt tipped the boy's chin up to hold his gaze. "Jake, I'd like your permission to marry your mother. I love her and I love you and I think we'd make a great family together. What do you think?"

Jake's face beamed as bright as the Bethlehem star, a symbol of a new beginning. A new hope. "I say yes."

"And," Matt shifted his gaze to the pretty woman in his left arm, a woman who'd known pain and abandonment but was wise enough to let God guide her through it all, step by step, "I think we should live here."

"Here?" Callie swept the model with the wistful look she'd tried to contain weeks before.

"Right here. If we're going to forge a family business, we need proximity. Affordability. And—" he let his eyes twinkle into hers "—it's a four bedroom, which means growth potential."

Callie blushed.

Jake laughed and fist pumped the air. "And I get to help you and Grandpa build, Matt!"

Matt ruffled a hand through Jake's hair and dropped another kiss to Callie's smiling mouth, wondering how he'd ever considered walking away. "You sure do, son. You sure do."

Epilogue

"Oh, look." Callie pointed to the left of the auditorium stage the following December and gave a momlike wave. "There's Jake. Right next to Jordan."

Chloe Wiseman leaned across her husband. "They're peas in a pod, those two. Have I mentioned often enough how happy we are to live in Cobbled Creek? Near you guys? To have such a nice friend for Jordan, so close?"

Callie laughed and squeezed the other woman's hand. "I feel the same way. And we've got a great bunch of neighbors with Phase One complete."

A tiny noise erupted from Callie's left. "Dad, you okay over there?"

Hank rearranged the pink-swaddled bundle in his arms and gave a sage nod. "Nothing a bottle and a burp won't cure. But I'm still not loving the pink camo."

"It's adorable," Callie protested.

"It's pink," Hank argued. "Camo should never be pink."

"Well, she is a girl," Matt reminded him. He shrugged and met Hank's grin. "Pink goes with the territory.

Doesn't it, Morgan?" Matt leaned in and ran a finger along the tiny girl's soft-as-down cheek.

"Dresses, fine." Hank kept his voice army-gruff, but his eyes twinkled as the newborn accepted the bottle with fisted hands and greedy tugs. "But army gear should be army gear. Never the twain shall meet."

Matt leaned closer to Callie. "What's he going to think of the pink leopard print stuff Hannah gave us?"

Callie laughed, Hank made a face and Matt watched with pride as Jake *Cavanaugh* stepped up to the microphone to welcome people to the eighteenth annual Christmas Concert for Veterans. And when Jake found them in the crowd and sent a grin their way, Matt felt like Grandpa Gus just clapped him on the back, showing his full approval.

And it felt good.

* * * * *

Dear Reader,

I love stories that laud success over failure, new beginnings and second chances! As a child of two alcoholic parents, I understand Matt Cavanaugh's childhood, but by the grace of God I attended a Catholic school filled with dedicated Christian staff. Their warmth, understanding and diligence taught me to move above and beyond. To grasp faith and hope when darkness surrounded me.

Callie Marek is a gal who can put her hand to any task, like my mother-in-law. I forged Callie's character to reflect Mom's strength and stoicism. Callie's mistake was falling for a man who didn't realize her worth, a woman unafraid to get dirty, dig out a pond or run power tools. Women like this helped build our country and I was determined that Hank's wonderful daughter would find a match worthy of her in God's good time.

And she did, she just had to slap some sense into our proud marine toward the end! A marine who determined the right course for life and stuck to it, doggedly, despite his early mistakes. Thank you for reading *Yuletide Hearts*, my first Christmas story for Love Inspired! Feel free to stop by Ruthy's Place at ruthysplace.com or check out things at www.ruthloganherne.com. We've got a constant party going on at www.seekerville.blogspot.com, where you'll find a strong Christian sisterhood sharing advice and cyber food! You can email me at loganherne@yahoo.com or snail mail me c/o Love Inspired Books, 195 Broadway, 24th floor, New York, NY 10007. I love hearing from you!

Ruth Logan Herne

MENDED HEARTS

Be still before the Lord and wait patiently for Him; do not fret when men succeed in their ways, when they carry out their wicked schemes. Refrain from anger and turn from wrath; do not fret—it leads only to evil. For evil men will be cut off, but those who hope in the Lord will inherit the land.
—*Psalms 37:7–9*

This book is dedicated to Melissa Endlich, whose patience and rolling pin have proved necessary on more than one occasion. Your continued confidence blesses me abundantly.

And to Amanda, Seth, Lacey and Karen, four wonderful high school teachers who've worked the front lines of adolescent development. God bless you guys!

Acknowledgments

Wonderful teachers are never forgotten. Special thanks to Mrs. Fenlon (now Mrs. Steiner), Sr. Mary Cordis, Sr. Mariel, (deceased), Sr. Natalia, Mrs. Bagley and Thomas Dowd. I'm grateful for your encouragement and kindness. And to Alice McCarthy, my Girl Scout leader, who became a stand-in at every parental function. Alice, thank you for treating an abnormal situation with sweet normalcy. God blessed you with a generous heart and I thank you for the times you sat with me, accompanied me and covered my "dues." There's a special place in heaven for people like you.

Special thanks to Mandy for traipsing the hills of Allegany with me, taking the time to meet perfect strangers with a smile and a handshake. Weren't those sheriffs adorable? To Beth and Jon for their constant help in so many ways. To Matt and Karen and Seth and Lacey for their continued support and help. And to Zach and Luke, who advise from afar and take the couch so I can have the bed when I visit them. You guys rock.

To the Seekers at www.seekerville.blogspot.com. Your light shines for so many. I'm blessed to have you in my life. Audra, thanks for the read. You rock. Andrea, for the steady belief for so many years.

And especially to Dave for his continued love and support. He makes a mean tuna-fish sandwich! Love you, dude.

Prologue

Jeff Brennan stood slowly, facing his illegitimate half brother, their gazes locked, a silent war of wills waging in their squared-off stature. Nice to see that twenty years of separation had changed absolutely nothing. "What do you want, Matt? What are you doing here?"

Matt Cavanaugh didn't match Jeff's caustic tone, but then he'd always had a way of wriggling out of things right up until he nearly cost Katie Bascomb her life. He did cost her a leg, but guys like Matt didn't worry about things like consequences. Ever.

Matt leveled a firm look at Jeff, not cringing. Not asking forgiveness. Not apologizing for all he'd put the family through two decades back. Which meant he might need to be punched. And with the current demands and conditions of Jeff's job as the chief design engineer for Walker Electronics, his business partner, Trent Michaels, called away for life-threatening family illness and the in-house rush to nail down a mobile surveillance system designed to keep an eye on threatened American borders, Jeff was ready to duke it out with just about anyone.

Throw in the matching funds library project his grandmother and CEO threw at him an hour ago, and Matt had no idea how close he was to risking his life.

Jeff swallowed a growl, glanced down, then up. The look in Matt's eyes said he might just be getting it, but on an already bad day, the last thing Jeff wanted or needed was the long-awaited showdown with his lawbreaking half brother. "I said, what do you want?"

Matt raised his hands in a conciliatory gesture. "I'm in town to scout out some possible work. I'm a housing contractor now, and I didn't want to blindside you or any-one else in the family by running into you in the street."

"You've grown a conscience?" Jeff's hands tightened. His skin prickled. The hairs on the nape of his neck rose in quiet protest. "Since when?"

Matt didn't answer the question. "I've come to make amends, Jeff."

"Too little, too late."

A tiny muscle in Matt's jaw tightened. "You could be right. I hope you're wrong. But I wanted to come here and see you face-to-face. Pave the way."

"So you're in town looking for work." Jeff mused over the words, wishing Matt wasn't so calm while he felt ready to jump the desk and settle old wrongs. "Or you're here because Walker Electronics is doing better and you want a piece of the pie."

Matt swiped Jeff's office a quick glance. "Right. I just now decided to fulfill a lifelong yearning to under-stand microchips, nanoseconds and satellite-fed commu-nications. Sorry, but that part of our father didn't bleed through to me."

"No." Jeff shut his desk drawer with more force than necessary. "You got the drinking, gambling, womanizing and lawbreaking genes. How's that working for you, Matt?"

Matt stepped back. "I didn't come to fight, Jeff. I just wanted you aware. And if you'll point me toward Helen's office, I'll let her know, as well."

What Jeff wanted was to show Matt the exit in no uncertain terms, but that would label him an even bigger jerk. He hiked a thumb left. "Out the door. Down the hall. I know she's there because we just finished a meeting about a matching fund drive for the Jamison library."

"Your grandfather's wishes."

"Yes."

Matt nodded and backed toward the door. "I'm not looking to get in your way down here."

"You already did."

Matt acknowledged that with a shrug and a straight-on look. "Those are your issues, then."

He turned, leaving Jeff with nothing but riled-up memories, twenty years of absence not enough to warrant Matt's presence as a welcome addition.

His grandmother would disagree. Jeff knew that. She'd always seen Matt as a broken soul, a lost kid, a troubled heart.

Whereas Jeff saw a conscienceless user, just like their father.

Long ago, Peter had asked the Lord about forgiving his brother, wondering if seven times was enough. And Jesus said no. Not nearly enough. Which only meant Jeff had some serious work to do if forgiving Matt was added to his already overflowing plate.

Chapter One

Megan Romesser's eyes brightened as Hannah Moore walked through the back door of Grandma Mary's Candies on this quiet September afternoon. Quiet equated good in Hannah's book, because she longed to vent loud and long, knowing Megan would listen, commiserate and then tell her to get on with it.

Megan understood the role of a good friend.

But venting would mean explaining why heading up a library fund-raising drive with weekly meetings and full immersion into what everyone else considered normal life thrust Hannah into an emotional tailspin. Opening that door meant facing things she'd tucked aside years ago.

If not now, when?

How about never?

Hannah shoved the internal questions aside. If keeping that door closed guarded her mental health, then so be it.

She nodded toward the trays of fresh candy and the wall of boxed chocolates shipped in from Grandma Mary's Buffalo-based factory. "Just being around this much chocolate adds inches to my hips. Why do I work here? To torture myself?"

"To see me." Megan sent her a quick grin, finished packing an order, then waved toward the back. "New sponge candy in the minikitchen. See what you think."

"I love the perks of this job. Have I mentioned that lately?"

"Which is why you run voraciously. Nothing sticks on you."

"A blessing and a curse."

"Ha." Megan sent a doubtful look over her shoulder. "Not packing on pounds is never a curse. Bite your tongue."

"Let's just say I'm not afraid to augment as needed," Hannah shot back, grinning. "Aiding and abetting my lack of curves."

Megan laughed out loud. "Seriously, Hannah, the way you look in a dress? In your running gear? Head-turning. Brat."

"Thanks." Hannah nipped a piece of fresh sponge candy, closed her eyes in appreciation and breathed deep. "Wonderful. Marvelous. Words escape me."

"That'll do for the moment. The chocolate is smooth enough?"

"Like silk."

"Sweet enough?"

"The perfect blend of slightly bitter chocolate to golden, sugary honeycomb. Need any more convincing?"

"I could use you to write my ad copy." Megan grinned, then turned to answer the wall phone. "Grandma Mary's Candies, Megan speaking. Hey, darlin', when are you coming home?"

Honeymooner talk. Hannah moved into the kitchen, removing herself from the inevitable love-yous and miss-yous of being separated for two whole days.

Right now, the last thing Hannah needed was another reminder of her empty life.

She tried to appear normal. She'd done a morning stint at the library, followed by a mandatory meeting with Helen Walker, CEO of Walker Electronics, which put her into this current tizzy. Now she would put in four hours of work helping Megan in the family candy store in Wellsville.

Working odd jobs offered a semblance of normal, but normal had disappeared on a rainy afternoon almost five years ago, taking a hefty part of her self-reliance with it.

Pretense worked now. Fake it till you make it, an old sales adage that applied. Only Hannah hadn't gotten to the "make it" part yet. Lately she'd been wondering if she ever would. Perhaps Helen Walker had been right, maybe shouldering this library fund-raising task would be good for her. Anything that pushed her out of her self-imposed comfort zone wasn't bad, right?

Depends on your definition of bad, her inner voice scoffed.

Oh, she knew bad. Been there, done that, had no desire to return. Not ever again. Keeping her responsibilities minimal meant downsizing risk, and that had become her current mantra.

"Hannah?"

"Yes?" She poked her head around the corner, then shifted her attention to the phone. "You done with lover boy?"

Megan laughed. "Yes, but he's not coming home until tomorrow. Problems with staffing at the Baltimore store. Wanna do a movie tonight?"

Hannah shook her head. "Too nice to stay inside. What about walking the ridge?"

"As in *walk*, not run?"

Hannah smiled as she weighed sponge candy into one-pound boxes. "Promise."

"I'm in. You're okay on your own here?"

Hannah glanced around the empty store. "Fine. You're leaving?"

"Just for a bit. Ben needs a ride home from the restaurant."

Ben was Megan's developmentally challenged younger brother, who lived in a group home a few blocks from the store. "You go get Ben. I'll do quality control on the sponge candy. And maybe the caramels, as well."

"Can't be too careful." Megan paused and gave Hannah a quick hug on her way out. "Are you okay?"

"Fine. Why?" Steadying her features, Hannah glanced up.

"You seem a little off."

"I'm a girl. That happens, doesn't it?"

"Hmm." Megan didn't look convinced. "If you need to talk…"

"Which I don't."

"Even so." Megan gave Hannah a look, her expression unsure. "If you do, I'm available."

"I know." Hannah turned her attention back to the task at hand, shoulders back, feet firm. "I appreciate it."

"Well, then." Megan sounded dubious but she'd never delve. More than Hannah's friendship, she respected her right to privacy, a wonderful plus in this age of girlfriends-know-all.

Hannah couldn't afford to have anyone know all. Bad enough she carried that burden on her shoulders. She refused to bring others down. But that weighted the yoke, and with the Allegheny foothills hinting gold and red, fall's beauty carried heavy reminders of love and loss.

The antique bell announcing a customer's arrival provided a welcome interruption. Hannah left the half-filled box on the scale and moved to the front of the east-facing store. A man stood scanning a new display kiosk, a man who'd become distressingly familiar two hours ago. "May I help you?"

Surprise painted his features as Jeff Brennan turned from a corner display. Hannah fought the rise of emotions his expression inspired. In three years she hadn't crossed paths with this man, and now twice in one day?

Obviously God had a sense of humor, because the last person Hannah wanted to be around was a rising young executive, no matter how great he looked in gray tweed, the steel-and-rose-pinstriped tie a perfect complement to the silver-toned oxford. She'd seen enough in the library council meeting to know he was self-confident, self-assured and slightly impatient, a condition that might arise from lack of time or lack of compassion, not that she cared.

His crisp, clean, business-first air had Brian's name written all over it, a CEO in the making, driven and forward-thinking. With the leaves beginning their annual dance of color, thoughts of her former fiancé only worsened matters. She shoved the memories aside, kept her expression calm and stepped forward, determined to get through this library fund-raiser somehow, since her library contract allowed her no other choice.

"You've got time to work here, but you're reluctant to help with the new library?" The hint of resentment in Jeff's tone said her lack of enthusiasm was unappreciated in light of Helen and Jonas Walker's sacrifices.

But then Jeff had no idea what dragons loomed in her past as summer faded to fall and kids marched off to school, pencils sharp, their backpacks fresh and new, a world she'd been part of until that dark November day.

She met his gaze, refusing to let the clipped tone get to her. "My library job in Jamison is part-time. Last I looked life was full-time and that includes living expenses. An extra job helps pay the bills since the county couldn't afford more hours in the library budget."

"And you tutor?"

He'd actually been listening when she'd tried to beg off the fund-raising committee earlier, but that shouldn't surprise her. You didn't get to Jeff Brennan's rung on the corporate ladder at thirty-plus without having a working brain. Of course being the boss's grandson couldn't hurt, but somehow she didn't see that happening at Walker Electronics. She slipped on fresh plastic gloves, ignored his question and indicated the glass-fronted candy display with a tilt of her head. "Would you like a hand-chosen collection, Mr. Brennan?"

His eyes narrowed, his look appraising once again. She got the idea that Jeff Brennan did a lot of appraising.

Well, he could stuff his appraisals for all she cared.

Feigning patience she waited, a box in hand, letting him make the next move. Which he did.

"Are you free for dinner tomorrow night?"

It took her a moment to register the words, shield her surprise, think of a response and then shelve the comeback as rude, a quality she chose not to embrace.

This is not Brian.

And yet the quick looks, the straight-on focus, the let's-get-down-to-business mode pushed too many buttons at once, especially with the distant hills hinting gold behind him.

He angled his head, his eyes brightened by her reaction. Which was really a nonreaction, and he seemed to find that almost amusing.

Dolt.

"I'm not, no."

"Wednesday?"

"The library is open until eight on Wednesday."

He sent her an exaggerated look of puzzlement, crinkled his eyes and moved closer, his manner inviting. "You can't eat after eight o'clock? Are you like one of those little aliens that couldn't eat after midnight?"

"Thanks for the compliment. Sorry. Busy."

"Look, Miss Moore…"

"Hannah."

A smile softened his features; he was probably remembering they'd had this conversation before, like two hours ago in the conference room of Walker Electronics.

"Hannah. Pretty name. It means favored. Or favored grace."

"And you know this because?"

"I looked it up on my computer when I got back to my office."

Add *smooth* to the list of reasons to avoid Jeff Brennan. Too smooth, too handsome, too winsome with his short curly brown hair, hazel eyes, strong chin, great nose and lashes that girls spent way too much money for.

Hannah flashed him a cool smile, not wanting or needing to dredge up a past best left buried, not this time of year. "You and the wife picking baby names, Mr. Brennan?"

He raised unfettered hands. "Not married, never have

been, nor engaged. And dinner is simply so you and I can go into Thursday's meeting on the same page with similar goals, if neither one of us successfully ducks this project. No strings, no ties, no ulterior motives."

The sensibility of his argument enticed Hannah to accept. Chronic fear pushed her to refuse. She waffled, hating this indecision, longing to be the person she used to be. Strong. Self-motivated. Forceful.

But that was before Ironwood, and nothing had been the same since. She shook her head, needing to decline and hating the cowardice pushing the emotion. "I can't. Sorry."

He'd tempted her.

Good.

She'd telegraphed the reaction as she weighed her response, a quick, vivid light in her eyes, quenched as seconds ticked by. Jeff liked the bright look better, but either way, something about Hannah Moore piqued his interest.

Which made no sense because shy, retiring women weren't his type, although something in her stance and bearing made him think she wasn't as timid as she made out. Perhaps hesitant was a better word, and that only made him wonder what caused the timorous look behind those stunning blue eyes.

And if he couldn't persuade Grandma that his sister, Meredith, was the better choice to cochair these weekly meetings, he had to establish a common ground with this woman. Clearly she shared his displeasure about spending the better part of a year on the project.

Even with her long blond hair pulled back in a ponytail for her candy store stint, she was lovely. And cautious, a trait he'd learned to deal with if not love because his mother embraced caution as her middle name. But beneath the carefully constructed and controlled features, he sensed something else.

Right now he needed a cooperative attitude with this whole library business, and since he'd happened upon her here, at the Romesser family's new tribute store, fate was obviously throwing her into his path. Or maybe it was the fact that he needed a box of chocolates for a friend's wife who'd just given birth. Either way, Jeff wasn't about to waste an opportunity. He shifted his attention to the chocolates. "I need a pound and a half of mixed chocolates including cherry cordials, if you don't mind."

Her face softened, dissipating the glimpse of worry. "Josie O'Meara."

He laughed, amazed. "How'd you know?"

Hannah leaned forward as if sharing a secret. "She stopped by for one cherry cordial nearly every day until she delivered. It was her way of rewarding herself for being a working mom with a baby on board."

"That's Josie, all right. Do you know all your customers like that? At the library and here? And the kids you tutor?"

She shook her head as she filled the box, then shrugged. "Yes and no. It's easy because I work at small venues. If they were bigger, it might not be the same."

Somehow Jeff doubted that. Hannah's soul-searching eyes said she was a woman of marked intelligence.

So why was she working part-time in an out-of-the-way postage-stamp-size library, gilding the lack of pay by boxing chocolates?

She wrapped the box in paper decorated with tiny dinosaurs, perfect for the mother of a brand-new baby boy.

"Tell her I packed extra cherry cordials in there from me. And that Samuel is a great name."

"Samuel was Hannah's son in the Bible, wasn't he?"

Her eyes shadowed, the hint of self-protection re-emerging.

"That will be eighteen dollars, please."

"Of course." He let the subject slide, not sure how or why, but pretty certain he'd prickled a wound. "And Wednesday night?"

She glanced away, then down.

"I can pick you up or we can meet at The Edge."

He waited, counting the ticks of the clock, then leaned forward. "And can you wear something that doesn't remind me of how pretty your eyes are? That doesn't augment that shade of blue?"

She jerked up, the shadow chased away by annoyance. "Maybe. Maybe not. I'll meet you there. Eight thirty."

"Perfect." He raised up the signature green-and-tan-striped paper bag bearing Grandma Mary's logo. "See you then. And thanks for the candy."

He felt her gaze on him as he left the store, the bell jangling his departure. He headed left toward the hospital, but refused to glance back to see if she watched him stroll down the sidewalk.

Nope.

Let her wonder if he'd totally forgotten her the minute he stepped through the door, which he hadn't. Give her something to stew over instead of whatever shadowed her expression.

Although he did understand the concept of shouldering burdens firsthand. His father's illicit drug and gambling habits turned Neal Brennan's brilliant mind into a disaster, nearly toppling their family business. Jeff intended to do whatever it took to polish the Brennan name until it gleamed. Matt Cavanaugh's sudden reappearance in the area didn't make his goal easier, but Jeff refused to dwell on that new twist. He'd meet with Grandma later, get her opinion. And he'd run an internet check on his half brother, see what he could find. Good or bad, he'd face any showdowns with Matt well-informed.

And Hannah…

Hopefully he could establish ground rules with her over supper. If they were on the same page, perhaps they could jump-start the library fund-raiser quickly. Start-up was always the most time-consuming part of fund-raising. Between his grandparents' and mother's philanthropy, Jeff had seen that firsthand. So he'd get together with Hannah, make a plan and set it in motion. And the whole dinner with a beautiful woman thing?

Not too shabby either.

Chapter Two

"Dinner with Jeff Brennan? At The Edge? Oh, girlfriend, you are travelin' with the big guns now." Megan nudged Hannah as they crested the hill at the edge of town, late-day shadows beginning to lengthen.

"Stop." Hannah scowled and increased the pace of the walk deliberately. Maybe if Megan was winded, she couldn't ask questions.

"Have you met before?"

Not winded enough. "No."

"Ever?"

"No. And don't look at me that way. I've only been here a few years."

"But he's everywhere. Does everything. And not only because his family is like the royal family of Allegany County, but because he's a people person. Jeff loves to be in the thick of things. A born manager."

The last thing Hannah wanted was to be managed. "Whereas I prefer the background, thanks."

Megan frowned, hesitated, then waded in. "You're great with people, Hannah."

"I've got nothing against people. I just don't like getting involved."

"But—"

"And I'm busy."

"Do you need me to cut your hours at the store? Would that help?"

"Not if I want to continue to pay my bills." Hannah started to surge ahead, then came to a complete stop, aggravated, wishing she didn't have to explain herself. Explaining meant she might slip back into the dark waters of things she avoided. "See, that's the thing. I love working at the library because it's small. Quiet. I help a few people here and there. It's perfect for me. If we make it all big and beautiful, I'll be expected to do all kinds of things, all the time. I like things the way they are, Meg."

"Why is bigger bad?" Megan wondered. "I would think you'd embrace the idea of helping more kids, more families, providing more books, more chances."

Megan's words struck deep.

Hannah had provided a lot of chances for kids back in the day. She'd gone out on limbs, taken the bull by the horns, encouraging, offering young adults a rare experience. She'd been a risk taker then, in her beautifully equipped classroom, before life flipped upside down.

She was a rabbit now. Emotional necessity ruled the cautious lifestyle she'd adopted. It suited her duck-and-cover personality.

"I'll be on the committee if you'd like," Megan offered. "Would that help? Then we could strategize while we're at the store together. Kill two birds with one stone."

"What horrible bird hater thought up that analogy?"

Megan laughed. "Don't change the subject. What are you wearing Wednesday night?"

"Nothing special."

"What about my blue sarong? The one I brought back from Hawaii?"

"Hmm. Show up at the library in a sarong. Perfect for children's hour." She flashed Meg a wry look. "End of story. And this discussion. Besides, I can't wear blue."

"What? Why?"

Hannah felt a blush rise from her neck and resented her fair complexion for the first time in several years. "We need another color."

"You've lost me."

Hannah sighed. "He said if I wear blue he'll have a hard time concentrating on anything besides my eyes."

Megan ground to a halt, pebbled stones skittering beneath her feet. "He said that? Out loud?"

Hannah stopped, as well, directed a bemused look to her friend and sighed. "He did, but it was most likely to throw me off track because he wants this project done. If he can't weasel his way out of it and pawn it off on his sister."

"Meredith's back?"

"If that's his sister's name, then yes."

"Huh." Megan frowned and resumed walking. "I'll have to call her, see what's up. You'll love her. She's funny and down-to-earth. And she does great hair and nails."

"Corporate boy's sister is a hairdresser? Why did I not see that coming?"

"She loves it. And she's wonderful, like I said. The Walkers aren't your typical rich family."

Jeff Brennan had seemed pretty typical earlier that day. Focused, frenetic and finite, a path she'd traveled once before. No way was she going down that road again.

"Is there such a thing as typical rich anymore?" Hannah asked. "There's some pretty weird millionaires running around these days."

"And some downright nice ones."

Hannah laughed. "Present company excluded, of course. Although I hear candy-store entrepreneurs maintain their delightful normalcy because of their choice in wives."

"Makes sense to me." Megan offered agreement with an elbow nudge to Hannah's arm. "And wear the blue. Call his bluff."

A part of Hannah wanted to do just that.

Another part couldn't take the risk.

The gold top Hannah wore said she had no intention of jumping into the water with him, metaphorically speaking. The fact that the soft knit looked just as good as the blue simply brightened Jeff's evening.

Watching as she wove her way through the tables of The Edge's second dining room Wednesday evening, it was impossible to miss the strength of her moves, athletic and lithe.

That inborn agility appeared out of step with her other body language, her careful facial movements belied by nervous hands and the inward expression that shadowed her eyes intermittently.

Edgy hands. Cloaked expression. A rough combination, all told, reminiscent of his mother in the bad days of his parents' publicly awful marriage.

He stood as she approached the table. The hostess smiled as she indicated a chair. Jeff pulled the chair out for Hannah, waited until she was comfortably seated, then sat in the adjacent chair.

"You had to choose that one, didn't you?" She met his gaze with a quiet look of challenge. "Being across from me wasn't close enough? Or intimidating enough?"

"I intimidate you?" Jeff unfolded his napkin, brow drawn, but not too much, just enough to let her know he could quirk a grin quickly. "Thanks, I'll remember that."

"Annoyed, possibly," she corrected, looking more sure of herself. "Intimidated? No."

"Good to know, although I was starting to feel pretty good about myself. I've been trying to intimidate my sister for years. No go."

"And yet still you try."

He grinned agreeably. "A brother's job. Would you like an appetizer, Hannah? The Edge has great stuffed mushrooms. And the owner makes Shrimp le Rocco, huge shrimp done in a wine and cream sauce with a hint of Cajun, just enough to give it life."

"Are you auditioning for the Food Network?"

"I'm a Paula Deen guy," he admitted, smiling. "All that butter. Cream. Southern drawl. And she's sweet but tough. Reminds me of Grandma."

"Your grandmother is one strong lady." Hannah looked more at ease talking about Grandma. She settled back in her seat and fingered her water glass, then smiled and nodded at the waitress as they gave their drink and appetizer orders.

The smile undid him, just a little. Sweet. Broad. Inviting. She had a generous mouth when it wasn't pinched in worry.

"She is." Jeff settled back, as well, surveyed her and sighed openly. "Which means you're stuck with me, I'm afraid. My attempts to get Meredith on board fell on deaf ears. Seems she's got other fish to fry."

"Aha."

"And your attempts? Still unsuccessful?"

She shrugged. "I didn't try. There's a part of me..." She paused, shifted her attention, then drew it back to him, reluctant. "That thinks this will be good for me."

Good for her?

Jeff considered the words, the look, then chose not to probe. Seeing fund-raising as therapeutic was beyond his understanding, but if they both had to be involved, at least they'd both accepted the fact.

Grudgingly.

However, sitting with her, watching her, eyeing the lights and shadows that played across her face, candlelight mixed with emotion, he didn't feel all that grudging. He felt...

Drawn.

But he couldn't be for two reasons: women of indecision annoyed him, which was precisely why he got on so well with his grandmother, and he had no time to devote to thoughts of a relationship.

If not now, when?

Jeff shut down the annoying mental reminder, thoughts of microchips, rare metal glazings and mobile communications taking precedence for the foreseeable future.

His grandmother was a thinker, doer and planner. Jeff followed her lead. Plan your work, then work your plan. He'd constructed his life that way, a goal setter to the max, doing anything to eliminate similarities to his narcissistic father. His appearance and affinity for inventive science labeled him as Neal Brennan's son, but that was as far as the resemblance went.

Jeff pushed himself to be better. Stronger. Wiser. Although lately a part of him felt worn by having to be on the cutting edge constantly, he couldn't afford the appearance of weakness. Not now. Not ever.

He leaned forward, elbows braced, hands locked, noticing how the freckles dusting her cheeks blended with her sun-kissed skin. "Hannah."

She noted his shift and a hint of amusement sparked in her eyes, a look that downplayed her nervous gestures. "Yes, Jeff?"

She was playing him in her own way. He leaned closer. "Since we're stuck with each other..."

"At weekly meetings." She drawled the words, her tone teasing.

He sighed, then nodded as if pained. "For the better part of a year until enough money is raised."

She met his look, but that small spark of humor in her eyes kept him moving forward. "Might I suggest we come to a mutual agreement?"

"That you buy me supper once a week? That sure would help my grocery budget."

He grinned without meaning to. "We'll put that on the negotiating table. Does that mean you'd cook for me once a week?"

"No."

"Obviously we need to work on your bargaining skills. You never say no right out. It puts the other players off."

"What if I'm not into games?" she asked. She eyed her water glass, then him. "Game playing isn't my thing."

"When it comes to raising funds, we're all into games," he assured her.

She sat back purposely.

"And when we're talking cajoling benefactors, you and I will need to be on the same page," he continued.

"Which means we stay open to any and all ideas as if they're workable, even if we know they're not."

"We lie."

He shook his head. "Not lie. Improvise."

"Lead people on."

"Not in a bad way." He studied her, and knit his brow, wondering. "As chairpeople, you and I need to appear open to others' ideas even if we've already planned a course of action."

"What if their ideas have merit?"

"We incorporate them, of course. But only if they don't take us off track."

His words quenched the spark of amusement in her eyes. "So as long as it's your way, it's a go."

"No, not really."

"That's what you said."

"What I said was spawned by your refusal to cook for me," he shot back, hoping humor would soften the moment, noting her withdrawal with a glance. "You said no too quickly. If you'd said, 'I'll consider that and get back to you,' at least then I'd feel like I have a chance. And that's how contributors want to feel. Like they're appreciated. Considered."

"So because I shot down your plea for a home-cooked meal, I'm being lectured on the ins and outs of fundraising?"

He sat back, confused. "Listen, I—"

She slid forward in her seat as if ready to do battle, a tactical move that surprised him considering her previous timidity. "For your information, I am perfectly capable of running this thing completely on my own. So feel free to take yourself back to Grandma and tell her I can fly solo, because it will be way more fun than dealing with a corporate know-it-all who pretends other people's opinions matter when clearly they don't." She stood, back straight, face set, determination darkening her blue eyes. "And as for cooking you dinner, not only would you be wise to not hold your breath, you might want to consider a weekly grocery delivery service so the inconvenience of shopping doesn't interrupt your goals and ambitions. Why should something as mundane as food interfere with total world domination? Let your grandmother know I'll be glad to take this on independently. End of discussion."

She strode out of the restaurant, shoulders back, head high, not glancing left or right.

Total world domination? Jeff sat back, mystified. Her reaction revealing two things. She had plenty of backbone, a trait he'd respect more when he wasn't being publically reamed out over nothing.

And someone had done quite a number on her and he was paying the price.

He refused to glance around, not caring to see the surprise or sympathy the other diners might bestow his way.

The waitress appeared looking slightly stressed. "Uh-oh."

"Yeah." He sent her a look of bemusement. "Can I have the appetizers to go, please? Looks like I'm dining on my own tonight."

"Of course. I'll be right back."

Her look of sympathy didn't help his deflated ego.

Smacked down in public.

Ouch.

That hadn't happened in…ever. Which made it almost interesting, despite the embarrassment factor.

Still…she hadn't looked faint or weak or intimidated

as she headed out that door after dressing him down. She'd looked strong. Angry. Invigorated.

Not exactly the emotions he'd been going for, but at least they were normal. Understandable. He glanced at his watch, nodded his thanks to the young waitress and tried to exit with his head high, fairly sure half the dining room was just too polite to stare.

They didn't need to. He felt conspicuous enough as it was.

Chapter Three

She'd call Helen first thing tomorrow, Hannah decided as she kicked off her shoes in her apartment fifteen minutes later. If she had to embrace this task, she'd take the helm and do it alone. The idea of dealing with a power-hungry ladder climber like Jeff Brennan touched too many old chords. Her teaching success. Brian's drive and goal-setting passions. The perfect couple when all was well.

No, being around Jeff nudged too many insecurities to the surface. She was better, she knew that.

But still scared. And scarred. Emotionally, if not physically.

The doorbell rang.

Hannah headed to the front entry, surprised. She stopped as her heart shifted somewhere closer to her gut.

Jeff stood framed in the glass, a to-go sack in his hand, his expression sincere, almost as if he was truly sorry for setting her off when he'd done nothing wrong except evoke bad memories.

Self-recriminations assaulted her from within. She

opened the door, and sighed, letting the door's edge offer support. "I shouldn't have walked out on you like that."

"Why did you?"

Hannah refused to open that box, although lately the cover seemed determined to inch off on its own, a concept that both worried and strengthened her. "You struck a nerve."

"Sorry." He didn't demand an explanation, just stood there looking truly apologetic. He hoisted the bag. "I can't eat these alone. I know you're hungry, and I don't want to start off on the wrong foot."

The gentility behind this surprise move softened her heart. Meg had proclaimed Jeff to be a downright nice guy, invested in the community. At this moment, Hannah couldn't disagree. "Come in."

He smiled, not triumphant or teasing, but amiable and friendly as if he'd teased her enough for one night. A part of her wished she could play those getting-to-know-you games she used to be good at, but she'd lost that skill and had no interest in resurrecting it.

Get it back.

She sensed the inner admonition, felt the internal thrust forward and resisted, her fear of risk standing its ground.

"Do not be afraid for I am with you..."

Isaiah's words tinkered with her heart, her soul.

"I will strengthen you and help you..."

"This is nice, Hannah." Jeff swept the front room an approving look, then raised the bag again. "Here or in the kitchen?"

"The kitchen's fine."

"Lead the way." He followed her, set the bag on the table, then faced her.

"I'm sorry about earlier. I shouldn't have run away."

"Interesting turn of phrase."

She grimaced acceptance. "A trait I'm trying to change." Tonight, with him here, delicious smells wafting from the to-go containers, a part of her longed to embrace change. And food. "I'll get some plates."

"Perfect."

It wasn't perfect, she knew that, but by coming here he'd leveled their playing field. Brian would never have swallowed his pride and come calling to make amends. She withdrew two plates from the cupboard and turned to find Jeff procuring silverware from the drawer alongside the sink.

"These okay?" He held up two knives and two forks. She nodded. "Fine, yes."

"Then let's eat." He drew her chair out, a gentlemanly gesture, then sat in the chair opposite her.

Hannah flushed. "You didn't have to do that."

"What?" He looked genuinely puzzled about her meaning.

"Sit over there. Here would have been fine." She indicated the chair to her right with a nod.

He raised a brow in amusement. "If you'd prefer..."

"Not what I meant and you know it."

The smile deepened. "I'm good here for the moment. The extra space gives me a buffer zone."

This time Hannah smiled. His banter was tinged with a hint of compassion, just enough to help calm the encroaching waves within. Her therapist had told her she'd know when to test the waters, dive back into the game. Hannah hadn't believed her then, and longed to believe her now, but mingled fears constrained her.

She wanted new memories. New chances. New beginnings. Wasn't that why she'd come to Jamison in the first place?

You came here to hide. Nothing more, nothing less.

Then she wanted to stop hiding.

A rustle of wind brushed the leaves against the windows. The sights and sounds of fall leveraged her anxiety, but only if she allowed it to happen.

Determined, she sat forward, met Jeff's gaze and nodded toward the food. "Will you say grace or shall I?"

He reached for her hand and it felt nice to have Jeff grip her fingers as he asked the blessing, his tone thoughtful, the strength of his hand a blessing in itself.

He smiled, released her hand and gave a delighted sigh as he opened the containers. "Since we're main-coursing this stuff, I had them pack two slices of strudel, too. I don't know about you, but I never have room for dessert if I eat a full meal, and Susan Langley's apple strudel is amazing stuff. I wasn't sure if you'd like raisins, so I got the one without them."

"Thank you, Jeff." She looked in his eyes and for the first time in ages didn't question the sincerity and integrity in another person, or the veracity of their smile. She let herself bask in the moment and realized how good she felt to be there.

So far as the east is from the west has He removed our transgressions from us...

She wanted to believe that, the sweet psalm anointing her, but she'd found out the hard way that simple faith was anything but easy.

And yet...

Something in Jeff's look and his manner made her want to take the chance she'd been refusing to contemplate for years.

"You'll know when," Lisa had promised, offering her professional and personal opinion before Hannah moved east. "And when it happens, seize the day. Grasp the moment."

Hannah hadn't believed her; the thought that time eases pain was too simplistic to embrace then, despite the therapist's assurance.

But maybe now...

"Try this." Jeff speared a piece of shrimp, leaned forward and held the fork up, his encouraging look somewhat boyish and endearing.

She shouldn't take the morsel. Sharing food was too personal, but she leaned forward, the moment charged with awareness. She paused at the last moment, rethinking her choice.

It's shrimp. Nothing more.

Hannah knew better, despite her recent holding pattern, like a jet circling O'Hare in a snowstorm. But she took the bite anyway. The combination of cream and spices was melt-in-your-mouth good. "That's amazing."

Jeff grinned. "I thought you'd like it. Try another."

She raised her fork, putting off another tidbit from his. "Feeding myself was one of my basic skills in college."

"Where I expect you did very well," he countered, following her lead, adeptly moving the conversation. "I did my undergrad and masters at MIT." His interested expression invited her to reveal the same about herself.

"I was at Penn."

"Philadelphia."

She nodded. "My father and stepmother live there. That got me the occasional home-cooked meal."

"Which always tastes better when you're away from

home. And you never fully appreciate the things of home until they're gone."

Hannah knew that firsthand. Her parents had split up amicably just shy of her ninth birthday. Both had remarried. Both marriages were still intact, but she'd never had a place to truly feel at home from that moment on. No matter which home she visited, a level of disconnect followed her as she figured out behavior that suited her stepfather and stepmother, a slippery slope for a kid. She'd hedged toward perfect, swallowing emotions, pasting on smiles, unwilling to make a scene, skills that turned against her later on.

As a science lover, she understood the intricacies of adaptation. What she didn't quite get was how to turn it off and move ahead. And if she couldn't do that, then all the adjustments in the world were of little importance because mere existence couldn't equate with life. Ever.

"The quieter you get, the more I delve." Jeff sent her a pointed look, his eyes amused but direct.

Hannah raised her fork in salute. "I only reveal things on a need-to-know basis, Jeff." She leaned forward before hiking one brow. "And right now, all you need to know is that I'm amazingly grateful for this food. Thank you."

"And the company?"

Ah, the company. She smiled, raised a glass of water and dipped her chin. "Even better."

His grin said more than words as he sampled a piece of stuffed mushroom. Was his look of delight meant for her or the delicious food?

She wasn't sure but a big part of her hoped it was for her. That sent her onto dangerous turf, but for the first time in a long time it felt good to laugh and tease with someone.

Real good.

* * *

Success.

Partially, Jeff admitted to himself as he headed back toward Wellsville later that evening. They'd exchanged fund-raising ideas, scoped out the time frame and brainstormed how to bring the library project to the forefront of people's minds. Spring and summer offered many opportunities, but winter in their mountainous foothills narrowed the selections. If they could target the Farmer's Fair at the end of October, the Christmas Salute to Veterans concert in December, then the Maple Festival in March as their big fall/winter projects, they should have a successful launch. Throw in the direct-mail campaign and fund-raising on the Jamison green on Sundays...

Jeff hoped it marked a strong beginning. His mother's ringtone interrupted his thought process. "Hey, Mom. What's up?"

"You know that Matt's back."

Jeff's gut tightened. "Yes."

"I've invited him to supper tomorrow night."

"Perfect. I'm busy."

"Exactly why I scheduled it then," Dana Brennan explained. "I won't have you boys fighting at my table, or have you make him feel like he's to blame for your father's actions."

Perfect. Just perfect. The prodigal comes home after two decades of doing whatever and gets the welcome-to-the-table speech while Jeff got the shaft. "I can lay plenty of his own actions at his door, Mom. He made sure of that twenty years ago."

"He's changed, Jeff. He grew up. And he paid his price."

"Tell that to Katie Bascomb. Every time I see her I remember that night, that weekend. He's lucky she wasn't killed."

"Yes. But Matt wasn't given an easy road to travel."

"And I was?"

Dana sighed. "That's not what I'm saying, honey. I know how rough things were for you and your sister. And maybe I tried too hard or stayed too long with your father, thinking he would keep his promises."

"Which he didn't."

"No. But you do, Jeff. You always have and I'm proud of you for it. I just wish…"

"That I would embrace your rainbow-colored world, forgive Matt and sing 'Kumbaya'? Didn't you just admit to trying too hard with Dad? I might be the one who looks like Dad, but Matt's got his personality down pat and I don't want to see you or Grandma get hurt."

"Or maybe you're protecting yourself."

"From?"

"Memories. Fears. Anything that reminds you of your father."

Jeff sighed. It had been a long day already, up early to get a jump on work Trent Michaels would have done if his foster father wasn't sick, but with Trent gone…

"I'm tired, Mom. While you're entertaining Matt, I'll be kicking off a fund-raising campaign I don't have time for. That seems to be the trend lately—'If no one else can do it, ask Jeff.'"

"You know I'll help. And stop feeling sorry for yourself. You love going 24/7, it's intrinsic to your nature. And Grandma and I both appreciate your time and your devotion to the library project."

Right then, Jeff didn't feel appreciated. He felt put out, put upon and a little put down. "Good night, Mom."

"Night, honey. I love you."

"Yeah." He paused before adding, "I love you, too." He disconnected the call, pulled into his driveway and sat back against the leather seat, considering the current circumstances. His brain refused to work without sleep. He'd catch a few hours, then jump into the specs for a new Homeland Security bid that included the mobile surveillance units his team designed. The forthcoming eight-figure contract would push Walker Electronics another notch up the ladder of military supply companies, and that meant more workers, more production, more jobs and a stronger local economy.

But it stunk big time that his good-for-nothing brother got invited to dinner, because with the library meeting tomorrow, Jeff would be lucky to have time to scarf down a deli sandwich on the run.

Sometimes life just wasn't fair.

Chapter Four

❧

"Jeff? May I see you a minute?"

The sound of Grandma's voice drew Jeff's attention in the library parking lot the next evening. He smiled and crossed the lot, surprised but pleased. "You're here. I thought you were attending that dinner for the Veterans' Outreach tonight."

Helen tipped a thoughtful look his way. "I decided it was more important to see you."

Her words puzzled him. "Except...we saw each other off and on all day."

"But not about personal things."

True enough.

He and Grandma didn't discuss family things on the job. And the only family things of note that had happened recently were Meredith's job loss and Matt's return. Since Meredith was avidly looking for a place to open a salon of her own, Grandma's visit could have only been spurred by one thing: Matt Cavanaugh.

Wonderful.

Jeff angled his head, silent. Waiting.

Grandma took his arm and headed toward the library. "Everyone deserves a second chance, don't they?"

He nodded. Shrugged. "Sure. It's the seventh, eighth and ninth that concern me, Grandma. Did he ask you for money?"

She paused and offered him a sharp, shrewd look. "First, it wouldn't be your concern if he did. I'm perfectly capable of making my own decisions and you need to respect that. Second…" Her frown deepened and she gave him a quick, appraising glance that said she was deliberately holding back. "You'll need to settle this thing in your head if Matt's moving back to town."

"He's not, is he?" Jeff read her expression and swallowed what he wanted to say. "Tell me you're kidding."

"He's looking for work."

"We didn't offer him a job, did we?"

Helen puffed an impatient breath. "What work does Walker Electronics have for a home builder? No, he's quite self-sufficient, but I suspect he'll be around awhile."

"Plenty of cause for concern right there."

Helen's look sharpened. "Matt's not the one I'm worried about."

Her words stung, just like his mother's the night before.

They weren't bothered by Matt's sudden reappearance? Then it was a good thing Jeff had enough concern for both of them. He shrugged off her comment, hid the hurt and angled toward the tiny library, which was in need of refurbishing. "I'm fine. You know that."

"Yes." She paused again, hesitant but straightforward. "And no."

"Yes," he countered firmly. "And this isn't a topic of conversation we can pursue right now." He straightened as a volunteer's car angled into the small lot. Fat rain-drops began to pelt them. "I've got a job to do."

Helen stepped back, nodded and opened her umbrella. "You do. And that's the reverend so I'll just walk over there and say hi before we get started." She gave Jeff's arm a light squeeze before she headed toward Reverend Hannity's car, as if her touch would soothe the prick of her words.

She was worried about *him*.

Not Matt.

The incredulity of that cut deep. Right now he needed to get inside, compare notes and goals with Hannah, dust off his bruised ego and get to work fulfilling Grandpa's dream, a well-set library system throughout Allegany County. And he needed to do it with the polished veneer of a leader, ready to forge ahead, when what he wanted to do was...

His hands clenched. His thoughts jumbled and frustration climbed his spine, settling in somewhere along the back of his neck.

He had no idea, so he buried the angst as best he could and headed through the door, a part of him wishing Grandma had gone to the veterans' dinner as planned.

"Are we ready?"

Hannah gave her heart a chance to come under control at the sound of Jeff's voice. His kindness the previous night was a delightful new memory that had managed to interrupt her sleep. But tonight he sounded gruff, and Hannah was savvy enough to know that any guy could appear nice for an hour or two. Maybe Jeff had exhausted his limit the previous night.

She turned, tamping her reaction. From the dozens of

wet splotches on his clothes, the promised showers had come to fruition. "You're wet."

"Rain does that." He peeled off an expensive-looking trench, then swept the room a glance. "I'd forgotten how small this place is because I use the Wellsville branch."

"And that's exquisite," Hannah acknowledged. The Howe Library was a shining star in the economically roughed-up town.

"We've really got our work cut out for us."

Did he realize his slight derision reflected her work for the past three years? She offered the tiny library a quick perusal. "It may be small, but it does the job."

"If it did, we wouldn't be here, Hannah."

"Ouch."

He huffed a breath, ran a hand across the nape of his neck, then shrugged. "I'm sorry. I didn't mean that the way it sounded, I just…" He stopped, glanced toward the exit and held up his jacket, pretending to head for the door. "Can we have a do-over? Please?"

No, they could not. "Unnecessary." She flashed him a cool, crisp smile. "Folders are on the table."

The door opened. Several committee members streamed in, lamenting the rain in mixed voices.

Jeff turned to greet them, his manner inviting, more like the guy she'd shared food with last night.

Just because he wears a suit, doesn't mean he's cut from Brian's cloth.

But he'd walked in here pretty tense and frustrated, and Hannah didn't do uptight or overwrought. Or driven, for that matter. Not anymore.

Jeff's attention veered left as another voice joined the group. Hannah watched as Helen Walker greeted people much like her grandson, offering a warm smile and a firm handshake. And having met Helen back when she interviewed for the librarian position and the other day, Hannah wasn't blind to the older woman's work-first focus and drive. But Helen's didn't bother her.

Jeff's did.

Because you're constantly comparing him to Brian. Move on. Forge ahead. There is nothing wrong with focus. Got that?

Hannah grasped Helen's hand. "Mrs. Walker, hello."

"Helen, please." Helen's grip offered warm assurance, the perfect handshake. "And as cute as this is, Hannah—" Helen let her gaze wander the children's corner, the faded carousel of computer stations and the narrow rows between labeled bookcases "—it's time we did better. You understand that, right? And how essential your input is to the success of the final product we hope to achieve."

Her words inspired Hannah's grimace. "I'm sorry I balked initially. I shouldn't have done that. Please accept my apology."

Helen beamed. "Accepted and forgotten. We all get a little intimidated now and again, don't we?"

"I suppose so."

Jeff shifted their way and indicated the school-style wall clock. "We should get started."

"Of course." Hannah offered him a polite nod and headed for her seat at the end of the table. He sent her an unreadable look as he took his place opposite her, the long library table creating a distance.

And distance is good, Hannah told herself, settling in. *Real good.*

"I love this concept." A primary school teacher raised Hannah's overview folder up. "Using the solar system to represent how the branches circle the main library in Wellsville is stellar."

A communal groan sounded at her joke. She grinned and turned Hannah's way. "Did you do this?"

"Combined effort," Hannah explained, feeling more like her old self than she'd expected. The realization buoyed her. "The analogy was mine. The graphics were all Jeff's."

"I love it," declared Helen from her seat midway down the table. "And what's more, Jonas would have loved it. The artwork embraces all the sciences, and that is the goal of a well-set library. So, Hannah..." Helen shifted her way. "Can you walk us through possible fund-raising ideas?"

"Of course." Hannah waved toward the far end of the table. "If I can direct your attention beyond Jeff, I've got a PowerPoint presentation of ideas, and then we can see how the committee feels about them individually."

"Excellent." Helen's warm expression went from one end of the table to the other, her enthusiasm obvious. "Financial constraints meant we had to wait much longer than I wanted to get this drive started, and I've felt guilty about it. And guilt isn't one bit fun."

It wasn't. Hannah knew that personally. With all Helen Walker had to do, the idea that one out-of-the-way, dot-on-the-map library meant something... That showed a whole lot of character. And Hannah respected good character.

"Jenny, adding a booth to next summer's Balloon Rally would be wonderful," Jeff assured the town council representative toward the end of the meeting. "And I don't think it matters that we'll be beyond our projected fund-raising date. Added funds secure future purchases, and libraries can always use help in that regard. Well, then…" Jeff scanned his notes, flipped a few pages and sat back, satisfied. "We did well."

"Very well," Hannah added, looking calmer now that the meeting had ended and nothing had self-destructed. Right until she looked at him, then the cool, flat facade fell into place. But then again he hadn't exactly been Mr. Friendly when he'd walked in tonight.

He stood, made small talk, then walked people to the door, feeling Hannah's eyes watching. Assessing. Probably figuring he was a total fake, pretending interest he didn't feel. On the plus side, the rain had stopped.

"Hannah, if you need anything at all, please call me." Helen gripped the younger woman's hands in hers. She leaned in just enough to show the sincerity behind her words. "Please."

"I will." Hannah's smile said Helen's authenticity bested her grandson's.

Helen headed for the door and nodded to Jeff. "I'll see you in the morning."

"I'll bring coffee," he promised, then turned back to Hannah, needing to close the evening on a positive note between them. Pinpoints of guilt prickled him for his earlier insensitivity.

He straightened his notes and his spine, slid his portfolio into his laptop bag and shouldered it before facing her. "I apologize if I was too blunt earlier. I had things on my mind, but I shouldn't have taken them out on you. Or this project. It was rude." He was ready to go home and collapse; the successive long days were wearing on him. "Thanks for offering to type up the notes and meeting minutes. If you email them to me once you've got them ready, I'll go over them with Grandma."

"Or I can 'cc' her a copy and spare you the time," Hannah suggested.

"She'll want to talk it out," Jeff told her. "She's very hands-on, as you can see."

"Then I'll forward them and you can proceed from there."

She kept her tone cool. Crisp. Concise.

Just what he wanted, right?

Except spending time with her last evening had put him in mind of other things. But those thoughts were best buried.

She'd readopted her business manner and kept her distance, sparing him from looking into those bright blue eyes. The dimmer lights by the library door kept him from seeing the sprinkle of freckles, or noting the long lashes, their shadow a curve against her tanned cheek. Obviously she hadn't read all the current warnings about skin and sunscreen, because her softly bronzed face and arms said she wasn't afraid to be in the sun.

He gave a quick wave as he went through the door, deciding not to linger with uncomfortable goodbyes.

She'd email him, he'd email her, they'd push forward. Perfect.

But it felt much less than that.

Dismissed.

Hannah watched him go and was tempted to throw something. Standing in a room full of books, her choices were numerous. But she couldn't throw books. She loved books. Loved learning. Knowledge. Sharing that love with others, children and young adults.

At least she *had* loved it until circumstances blind-sided her, stealing her livelihood, her heart and a share of her soul. Melancholy threatened, but she pushed it aside, determined to stay in the here and now.

She didn't like being shrugged off by the electronics wizard as if she were some ordinary business partner.

Which she was.

Or some underling who depended on him for her live-lihood.

Which she did. Kind of. Since his grandmother was head of the library council and approved her hiring three years back.

But the fact that he made her feel like that was ag-gravating. Exasperating. She shut off the lights of the tiny house, set the lock and headed for her car. Usually she walked from her apartment to the Jamison Farm-ers Free Library, but she'd known she'd be late tonight, probably tired, and rain was in the forecast, so she'd driven over. She'd get home, sit down, hammer out these notes, email them to Jeff and be done with things until the various committee members got back to her with their plans. Then she'd compile them into a semblance of order, send them on to Jeff and move to step two for next week's meeting.

Easy.

She fumbled in her pocket for her set of keys and stopped, chagrined.

Not there.

She tried again, then groped for a nonexistent purse.

Nope, she'd left that home on purpose, wanting to be unencumbered.

No keys.

Either she left them inside…

Or she'd locked them in the car.

She went over to the car, pressed her nose to the glass and tried to scan the interior.

No luck. Darkness had fallen hours ago, the fall equinox behind them. The one lone dusk-to-dawn light was set near the library entrance, leaving this corner of the gravel lot in complete darkness.

Split. Splat. Split. Splat.

Fat raindrops began to pelt her head, her face, her arms. And of course she hadn't brought anything along since she was driving back and forth. No sweater. No hoodie. No sweatshirt.

Grumbling, she tucked the important papers under her shirt to protect them, and started jogging for home, the thin manila edges cutting into soft skin with every running step.

She had a spare key at home, but that thought didn't make her any drier, warmer or smarter at the moment. By the time she got home, fumbled her hidden key into the apartment lock and closed the door behind her, she was cold, soaked and fairly miserable, a combination that brought back too many memories.

Shoving aside mental images that had owned her for too long, she headed to the shower and let warm water ease the chill and the frustrations.

The images she left entirely up to God.

Chapter Five

Jeff spotted Hannah as he cruised down McCallister Street the next afternoon; the pretty blond hair was a giveaway.

He pulled over, opened his window and called her name.

She turned, surprise lighting her face. The way his gut clenched on seeing her told him that instead of waning, the appeal was growing. Of course, the fact that he was showing up out of the blue on his lunch hour to thank her for the copious notes she'd sent him might have something to do with that.

Polite, he told himself.

Nice try, his conscience replied.

He jumped out of the car, rounded the hood and opened the passenger door for her. "Come on, I'll give you a ride. It's cooking out here today."

She looked trapped but grateful. The midday sun was blazing hot, a late September anomaly. "Thanks."

"You always walk?" he asked as he climbed in the driver's side a moment later.

"Umm. No."

He frowned, then nodded. "That's right, I saw your car last night."

"How did you know it was my car?" She tilted her head, her freckles darker in the bright light of the noon sun.

"Because it was the only vehicle there when I left last night?" He shot her a grin, angled down Whitmore and pulled into the library lot along the curve heading toward Route 19. "Sitting right where it's sitting now. Car trouble?" he asked, brows bent, his look encompassing the car parked exactly where it had been fourteen hours before.

She sighed and made a face. "I locked my keys in it."

"Last night?"

"Yes."

"So you walked home? At ten o'clock?" He didn't try to temper the concern edging his voice.

She turned more fully, surprised by his reaction. "My options were limited. Because it was ten o'clock."

"You could have called me." The suggestion made her sit back farther, a touch of awareness brightening her features. But right now he was too busy thinking about what could happen to a woman alone on country roads at that hour. "I was minutes from here. I could have swung back, picked you up and got you home safely."

"Which was the outcome as you can see from my unscathed body." She waved a hand toward herself. "And since you were decidedly cool last night, why on earth would I have called you for help?"

"Because..." He paused. "Because I want you safe," he went on, meeting her gaze, letting his eyes say more than his words. "It was pouring rain before I got three blocks away. You had to be soaked."

"Drenched." She sighed, her face a mix of resignation with a touch of sorrow.

Why sorrow?

He had no idea, but a part of him longed to wipe it away, replace the look of anxiety with joy and youthful abandon. Although at thirty-five, youthful abandon had escaped him about twelve years ago, when his father's ignominious death marked the end of a dark era.

But something about being around Hannah made him want to embrace that lost joy. That family camaraderie. Since that was impossible, he'd try to figure out what was going on here. Looking at her, it seemed fairly obvious, but was that emotion or hormones?

Both.

"So you walked home in the pouring rain, then sat down and typed up copious notes for my benefit?"

"I like to stay on top of things." She shrugged as if it was no big deal.

Jeff had been in business long enough to know a good work ethic was key to success. Hannah's drive and determination belied her fragmented lifestyle. She obviously embraced her privacy, a concept he respected. He climbed out of the car and circled the hood, meeting her as she emerged. "Thank you, Hannah."

She glanced up, those blue eyes meeting his, a flash of awareness in her manner. She looked flustered again, only it wasn't the insecure agitation he'd seen before. This implicit nervousness stemmed from him, their proximity, the look he offered that probably said too much.

He leaned down, holding her attention, deciding direct and to-the-point worked best most of the time. "Spare me the lecture of how this could never work, we have nothing in common, we barely get along and you're not at a point in your life to consider a relationship with a stuffed shirt like me."

A tiny smile softened the awareness. "Thanks for saving me the trouble of the summation."

"Except..." He moved closer, crowding her space, watching her pretend he wasn't encroaching on her emotions, her equanimity. "I want you to promise me something."

"What?"

Those eyes, that summer-sky blue, with tiny points of ivory offering inner light. "If you ever have car trouble, locked keys, a breakdown, a flat tire... Call me. Okay?"

She raised her cell phone and waggled it, then headed for the library door. "A little tricky since I don't carry your number around."

He snagged the phone, ignored her protest and proceeded to program his number into the speed dial.

He grinned and handed her phone back once she'd unlocked the library door. "I actually stopped by today with a purpose in mind."

"Because men like you always have a purpose."

"Since when did that become a bad thing?"

"Not bad, predictable. What was this purpose that dragged you out of your office and brought you here in person when you have a perfectly good phone at your disposal?"

He maintained a strong, sincere expression. "To thank you for the notes. They're perfect and I realized from the time stamp that you stayed up late to finish them. And now I know that it was after you got soaked to the skin."

"No problem."

"I'm grateful, Hannah." He reached out as the door swung open and laid a gentle hand on her left shoulder.

The feel of her sun-kissed skin was warm and smooth, a summer touch in the grip of fall.

Her look said she wasn't immune to the buzz and that almost made him take that last step forward, but they both knew that wasn't a good idea. The look she gave him, yearning mixed with caution, made him go slow, which was for the best, right?

A car pulled in behind his. A woman tooted the horn in welcome, and a young boy waved from the front seat, his face a blend of excitement and eagerness.

Hannah smiled, the anxiety erased, wiped out by the smile of a child. A part of Jeff's heart melted on the spot. He released her arm, stepped back and nodded toward the car. "One of your young suitors?"

Her grin delighted him. "This is Jacob. We're working together on some really cool projects and he had a half day of school today so we're meeting earlier than usual."

One of her tutoring duties, Jeff realized. The boy dashed up the steps, ignored Jeff completely and launched a hug at Hannah. "I got them all right except the one about the gasoline."

She laughed and squatted to his level. "I saw that. Two hundreds and a ninety average out to ninety-six." She watched as he absorbed what she was saying. When he nodded agreement, she ruffled his hair. "That's an A, kid. Pretty solid."

"An A." He turned and sent his mother a smile that she matched. "I got an A, Mom."

"I'm so proud of you, Jake." She stooped, planted a kiss to his hair, then shooed him inside before facing Hannah. "He has never been this excited about learning. Not ever. His teachers are ecstatic and his grades are wonderful. I can't begin to thank you enough, Hannah."

Hannah's smile said she expected no thanks. "That A says it all. Head on in, Callie. I'll be right there."

"All right." The mother smiled and nodded to Jeff, then stuck out her hand. "I'm Callie Burdick and that whirlwind was my son, Jake."

Jeff shook her hand, nodded appreciation toward the boy and grinned. "Jeff Brennan. Hannah and I are co-chairing the library fund-raising for this branch. He's an excited whirlwind, for sure. I was just thinking that if my third grade teacher looked like Hannah, I might have paid more attention myself."

Callie laughed.

Hannah blushed, then scowled. "Don't you have a job to get to?"

"I do."

"Then might I suggest—"

"I'm gone." He switched his attention to the other woman. "A pleasure, Callie."

Callie nodded and swept them a look. "May I help? On the project, that is?"

"Of course." Hannah grinned, surprised but pleased. "We'd love it, Cal. Do you have time?"

"More than I'd like right now, and working on this would be a good distraction," the other woman admitted. "With Dad's construction business taken over by the bank, there's literally nothing to do right now except pray the economy improves and Dad can get back on his feet. Since I crewed for him and worked in his office, we're taking a double hit. Waitressing doesn't come close to covering the bottom line, so a well-intentioned distraction would be heaven-sent."

"We'd love your help." Jeff made a mental note to see if he could track down her father's business based on her name. The nice thing about small communities was the way they looked out for each other whenever possible. He turned back toward Hannah. "Can I call you later?"

"I'm swamped."

Callie flashed them an understanding smile before she headed inside.

Jeff understood *swamped*. "Aren't we all?"

"I'm here until four, then at the candy store until eight," Hannah explained. "And I have every reason to expect to be tired by then."

Remembering the time on her emailed notes, he nodded. "All right. Tomorrow?"

"No can do. I've got library hours in the morning, then I'm overseeing the mock-up of a weekend camper science project at Dunnymeade's Campgrounds."

"You work there, too?"

She glanced inside, her look saying she didn't want to keep Jacob and his mother waiting. "They needed someone to help lay out their minicamp so I volunteered."

"You like science?"

Her expression told Jeff he was on shaky ground. "Yes."

He nodded as if he hadn't noticed. "Me, too. Hence the degree. Maybe we can experiment sometime? Together?" He grinned, lightening the moment, enjoying the bemused smile she shot him.

"My experimental days are over."

"We'll have to see about that." He smiled, winked and headed for his car while he scolded himself silently for more reasons than he could count. "I'll catch up with you soon."

"We have a meeting scheduled next week." Hannah tapped a nonexistent watch. "Soon enough."

Jeff laughed at her from across the gravel. "Should we make it a contest? See who caves first?"

"I never lose, Mr. Brennan."

"Neither do I, Miss Moore." He grinned, opened his door and met her gaze. "You're on. The first one to call or contact the other for reasons other than the library fund project buys dinner."

"You'd make me pay for dinner? On my salary?"

"To make a point, yes. We'll consider it valuable education."

"Since it won't happen we'll consider it moot. Goodbye."

She went into the library without a backward glance, at least not one he could see. But it wouldn't surprise him if she tipped a blind, watching him. Grinning.

And yeah, he knew there wasn't time to pursue this. Not now. *But if not now, then when? When will you let yourself embrace life?*

Reverend Hannity had done a series of sermons making that very point this fall. Thoughtful and thought provoking, his gentle words had tweaked Jeff's conscience. The work demands that used to nibble his free time now consumed it.

Was his dedication to work extreme?

The fact that he didn't want to answer that question said plenty. Sure, he'd grown up in the shadow of his father's misdeeds, and their physical resemblance was so strong that Jeff felt required to establish degrees of separation. He accomplished that by being honest, faithful and self-reliant, qualities his father could have embraced.

But chose not to.

Hannah was right. He should squelch this attraction and cite bad timing as the reason. He needed to cover for Trent while putting the company's best foot forward on current bids.

Plus, the girl wasn't interested. Correct that, she *was* interested, but didn't want to be and Jeff sensed that reluctance. He didn't need distractions or aggravations. Neither did she. And since they'd thrown down a challenge to see who'd cave first, maybe it was for the best if neither caved.

It wouldn't be easy to let things slide. And the thought of her walking home, even though it was only several blocks away…the image of her alone, on the streets, in the rain, the dark of night…

That brought out his protective instincts. But she'd made it this far without his help, his protection. The fact that he wanted, no, *longed* to help and protect needled him.

But he'd let it go. They both would. He knew she wouldn't call. If self-preservation was a lock, Hannah Moore turned the key long ago.

Sometimes God offered a distinct picture of right and wrong, and sometimes He let you figure it out for yourself. This time, Jeff was pretty sure of the message he'd been getting from Hannah.

Put it on hold, as much as it scorched his take-charge mind-set.

And with work tugging him in different directions, it might not scorch as much as he'd have thought.

Chapter Six

Hannah moved to the candy store counter and smiled at the teenage boy who walked in with his mother on Monday afternoon. He didn't return the smile, just gave a semi-embarrassed "what am I doing here" half shrug.

Hannah understood the adolescent gesture. When the woman moved off to examine preboxed candy, a note of desperation darkened the boy's eyes, a quick flash, as if weighing escape routes and finding them lacking.

A cold shudder coursed through Hannah; an icy prickling climbed her back, clawing her gut.

She stood on her side of the counter, wanting to move, wanting to help, frozen in the press of memories, the boy's stark look familiar.

The boy read her expression and jerked his features into a quick semblance of normalcy. Then he ducked his chin.

He's a kid, Hannah reminded herself as she stepped forward. *They're all a little whacked-out at this age. Puberty does weird things to kids' heads. You know that, Hannah. Get a grip.*

"May I help you?"

He shrugged again, glanced around, then settled a look on his mother. "I'm just waiting for her."

His detached tone told Hannah he wasn't here by choice. She nodded and raised a tray of freshly done candies. "Well, I've got a sampling here of some new twists on old favorites. If you'd like to try a couple for me, I'd value your opinion, sir."

Mixed emotions crossed his face, a hint of hope and pleasure marked with surprise. "Like, free?"

Hannah's laugh drew the woman's attention. "Absolutely free. The only way we find out what works for people is a good old-fashioned taste test, so you're my current guinea pig."

He smiled as he reached forward. Her banter had eased the hopeless expression she thought she'd seen. "I'll try this and this."

"Perfect." She nodded his way, then offered the tray to the woman. "How about you? Can you be tempted as easily as your son?"

"Stepson," the woman corrected too quickly.

Hannah felt the swift bite that took the wind out of the young man's sails. She wanted to give the woman a piece of her mind, but that would only make matters worse. The boy kept his gaze trained on the candy, but Hannah could read the set of his shoulders that said he couldn't wait to be old enough to be out of his current situation.

Holding the plate out, Hannah wrestled the Holy Spirit's attention with an SOS. *Cover him, Lord, soften him, shelter him, guide him, give him Your grace, Your courage, Your temperance, Your strength. Take this boy by the hand and the heart and carry him through whatever darkens his path.*

The boy shrugged and sent a sheepish look Hannah's

way as he headed for the door. "I'll tell you which ones I like next time I come in."

Hannah nodded with appreciation. "Thank you…?" She ended the sentence on an up note, wanting his name.

He stepped outside and the door swung quietly shut behind him.

The woman sighed, tired, bored, rude. Hannah longed to smack her, but reminded herself she needed to cut the woman some slack, although right now that was the last thing she wanted to do.

"My husband tolerates far too much. If it were up to me he'd be doing more manual labor to teach him a lesson or two."

Hannah fought off a sharp retort, knowing it wasn't her place. Her heart went out to the boy. "Oh, he seems all right. Fairly normal for a young teen. What's his name?"

"Dominic."

"Nice. Strong."

"It's his father's name, handed down like some sort of crown. Ridiculous, really. Can you pack me a pound of mixed caramels, too?" she asked, pointing down the display case. "I'm hosting a dinner tomorrow night and chewy caramels might quiet some of the more annoying wives."

Hannah bit back words and nodded, filling the box quietly, not daring to speak.

The woman made a show of surprise at the final tally, handed over a debit card with obvious reluctance, then left the store in her designer shoes, her attitude a cartoon depiction of the fairy-tale stepmother.

Except this was real life and Dominic was on the receiving end of that harsh attitude.

Help him, God. Guide him. Soften the days, gentle his nights. Don't leave him alone, please.

Another customer walked in, followed by another. The late September day highlighted autumn's dance of color, summer's verdant green becoming fall's rainbowed majesty.

Hannah used to welcome fall, embracing the seasonal changes, the excitement of a new school year, ripe with opportunity. New classes, different students, fresh opportunities. Now she confronted the capricious season, willing herself through the beauty by way of prayer and self-therapy methods her psychologist taught her.

Day by day.

Seeing this boy's sorrow and angst, hearing the disdain in the stepmother's voice and seeing the kaleidoscope of color in the trees beyond the east-facing stores on Main Street drummed up a lot of memories.

But she disengaged herself from each twinge, taking care of customers and praying for strength, wishing for equilibrium, wanting more than anything else to move the clock back five years, to make a difference where it mattered most.

But that would never happen so she'd pretend to be brave and bold outside while her cowardly soul huddled within, wishing she'd done more, knowing she hadn't.

And she couldn't forgive herself for that.

Hannah felt the air change the minute Jeff walked through the door Thursday night. She had to squelch twinges of anticipation. Luckily, two other committee members walked in with him.

Perfect. Their presence precluded personal talk. She stepped forward and perked a smile that encompassed all three. "Good evening. I've got things set up at the round table tonight."

Jeff took her cue and stayed matter-of-fact. "And Grandma sent cookies from the Colonial Cookie store. Cookies you may have helped make."

Hannah kept her smile easy and her voice neutral. "I do the candy store more often now, so probably not. Although I've been known to warm up the cookie ovens at the bakeshop when Megan's shorthanded."

"Altruistic."

"More like thrifty," she told him. "Paying the bills. Hey, Callie, glad you could make it." Hannah shifted her attention to Jacob's mother as she hurried in, her hassled expression saying there weren't quite enough hours in a day.

"Glad to help, although I'll miss this place when it's all dolled up and fancy," Callie told her, grinning. She gave the small, cramped library a fond look. "This was the Farmers Free Library before I was born."

"And before I was born," added an older woman who followed Callie through the door, a newcomer to the committee. "And since I remember your mama pushing you in a stroller, Callie Marek, my memory stretches longer. But not with the same level of accuracy as you young folks."

Jeff stuck out a hand to the older woman. "I beg to differ, Miss Dinsmore. Your wealth of knowledge puts us youngsters to shame. How are you?"

She waved off his hand with a shrug of impatience. "I'm not being unfriendly, Jeffrey, but I've had a cold hanging on for the better part of a month and while common sense would say I'm not contagious, it also warns me not to be careless with others, so I won't shake your hand tonight."

"Is this the same cold you had in August?" he asked, his left brow shifting up.

"Or another one piggybacking the first. In any case, catching colds when you're a teacher isn't a bit unusual."

"But not getting better is," warned Jeff.

His concerned manner intrigued Hannah. Was this a family friend? A relative?

"Hannah, this is Miss Dinsmore, Wellsville's beloved high school science teacher." Jeff offered the introduction easily, his affectionate tone respectful but friendly. "There are few people here who haven't benefitted from her wisdom and patience during adolescence."

Science teacher?

A cool chill crept up Hannah's spine. "Nice to meet you."

The other woman met Hannah's gaze with a pointed look of consideration before she softened her expression. "And you. I've heard a lot about you, my dear."

Jeff's look sharpened, but one of the other committee members drew his attention, interrupting the moment.

She knows.

Hannah met Miss Dinsmore's eyes and nodded, not willing to pursue the feeling but fairly sure she had no secrets from the wizened woman facing her. "Do you teach all levels?"

"Yes and no." Miss Dinsmore withdrew a chair and settled into it, a glimmer of discomfort darkening her features before she took a deep breath, let it out slowly and smiled. "I have over the years. Right now I'm doing bio and chem."

Hannah slid into the seat alongside her, reluctantly drawn. "I love biology."

"I know." Miss Dinsmore looked at her and broke her

no-touch, I've-got-a-cold rule. She laid her hand atop Hannah's, commiserative. "You're quite gifted."

A sigh enveloped Hannah from within, a silent inner wince that didn't seem quite so harsh in Miss Dinsmore's presence. "Thank you. It looks like we're ready to get started." She nodded toward the opposite side of the table where Jeff stood waiting, a folder in his hands, his quick glance taking in the scene with Miss Dinsmore but too far away to hear their conversation.

Just as well.

Miss Dinsmore nodded, and turned her attention toward Jeff. Callie slipped in next to Hannah, her bright smile pushing harsh memories aside. Hannah was pleased that the old thoughts shoved off with barely a whimper, a good step forward.

Progress.

She thanked God for baby steps of strength while Reverend Hannity offered a prayerful request for wisdom and cooperation; his warm words advised open minds and prayed for open wallets to help augment the cramped library surrounding them.

And when Jeff's eyes sought hers at the mention of open minds and forward progress, his expression sent her heart into a crazy spiral of what-ifs and could-bes. Hints of breaking out and busting loose tugged at her self-containment.

And it felt good.

"So." Jeff stood with his back to the exit, arms folded, legs braced, facing Hannah and the now-empty room, seizing the opportunity to talk to her alone. "The meeting went well."

"Quite." Hannah finished gathering her notes, slipped

them into her shoulder bag and jangled her keys. "And we finished early, which is always a plus."

"Except we're not quite finished."

She stopped halfway across the room, as if the short space marked neutral territory. "You had something to add?"

"You didn't call."

His words sparked a bemused smile. "Neither did you."

"Why?" He didn't move forward but he didn't step back either, his stance was solid, determined to find answers.

Hannah shrugged. "We've got jobs to do. There's no reason to let this—" she waved a hand from him to herself and back "—interfere."

"What is *this*?" He mimicked her hand gesture, his expression questioning.

Her gaze tightened. Her shoulders straightened. His question bothered her, but why? He had no idea.

He took the first step forward, figuring she was probably too stubborn to make the first move. He wasn't sure if that was good or bad, but it *was* intriguing. He halved the space between them in two quick strides. "Well?"

"We've got jobs to do."

"You mentioned that." He took another half step forward. "And I can't deny that work's been pretty demanding on my end, with no letup in sight. Why didn't you call?"

"Because I'm hideously old-fashioned and think the man should call?"

"Nice try. What's the real reason?"

She studied him, something in her expression saying mixed feelings had become the norm rather than the exception.

That realization made him want to change things up, make her happy. Keep her happy. Which was silly because he barely knew her, and yet... Seeing her talk with his grandmother. With Miss Dinsmore. The way Callie Burdick opened up to her. All of this pointed to how special she was, while she tucked herself out of the way, skirting the edge of life.

"I'm not a big fan of heartbreak, Jeff."

A clue. He nodded. "Me either. But that's a big jump from a nice dinner, a few evenings together—"

She raised a hand to stop him and went all serious and cute. "Which seems presumptuous, I'm sure... Or just plain silly."

He shook his head. "It's not either. It's simple caution. But how do we know where this—" he did her hand gesture again, teasing her "—might lead if we don't talk." He moved forward. "Date." Another step put him within a hairbreadth of her, those blue eyes inviting him to drown in the depths.

"I don't date."

"Perfect time to change that." He softened his voice to a whispered invitation, then grasped her left shoulder with his right hand. "We have nothing to lose, Hannah."

She stepped back, eyed him, ran a hand through her hair and shook her head. "I have a lot to lose, Jeff. I don't take risks. I don't buy raffle tickets, I don't play the lottery no matter how much of the money goes to education. I play it safe and sound now. It's the best I can do."

"Now." He held his ground. Another piece to the puzzle. "Which means you used to take chances. What made you stop?"

She didn't cringe, wince or do any of the moves typical of a wounded animal, yet he instinctively felt the moves unseen. She settled a look of pained strength on him, an expression that said she'd examined her options and chose the only one available.

And it wasn't him.

"Life changes people, Jeff."

No disagreement there. Life had certainly done a number on him, but he'd survived. "Doesn't free will give us the power of choice?"

She contemplated his words, glanced away, grimaced, then nodded. "Within reason. But sometimes those choices are beyond our realm."

"Only if we let them be." He closed the space she'd created with her small step back. "God puts that road before us, broken or clear, and then we make the choice of how to maneuver the path. Hurdle the potholes. Climb the hills."

"Some hilltops are inaccessible."

He shook his head, decided he'd said enough and gave her shoulder one last gentle grasp. "With the right shoes and training, all hills are attainable. How about dinner Saturday night?"

"I just said—"

"I'm ignoring your lame protests in favor of my desire to get to know you better. And you owe me dinner."

She straightened, shrugging his hand away, a half smile brightening her features. "I don't. I didn't call."

"You walked out on our first dinner together, meaning you still owe me a date."

"It wasn't a date so your reasoning is illogical."

"Really?" He grasped his laptop bag and winked. "My game, my rules. I say it was and we need a do-over."

"And if I disagree?"

"I'll pester you until you cave. You could—" he leaned her way as they headed for the door, smiling inwardly as she tried to hide the look of enjoyment his teasing inspired "—save us a whole lot of trouble and go out with me on Saturday. It's the weekend, we both have to eat, it's a perfect excuse to wind down before Sunday." He waited as she locked the door, tested the handle, nodded satisfaction and turned smack into his chest. "And we could talk." He dropped his gaze to her cheeks, her mouth, then raised his free hand to graze her chin ever so lightly. "Get to know each other."

"But—"

"Please?"

The little-boy *please* did it. She caved, her eyes searching his, saying more than she wanted them to, he was quite sure of that. "Okay."

He smiled, the whispered response exactly what he'd been hoping for. The fact that he had no idea why he needed to chase those shadows from her eyes wasn't lost on him.

Why was he drawn to a woman with issues?

Because she needed him. But didn't want to need him. And that raised the stakes.

Watching Hannah ease her aging car down the road, the memory of their banter fresh in his mind, he realized that a big part of her wasn't playing games, and that sobering thought meant he better make sure he was on solid ground himself. That was easier said than done.

He called in an order for sandwiches from the Beef Haus. By the time he pulled up to the curb, his growling stomach reminded him lunch had been a long time ago. A waitress smiled his way, grabbed a to-go sack and handed it to him. "Two beef on wecks with extra horse-radish on the side and an order of fries, right?"

"Exactly," Jeff told her. He pulled money from his wallet and handed it over. "Here you go, and keep the change. I was hoping I'd catch you guys before you closed up."

"And you did." She smiled at him, then shifted her attention to someone behind him. "You're all set, Matt?"

"Yes. Thank you. I left money on the table, Gail."

She swept Jeff a quick look, then nodded, understanding. "I'll take care of it. Thanks for coming in."

"No problem. Great food. Brought back a lot of memories. Good night." He turned to acknowledge his half brother, his gaze steady. "Jeff."

"Matt."

Matt noted Jeff's bag with a glance. "Seems eating late is a family habit."

Jeff didn't want to share any habits with Matt Cavanaugh, but seeing Matt here, unexpectedly, resurrected his mother's words from last week. Moving on sounded great in theory. In reality, with Matt standing toe-to-toe with him?

Much harder.

Matt headed out the door. Jeff followed more slowly, giving Matt time to get to his truck and pull away, not wanting a confrontation this late at night. Maybe not wanting one at all. He climbed into his car, set the bag down and eyed the town.

This was home. His home. His place.

And his, an inner voice scolded.

Was his, Jeff corrected. And that was a long time ago. He gave up the right to call this home by breaking laws. Going to jail. Being a jerk.

A lot of kids are jerks, his conscience persisted. *Luckily, most of them grow out of it.*

Had Matt?

Jeff sighed. Christ had come to forgive man's sin by offering Himself in sacrifice. Embracing the cross. Out of grievous wrong had come great good, so why couldn't he look at Matt Cavanaugh without cringing?

Help me, Father. You've given me strength and focus, You delivered me from rough situations with my father, You anointed me with intelligence to create amazing things. Why can't I do this little thing, to forgive my brother?

Cool silence answered his prayer. The chill of October pushed thermometers down. He stared into the quiet night, sighed again and put his car into gear, not nearly as hungry as he'd been ten minutes ago.

Chapter Seven

"Jeff, is that you?" Delight brightened Dana Brennan's features as Jeff walked into his mother's house midday Saturday. "I was just telling Meredith I needed to see you and here you are."

He eyed the clock and sent her a not-so-pretend look of disbelief. "Since I said I was coming by, it's really not a big surprise, right?"

"You said you *needed* to stop by, not that you *would*, and I've been your mother long enough to know that work sometimes interferes."

He couldn't argue with that. He grabbed a handful of homemade pizzelles and followed her into the kitchen. "Where's the brat?"

"Seriously, Jeff? I'm thirty-two. I stopped being a brat last year." Meredith grinned at him from her spot at the island counter, a bowl of fresh green beans making her look way more domestic than she'd ever thought of being, but that was before she'd been dumped as the manager of an exclusive spa when the owner's daughter took over. Sometimes nepotism wasn't a good thing. In Meredith's case, it brought her home with little money in the bank, no furniture because she sold it rather than move it, and great hair. Jeff matched her grin, then scrutinized the bowl. "You're helping Mom cook?"

"She's trimming the beans so we can grill them," Dana explained. She settled a fond look on Meredith, obviously pleased to have her home. "I'm going to brush them with garlic oil and a dusting of salt and fresh-ground pepper. Wonderful stuff."

"It sounds good," he admitted, snatching a pair of beans to go along with the pizzelles. "I've never met a green bean I didn't like. So why are you playing kitchen domestic when you said you'd be hunting up possible sites for a beauty shop?"

"A salon, Jeffie, not a beauty shop. How fifties can you get?" She sent him a look of dismay, then shrugged. "I was examining possibilities with Mary Kay this morning, but we didn't find anything that fit my vision."

"How about your pocketbook?"

She made a face. "Since it's empty, Grandma's start-up loan and a mortgage will be my launchpad. I knew times were fundamentally tight, but I didn't realize that funds for small-business loans had dried like the Sahara."

"Grandma's okay with up-front money?"

Meredith trimmed the ends off the next pair of beans and eyed him, puzzled. "You work with her. She didn't tell you?"

Jeff shook his head. "We don't discuss personal stuff. If it doesn't involve Walker Electronics, I don't ask and she doesn't offer. We don't mix personal and business."

"Seriously?" Meredith smiled at him and Jeff realized it was the first smile that had reached her eyes since she'd come home weeks before. "That's classy of you."

He waved that off. "Just good sense, Mere. Why muddy water we've worked so hard to clear?"

Her smile faded and Jeff backtracked. "Wait, I didn't mean it that way, like your business would muck things up. It just seems smarter to keep things separate."

His mother leaned in. "Stop talking. You're only making it worse."

"I see that. Silence is my new middle name."

"Ha."

"So what brings you by?" Dana gave him a look as she chopped peppers with finesse. "Nothing serious, I hope?"

"You know I'm doing the library fund-raising for the Jamison branch?"

Dana nodded. "Of course. I'm planning on being a two-time Austen sponsor."

"Say what?" Jeff exchanged puzzled looks with Meredith.

"You've established levels for donations, right?" Dana looked up, her expression saying her intent should be obvious.

"Yes. Lee, Twain, Alcott, Cooper, Austen, Fitzgerald."

Dana nodded as if her reasoning made perfect sense. "I wouldn't read Fitzgerald if you paid me, but I love Austen, so I'm signing on to be an Austen contributor twice. Once in my name, and once in honor of you and your sister. That way it's the same money and none of the negativity. Have you ever read an Austen book?"

Jeff didn't fake his shudder. "Not on your life."

"Read one and you'll understand." She waved a knife at him that looked more like a meat cleaver than a veggie dicer.

"Why so much for Jamison?" Jeff settled into the chair

opposite her while he munched a bean. "You didn't give that much to the Wellsville branch."

"Two reasons." Eyes down, she chopped until a small mountain of green pepper stood ready to layer over a bowl of slightly warm Yukon gold potatoes. "Wellsville had plenty of donors because it draws from a bigger population and I knew they'd do fine once the idea took hold."

She was right. The Wellsville library was now refurbished, its terraced patio seating a work of art.

"Second, most of my friends are from Jamison. And your dad and I were married there. I've got a lot of old memories in that little town."

Jeff knew they'd been married there. He'd assumed it was because his mother had been in the family way and they wanted to keep it quiet so they'd opted away from the beautiful cathedral-like church in Wellsville. He'd always wondered what would have happened if she hadn't gotten pregnant. It wasn't like he felt responsible for the whole mess, but if he hadn't been conceived, what would her life have been like? Would she have married his dad anyway, following a road of broken dreams and empty promises?

Knowing his mother's gentle heart, he recognized the likelihood; her hopeful nature was optimistic to a fault. And while Jeff had no memories of his father's early engineering brilliance, some of Neal's initial concepts had been the starting ground for later projects, so there was no faulting his mind. His weakness for drugs, gambling and women? A whole different scenario.

"We're planning a Harvest Dinner to wrap up October at the Farmer's Fair and I was hoping you would chair the food end of it. Nobody puts together a fund-raising dinner to rival you, Mom."

Dana smiled with delight. "I'd be glad to. And if it's successful, maybe your committee could stagger a few more throughout the year. Something like that in January or February makes a great transition into spring."

Just the idea and enthusiasm Jeff was hoping for. He grinned and looped an arm around her. "I'll talk to the committee. Thanks, Mom."

"You're welcome." She liberally ground fresh pepper until dark specks dotted the vegetables below, the enticing smell jump-starting Jeff's appetite.

"I plan on helping with the later part of your campaign." Meredith interrupted his thoughts as she stood, rolled her shoulders, frowned at the high, barlike stool and settled her green beans into the sink for a quick rinse. "You've got stuff going on over the winter, right? And at the Maple Festival?"

"Yes."

"Well, count me in on that. I know I can't handle a lot right now with trying to find, develop and establish my—" she wagged two fingers of both hands in quotation marks "—beauty shop."

Jeff grinned. So did Dana.

"But once I've got things underway I can give you time. Donate services. Whatever you need as long as it isn't cold, hard cash. I'm leaving that one to you, Grandma and Mom."

Dana nodded. "We'll cover cash donations from the family. You donate great hair and nails. And massages. People love them these days."

Jeff wouldn't argue that point. A great massage after a strenuous workout?

Stellar.

He took his sister's cue, stood and bent to kiss his mother's cheek. "You smell like potato salad."

She grinned. "Story of my life. Let me know dates and times, menus, et cetera. I can come up with my own or follow the committee's direction. Either way works for me."

"Will do."

Jeff turned toward his sister. "Mere, love you. Let me know when you narrow sites down. I'll come and look them over for you if you want."

"I'd love it," she admitted. She blew him a kiss from wet hands. "And I'm getting together with a bunch of the gals tonight, so I'll most likely have any and all current info on you by morning."

He grinned and sent her a mock salute. "Lotsa luck. Nothing to tell."

She matched his smile with her own. "That's what they all say, honey."

Hannah eyed the clock, set down her brush of pink-toned white chocolate and took off her apron. "Meg, I've got to get this stuff to the post office before two. Are you okay here?"

"Fine. And make sure you leave time to get ready for your date tonight. And let me just add, it's high time you started dating. I don't think you've had a date in the three years you've been in town."

Meg was right, and hearing it said out loud made her sound pretty lame. Still… "You don't think it's risky for me to date Jeff?"

"I think it borders on ridiculous for two thirtysomethings to *not* explore the possibilities. Seriously, Hannah, do I have to spell this out for you? Ticktock, ticktock?"

Hannah couldn't resist. "So, speaking of biological clocks…"

Megan's grin said it all.

"Dork, why haven't you said anything?" Hannah rounded the counter and hugged Meg. "Why the big secret?"

Megan shrugged, but still looked delighted. "We agreed to wait until we got to three months along because my mother miscarried twice. We just wanted to be as sure as we could be that things were okay."

Totally understandable. Hannah looked at the wall calendar. "And?"

"Three months tomorrow."

"Yee-haw!" Hannah spun her around, gave her another hug, then headed back to the kitchen, laughing. "I knew it, of course, but I'm glad you finally owned up."

"Oh, I figured you did." Megan nodded ruefully. "Something about morning sickness and pasty white skin says so much."

"Yup. So. End of March?"

"Thereabouts. And Danny's family is over-the-top excited. My parents are dancing in the streets and Grandma Mary…" Megan grinned, her face a telltale sign of her great-grandma's approval. "She's hoping for a girl, named for her, of course."

"Mary." Hannah smiled. The sound of the soft, Biblical name was a whisper on the wind, hinting new life, new beginnings and established roots. Wonderful things. "I love it."

"Me, too. Danny was a little goofy about it, thinking the name was kind of forced on me, but I love tradition and family heirlooms. And what's a better gift for a new-born child than a timeless name?"

"I agree." Hannah headed for the door. "I'll be back in a few minutes. Anything you want? Need?"

Megan shook her head, her look of satisfaction born from within. "Nope. I'm good."

Pure delight pushed Hannah's steps. Just shy of the post office, a voice called her name. She turned and spotted a certain science teacher. "Miss Dinsmore, hello."

"You remembered."

"Of course." She smiled and put a hand out. "Nice to see you."

"And you." Miss Dinsmore half smiled, half frowned at Hannah's left cheek. "Been working with pink frosting today?"

"Oh, no. Seriously?" Hannah scrubbed her hand over her cheek and sighed. "Wouldn't you think I'd know enough to check my face in the mirror?"

"Well, it's fine now," Miss Dinsmore assured her, falling into step alongside. "And my car is parked around the corner, so I'll walk with you, if you don't mind?"

"Not at all."

"Lovely day. A nice hint of cool and crisp, tinged with warmth, the sun still high enough to toast the air."

"For a few weeks yet."

"Yes." Miss Dinsmore breathed deep, her gaze trained on the kaleidoscopic hills that backdropped Wellsville. "I love fall."

Hannah was just about to agree, the words on the edge of her tongue, but then she realized it was an old feeling, now abandoned.

She *had* loved fall. And she never minded winter. As an athlete she'd embraced cooler days for multiple reasons, but fall's show of color, the chilled starlit nights, the wanton winds of change, tempestuous storms pummeling trees and homes… She'd loved it all.

"Fall's hard for you, I expect."

Hannah's suspicions were confirmed. Miss Dinsmore knew who she was. "How did you know?"

"Two ways. I was on the hiring committee for the library and your background check offered your history at Ironwood."

Hannah knew it would, but no one had said a word. Not to her at least. "And the second way?"

"I kept a scrapbook with my class back then of what you and your class accomplished. Your classroom projects on the effect of mood-altering meds on the human psyche were wonderful."

But not wonderful enough, Hannah thought, a wellspring of emotion surging upward.

"And the fact that so many of your students came to an understanding of the cooperative inner workings of the human brain and of nature versus nurture were just wonderful. Were they all honors students?"

"No." Hannah took a breath and paused, seeing the sights and sounds of Wellsville while her brain wrapped itself around memories of Ironwood High. "Most of them were regular students, although a lot of them were overachievers in things that may or may not have been school oriented."

"I've had my share of those." Miss Dinsmore nodded, agreeable. "We always called them late bloomers, and it's not a bad analogy in retrospect. Sometimes we tend to overanalyze what history has taught us are simple aberrations of the norm."

"Which is exactly what our study showed." Hannah

sent her a look. "But then we learned the hard way that nothing is really simple."

"And that no one teacher, one school, one community has all the answers," Miss Dinsmore replied, matter-of-fact. "I trained myself to recognize that when I get a student at age fourteen, I have four limited years of influence on his or her life. The family has had fourteen years to mess the kid up or strengthen him." She stepped closer, stopped Hannah's progress with a firm hand and looked deep into her eyes. "In other words, it's not our fault. Rainbows occur because of a finite grouping of events dependent on time of day, angle of light, prismatic function and saturation. If it takes all those accidents of time to make such a natural occurrence, how much more must it take to twist a child's thinking into total lack of conscience?"

"You're saying it wasn't my fault." Hannah tilted her head back, eyeing the sky, visualizing Miss Dinsmore's arced covenant in her head. "And I know that fundamentally. But I can't silence the cries. Or the sounds of the gun being fired repeatedly while I did nothing to stop them."

"You kept safe those you could," Miss Dinsmore offered, empathetic. "No one could have saved them all, not in a human context. That's why we've got God." She shifted her gaze, then brought it back, an air of quiet satisfaction marking her expression. "I've worked here a long time. I've made a difference. I know that. So I'm doubly glad you've come along now. I don't believe in fate, Hannah, but I put great stock in God's plan. His timing."

Hannah smiled, a bit of her gloom slipping away with this open discussion. Funny, she hadn't realized that *not* talking about Ironwood kept the memories closer at hand.

Somehow sharing this information and testimony made her heart and soul feel lighter. "Megan was telling me the same thing at the candy store just minutes ago. I'm going to trust that you've both been put in my path to knock some much-needed common sense into me."

Miss Dinsmore grinned. "Oh, I think you're well equipped with common sense, but when our emotional well-being gets broken, it's hard to rebuild. It takes time. Prayer. Patience. And a good-looking guy is never a bad thing." A look of female appreciation brightened Miss Dinsmore's aging features.

"A—" Hannah turned, saw Jeff approaching them looking both surprised and pleased, then tried to contain the blush of pleasure she felt at his approach, his presence, his easy but purposeful gait. "Hey."

"Hey, yourself." Jeff stopped short of them and angled them a look of mock suspicion. "This isn't an impromptu committee meeting, is it? With no quorum? No reading of the minutes? Aren't there rules about such things?"

"Would it bother you if there were?" Miss Dinsmore's fond expression marked him as a favorite, but that was no surprise. Jeff had charm.

Or was he just another glib schmoozer, standing on the backs of whomever, wherever, to get where he wanted to be? Hannah's past record said her judgment in men might be off.

"Not in the least, especially with such lovely ladies."

Hannah made a choking sound and stepped back, only half faking. "Is that the best you've got?"

He settled a look on her that said plenty. "I'm saving the best I've got for our date tonight."

"And on that note—" Miss Dinsmore winked at Jeff, smiled at Hannah, patted her hand and gave it the lightest squeeze of understanding "—I'll leave the antics of youth to the young. Nice seeing you, Hannah."

"And you, Miss Dinsmore."

"Jane, please. For most of the area I'll always be Miss Dinsmore, but I'd love for you to call me Jane."

"Then I will, Jane." On impulse, Hannah reached out and hugged the older woman. "Thank you."

"No thanks needed."

Oh, but there were. They both knew it. Hannah appreciated Jane's gentle compassion for what it was. God-sent. Perfectly timed. They exchanged smiles of understanding.

Jeff turned her way, his expression quizzical, inquiring and totally good-looking. "You girls were discussing…?"

"Men."

"Ha."

Hannah grinned, turned and continued toward the post office just to see if he'd follow.

And he did.

"Any special men?"

"I don't know any special men."

He faked a shot to the heart. "'Teach not thy lips such scorn, for it was made for kissing, lady, not for such contempt.'"

Hannah laughed. "You like Shakespeare?"

"Some, not all. Great quotes, though."

"I'm a Franklin fan myself."

"Sage, science and certainty. Your Philadelphia roots are showing."

"A little." Hannah shrugged. "Since my father works for the university, my tuition was reduced, and he's got a pair of rental properties near campus so I didn't have housing expenses."

"That's a huge plus right there. Sweet education, Hannah."

"It was." She stopped just shy of the post office and turned his way, determined to keep this light. "So, about tonight—"

"Wear the blue. Please."

"Whereas I was thinking of canceling."

"Nope." Without a moment's hesitation he leaned in and scraped a gentle kiss to her cheek, his lips grazing ever so slightly. The spontaneous gesture tweaked everything she'd put on hold a few years before, sedated emotions resuscitated by his gaze, his voice, his touch. "No chickening out. Promise?"

A part of her wanted to do just that, but another part longed to push aside old pain and shadowed loss. "I'm not a chicken."

"Then don't act like it." He said the words lightly, but the challenge shone through his eyes and the set of his jaw. "I'll pick you up at seven thirty."

"Eight."

"Nope. I'm not losing a half hour with you if I don't have to. Grandma Mary's closes at six on Saturdays— that's plenty of time for you to get home and do whatever it is women do. And since God gifted you with good looks, I'd say your prep time is minimal. Seven thirty. And dress casual. In the blue top." He stepped back, raised a hand in salute and strode away, leaving her watching. Waiting. Wondering.

But smiling.

And when he turned at the corner, he caught her watching his retreat. He grinned and winked, his confident attitude part bane, part blessing.

But sometimes confidence equaled selfishness, and

she didn't dare let herself mistake one for the other again. Since she was obviously drawn to strong, successful types, men not unlike her father, she needed to be careful in matters of the heart. Her parents got along quite well despite their failed marriage, and their second marriages had both worked out so far.

But the little girl inside Hannah wanted the happily ever after, a knight in shining armor.

She finally felt like she belonged in Allegany County. She loved Wellsville; its gradual resurgence sparked all kinds of new business ventures. And Jamison was too sweet for words, the historic town embracing its past to provide for its future.

One broken heart could taint all that. When she was on her own, she could drum up a gazillion reasons why exploring this attraction to Jeff Brennan made no sense at all.

Ten seconds in his presence chased them all away.

So, okay. She'd go out with him tonight. Spar with him. Laugh with him. Have an easy conversation with a sharp, good-looking guy who made her heart jump at a simple word or a long, slow look.

But no way was she wearing the blue.

Chapter Eight

"You wore it." He hoped his look of appreciation said more than his lame words. "Thank you."

"It was the only thing clean."

"I don't believe you for a minute, but I refuse to gloat because good guys don't do that on a first date."

She shifted her position to meet his gaze. "I told you that other fiasco wasn't a date. So now you agree."

"Now that I've got you in my car for a real date, I concur. But it got you here, and that was not an easily won battle."

"Nothing's been won, Jeff. We're just…going out. To-night. On one single date."

"Honey, every long-term commitment starts with one single date, doesn't it?"

"Or a guilty verdict by a jury of your peers," she shot back, her look saying she wasn't sure which was worse, dating him or serving a long-term sentence in a federal penitentiary.

He laughed out loud. "Either way, I've got you here. Now what am I going to do with you?"

"You said casual, so that limits your possibilities.

And don't tell me you don't have every minute of tonight planned out. Guys like you always do."

"Guys like me..." he mused, keeping his eyes on the twisting road, but letting his voice weigh her word choice. "Who hurt you, Hannah?"

"Off topic."

"Call it a change of subject."

"Then consider it off-limits."

"For now."

"Jeff, I—"

She twisted in her seat. Once again he knew not to push. "How do you like your steak?"

"I'm a vegan."

"Wrong answer."

"I don't eat meat for humanitarian purposes."

He lifted a brow. "Since this morning when you wolfed down a bacon, egg and cheese muffin?"

"You're stalking me?"

He smiled, amused. "If stalking means I passed you on the street as I was heading to my mother's place, then, yes, I guess I am." He eased the car onto the entrance ramp for I-86 and headed west. He shifted the car, then his attention. "I didn't mean to put you on the spot, so food seemed a safe change of subject. Okay?"

"Maybe."

"Pretty please?"

"You're such a little boy inside. How did your mother resist your charms?"

"Didn't. Still doesn't. You'll find that out when you meet her. She's doing a double Austen sponsorship for the library and she's agreed to head up the food organizing for the Harvest Dinner."

"Wow."

Mended Hearts

Jeff frowned. "You didn't ask why a double Austen? I did."

Hannah noted the quizzical look and had to remind herself to take a breath. Even in profile the guy was a stunner. Great hair, strong forehead, laugh lines edging his eyes, perfect nose, square jaw. Jeff Brennan was every woman's dream choice to father their children. She cleared her throat and the imagery of two Jeff Brennan "mini-mes" wearing matching polos in her head. "She picked two Austens because Jane Austen was an amazing female novelist who set the bar for great romantic comedy and women's fiction. Do you know anyone who reads Fitzgerald?"

"Lots of people."

"Anyone you'd like to spend more than five minutes with?"

He grinned. "There you have me."

"Exactly." She pressed forward to make her point, humor coloring her tone. "Your mother sounds quite astute to me. And I like my steak medium rare. With onion rings."

"The only way to eat it." He reached out a hand to cover hers, just for a moment, but long enough for her to feel the blanket of warmth and zings of attraction rolling through her system.

Why him?

Why now?

When I was waiting quietly for the Lord, His heart was turned to me, and He gave ear to my cry. The sweet psalm enveloped Hannah, words of promise and patience.

Part of her felt undeserving, but these last few weeks had diminished the old negativity somewhat. Without the shadow of guilt looming like a gathering storm, she saw possibilities with greater clarity, the prospect of a future she'd denied herself to this point. "And do they have baked potatoes?"

Jeff smiled. "Idaho or sweet?"

"Either."

"They do. Are they on your training regimen?"

"I don't have one."

"Anyone who runs daily has one whether they recognize it or not."

"Not true." Hannah settled back into the seat and watched him. "I run to pray. To think. To absolve."

"Penance?" The tiny clench to his jaw said he had read too much into her statement. Or maybe just enough.

"I prefer the term *therapy*. I keep it controlled because I know I'm a little OCD. I like to do my best at everything and that can become obsessive. So I don't allow it to."

"Hence the onion rings and baked potato."

She grinned in agreement. "And don't forget dessert."

His smile said more than words could. "I'm looking forward to it, Hannah."

She waved a hand as they angled onto Route Sixteen. "I've never been to Olean."

"Seriously?" He glanced her way, the quieter road allowing him more leeway. "How long have you lived here?"

She hedged. "Three years."

"Where do you shop?"

"Wellsville. Jamison. Online." His expression said her response surprised him again, prompting an explanation. "I don't shop much."

"Another anomaly."

"Not true. I just have simple needs."

His appreciative look dispelled her twinge of concern.

"In your case, simple says style." He pulled into a parking spot, climbed out, rounded the car and opened her door, the action old-fashioned and sweet. As she stepped out, he reached for her hand and held it overlong, his warm expression smiling into her eyes, her heart, thawing a corner she'd kept on ice for too long. He winked, grinned and tugged her toward the Millhouse. "Let's eat. I'm starved."

She couldn't help but smile back. He tugged her closer and swept a gentle kiss to her cheek. "You're amazing, Hannah."

Right then she *felt* amazing, invigorated by his attraction. For tonight she'd put aside concerns that echoed from her disaster with Brian. For tonight she'd dwell in the here and now, a move that seemed easier in Jeff's presence. For tonight, she'd be Hannah Moore, librarian and fund-raiser, out on a date with a delightful man. For this one night, it would be enough. And it was, for about thirty seconds, right up until they stepped inside the gracious and updated eatery in the former grain mill storage facility.

"Mr. Brennan, good evening."

"How are you, Maggie?" Jeff smiled at the hostess.

"Fine, sir. I've set aside the customary table."

"Thank you, Maggie. This is my friend Hannah Moore."

"Miss Moore." Maggie extended her hand. "Is this your first visit here?"

"Mine? Yes." Hannah gave Jeff a pointed look that inspired his grin.

"Whereas my *family* has been coming here for years," he cut in. "Grandma grew up in Olean and she and

Grandpa liked to bring us here for special occasions. Birthdays. Holidays. Family reunions."

"And your grandmother is well?" Maggie asked as she led them to a quiet table.

"Quite well. And your family?"

"All fine." She waited as Jeff held out Hannah's chair. When Jeff took the spot alongside Hannah, she sent him a relaxed grin. "And I know business is booming for Walker Electronics. I read the feature article in last Sunday's *Herald*, but I'm glad to see you get away from your desk now and again."

"This coming from a woman who works every holiday known to man," Jeff quipped back.

Maggie acknowledged that with a wry smile. "Too true. Family businesses are nothing to be taken lightly. But a nice heritage, all in all."

"It is."

Was it? Hannah wondered. The thought of Maggie working every holiday, the rush of business on weekends... There was no such thing as a weekend off in the restaurant business, but Maggie's words said something else.

She saw the work, the dedication and the diligence as part of her heritage, and that put a new slant on Jeff Brennan's ambitions. Inheriting a family business would come with no small level of responsibility, and that made working his way up the ladder of success more amenable.

A college-age waiter approached them for their drink orders. Jeff sat back, letting Hannah take the lead. "Do you serve lattes?"

The young man nodded. "Flavored?"

All the better. Hannah smiled. "Yes, please. Caramel?"

"Of course. And you, sir?"

Hannah leaned closer. "Someone who doesn't know you. Must not be part of the family."

Jeff smiled, grasped her hand and squeezed before answering the waiter. "Regular coffee, please. And I think we're going to forgo appetizers tonight because the young lady mentioned a hankering for dessert later."

"Or now." When Jeff turned her way, she quipped, "Life's short. Eat dessert first."

"Whatever you'd like, Hannah."

His easy words melted another corner of her taut heart. Something in his comfortable gaze, his winning manner, his gentle touch reminded her this wasn't Brian.

And then he withdrew a vibrating cell phone from his pocket, negating the little glimmer of reassurance she'd grabbed. He scanned the phone, let the call go to voice mail and turned the phone off.

Now she felt guilty. What if the plant needed him? What if some very important person had to wait to talk to Jeff and then called another supplier instead? She reached a hand toward the phone. "You can keep it on."

Jeff swept her and the phone a look before slipping it into his jacket pocket. "Why?"

"In case something important happens."

"Then they'll leave a message and I can check it later. And the plant manager has Grandma's numbers, as well. And Trent's. We're covered."

"But Trent is out of town."

Jeff nodded slowly. "Yes."

"And what if your grandmother falls asleep or something?"

"Then she'll awake to the same message I find later. What's this all about, Hannah?"

She frowned, not sure herself. "I just don't want you to think you can't work if you need to."

"Well. Thanks. I think. What if I'd rather spend the evening talking with you?" He leaned back but kept her fingers loosely in his. "Getting to know you? Teasing you?"

"I'm not interrupting something important?"

He eased forward, lamplight softening the strong planes of his face. "Hannah, you *are* something important. For tonight, everybody else goes on hold. Not you."

By the time they got to dessert, Hannah realized she shouldn't have jumped to conclusions about Jeff Brennan, and that he might be just about the nicest guy she'd ever met, which might make holding to that just-one-date scenario a little tricky. Or downright impossible.

He'd wanted to get to know her better tonight.

He had, somewhat, but her reaction in the car on the way to Olean had cautioned him to hold off. Take his time. And since taking time with Hannah wasn't exactly a hardship, Jeff was okay with that for now.

He pulled into the driveway of her apartment house, switched off the engine and rounded the car to walk her to the door.

"I had a great time tonight." She withdrew her keys from her bag and smiled up at him. "Although that crème brûlée was probably an indulgence that will push me to an extra two miles of running tomorrow."

Jeff laughed. "This from the lady who doesn't have a training regimen."

"It's not a regimen. It's…common sense."

"Uh-huh." He stopped talking, letting his eyes wander her face, her eyes, her mouth. Settling there, wondering what it would be like to kiss Hannah, then deciding that wondering wasn't enough.

Her gaze flicked up to his, and he saw his question reflected in her pretty blue eyes. "Hannah."

Her answering expression offered silent permission. Jeff lowered his head, his hands gently grasping her shoulders, the nubby feel of her tweed wool coat a kiss of fall while Jeff lingered over a different kind of kiss.

Sweet. Soft. Warm.

The adjectives that filled his mind softened his heart; his worries about work, time and Matt disappeared in the wonder of kissing Hannah. And when he stopped, he didn't pull away, couldn't pull away. He embraced her in a hug, one hand cradling the back of her head, the other arm wrapped around her, glad they'd taken this step.

She dropped her forehead to his chest, then eased back. "Thank you for a lovely evening."

"It was fun. And the kiss speaks for itself, I hope."

Her blush said it did.

Jeff straightened his shoulders and tweaked her nose. "Can we plan the next date now, or do you have to put me through the wringer again?"

She thought a moment, then arched a brow. "Church in the morning?"

He ahemmed out loud, daring her to smile.

She did.

"Big step."

"I'm feeling braver by the minute."

"I see that."

When he took a few seconds too long, she stepped back, lifting her left shoulder in a light shrug. "Sorry. It's one of my litmus tests and you just failed."

He gripped her shoulder, not allowing the retreat. "I

wasn't hesitating on saying yes or no. But which one? Yours or mine?"

"Oh."

"Yeah. Oh."

"Mine," she declared, sure and certain. "You're the guy, you're supposed to go the distance. And Reverend Baxter is a sweetheart."

"And Reverend Hannity isn't?"

"Since they're related, the point is moot. And I'm second-guessing the invitation in any case."

"Rude, Hannah. No take-backs allowed."

"Who's making these rules?"

"We are." He leaned forward, wanting to kiss her again, knowing he'd best refrain.

"So you're in?"

"Their service starts at ten?" At her nod he winked and gave her hand a light squeeze. "I'll be here at nine thirty. Be prepared."

She frowned, confused. "For?"

"The talk and speculation. A marriageable man and woman walking into church together in a small town, well..." He let the twinkle in his eyes say the rest.

Her composure wavered. Her expression stilled. "I didn't consider that."

He shrugged. "No big deal."

Maybe not to him, but it was huge to her. Hannah stepped back. "No, it *is* a big deal. If I'd been thinking clearly I'd never have suggested it."

He'd been edging toward the step, but now he moved forward again. "Are you afraid to be seen with me, Han?"

The nickname almost pierced her armor. No one besides her Grandma Grady called her "Han." Until now. "It's not smart. Not at this stage of the game."

"I don't play games."

Um, right.

Maybe guys like Jeff and Brian finagled so often, they didn't see it as game playing, but Hannah refused to be maneuvered ever again. She took a firm step back. "I had fun tonight. A lot of fun," she admitted. She glanced left, then down, bit her lip and drew her gaze back to his. "But remember what I told you? I don't take chances. I don't guess the sure thing because it doesn't really exist. Maybe we can go out again sometime, but maybe we should just smile and nod, say we had fun, part ways and leave it at that."

His expression shadowed. A hint of reluctance darkened his eyes. But then he squeezed her shoulder lightly, nodded and stepped away. "You're probably right. Thank you for a wonderful evening, Hannah. I had a great time."

"Me, too."

She let herself into her small apartment. The neighborhood was silent in the cool fall night.

Her phone blinked a welcome as she crossed the room. She lifted it, pressed the code for her voice mail and smiled when she heard her younger brother's voice. "It's a girl! We named her Caitlyn Jean, for Mom, of course. She weighs seven pounds, two ounces, she's twenty inches long and Leah says to tell you she looks like you, which is perfect because we'd like you to be her godmother. Are you available in late November for a baptism?"

Hannah glanced at the time, decided congratulations would have to wait until morning, then slipped into the big easy chair she'd found at a moving sale up Route Nineteen.

Tears stung from nowhere, part joy for Nick and Leah's news, part pity party, wondering why she'd just turned away from the nicest thing that had happened to her in years. Was she totally crazy or just a little unsure of herself?

She didn't know anymore.

Going to church with Jeff wasn't earth-shattering. It would be nice. Typical.

Had she contained herself so long she'd forgotten that ordinary, customary things weren't out of the norm? Perhaps.

Time to change that. She swiped her hands over her cheeks and headed for the bedroom.

She'd told Jeff no in no uncertain terms, but a woman's prerogative was to change her mind. To that end...

She'd go to services at Good Shepherd tomorrow. Reverend Baxter would totally understand since Reverend Hannity was his father-in-law.

Now the big question would be what to wear since she'd already worn the blue...

With work demands pressuring him, Jeff almost didn't make the longer drive to Jamison when Wellsville churches were more convenient.

But he loved Reverend Hannity's homilies, so he'd cruised up Route Nineteen, figuring he'd make up time later.

He was glad he did when Hannah slipped into the worn chestnut pew next to him wearing a fall floral dress shot with bronzed thread that sparked light when she moved; her thin ivory sweater a tribute to the cool fall morning.

He edged closer, facing forward, part of him wondering if this was a good idea while another part warned him not to blow it. "You caved."

She nodded, thumbing through the prayer book, her face serene. "I did."

"And you admit it." He colored his whispered tone with surprise, pleased when her lips quirked up in a smile. "That's a big step forward."

She turned and looked up at him, right at him, her gaze making him feel ten feet tall and hideously unprepared, an odd pairing. But then, he'd already figured out that Hannah was no ordinary woman. Soft, lilting notes of a flute stopped her comeback, the gentle call to worship commanding in simplicity.

He'd have to work to concentrate this morning. He'd figured that out the minute she took the seat alongside him. His urge to shelter and protect elevated to "high" in her presence.

Why was that? He snuck a glance left and sighed quietly, noting the dip of her chin, the sweep of dark lashes, the soft, slow blink she did when lost in thought.

It didn't matter why. They were in the getting-to-know-you stage, except he knew next to nothing about Hannah while she'd learned a great deal about him.

But did she? his conscience scolded. *Did she discover anything of substance, or just the face you want the world to see? The strong, successful good guy who's nothing like his father.*

Except you are. And you know it.

Jeff shoved the admonition aside. He wasn't like his father, despite the mirror image. He'd worked strenuously to prove that, day by day.

And he'd keep doing it, making sure the world understood that Neal Brennan had passed on nothing more than a last name.

Well, there is that little wrinkle of an illegitimate half brother back in town.

Jeff fumbled with the songbook as the congregation stood, trying to put thoughts of his father aside, but Matt's presence in the area made that harder to do.

A light, chill rain started midservice, the steady sound drumming on the church's roof. "Did you walk?" Jeff asked when the service had concluded.

Hannah tugged her sweater closer. "Yes, but it's not really cold. I'm fine."

He sent her an "are ya serious?" look before pushing open the back door of the old church. Reverend Hannity stood on the broad top step, only partially covered by the overhang. He greeted people with one hand clutching an umbrella. Jeff cast the umbrella a wry look. "Change is in the air, it seems."

"In many ways." The reverend swept the pair a smile.

Hannah's shoulders tightened.

Jeff defused her reaction with a light shoulder nudge. "I was referring to the weather."

The reverend's smile deepened. "Duly noted, of course. My vantage point on the altar allows me greater perspective so I find myself aware of subtle change before the majority of people. But sitting in church together? That's like putting your new friendship on the Jumbo-Tron at a football game."

"Speaking of which, there is a four o'clock game today and I've got work to do if I want to catch it." Jeff raised his hand, indicating his watch. "Have a good day, Reverend."

Reverend Hannity reached out and grasped Hannah's hand, his expression intent. "While I don't have the youthful verve and vigor of my son-in-law across the way—" he angled his head toward Holy Name where his daughter and son-in-law served "—I've got age on my side. Wisdom. And a wife who makes great cookies. Thanks for coming over, Miss Moore."

His sincerity softened the set of her shoulders. She smiled, a small dimple flashing in her right cheek. "My pleasure, Reverend. You won't tell, will you?"

He grinned. "Oh, I will. I'll brag it to the heavens to keep that son-in-law of mine humble. And if my team wins today? All the more reason to crow."

"The stadium will be washed in red, white and blue this afternoon. You're not going to the game?"

The reverend shook his head. "I go once a season as a gift from my wife. Stadium crowds get rowdy and I can jump up and shake my fist at the TV screen in the rectory with no fear of knocking over someone's soda. Other than my own."

"And the living room is climate controlled. Definitely a plus as the weather turns." She smiled up at him and Jeff watched the pastor's smile bloom.

"Never a bad thing at my age. You folks have a nice day, okay?" The hint of blessing in his tone reflected the gentle look in his eye as he released Hannah's hand.

"We will." Hannah started toward the parking lot. "You, too."

"See you on Tuesday night, Reverend. We've got that council meeting at seven, right?"

"I'll be there."

"Good. Between you and me maybe we can keep Hank's subdivision off the auction block."

The reverend frowned. "I don't think that's possible, but I've been praying for a good outcome all around. Sometimes the worst wrongs produce wondrous good."

Christ's life epitomized the saying. Jeff nodded. "I can't argue that. See you then." He loped down the stairs and across the lot until he caught up with Hannah. "You know football?"

"I have a father, a stepfather and a brother. It was inevitable."

He grinned, grabbed her arm and headed toward his car. "Hop in. I'll drive you home."

"It's a five-minute walk and the rain's letting up."

"It's cold and you're only wearing a sweater. In." Before she could set her face in what he was coming to recognize as pure stubbornness, he bent a smidge lower and met her gaze. "Please?"

The *please* did it. She smiled, rolled her eyes and climbed in, but she was pleased he insisted. It showed in the curve of her jaw, the twinkle in her eye. "Breakfast? My treat."

Like he was about to let her buy him food on the slim paychecks she brought in from two low-end jobs. Right. In any case...

He grimaced, reluctant. "I can't. We've got a final bid due tomorrow and I've got to number crunch today, make sure I'm on target. And then there's a second one due on Tuesday. Trent's due back then, but not soon enough to shoulder any of this."

"Of course."

"Normally it wouldn't be a problem," he began, then wondered why he felt the need to explain. Could it be because she'd edged away the moment he cited his work schedule? That she'd taken a dislike to his responsibilities?

With military contracts, time equaled money and sometimes lives. Jeff took both seriously, knowing the future of Walker Electronics and Allegany County loomed brighter with the continued partnership with the armed forces. Trent's vision had become the new normal, and Jeff couldn't let anything interfere with that. Too many people depended on them for paychecks, benefits, opportunities for advancement. Not to mention the soldiers in the field, manning front lines, whose communications capabilities might mean life or death.

He pulled up in front of her apartment not sure what to say, an unusual circumstance for him. She climbed out before he could round the front of the car. He caught up with her as she climbed the first step and caught her hand. "You're mad."

"I'm not."

He held tight to her hand and just waited, silent, watching her. She sighed, blew out a breath and eyed the dripping trees. "I understand you have responsibilities. I'm sorry for trying to infringe on them, Jeff."

Part of him wanted to turn the clock back ten minutes and just say yes to breakfast.

Although no way would he let her buy.

But another part of him recognized the hurdle she'd erected.

Yeah, he worked hard. He had to, partially to continue Walker Electronics's growth and partially to repair the family name. And even harder right now because Trent was gone.

But he didn't feel compelled to justify any of it. That rubbed him the wrong way. His work ethic was part and parcel of him. It wasn't about to change.

She was obviously unsympathetic to that.

He stepped back, a sense of déjà vu blindsiding him,

because hadn't they just done this same dance last night? And come to the same conclusion?

She beat him to the parting line. "Thanks for the ride home. I appreciate it."

"Anytime."

They both knew he didn't mean it. She'd put up a barrier he wouldn't try to scale. Hard work and industry were part of him, a piece of the whole.

Her reaction said she only dealt with fragments.

Jeff wanted the whole pie graph. He headed back to the car, waved his hand, climbed in and refused to beat himself up over shouldering needed responsibilities, his gut reaming him for thinking this could have gone anywhere, been anything.

He pulled away from the curb with his foot on the gas while he worked to put the brakes on his heart. He'd see her each and every Thursday night, and at fund-raising events no doubt, but her reaction to his work constraints added further bricks to her walled-in existence. Right now, Jeff didn't have the time needed to make the climb.

And because he actually liked himself, who he was and what he'd accomplished so far in life, he was pretty sure he shouldn't have to.

Chapter Nine

Hannah's phone rang as she closed up the library a few days later. She fumbled with her keys while juggling the phone and answered just in time, sounding rushed when she wasn't even close to rushed, a sad scenario at age thirty-four. "Hello."

"Is this Hannah Moore?"

Hannah paused, the unfamiliar voice reminding her of intrusive reporters and media hounds relentlessly pursuing a story, only she saw nothing about her Ironwood actions as noteworthy.

"Yes." Caution tainted her tone.

"Hannah, this is Dana Brennan. I volunteered to oversee the food preparations for the Harvest Dinner the library group is holding in conjunction with the Farmer's Fair."

"Jeff's mother."

The other woman's microsecond hesitation said she found it interesting that Hannah classified her that way, which was totally understandable because...

Because Hannah hadn't stopped thinking about Jeff since her rude about-face Sunday morning, making him feel guilty about his job when scores of people depended upon his business. She bit back a sigh of recrimination and covered smoothly. "Jeff mentioned he was going to sign you up for food because, in his words, nobody does it better."

Dana laughed but Hannah was pretty sure the older woman had picked up more than Hannah meant to say with two little words. "What a lovely compliment. And that sounds like my son—hardworking, industrious and appreciative of a good meal."

Hannah had watched him down a twenty-ounce steak at dinner the other night, so she was no stranger to his formidable appetite. "Sounds like the same guy. Do you need help with the dinner planning? There are committee members who'd love to talk with you tomorrow night."

"I've actually got everything planned out," Dana replied, her gentle voice self-assured. "There's a local group of gals who love to put on this sort of thing and we haven't had the chance in a while. If I could come to the meeting and present my plans and ideas for approval, that would be great."

"I'll put you on the agenda when I type it up today and add you to our volunteer list, Mrs. Brennan."

"Oh, Dana, dear, please. If we're going to be working together, first names are so much more fun."

"Dana, then. I'll see you tomorrow night."

"Wonderful."

Hannah headed for home, the crisp October day beautiful, the hillside colors deepening with time.

Her mother's distinctive ringtone interrupted her musings as she neared the apartment. "Hey, Mom. What's up?"

"Just checking in." Jean Moore's voice held warmth

and reassurance. She'd obviously been eyeing the calendar, watching the days advance, a family habit every autumn. "How are you doing, honey?"

"I'm doing well, actually," Hannah told her and was surprised by how true that was. "Very well, in fact."

"Hannah, that's wonderful. I'm so happy to hear you say that."

She didn't add "at last," but they both recognized the inference.

"Are you busy with work?"

With work and life, Hannah admitted to herself, another thought of Jeff's quirked grin and bright eyes making her squirm inside since she'd mucked that up. "Yes, we've got a library fund-raising project going on that's eating up my spare time and it's been good for me. All around."

"I'm glad, Hannah."

Hannah read her mother's relief and couldn't disagree. "Me, too. Hey, I've got to go. I just got home and there's a package on the step. But first, tell me how adorable this new baby is, our little Caitlyn Jean."

Jean laughed out loud, embracing the new subject matter like any first-time grandma would. "She's precious beyond belief. She's like a mix of you and Leah, absolutely adorable, and Nick is going to be a wonderful father. I can just tell."

"I agree totally," Hannah replied. Her brother Nick's fun, gentle nature was perfect for fatherhood. "And I can't wait to see her, to see all of you. I'm looking forward to Thanksgiving."

"Well…"

The single word said something had gone awry with

Nick's well-laid plans. "You're not coming up to Philly for the baptism?"

"We're doing Thanksgiving with John's family this year and it seems rude to head up north right after we've arrived, don't you think? And since we're coming up at Christmas, it gets a little expensive."

And right there was reason enough to hate the long-lasting effects of a broken family. Her stepfather's discomfort around her father dictated her mother's actions, and as wrong as that seemed, Hannah knew better than to expect anything else. "Is it less rude to miss your granddaughter's christening?"

"Unfortunately we don't have limitless funds, travel's expensive and John's pension fund took a huge hit, so we've got to pick and choose. And we'll see you at Christmas if you make the drive to Nick's house in Bucks County."

"I understand." And she did, although a part of Hannah wished they all lived closer. "I'll let you guys know about Christmas. It mostly depends on the weather. Getting caught on I-81 in a blizzard isn't my idea of fun."

"Me neither. And Hannah?"

"Yes?"

"It's nice to hear you sounding so good. So strong."

Her mother's approval added a layer of strength to her growing confidence. "Thanks, Mom. I think so, too."

She pocketed the phone and stared at the box on the stoop, the bold, black marker address way too familiar. *Brian.*

She sighed, lifted the box, felt the lightness of it and wondered what on earth he might have sent her at this late date. She'd left nothing of consequence in Illinois, except a good part of her heart and soul, unboxable items she was reclaiming step by step.

Toss it.

The advice seemed timely. No way did Hannah want her growing initiative blindsided by the parcel's contents. She made it halfway around the house, then paused and shifted her gaze up, the bright blue sky edged by an incoming storm system.

Was fear driving her thoughts of dumping the box? Or common sense, a necessary attribute touted by therapy?

"Do not fear what they fear; do not be frightened." Peter's presence in the Bible was brief, a span of two letters, but his encouragement to face fear and bind to courage touched Hannah's heart. Sighing, she took the box inside and pushed it into a closet for another day, another time. Right now, basking in her mother's words of pride, she had no intention of interrupting the current upward cycle.

She'd deal with the box later. The packaged presence was unable to hurt without her tacit permission. But for the moment, setting it aside shielded her from memories that had owned her for too long.

Hannah looked lovely and that seemed so unfair, Jeff thought as he strode into the library Thursday evening, determined to keep everything quick, friendly and business oriented. One look at Hannah in some kind of fitted dress tossed those well-scripted plans out the window.

He'd come early on purpose, wanting to go over a couple of points with her. But when she met his gaze he morphed into a tongue-tied teen boy, captivated by her grace, her charm, the look of her.

She moved his way, seemingly unaware of the war raging within him. So why did he lean forward as she drew near, take a deep, slow breath and sigh, his mouth a whisper's breadth from her cheek? "You smell delightful."

Her answering smile feathered her cheek against his mouth, the sweet softness sublime, but common sense reminded him he'd walked away on Sunday with good reason. Hannah had issues with the constraints of his job, her reaction made that obvious, and his job wasn't about to change. So why did that reason seem to vaporize in her presence?

"Thank you."

"Nice dress."

She smiled and her left hand came up, twisting a thin lock of hair, a habit he'd noticed at each meeting. "If I admit I wore it on purpose, do I gain or lose points?"

"I thought we decided to stop keeping score on Sunday." He leveled a straightforward gaze on her. She released her hair and the spiraled curl sprang forth, turning and dipping its way to her shoulder.

"I was rude on Sunday." She paused, glanced away, then drew her attention back as if deliberately choosing her words. He didn't note any reluctance to engage face-to-face or the hesitation he'd sensed at previous meetings. Instead she faced him with a look of understanding. "And I didn't mean to be. Sometimes my emotional buttons get pushed by circumstance, triggering out-of-line reactions."

"And my needing to work triggered you?"

"On a Sunday, before watching football," she explained. "Which probably seems ridiculous, but…"

"It reminded you of someone else."

"In part, yes." Her expression said she wasn't proud of her reaction, but understood it.

"And he did quite a number on you."

Her face shadowed. She pursed her lips, the flash of pain in her eyes brief but real. "Life did a number on me, Jeff. Brian's actions just added fuel to the fire."

Brian.

His nemesis had a name. But Jeff had no intention of fighting the past. He'd taken his past on headfirst, moving forward, refusing to let the father's actions shackle the son's choices. Well, until Matt showed up.

Hannah would be wise to do the same.

He stepped back, because the scent and sight of her made him want to help, but he'd learned the hard way that God helped those who helped themselves. It was a belief system he embraced.

"Jeffrey." His mother's voice pulled his attention toward the door. She walked in, her step light, her smile infectious, her warm look taking in the situation at hand. Hannah. Jeff. The mood.

Great.

"Dana, good evening." Hannah moved forward, a hand extended, her surety surprising Jeff. "I'm Hannah Moore, Jeff's cochair."

"Hannah." Dana grasped Hannah's hand and squeezed lightly. "I've heard so much about you."

Hannah worked to keep her voice easy. "All good, I hope."

"Marvelous." Dana squeezed her hand again and shifted her gaze back to Jeff. "I had lunch with Grandma and she's delighted with how quickly you two got things in motion. She's quite impressed, and my mother is not easily impressed."

"That's for sure." Jeff grinned, his manner gilding the words, but Hannah read the distinct difference between the two women now that she'd met both. Martha and Mary, mother and daughter, opposing points of view. The scientist in her said that had to make for interesting holiday conversation and the pacifist within warned those meals should be avoided at all costs. Which wouldn't be a problem because Jeff had shrugged her off, right?

The door swung open and Hannah moved to greet more arriving committee members.

Jeff caught her arm. "May I see you for a minute?"

"Umm…" She glanced from his hand to his face, letting her cool expression speak for her. "You just did."

He flushed slightly. "I was distracted. My bad." He indicated the brightly toned children's area to his right. "For just a moment, Hannah. Please. I wanted your advice on an Advent Walk project before we convene."

"Oh. *Business* talk." She led the way to the children's book nook, then turned and caught him noticing the dress.

That made her smile. The way Jeff managed to stumble over his first words widened it even more. "Listen, I, um…"

"Yes?"

He ran a hand through his hair, the rising voices of the committee members forcing him to speak up. "I was thinking of introducing a buy-a-brick campaign in conjunction with the Advent Walk."

Hannah frowned. "Explain."

"Jamison schedules an Advent Walk every year."

"Right." Hannah drew the word out deliberately. She'd only been in town a few years, but the quaint tradition of people walking from church to church around the town green, carrying candles for light and greens to decorate the church doors had proven delightful. The gathered group caroled as they walked, and once a church door had been decorated for the Advent season, they paused within that church to pray before proceeding to the next house of worship. The evening concluded with a dessert hour in the newly refurbished youth center, a marvelous finishing touch to a small-town celebration.

"But because there's no sidewalk, we walk in the street."

"We do," she agreed slowly. "But it's not like there's a lot of traffic in the street, Jeff. On a weekend December night."

"But what if we sold pavers to create an Advent walkway for next year?" His animated gaze said he liked the idea, and it was village-centered enough for people to embrace. "I called Winchell Brick and the owner said we could get the pavers at cost and they'd donate the underlayment stone and sand. That way we could build the walk next summer, have a pretty path to do the Advent Walk from that point on and a safe path for kids over the summer when traffic to and from I-86 does get busy."

Hannah recognized the merit in his well-considered plan. "I like the idea," she told him. "And we could sell the stones for a fifty percent profit with the proceeds going to the library fund, staying community-based with a positive outcome as a benefit."

"Exactly."

The grouped tables were rapidly filling with committee members. Hannah headed that way. "It's a great idea, Jeff. Go ahead and introduce it. I've got your back."

She crossed the room to get the meeting started. Her defined movements warred with the undertone of hesitancy he'd witnessed, but he wasn't good at reading hints and signals. He needed straightforward direction.

Hannah threw curves.

His current time constraints might be temporary, but as a company executive and design team leader, they'd resurface as business grew. And he couldn't afford to mess up, not with so much at stake.

"I waited patiently for the Lord. He turned to me and heard my cry."

The psalm mocked Jeff. He'd stopped waiting patiently for anything years ago, needing to be in charge. But right now, watching Hannah's ease with the other committee members, he wondered what he hoped to gain by rushing through life. Did he want his measure of success to be in business only?

"Imagine what my parents thought," his mother exaggerated, amusing the group as he approached, "when they got me instead of the science-loving prototype they envisioned. While my mother devoured every issue of *American Scientist*, I was hiding in my room reading romance novels and practicing the piano, imagining myself a modern-day Elizabeth Bennett."

Hannah laughed with the others, lilting and sweet, the kind of reaction he'd like to inspire. Of course, he was a stuffed shirt scientist, like his grandparents. But Hannah liked science. She'd said so.

Which meant he might still have a chance, although after tonight's fiasco, his opportunities appeared dim.

"Do you still play, Dana?" Miss Dinsmore asked as she settled into a seat, a huff of breath making her sound tired.

"I do." Dana smiled at her old teacher before indicating Jeff with a wave of her hand. "And I forced Jeff and Meredith to learn because as much as I respect the periodic table and great haircuts, the arts and a nice garden are food for the soul. A good life should embrace balance."

Jeff read her message, but wouldn't pursue that now. He called the meeting to order and went through the customary procedural notes before offering his idea up for a vote.

Reverend Hannity raised his hand. "Yes, Reverend?"

"The idea of a walkway is wonderful, Jeff," the reverend exclaimed. "I know the other pastors will offer full support. We've talked about it among ourselves, but the village right-of-way made it impossible to do without board permission."

"Can we get permission?" Hannah asked Jeff. "Do we need to attend a board meeting to present the idea?"

He nodded, hearing the word *we* and wondering if she'd deliberately just offered him another night of her time. Most likely not. "They meet on the first and third Wednesdays, so if we can put together a prospectus with Winchell Brick, we could present it to the board next week and get things rolling. This would be a carryover-type fund-raiser that we'd work on throughout the winter."

"Who would build the path?" Miss Dinsmore wondered out loud. "Volunteers are fine, but a permanent path needs to be carefully graded."

"We could help with that," Callie offered. "My dad and his crew are great at putting in landscape walls and paths and this is the same idea, just wider and longer. I'll run it by him, but I'm sure he'll say yes."

"Thanks, Callie." Jeff smiled at her, then scanned the group. "Objections?"

No one raised their hand.

He nodded before shifting his attention back to Hannah. "Then we'll approach the town board next week and seek approval contingent on raising the necessary funds by selling the bricks."

He included her on purpose, she was sure of it, and there was no wiggle room when they were surrounded by a room full of people. By the time the other committee members headed home, she'd forgotten the list of reasons why she *shouldn't* accompany Jeff to the meeting.

That meant they'd be together two nights next week, and while a part of her thought of that with anticipation, another part urged caution. She decided to ignore both as she stowed her paperwork and notes in her shoulder bag. Jeff gathered his things in similar fashion and headed her way, a glance at his watch telling her she was taking too much time.

Well, too bad. She'd been walking to her car for three years; she hadn't needed an escort before and didn't need one now.

Jeff glanced at his watch again. Hannah swept him a quick glance. "You don't have to wait for me. I'm fine."

He frowned and looked at her, then the watch, before an "aha" expression brightened his features. "I wasn't in a hurry. My watch seems to have stopped at seven fifty-two."

His watch broke. Suddenly Hannah felt foolish.

He wasn't trying to push her along. Or lamenting the time like Brian had done so often, making her work seem less vital.

"And I was thinking we should get together this weekend," Jeff continued, "to put together an intelligent proposal about the sidewalk fund-raiser."

"I know nothing about building sidewalks," Hannah said as she approached the door. "You'd do better to find somebody else."

"We don't have to know the how-tos," Jeff explained, following her outside. "Just the basics. And it would look better to the town board if we both attend the meeting since we're cochairs."

Jeff had a good point. Their old-school town officials might need some convincing, and two was better than one.

"All right."

"Can we get together this Saturday to check out Winchell Brick?" Jeff asked as they crossed the parking lot. "Once we've got sizes and prices figured out we could head to my place or yours, figure out the square footage and the application process and then present the full package to the board. What do you think?"

"I'm here until three."

"And Winchell's closes at four on Saturday," Jeff mused as they reached her car. "How about if I pick you up here and we go straight to Winchell's? I'll let Ted know we're coming and he can advise us."

She couldn't dispute the plan, and since she didn't exactly find spending an evening with Jeff a hardship, that meant they'd be together three of the next six nights. Well. She could keep things together for three evenings. Right?

One glance up into his eyes nixed that assumption.

"We can get takeout and have a working supper," Jeff continued. "Chinese, Italian or pizza."

Hannah smiled. Jamison didn't sport much in the way of Indian, Thai or sushi. "Chinese. From Happy Garden. Because I like the name."

Her answer drew his smile. "Happy Garden, it is." He watched as she climbed into her car, then raised a hand. "I'll see you Saturday. Drive careful."

"I will. The whole three blocks." She offered a quick wave and left him standing as she drove off, mixed feelings vying for her attention.

She wanted to see him. The spark of attraction that burned brighter in his presence felt good.

But she was driving herself crazy trying to read something into his every movement, hunting for signs that made him more or less like Brian, and that wasn't healthy. "Father, help me. You know me, Lord, You know what I've seen. What I've done. You know the cowardly soul that lingers inside. I don't want to be that person anymore, but I don't know how to take full command again. Show me. Please."

You know exactly what you need to do, her conscience retorted. *And until you walk into a school and take your place in front of a classroom again, you let evil win, letting fear stand in your way. You know what needs to be done. You just won't do it.*

Not won't. Can't, thought Hannah. *I can't do it. There's a difference.*

But her heart knew there wasn't and while she might be able to turn off the mental scoldings, there was no way to silence her heart. Like it or not, she was a teacher. And a tiny part of her dared to dream of doing it again.

Chapter Ten

Hannah pretended to scowl at a make-believe watch when Jeff rolled to a stop in front of the library entrance at 3:07 p.m. on Saturday. He started to climb out but she hopped in before he had a chance.

"Chivalry later." She buckled her seat belt and shot him a glance. "Clock's ticking."

"I know. I worked this morning and gave the yard one last mowing. At least I'm hoping it's one last mowing, and the cold front headed our way seems to agree. And by the way—" he gave her gold top and dark brown sweater a quick look "—you looked wonderful standing there with the trees turning color behind you."

"Really?" He had no idea how much that compliment meant to her. She beamed. "Thank you."

"You're welcome. Got your notebook?"

"Right here."

"And Ted Winchell knows we're running short on time so he's gathered information for us. And once we're done, we can head to my place if that's okay, eat and outline our presentation?"

"Sounds like a plan." She leaned forward, then paused, one finger ready to hit Play. "Music?"

"Sure."

She hit a switch, heard the music playing and sent him a sideways glance. "VeggieTales? Really?"

He laughed and hit Eject. "Trent and I worked this morning. We had his daughter Cory with us so Alyssa could have time with baby Clay because he was running a fever. Five-year-olds like listening to the same CD over and over again. Kind of like women."

Hannah raised a hand. "Guilty as charged. I have my favorites and Cory Michaels is one smart little girl. And adorable. How Alyssa handles three kids and a full-time job with Trent out of town is a marvel."

"You're right." Jeff pulled into the parking lot abutting Winchell Brick and turned the engine off. "And that realization should be enough to make me feel guilty. I've only had the increased workload at the factory."

"'A man works from sun to sun...'" Hannah started the quote and laughed.

"Yeah, yeah." Jeff sent her a grin as they headed up the walk, sweet and sincere, a smile that faded as soon as he stepped in the door.

"Thanks for all this, Ted." A dark-haired man reached out to shake Ted Winchell's hand. "Hank Marek began this project with solid goals and I want to follow that lead. Having the current prices on materials is crucial."

"Yes, it is." Ted turned, saw Jeff, smiled, gave him a quick "just a moment" hand sign, then turned back. "Matt, if you need anything else, give me a call. I can honor that quote through next spring unless something unforeseen happens in the market. In that case, I'll call you."

"Sounds good."

The dark-haired man turned and spotted Jeff and Hannah at the door. He drew a deep breath and looked ill at ease, his right hand clutching a fistful of papers in an iron grip. "Jeff."

"You're buying the Marek subdivision?" Jeff stepped forward, shoulders taut, wondering why he had to run into Matt right now. "You'd stoop that low?"

"The bank's already taken it over. It's falling into disrepair. So, yes, if I can crunch the numbers, I'm going to buy it and complete it. Until this moment it was a quiet deal—"

"I'm sure of that," Jeff retorted.

Matt continued as if Jeff hadn't spoken. "And because we're at a sensitive part of the negotiations, I'd appreciate you keeping this confidential."

Ted shot Matt a look of chagrin. "I'm sorry, Matt. I should have finished this with you in the office."

Matt shook his head. "My brother understands the art of careful negotiation, Ted. I'm sure he'll respect my wishes."

The word *brother* drew Hannah's attention. Jeff felt her eyes on him, sensed the shift of emotion. And he knew better than to make a public spectacle. Wasn't that exactly why he worked so hard to spit-polish the family name, trying to erase Neal Brennan's high-profile mistakes? But it was a tough go when one of those missteps stood larger than life before him, way too self-assured for an ex-con.

Jeff's mother believed Matt had paid his price by doing eighteen months in juvie.

Katie Bascomb was sentenced to a lifetime with a missing right leg.

Jeff had a hard time seeing justice in that equation, but he ground his jaw and shut his mouth, eager to maintain the family dignity. He'd been doing fine with that until Matt showed up.

He moved to let Matt by, refusing to introduce him to Hannah. As he passed, Matt dipped his chin Hannah's way in a nod of respect. "Ma'am."

She nodded back, then shot Jeff a look that hinted at disappointment.

Her look cut deep. Once again Matt's presence cast him in a bad light.

"Jeff." Ted stepped forward, determined. "I've got your facts and figures back here in my office, but let me show you guys a few ideas first."

"Thank you." Hannah smiled at Ted and extended her hand. "I'm Hannah Moore and I'm helping chair the fund-raising."

"Nice to meet you." Ted shook her hand before leading them to the far wall. "I stopped up in Jamison the other day to examine the existing masonry work on the churches. Fundamentally you can use anything for the path. Aesthetically, I'd go with fieldstone pavers." He pointed to the wall display. "You could go with the pink-tinged or gray-tinged stone. Either would draw together the preexisting aged conditions of the five churches surrounding the round green of the park."

"Could we combine them?" Hannah asked.

Ted grinned. "You've got a good eye. Yes. Either works fine, but blended they'd carry the right color balance. They're made for long-lasting good looks and foot traffic, and with the proper underlayment they won't shift and gap with repeated frost, ice and snow. Sound good?"

"It does." Jeff nodded, determined to focus on the

task at hand. He shifted his attention to Hannah, wishing he hadn't caused that guarded look in her eye. "Do you think we need to present the board with various options or go with this one alone?"

"Good question." She scanned the other displays, frowned and shrugged. "Nothing else is exactly right, correct?" She met Ted Winchell's gaze.

He shook his head. "Not in my estimation."

"And you're the resident expert."

He smiled. "Well, I don't like to brag…"

Hannah laughed and waved her hand at the stone they'd chosen. "Let's go in with this. The more decisive we appear, the more confidence we'll inspire."

"I like how you think." Ted led them into the office, typed a few figures into an existing spreadsheet, then printed the results. "This gives you the information you'll need to present to the board." He handed Hannah a brochure from the stone company. "And this one is the cost of what we're donating."

Jeff looked at the donated figure and whistled. "Ted, that's mighty generous of you guys."

Ted shrugged. "My brother is buried in the graveyard behind Holy Name. My parents got married in Good Shepherd just before Reverend Hannity came. My grandmother still goes to the White Church at the Bend each and every Sunday." He indicated the figures with a nod. "Family takes care of family, right? It was the least we could do."

His words stifled Jeff's reply, and Hannah stepped into the silence.

"Thank you."

"You're welcome. And good luck," he told them as he walked them to the door, his keys in hand. "Between

Councilman Bascomb and Councilwoman Jackson, you might have your work cut out for you. They pretty much say no to everything, and that leaves Cyrus as the tie-breaker, and Cyrus can't make a decision to save his life."

"You're kidding, right?" Hannah scanned Ted's face, then turned to Jeff. "Please tell me he's kidding."

"I wish I could."

"So we did all this and they're going to say no? What was the point?"

Jeff exchanged looks with Ted. "Because we're going to schmooze them into saying yes."

"More games?"

"Let's call it strategic planning," Ted told her. He exchanged a frank look with Jeff before returning his attention to Hannah. "Small towns have advantages and disadvantages. An advantage is knowing everyone because there is no such thing as hiding in a small town. So you play to the council's sensitivities to win their individual votes."

"And the disadvantage is?" Hannah arched a brow.

He shrugged and laughed. "Secrets don't really exist. No one comes here to hide because everything's an open book. And no council member is going to want the smudge of being the one person to vote down a good thing for the town because that's political suicide."

She pointed a finger at Jeff. "You got me into this on purpose, didn't you?"

"Absolutely. I wasn't about to take them on alone, Hannah. I'm brave, but I'm not stupid."

His words brought his confrontation with Matt back to mind. He hadn't been brave then. He'd been contentious and ornery, both of which equaled stupid.

And he'd done it in front of Hannah and Ted, after

he promised himself he'd get a handle on these feelings about Matt.

Hannah's quiet look of appraisal said he'd lost points, which was fine, wasn't it?

Define fine, his conscience niggled. *And get a grip.*

Easier said than done.

Saint Peter's question popped into his mind again. *"How many times must I forgive my brother, Lord? Seven?"*

Jeff knew Christ's answer. He understood the severity behind the response, the virtually limitless cache of forgiveness. Now he just had to find the strength to go along with the understanding.

"Jeff, this is lovely." Hannah surveyed the stately Colonial from the driveway a half hour later as the late-day light danced beams across the west-facing house. She turned to face Jeff, her right hand indicating the house and the yard. "This is yours?"

"You like it?"

"Try love it. Is it as sweet inside?"

"Let's find out." He grinned and lifted the two bags of takeout. "Since it appears I'll be eating leftover Chinese for a week, we might as well start putting a dent in this."

"I told you not to get the cashew chicken or the sesame shrimp," she scolded as they reached the front door. "Just because I said I liked them didn't mean we needed four entrées."

"I enjoy choices, and I lived through many a college weekend on cold Chinese," he told her. "So I actually like having leftovers in the fridge."

"You surprise me."

"How's that?"

Hannah shrugged. "You live in a big house you probably rarely see and you eat cold Chinese out of paper cartons."

"The house was a wise investment about seven years ago when prices were down and the former owners moved south. The Chinese food, well, I like cold Chinese."

"It's beautiful, Jeff." Hannah turned in a slow circle once inside, taking in the entry hall, the oak-trimmed rooms embracing the foyer and the staircase before her, a nod to older times and more stately bearings. "And what a staircase."

Jeff grinned boyishly. "That's what sold me. I could just see me as a kid, sliding down that banister, listening to my mother scold me."

"Having met your mother, I can't imagine she scolded too loud or too long. She's sweet and gentle."

"Unlike me?"

Hannah heard an almost plaintive note in his voice. "I think life might have handed you a two-sided coin and you're not too sure how to handle that."

"You mean that scene with my brother."

She made a little face. "Your business. Not mine."

He crossed the large and fairly empty dining room and entered a big, homey kitchen. Hannah followed, appreciating the welcoming stature of the elegant old rooms. The inviting maple table and chairs said the kitchen was his room of preference. He set the bags on the kitchen table and indicated them with a wave as he withdrew plates from ivory-stained cupboards. "Buying beef, shrimp, chicken and lo mein should be considered at least a little sweet."

"Since food is a necessity, and I've witnessed your

confession about loving leftovers, I'm afraid buying too much doesn't measure up."

"How about this?" He handed her the plates, opened the fridge and withdrew a string-tied white box. He slit the string, lifted the cover and withdrew a chocolate enhanced cannoli. "When it comes to desserts, I like Italian best." He held the pastry to her mouth and Hannah bit down carefully, letting the mingled tastes of dark chocolate, crisp cookie and sweet filling meld before she swallowed.

"Amazing. Gimme." She took the cannoli from his hand, took another bite and laughed at his look of chagrin as she began opening bags one-handed.

She fit, Jeff decided, seeing her there in front of the charming glass-fronted kitchen cabinets surrounding the kitchen on three sides. Her long braid dipped and swung with her movements, fetching atop the gold knit turtleneck beneath a dark brown nubby sweater. He grabbed silverware from a drawer, then plunked them onto the table with a deliberate lack of finesse. "Casual okay?"

She laughed, licked the last tidbit of cannoli cream from her fingers and agreed. "I love casual."

So did he. The smidge of pretentiousness that sometimes accompanied his job annoyed him. Over the years he'd dated a few women who fawned over that aspect of his career.

Not Hannah. She filled a trucker-size plate from the various cartons and then nailed him with a scathing look when he scanned the plate. "I do believe we've already had this discussion. I like to eat."

"I remember. You just surprise me because most women pretend they don't eat, then wolf down a bag of chips when they get home because they're starving."

"And you know this because?"

"I have a sister."

"Meredith." Hannah nodded, pulled out a chair and took a seat. "And Megan says she gives great haircuts. That's an art right there."

"You're not thinking of cutting your hair, are you?" It was no concern of his, but the very idea sat wrong with Jeff. In an age when so many women went short and sassy, he loved Hannah's long, tumbling curls. Today's braid just reminded him that braids could be undone.

"Maybe. Why?"

He kept his tone neutral with effort. "Your hair is beautiful, Hannah. It's perfect."

Surprise and pleasure infused her cheeks with color, but he was pretty sure she veered from serious talk for the same reasons he did, because this could never work. "Well, thank you, Jeff. I like your hair, too."

She was laughing at him. Oh, not out loud, she was too nice for that, but inside? Yeah, he was sure of it. But he'd been around the block often enough to know how far he could bend without breaking.

He sent her an easy grin over the paper cartons, gripped her fingers lightly and tried not to think of how cool and soft her skin felt as he said grace.

"Done." Hannah settled the last carton into the refrigerator. "Would you mind if we take a quick walk around the neighborhood? Otherwise I might fall asleep while you factor stones and dimensions."

Jeff grabbed her jacket and his. "Works for me. Our days of nice weather are dwindling."

"That's for sure." Hannah fastened her coat, stepped outside and drew in a deep breath. "But this is wonderful, isn't it? What a great neighborhood you live in. All these old homes. The trees. The streetlights. Positively poetic."

"You like poetry, Hannah?"

"Doesn't everyone?" She read his expression and burst out laughing. "Guess not. I expect your mother had a time with you, trying to balance your quest for scientific exploration with 'Twinkle, Twinkle, Little Star' on the keyboard."

"I didn't make it easy for her," Jeff admitted. He kicked a tiny stone off the sidewalk and watched it skitter away. "I love trying new things. Reinventing the wheel. I had a hard time understanding why she wanted me to do things I wasn't naturally good at while messing with the time I wanted to devote to what I liked."

"Because variety *is* important." Hannah eyed the starlit sky between gold-tinged maple boughs; the changing color intensified with each passing day. "And a parent's job as primary educator is to create that balance because they have an adult vantage point."

"You're a teacher."

He studied her, surprised. She pulled in a breath and fought a wince. "Yes."

"What did you teach?"

"High school science."

"Ah." He nodded, appeased. "I wondered why scientific jargon slipped into your speech so easily. I expect you were good."

Her face showed mixed emotion. "It was a long time ago. I like what I do now. It's peaceful."

"But is it exciting?" Jeff wondered out loud.

Hannah shook her head. "No, and that's just another reason to love it."

He accepted her words, as if it was the most natural

thing in the world for a science teacher to be working part-time in a hamlet-size library. Should he ask why she stopped?

Her expression told him to hold back.

He had time, as far as he knew. Now what he needed was patience, and that had been on his mother's prayer list for decades. Walking with Hannah? Talking with her? Getting to know the woman within?

That was worth every patient moment he could muster.

Chapter Eleven

No way could he wait until Wednesday night's board meeting to see Hannah again. The fact that this was his first thought on a bleak Sunday morning made Jeff take notice.

He called her cell phone but when his call went directly to voice mail, he realized her phone was either off or uncharged. He left a message, got cleaned up and headed toward Jamison for church, not even trying to pretend he wasn't hoping to see her. Maybe grab that breakfast she'd offered the week before. He headed over to Holy Name, slipped into the back of the old stone church and realized it was rock-band Sunday when the pounding of drums nearly pierced his ears.

Then Hannah slipped into the pew beside him.

"You're late," he whispered, refusing to disguise his pleasure.

She shook her head. "Nah, I'm not. I went to Good Shepherd to sit with you and avoid the first-Sunday-of-the-month amplifiers over here. But then I saw you racing up the steps…"

"Running a touch behind," he admitted, wondering if

she knew how perfectly her mottled blue scarf matched her eyes. "So you came over here to join me? Without earplugs?"

Her answering smile said enough. The way she turned her attention to the altar meant she didn't dare pursue this line of conversation at this moment.

Which only meant there'd be another time and another place, and Jeff was okay with that.

"Breakfast?" he asked as they headed down the church steps later, his ears reverberating from the church's less than perfect acoustics. "My treat."

Her bright smile encouraged him to edge closer, but she shook her head, regretful. "Not today. I've got a gazillion things to catch up on, and I promised myself I'd do them today because we have the Wednesday night council meeting, the Thursday night fund-raising meeting and next weekend is the Farmer's Fair and Harvest Dinner. I'm swamped."

"I'll help."

"With my laundry? Umm…no."

He laughed. "Then I'll help with other stuff. If we work together we can spend the later part of the day doing something fun."

"You don't have anything to do today?"

Her words reminded him of last Sunday's debacle, but he wouldn't lie to her. "I've got contract bids I need to go over, but I don't want a repeat of last week."

"And it's football season."

"So?" He paused at her car, watched as she unlocked the door and then offered a solution. "You go home and do your laundry and whatever else you need to get done. I'll go over my contracts and pick you up around two."

"Make it four."

He shook his head. "Too late and too long to wait." Color invaded her cheeks at his words and he smiled, grazing a finger against the flushed skin. "Three. And that's four hours longer than I care for."

Her gaze melted. She squared her shoulders, trying to look businesslike, but from the occasional looks Jeff intercepted from passersby, no one mistook their conversation for library business. "Three o'clock. I'll pick you up. Wear jeans."

"Bossy."

Her pleased smile softened the crisp response. He pushed her door closed, leaned down and grinned, giving her mouth a look of longing that seemed to deepen her expression. He nodded, letting his appreciative look speak for him. "See you then."

Jeff Brennan managed to put her in a tailspin with a simple look, a gentle smile, despite her best efforts to keep him at bay.

Keep him at bay? You ran over to Holy Name the minute you caught sight of him. That's not exactly maintaining an arm's length.

Hannah pressed cool hands against her warm cheeks as she decided she was not sick, just flustered.

It was delightful.

But also scary.

You will not dredge up fear and foreboding. Weren't you listening this morning, hearing Isaiah's words? "Do not be afraid. I am with you always. Follow me, and I will give you rest."

Hannah settled laundry into various drawers and took a clutch of hangers to the closet. She withdrew several summery tops with one hand and refilled the spot with long-sleeved blouses and turtlenecks. Her toe caught the box she'd stuffed in there, edging it forward. The closet floor was too shaded to see Brian's bold, black script, but she didn't need a visual to picture the slanted *H* and *M*, evidence of Brian's decisive flair.

Open it.

Not today. Today she was outdistancing the past by embracing the future. No matter what might come of this attraction to Jeff Brennan, wallowing in the past was no longer an option.

She finished stowing things away and barely had enough time to brush her teeth and fluff her hair before her doorbell rang at two-fifty. She strode to the door and yanked it open. "You're early."

He grinned and unlatched the screen door. "Couldn't wait any longer."

His words lifted her heart, soothed her soul. The feeling of being cared for was one of God's most natural highs. She waved him in, scurried into the bathroom for a hair clip and scolded, "Do you know how much a girl can get done in ten minutes, Jeff?"

He laughed from the living room and shot back, "Considering the girl's God-given beauty, there's little that needs doing."

So sweet of him to say so. She clipped back her hair, touched up her mascara and rejoined him in the front room. He gave her an appreciative smile, then motioned to Nick's family photo on the bookshelf. "This wasn't here a few weeks ago."

Add great powers of observation to his list of many talents, Hannah decided. "My brother, Nick, his wife, Leah, and their brand-new baby girl, Caitlyn Jean. I've got the honor of being her godmother on Thanksgiving weekend."

Jeff traced the baby's face with one blunt finger, the gentle action sweet beyond words. "She's beautiful."

Hannah smiled. "She is. My mom says she looks like a combination of Leah and me."

Jeff eyed the photo, tilted it, examining the baby's profile. Then he frowned and shook his head, humor glinting in his eyes. "You drool more."

"Stop." Hannah snatched the picture out of his hands. She waved to her jeans, turtleneck and thick, fleeced hoodie. "Is this good for whatever we're doing?"

"Perfect. Let's go."

"What *are* we doing?" she asked as they headed down the porch steps.

His car wasn't there. Instead he opened the door of a pickup truck that had seen better days. "We're driving this?"

He grinned. "Yup."

"But..."

"In." He waved a hand, then pretended to wince as she clutched his shoulder to climb up. "Nice grip, Han."

She waved his complaint away as he climbed in the driver's side. "What's the plan?"

"You'll see."

A surprise. Hannah had been alive long enough to know that surprises could either enchant or disappoint, but the gleam in Jeff's eye said this one should be fun. And when they pulled up to Breckenridge Farm a few minutes later, she was sure of it.

"Okay." Jeff looked around, puzzled, then waved a hand to the gorgeous fall displays and Hannah. "Pick."

"Pick what?"

"I don't know. Stuff. We're going to decorate our porches for harvest season. It's one of the things we do down here before the Farmer's Fair. Your landlord won't care, will she?"

"No."

"Good. It's silly to have unfestive porches, right? Downright unpatriotic."

"I couldn't agree more. Where do we start?"

"Straw," Jeff decided. He walked to a stack and removed four bales of straw and stacked them in the back of the pickup.

"And cornstalks for the pillars," Hannah told him. She moved to a huge tepee-style display and handed Jeff eight bunches of cornstalks.

"You don't think this is too many?" he asked, stretching his neck around the cumbersome bundles to see her.

"You have four pillars. I have four pillars. We both have lampposts, and you have that cute decorative fence by the front sidewalk. You can't decorate your porch without carrying the theme throughout."

"Far be it from me to mess with a theme." He hauled the bundled cornstalks into the bed of the truck. "And now pumpkins."

"And squash."

"I love squash," he told her as they lined up an assortment of pumpkins, then balanced the effect with a mix of squashes. "Butternut is my favorite."

"Mine, too." She smiled up at him, the thought of sharing a favorite squash far more pleasant than it should have been. "I like it with brown sugar and butter. And lots of cinnamon."

"I'm getting hungry just thinking about it." He eyed their stash and shook his head. "Something's missing."

"Whimsy."

"Say what?"

Hannah waved toward the far side of the quaint, aged barn. "Fanciful. Fun." She led him to a shed display of scarecrows and birdhouses surrounded by seasonally toned ribbons in nylon and raffia. "I think for your house we should get him." She pointed to a funny-faced scarecrow on a stick, perfect for posing in the hay, his blue jeans topped by red hunter plaid. A bright yellow hat completed the straw man's ensemble.

"And she would look great on my porch," Hannah explained, withdrawing a slightly stout straw woman in a blue flowered dress, her dark green hat embellished with fall-toned flowers.

"Why can't she stay on my porch?" asked Jeff. "They could keep each other company."

Hannah leaned close, whispering the obvious. "They're not married."

It was an innocent bit of teasing, so why did he turn her way, his expression all sweet and serious, as if the fate of two wooden stick scarecrows meant something?

Hannah swallowed hard. Jeff's questioning look pushed common sense and fear aside.

"I know a preacher." Jeff matched her soft tone as he moved closer, his gaze roaming her face until it settled on her lips. "Several, in fact."

"Do you?" She read the question in his eyes and couldn't pretend she wasn't thinking the exact same thing. She raised one hand and traced his face, his jaw, the sandpaper feel ruggedly male beneath her fingers.

Jeff slipped an arm around her waist, waiting for her to object or duck away, but that was the last thing Hannah wanted to do, although she knew she should. She puffed a breath, a tiny sigh that made him smile and draw her closer before he slanted his mouth over hers, the gentle pressure of his mouth, his embrace, like a wanderer finding home.

The strength of his hands, the stubble of late-day skin, the scent of him, all fresh air and hay with a hint of coffee. Standing there in the privacy of the rustic shed, with Jeff's lips on hers, it was almost easy to think about things like preachers and weddings.

For the scarecrows, that is.

Hannah drew back, ending the kiss, but she trailed a finger of contentment along his cheek, his chin, before indicating the straw woman with a quick look. "What if those two want a big wedding? Neither one of us has time to plan that."

Jeff smiled at her. "Then we find people to help. Did you pick out enough ribbon?"

"This, this and this." She piled the rolls into their woven basket, then glanced around, satisfied. "We did well."

Jeff sent her mouth a teasing glance. "Very well."

Her blush deepened his smile. He grabbed his scarecrow and hers, then headed toward the huge apple display. "Except for apples."

"Apples on the porch?" She frowned and shook her head. "They'll go bad."

"Apples to eat," Jeff told her. He grabbed a half peck of Honeycrisps as they headed inside to pay for their truckful of autumn fun. "And an apple pie for dessert."

"I love apple pie."

Kim Breckenridge added a fresh-baked pie to the basket, then swept them a quick look of question. "Anything else?"

Hannah nudged Jeff. "Cider."

"Great idea."

"A half gallon or whole?"

Jeff eyed the whole gallon and shook his head. "Half. We don't want it to sour and we can always come back for more."

"Which makes my entire family very happy," Kim told him, grinning. She withdrew the cider from an adjacent cooler. "There we go. All set now?"

Jeff eyed the pickup truck and the various things they had on the counter and gulped as he handed over his debit card. "Yes. Please."

He rearranged the truck bed to accommodate the vegetables and straw people while Hannah packed the front seat with food. She settled back into her seat as he shut the tailgate, wondering when she'd last had this much fun.

Maybe never, she decided, smiling as Jeff shifted the peck of apples to make room. She leaned across the front seat and surprised him with a kiss, just a little kiss, a feathering of her mouth against his somewhat grizzled skin. He smiled his thanks, his expression saying more than should be possible with the short weeks they'd known each other. But Hannah read the look in his eyes, the warmth, the caring, the invitation to travel a new path. And for the first time in nearly five years, she felt strong enough to take the chance.

"Oh, Jeff, I love it!"

Since Hannah rarely got this excited about anything, Jeff enjoyed hearing the uplift in her voice when they finished her porch in the lamplight that evening. He stood back, surveyed the effect and nodded, pleased that she'd enjoyed the afternoon. "It looks good."

"It looks great," she corrected him. She crossed the porch, then indicated the house with a wave. "Do you want to order a pizza and watch the beginning of the Sunday night game here?"

Jeff digested the invitation. She'd gotten weirded out last week by his work and football. Sure, she'd apologized, but no way was he about to mess with a great afternoon by chancing a bad evening. "Pizza's good, but I've got an early morning and unless I'm really into the team, I don't do late games."

"Pizza it is." She withdrew her phone, hit a number on her speed dial and placed the order. "I'm having them deliver it so we can tip the driver."

"Because?"

"It's Callie's cousin. He usually does construction but with the slowdown he hasn't had much work, so he's going to trade school for electricians and delivering pizzas at night."

Add kind and thoughtful to her growing list of wonderful attributes. She worked two jobs and drove a low-end car, but was willing to shell out five dollars she didn't have to help a young man's dream.

When the doorbell rang, Jeff moved quicker and waved her off. "I've got it."

"But you paid for all the stuff this afternoon," she protested, her chin thrust up in a really cute pout.

Jeff paid the young man, added a considerable tip and a nod of thanks, then turned. "My day, my decision. What kind of guy takes a girl out and makes her pay?"

She smiled, unwilling to argue that. "The worst. Thank you, Jeff." She surveyed the decorated porch and lifted one shoulder. "I'll smile every time I see that porch. Or think of it."

"Perfect."

A part of him longed to jump into hyperdrive, a typical Jeff Brennan move. The wiser portion urged him to pay close attention to laying a foundation of trust, the brick and mortar of a good base. Watching her devour a hefty share of the pizza, he waved outdoors. "Are you intent on making me walk off supper tonight, too? Because the rain just started and I didn't bring an umbrella."

"I have umbrellas, but no. I think we should just sit here with the curtains open and enjoy the fruits of our labors—"

"Vegetables, in this case," he interrupted, smiling.

She accepted his correction, looking really pretty and serious. "*Vegetables* of our labors and spit-polish our presentation."

"Gotcha." Jeff stood and cleaned up the paper plates and napkins, then reached down and hauled her to her feet. "Since we did our civic duty by improving the appearance of both Wellsville and Jamison with great-looking porches, I suppose work is in order."

"I concur." She moved across the room and drew open the drapes, the front porch light showcasing the fall array. "And if we sit here, we can enjoy the view."

"I already am."

She flushed, embarrassed and charmed, her beautiful smile a gift he hadn't expected and probably didn't deserve, but that only made him want to be more deserving.

His mother kept telling him to forgive and forget. To leave the past alone.

He thought he'd done that, but Matt's reappearance proved him wrong. Jeff followed Hannah across the room, took a seat and wondered if he had what it took to make things right. Go the distance. Be the peacemaker his mother and grandmother wanted him to be.

"Blessed are the peacemakers, for they shall be called the children of God." He'd learned that as a child, not understanding the depth of its meaning. Now, as Hannah leaned over the projected notes, her fall of hair curtaining half of her face, he understood the import more fully. He was letting his past dictate his present. Was that Matt Cavanaugh's fault?

Hardly.

But Matt had wreaked havoc back in the day, ruining lives in the process.

"I've lost you, I see."

Jeff pushed the puzzle of his life off to the side. "Only temporarily."

"Thinking of work?" She tipped him a look before noting the clock. "If you need to go home and get things done, I can finish this. We're almost done, anyway."

"Not work," he admitted, taking his time. He glanced away, then back. "Family stuff."

"Ah." Hannah sat back, steepled her fingers and met his gaze. "Meeting your brother yesterday."

"Half brother."

She considered his words then leaned forward. "I think you've nailed a big part of the problem right there. My parents divorced when I was nine years old. Both remarried. My father never had more kids, but my mother did." She indicated the picture of Nick on the small table beyond Jeff. "And I've never in my life thought of him as a half brother."

"But you lived with him, right?"

"Part of the time. But that's just geography, Jeff."

Jeff didn't want to concede that. "You knew him since he was a baby."

"Yes. But even if I hadn't—" she met his look, determined "—he'd still be my brother. I don't do halfway, Jeff. Ever."

Her words speared him.

He'd have thought the same about himself, but right now he wasn't too sure. Maybe he went full tilt when he had control, and pulled back when uncertainty loomed. Either way, he wasn't a big fan of this conversation. "So. For Wednesday. Do you have time to do a volunteer time chart?"

Did his quick shift back into business mode put that shadow on her face? He thought so. She bent her head, made a few marginal notes and put together a packet of information for him. "I can if you manage to put this into a semblance of order for us."

"I'd be glad to." He stood, wishing they'd never brought up family, wishing...

"Then I'll meet you at the Community Center. Is six thirty good?"

"Yes."

"Perfect."

"Hannah, I—"

"I loved the decorating." She smiled toward the front porch as she led the way to the door. "And the pizza. Thank you."

He wanted to say more, but good sense told him to hold off. He shrugged into his jacket. "You're welcome. See you Wednesday."

"Yes."

And that was it. He strode across the porch, remembering how carefree she'd looked as they decorated, the innocence of the day reflected in her face, her emotions. The memory of that kiss made him think all kinds of things.

Right up until they started talking about family and she realized he was a jerk of the highest proportions.

Maybe he was, maybe he wasn't, but most days were too chock-full of work to dwell on things like old wrongs.

But you do, his conscience reminded him. *Your quest for bigger, better, stronger is nothing more than trying to best your father. Get over it, already.*

Easier said than done when his life echoed with constant reminders. But whose fault was that? Hadn't he deliberately chosen a similar career to prove to himself and the world that he could do it better?

He headed home, tired and a little miffed that Hannah didn't quite get it. His conscience took great delight in reminding him that the problem probably wasn't Hannah's at all, and that just made him feel worse.

Chapter Twelve

Hannah drew her lightweight jacket snug as she hurried into the Jamison Community Center on Wednesday evening, the sudden dip in temperature a chill reminder. She spotted Jeff and headed his way. "Have you seen the weekend forecast?"

He gave her one of those steady, long looks and quipped back, "Hi, Jeff. How are you tonight? How was your day? Oh, and by the way, have you seen the forecast?"

"Sorry. I'm in business mode. First things first. We've got this nailed—" she held her presentation folder aloft "—and I'm projecting ahead. The weekend forecast is dire and we're putting a lot of stock into this big opening fund-raiser. Are we going to bomb?"

"We're hardy stock here, Hannah." Jeff shrugged off her concerns. "A little rain's nothing to get steamed up over."

"We're not talking scattered showers," she retorted. "We're talking monsoons. Flood watches. The real deal."

He still didn't have the decency to look worried. "Everything moves inside the high school if it storms. The performers use the auditorium and we move the dinner to the high school cafeteria."

The high school. Hannah hadn't bargained on that, hadn't given it a thought, actually. His words sent an adrenaline shot to her heart. She had to work to find her voice and when she did, she hoped it didn't tremble. "Where do the vendors set up?"

"Along the hallways," he explained. "It gets a little crowded and the fire marshal turns a blind eye for those two days, but it's doable. And Megan's got a candy booth and a cookie booth this year, so you'll have your hands full between those and the library fund-raising booth. You've never driven down for the Fair before?"

Hannah refused to explain that she avoided anything to do with fall or schools, that this was the first time she'd actually felt somewhat normal watching the march of color enrobe the surrounding hillsides. "No. Megan only did one booth in the past, so she didn't need me."

Her excuse was partially true. She was doing better, but the thought of being closed in in the high school during a rainstorm iced her from within, a condition that had nothing to do with external temperatures and everything to do with one young man's murderous rampage. "When do they decide?"

"Friday. If the forecast seems extreme, we go for the indoor venue. How's your scarecrow lady doing? You might want to consider giving her a raincoat for the weekend."

Yes. Concentrate on funny. Sweet. Mundane. Do not think about the high school, do not perseverate, do not allow the past to ruin the present. "The Lord is my light and my salvation; whom should I fear?"

That psalm verse was inscribed on a wooden plaque

over her bed and the words engraved on her heart. But despite her push forward, the thought of being entombed in that high school for hours on end blindsided her.

Then it's high time it didn't, her inner voice scolded. *You will be surrounded by people you've come to know and care for. One, especially.*

"Hannah, you there?"

She flushed, painful emotions rising within. "Yes, just thinking of how to do this and make it the best possible experience for all."

"Which for me, just means you're there." Hannah flushed. "Are you hungry?" he asked as the town clerk opened the meeting room door, allowing them to enter. "We could grab something after the meeting."

She shook her head, the idea of food a worst-case scenario right now. "I can't, thanks. I've got to stay ahead of things this week because I'll be working the Fair the whole weekend. I've got the library hours covered, but that means having everything organized for the gal who's stepping in for me."

"Understandable," he agreed. "And since we'll have you trapped indoors, you'll be fairly inaccessible this weekend."

Trapped indoors.

Her heart clenched; the common phrase was uncommonly chilling.

Jeff touched her arm, slowing her progress, letting others move into the room before them. "You okay?"

"Fine." She wasn't. She was about as far from okay as she could get, but she hoped, no, *prayed* it wouldn't show, that she could present a normal face to the world. And right now the world was Jeff Brennan.

King David had wondered out loud what could mortal man do to him, what should he fear?

Hannah had seen what mortal men did firsthand; she'd watched, listened and smelled the horrible aftereffects of man's depravity. And yes, she feared, that was painfully obvious when the prospect of being in a totally unrelated high school during a rained-out festival messed with her emotions.

But she'd grown strong enough now to regain control. Heading into the meeting room, she was determined to push through the wall of sensations steamrolling her. It was a building, no more, no less.

And she was so much better now.

Bright blue morning sky provided a backdrop for the riot of fall colors surrounding the high school. Hannah parked her car and headed inside, then turned in surprise. Her red car had become silver, and it was newer. Longer. She frowned, waved to a colleague and ducked into the teachers' entrance at ground level, the familiar hallways her home away from home.

As she reached the third level, a voice called her name. She looked around but saw no one, the hall empty and dark as if maintenance forgot to switch the lights on.

She unlocked her classroom door and opened it.

Ten faces looked up at her, expectant.

She frowned and glanced at her watch, but she wasn't wearing a watch. She moved into the room as dark clouds blotted out the sun beyond the long bank of windows; the predicted midday storm arrived early.

Except it wasn't early. The wall clock said 12:32, which meant she was late. Very late. She did an about-face, confused. Then she hurried to her desk as the silent class watched her. Waiting. Wondering. She had to say something, apologize for keeping them waiting. It was unspeakably rude behavior and she was never late for anything. Or rude.

The clouds opened up beyond the glass wall, unleashing a torrent of rain, the dismal sight and sound dulling the day in shaded grays.

She never heard the first gunshot. She was sure of that. Maybe the thunder blotted the noise, masking it.

But she didn't miss one scream, one plea for help as the kids in the adjacent lab room begged for their lives.

She ran for the adjoining door. When she got to it, she didn't open it, fearlessly running in to save the day.

She locked it, using the set of keys clutched in her hand, saving herself and the ten students in her room, but sealing off a possible avenue of escape for nine others.

Their screams echoed as she locked the hallway door, their pleas lost in a volley of gunfire, breaking glass and pouring rain, a cacophony of blended sounds. She scurried, gathering her ten students like baby chicks beneath a falcon's shadow, huddling them behind the half-wall bookcase in front of the windows, while chaos reigned in the lab next door, the eventual silence more formidable than the noise ever thought of being.

Hannah struggled awake, fighting her way out of the dream, clawing through blankets to escape. It took long seconds to realize she'd been dreaming, a dream she hadn't had in over a year.

She sat up, cradling a pillow, wanting to cry, longing to turn back the clock and think of something she could have done other than turn that key.

Many labeled her a hero in the aftermath. That made

her sick to her stomach. She was no hero. No matter what she did, she couldn't forget how she used those keys in her hand to lock out three crazed killers, one innocent lab instructor and nine innocent kids.

God forgive her, she'd turned that key, barricaded the door with the help of two sturdy boys, gathered the ten kids in her charge and crouched like a frightened rabbit behind a makeshift bookcase blockade while gunfire shattered the windows above them, showering them in a volley of crushed glass and cold, teeming rain.

Sure, she'd saved some, and everyone told her she should focus on that. Grab the positive and avoid the negative. Scientifically speaking, she understood their reasoning.

But she couldn't forget that *she* was Brad Duquette's intended target, the one he came gunning for because she'd turned down his application for her elite science class. He'd reminded her as he targeted the teacher and students in the adjacent lab, counting them off nice and loud for her benefit.

Dark thoughts invaded her heart, her soul, the memories of so much lost in so little time.

"Father, help me. Be my strength, my heart, feed my soul. Shelter me from this mayhem, from these memories, from this fear. Strengthen me, uphold me, uplift me."

Lisa had told her that life would trigger strong emotional reactions sometimes, that she'd have to bolster herself to push through. "And each time you do, you'll gain strength and momentum," the young therapist promised. "But you need to take it step by step."

The impending weekend loomed before her, the thought of rain beating on the school roof, darkening the windows, weighing heavy.

Because you're letting it, her conscience scolded. *It's rain, nothing more, nothing less, in a building that's common to every community in the world. A school. Go. Do good work. Be at peace.*

Could she?

Hannah clutched the pillow tighter and sighed.

She had to. She knew that. Eyeing the clock she noted the predawn hour and climbed out of bed, knowing there'd be no more sleep this night, praying she wouldn't repeat this performance every night this week in anticipation of the indoor setting.

But if she did?

She would not cave. Not ever again. She'd move forward. No more would she let fear and guilt dog her steps or impede her way. She was determined to take charge of her life, once and for all.

She washed her face, made coffee, opened her laptop and sat down to do something she should have done long ago: write notes of apology to those families whose children died that day, seeking their forgiveness. She hunted through files, found most of their addresses and withdrew a pad of notepaper from her desk drawer.

She'd felt better after talking to Jane Dinsmore about Ironwood, and while she hated what she felt compelled to say to these parents, she knew she had no choice. With God as her witness, she needed to face the enormity of her guilt head-on. And it was high time she did just that.

"I'd prefer snow," Megan grumbled as she and Hannah removed wet, protective plastic sheeting from the stacks of cookies on Saturday morning. "At least snow can be brushed off. This—" she held out a dripping sheet of plastic and shook her head as she glared toward the windows "—borders on ridiculous."

Hannah handed over a fresh roll of paper towels. "Don't talk. Wipe. We need to get set up down the hall and some bossy gray-haired man is standing guard at the hall door to make sure we don't mess up his floors."

"Ray Bernard, head custodian. And believe me—" Meg leaned closer "—I wouldn't have the nerve to mess up his floors." She looked up and her smile broadened. "And what a coincidence, Jeff Brennan just happens to be coming this way. In all the years I've been manning the Farmer's Fair, I don't recall seeing Jeff this early or this excited."

"Stop." Hannah met his gaze and knew their mutual reaction was ill-hidden.

"You made it." Jeff didn't even pause, just grabbed Hannah's hand and swept a quick kiss to her mouth before offering his help, as if kissing her in public was the most natural thing in the world. He squeezed her hand, hefted multiple boxes of cookies onto a dry cafeteria cart and led Hannah past the grim-faced custodial sentry and down the hall. "They put the cookie booth down here and tucked the fudge tables in the clump of food booths just beyond the gym." He withdrew a floor plan from his pocket and marked her spot with an X before handing it over.

"A cheat sheet. Excellent."

He nodded as he shifted the boxes aside to make room for a volunteer lugging the rest from the kitchen. "Thanks, Cheryl. And yeah, the cheat sheets are a must because a lot of the vendors don't know their way around the high school and it's easy to get yourself turned around."

"Thank you, Jeff."

"You're welcome." His gaze lingered on her face, her eyes, as if wondering… What? What was he thinking? She had no idea, but the look disappeared as someone called his name from down the hall. "I'm in and out today with stuff going on at the plant. The library fundraiser booth is near the front, but if you need me for anything—" he moved closer, his gentle expression a promise "—just call me, okay?"

Hannah drew a deep breath, refusing to look around, not wanting to see the lockers, bulletin boards and trophy cases. Today her eyes would face straight ahead or be trained on cookies. She swept the stack of boxes a look. "By the time I get set up here, people will be coming in droves, keeping me so busy I won't have a spare minute to think of you."

He cupped her cheek with one broad hand, his gentle look strengthening her. "I hope that's not true."

She flushed, saw his grin and felt like her world edged a little more upright. "Go. We've got work to do."

"See you later."

Her heart skipped a beat at that thought, the simple phrase a blessed promise. And just like she'd assured Jeff, by the time she got the booth festooned with harvest plaid tablecloths, Indian corn and silk mums, then set out baskets of individually wrapped supersize cookies, customers were wandering by in thick groups, undaunted by the gloomy weather and ready to enjoy a weekend of good food and innocent fun. By day's end, she'd almost forgotten the setting, the press of people, talk and laughter shifting the feel from academic to festive more than she would have thought possible, right up until a voice startled her from behind.

"I liked the vanilla caramels best."

A flicker of unease prickling her neck, Hannah choked down a sigh at the familiar boy's needy expression. "Dominic, right?"

He smiled, pleased she'd remembered, embarrassed almost, then gave a quick jerk of his head. "Yeah. Do you work at the cookie store, too?" His question referenced the banner displayed behind her, the words *Colonial Cookie Kitchen* flowing in old-world script.

Hannah nodded. "Sometimes. I work in the library in Jamison and the candy store, but when Meg has weekend festival booths, I try to help out. Would you like a cookie?"

He eyed them, hesitated, then flushed when she handed him two. "They're on the house."

"I've got money," he protested, but Hannah waved that off.

"Save it for something else or donate it to one of the good causes at the front. We have to start with fresh stock tomorrow so you're actually doing me a favor."

"Thanks." He took the cookies, his expression saying he wasn't sure how to handle her magnanimous action. In the end he headed down the hall, his shoulders a little straighter than they'd been. Several strides away, he swung back. "Thanks again, Miss—"

"Moore," Hannah told him. She widened her smile and shooed him away. "Go. Enjoy. And thanks for stopping by."

Her words surprised him, as if he couldn't fathom someone thanking him for just being there. Then he headed out the side door, one cookie rapidly disappearing.

Hannah noted his thinness and filed that alongside

the personality quirks, the hand twitches and the uncertain eyes.

Was it something?

Nothing?

She had no clue, but instinct told her Dominic needed
a friend.

"Time for supper." Jeff's voice broke up her thoughts,
a welcome diversion. "And don't tell me you snacked
on cookies all day and don't want to eat because I'm
starved."

"First, you're bossy," Hannah told him, sliding the
meager remnants of the day's leftovers his way. "These
are for you. Meg's dad already gathered my boxes and
cash to take back to the store for tomorrow's load so
we're good to go."

"As nice as this is," Jeff replied, hoisting the small box
of cookies for her benefit, "it's not supper. And I don't
know about you, but I didn't have a chance to eat all day."

"Me neither."

"Then I'm assuaging my guilt for not feeding you
lunch by taking you out. I should have gotten over here
midday but I got tied up at work. I know how crazy it is
when you're running a booth on your own. It's hard to
find a moment to get away."

"The hall runners offered to spell me so I could get
food," Hannah admitted, but she wasn't about to explain
why she refused, that the thought of walking the halls to
get to the improvised food court made her go weak in the
knees. "But I hate to eat on the run, so I figured I'd wait."

"All the more reason for me to feed you now," Jeff declared as he led the way out the front doors. The rain had
let up slightly, but the late hour and thick clouds hung
dark and foreboding. Jeff grasped her hand and headed

for the shuttle bus at a run. "We'll grab our cars and head to the Texas Hot, okay?"

"Perfect."

"Callie said we signed up twenty-two significant sponsors today," he told her once they'd settled themselves into a booth at Wellsville's old-style restaurant. "That's a huge plus for little investment of time or effort."

"I'll say. And despite the bad weather, the fair did well. I was surrounded by happy vendors."

"I think the rain actually helped us," Jeff replied. "The local corn mazes and hayrides got rained out. Since we had an indoor location, we got the spillover."

"And tomorrow…"

"Shorter hours, ten to three, then the Harvest Dinner."

She smiled, rimmed her water glass with a finger and sat back. "I'm glad I had time to help this year."

"Me, too." He glanced up as Ellie Ramos headed their way.

"You guys worked the festival and you're still hungry?" she asked, surprised. She handed them each a menu and shook her head. "Which means that business was so good there was no time to eat or they ran low on food around four o'clock."

"Right on both counts." Jeff grinned and didn't bother with the menu. "Ellie, nothing sounds better on a cold, wet day than your chicken and biscuits, smothered in gravy with a side of slaw."

"Make that two." Hannah handed her menu back to Ellie and added, "And if a chocolate cola happens to come my way, I wouldn't refuse it."

"Coffee for me."

"I'm on it."

Jeff studied Hannah once Ellie had gone, his gaze questioning.

"Why are you staring at me? Do I have something on my face?"

"No." He wavered, the tiny furrow between his eyes hinting concern, then said, "You looked a little shell-shocked at the school this morning and I was wondering if it was something I said. Or did."

Tell him.

A part of her wanted to, but not here. Not now. Revealing her part in the Ironwood massacre couldn't be relegated to casual dinner conversation. She met his look of concern and shrugged. "It pushed some old buttons."

"Do you want to tell me about them?"

"Another time?" She sat back as Ellie delivered their drinks, then glanced around the restaurant. "And in a more private setting."

"I'll hold you to that." His look of promise meant business. After talking with Jane the week before, Hannah realized that some people already knew her past and respected her privacy. She didn't want Jeff to hear about it from someone else, but Ironwood wasn't a subject she delved into lightly.

She took a sip of her blended soda and raised her glass in a toast. "To a successful day."

"Hear, hear." Jeff tapped her glass with his coffee mug. "I can't remember ever enjoying a Farmer's Fair so completely, Hannah."

Heat rose again. "You were barely there," she scolded lightly.

"In body, yes. But in thought?" He met her gaze with a sweet look of warm appreciation, his eyes saying more than mere words. "I was by your side all day."

His gentleness melted her, but did it make up for the dogged determination he gave to his job?

You equate too much with Brian, with the past. A good work ethic is something to thank God for.

"Food." He tapped her hand as Ellie approached. "And stop looking so serious. It's bad for your digestion."

She smiled in gratitude. "We'll talk sometime soon, okay?"

"It's fine, Hannah." His tone bathed her in reassurance, as if nothing she said or did could possibly make a difference. Hannah knew better, but was willing to take the chance because keeping her secrets was no longer possible. And maybe that was a good thing.

Chapter Thirteen

Jeff strode into the library for the scheduled Thursday night meeting, his expression grim. Protective instinct pushed Hannah forward, wanting to soothe his angst.

He spotted her and smiled, a heartfelt smile that softened the hard lines of his face for just a moment. He took his place at the end of the table, settled his notes, then addressed the group. "I apologize for being late. I was on the phone with my grandmother. She called me a few minutes ago to tell me Jane Dinsmore is gravely ill."

All eyes moved to the empty chair next to Hannah.

"She's in the hospital right now. According to my grandmother, she's been quietly fighting cancer for over three years. She'd been doing better until this summer, when a recurrence showed the cancer had metastasized to other parts of her body."

His expression reflected the pain of his words. "Most of us have known Miss Dinsmore since childhood, and we all understand what a loss her death would be to our community."

Reverend Hannity stood, apparently unsurprised by this news. He reached for the hands of those seated alongside him, then waited as the rest of the group followed suit. Silent for a moment, he lowered his chin and closed his eyes. "Father, we beseech Thee on behalf of our dear sister Jane, to love her, watch over her, care for her and guide her. We ask Your healing hands upon her if that is Your will, but more than that, Lord, we thank You for Jane Dinsmore, for her selfless life, her unselfish acts, her kindly, straightforward ways and her tireless commitment to the youth of our community. You blessed us with her love of science and teaching, and while our hearts grieve her illness, our souls appreciate what she has sacrificed for our children. Amen."

Hannah stared at the empty chair, little things suddenly making sense. The cough. The pale look. The breathlessness.

For a brief moment, Hannah wondered if her presence in Jamison, Jane's illness and now Hannah's gradual healing was all part of God's greater plan?

Of course not.

And yet...

She shut those thoughts down and concentrated on what Jeff was saying as he outlined the town board's approval of their stone walking path proposal, but the pall of Jane's illness took the shine off the excitement. By meeting's end, everyone was ready to go home, digest the news and think. Pray.

And that included Hannah. She stepped up to Jeff once the others had left and quietly put her arms around him from behind, hoping her presence offered comfort.

He didn't turn. He covered her hands with his and she felt the tremor within, the emotion he'd tamped down while conducting the meeting. She moved around front, laid her head against his chest and felt those strong arms engulf her. This time she was pretty sure she was holding him up, not vice versa. "I'm sorry, Jeff."

He tightened his grip. "Me, too. Jane's been Grandma's friend forever. They're peas in a pod, two of the most industrious women I've ever met. Grandma's not handling this well and Grandma handles everything well, so that's a real wake-up call."

Having met both women, Hannah saw the parallel. "Death's a tough thing to face. We can rationalize it through our faith but it's hard to minimize the physical loss of someone we love."

"Exactly." He held her close; the steady beat of his heart beneath her ear was a source of comfort and strength. When he pulled away, she saw the reluctance in his face, his eyes, and smiled.

"Thank you."

She moved back to the table, grabbed her jacket and shrugged into it while he gathered his notes in an uncharacteristic slapdash fashion.

He walked her to her car, pensive, and Hannah wished there was some way to help him through this. She might be a relative newcomer, but she'd sensed the feelings of the volunteers gathered tonight, and their heartfelt reaction said so much about Jane's effect. Hannah knew firsthand the positive ramifications of a good teacher. She rolled down the window to bid Jeff good-night, and his sad look made her wish she could help make this better.

"I'll talk to you tomorrow."

Hannah nodded, unable to smile, wishing things were all right. "Okay."

Jeff stepped back, watching as she drove away, but not really seeing her, Hannah was sure of it. As she climbed the steps to her apartment, she heard the sound of an

engine. She turned, noting Jeff's car, and that made her
smile.

He'd taken the time to make sure she'd gotten home
okay. She raised her hand in acknowledgment, unable to
see his answering wave, but for tonight, just the knowledge that he'd followed her home was enough.

Do it, her inner voice scolded the next evening.

Don't you dare, argued its alter ego.

She'd been living a tug-of-war since the previous
night. She'd contemplated, stewed and prayed, unable
to decide. Should she offer to take over Jane's classes,
be the helping hand the school desperately needed? She
was professionally self-confident enough to know that
no one could do it better, but the question boiled down
to could she do it at all?

She dropped her head into her hands, pensive, the late-
day shadows marking the library's closing time. She'd
locked the door but hadn't gone home yet, determined to
sort this out. If only she could talk to someone.

Jeff.

Her heart agreed, but her head scolded. *He's going to
find out eventually, why not just tell him? See what he
thinks? He's the kind of guy who views the whole picture.
He'll give you a fresh vantage point.*

And then maybe walk away forever, like Brian.

That thought crushed her fervor, but she couldn't let
it die, so in the end she hit her speed dial and prayed.
He answered right away. "Hey, I was just thinking about
you. What's up?"

His gentle warmth, his choice of words, the way he
looked at her when they were together… Could she risk
losing that by revealing her past? Would the truth set

her free or send him running? Either way, she needed to know, so she took a deep breath. "Can I talk to you?"

"Of course. Now?"

He didn't tease or joke around, unusual for him, but maybe he read the need in her voice. "Yes. Are you home? Can I come over?"

"I'm actually just pulling into the library parking lot because I knew you'd be closing up."

His thoughtfulness tightened her throat, making this confession that much harder. She had so much to lose, but she knew they didn't dare take this relationship further with Jeff in the dark. And right now she needed a friend, a confidant. Who better than the man she loved?

Loved? Admitting that sent anticipation shivering up her spine and fear roiling into her gut. "I'll be right out."

"I'll be waiting."

He met her by the steps, smiled and hauled her in for a bracing hug, his strong arms and broad chest warming her. "Rough day?"

"No. But I need to talk to you."

"Your place is close. Shall we head there?"

"Sure."

She climbed in her car and headed home, half wishing the drive was longer. Her festive porch lightened her mood as she climbed the steps. No matter what happened after today, she'd shared a wonderful time with Jeff, a delightful reprieve. And if that was all he was able to give after hearing her story, she'd be grateful.

You'll be brokenhearted, warned her conscience, more than a little self-righteous.

Yeah, but honest, shot back her good-girl ego. *The truth shall set you free, Hannah.*

He followed her in, set a bag in the kitchen, then

grabbed her hand and led her to the couch in the front room. "Sit."

She followed his direction, not like there was much choice. He sat alongside her, leaned back and tugged her with him. "Okay. What's up?"

She couldn't do this sitting back, unable to see his face or read his reactions. She pushed forward and turned to face him. His left brow arched, wondering. She clenched and unclenched her hands, then dove in. "I told you I was a teacher."

He nodded. "Yes."

"I taught high school science for eight years."

"Impressive. Not an easy task."

"It was very easy," she corrected, working to keep her voice level. "I loved it. I loved it so much." Her voice cracked with that admission. just a little, but he noticed it. She could tell from the way his brow furrowed, the way he hunched forward slightly.

"Why did you stop, Hannah?"

Five little words that either led her forward or offered her an escape. She chose to move forward, fully aware of the risks. "I taught at Ironwood High."

He reached for her hand, his strong, sure fingers giving her strength, but the gravity in his eyes said he remembered Ironwood High, along with the rest of a grieving nation.

"We had developed a special class in conjunction with a program at Penn. It was an elective for students who met certain criteria, but I had the power to approve who should be in the class. The mission of the class required outside fieldwork and we developed a thoughtful selection process to give us a variety of kids. We were excited about this concept, because the class selection was actually part of the team research, the effect of nature and nurture on the human brain."

"To do this with high school kids half fascinates me and half scares me to death," Jeff told her, his gentle tone saying she could continue. "So you chose the class…"

"We had a committee," she explained, "but I had veto power because I was the teacher who would be out and about with this group. The administration let me weed out kids whose application might look okay, but whose personality might be detrimental in less structured settings. We had tons of applications but we limited the class to twenty, a nice number to work with."

"If you say so." His face said there was little fun involved with teaching twenty kids anything, but he squeezed her hand. "And then…"

She hauled in a breath and let it out on a sigh. "Brad Duquette was the mastermind behind the Ironwood massacre. Steve Shelwyn and Dave Mastrodonato were his disciples, but they didn't have the vision to put it together. Brad did. He was such a smart kid, but there was something about him. Something not right, as if he wanted help, but laughed at anyone's efforts because he knew he could outsmart them."

She shook her head, thinking back and still coming up short. "I saw that in him, and that's the reason I vetoed his application, because it always felt like he was trying to trip me up and I couldn't take that chance if I was out on my own with the kids, you know?" She met Jeff's gaze.

He nodded in support, and Hannah gripped his hands tighter. "What if I'd accepted him? Would it have been the tipping point, the one thing that gave him hope, that lessened his anger?"

"You can't take that on yourself, Hannah." Jeff closed

the narrow space between them and pulled her in for a hug. "Out of all those applications, you could only accept twenty. The odds were against *all* of the applicants, but none of the others went on a shooting spree, right?"

"I know that." She pulled back and held his look, wishing she didn't have to burden him, but having little choice now. "But this one did. And when they entered the school during lunchtime, my research class was split, half in the lab, half in the adjoining classroom with me. We heard loud voices, then screaming, then gunfire. Karen Krenzer, the lab instructor, liked to keep our linking door closed during labs so my voice wouldn't distract her group. I'd left my keys on top of my desk because I was running late that morning, so I grabbed them and locked the adjoining door to the lab. A couple of boys barricaded it with a filing cabinet and a bungee cord while I locked the hall door.

"Between the bombs they rigged, the guns they used and the sheer surprise of the attack, they managed to kill three teachers, nine students and two police officers who tripped a bomb as everything was happening. Fourteen people died that day because I denied Brad Duquette's application into my research class."

Chapter Fourteen

Her face had grayed. The pain of retelling the story was an obvious drain.

What a thing for her to carry around, this kid's lack of conscience, his deep-seated anger. None of that was Hannah's fault. "You can't shoulder that, Han. It's not fair. Whatever messed those kids up happened long before you came on the scene."

A tiny smile softened her face. "That's what Jane Dinsmore told me. She's known all along who I am, where I came from. So did your grandmother."

It didn't surprise Jeff that Grandma knew. She was thorough with everything she did and she chaired the council that hired Hannah, but the fact that she didn't say anything...

That felt a little off.

"They also knew Jane was sick, that she might not beat this cancer and if she didn't, I would be here, waiting in the wings."

The idea that Jane and his grandmother plotted to keep Hannah here because they wanted a teacher to step into

Jane's shoes if she didn't win the battle with cancer... Of all the pompous, power-wielding—

"It was a brilliant idea, actually."

Hannah's words stopped his inner tirade. "What do you mean?"

She lifted her slim shoulders in a slight shrug. "They gave me a chance to heal, to reconnect with people, with God. With life. And you."

"Hannah, I—"

"I need to finish before you say anything else, Jeff. Please?"

Her soft and earnest plea made him relax his hands, his emotions. "Of course."

"Ten of my students were with me. Nine were in the lab with Karen, the lab instructor. One was absent. Once we barricaded the lab door and locked the hall door, we hid behind a half wall of shelving that was built like a study nook along the last three windows. We huddled there, crouched behind the shelving, listening to what happened in the lab, step-by-step."

Jeff didn't need to hear the details of that carnage. He remembered the ceaseless minute-by-minute news coverage and read the reality in her gray pallor, her heavy eyes.

"And while Brad tormented and shot Karen and those lab students, he shouted we'd be next, that I'd never get the chance to keep a kid out of a class again."

"Oh, Hannah." Jeff pulled her into his chest, needing to hold her, not sure what to say when words weren't enough. "Hannah. I'm so sorry."

"He couldn't get through the lab door. He sent Dave to the hallway to see if they could infiltrate our room through the hall entry doors, but the hall security gates came down when the emergency was sounded, and our security chief was a former county sheriff licensed to carry. He shot Dave as he approached our classroom door with a sawed-off shotgun and two homemade bombs. Ironwood is a huge school, and I found out later the reason Dennis found the shooters so quickly was because he followed the trail of bodies up the back stairs."

Jeff hung on, praying, begging God to bless her, help her, help those families whose lives were altered in the space of a few hours.

"When Brad realized he couldn't get through the lab doors, he started shouting the names of the captive students before he shot them. He made sure we heard them cry and plead. Beg for their lives. He had Steven list the names on the blackboard with the time of death, taunting the police for their lack of speed."

The magnitude of the combined depravity gripped Jeff, making him wish he could do something, anything to make this better. But no one could.

Except God.

"When Brad realized he'd lost Dave, he and Steve started raining bullets on our room through the wall. They managed to hit the windows above us." He didn't think she could pale further but he was wrong. Her eyes went wide, the sights and sounds of that horrific afternoon painting a mental picture he could only imagine. Hannah had no choice but to replay the events. She'd lived them. "We clung to one another, crouching low in a bed of sharp, broken glass while the rain poured in, lashed by forty-miles-per-hour winds."

"Lord, bless Hannah, help her to stay strong, to see Your words, Your truth in the goodness that lives in her. The strength, the wisdom, the amazing intelligence You've given her and the gift of giving she shares with others every day. Help her, Lord, take away the guilt she carries wrongly, help her see that evil cannot always be explained and that the devil's work should be condemned, not that of the innocent."

"Was I innocent, Jeff?" She pushed back and searched his gaze. "What if I let him into our room? Would he have still shot Karen and those students? Would it have bought time so that help could arrive?"

"You did the right thing, the brave thing," he insisted, amazed she'd think differently. "You saved lives that day, the lives of the kids in your classroom. You didn't cause the other deaths, Hannah. The shooters did. Don't take that on yourself. You reacted to a horrible situation with guts and brains. How can you think less of yourself?"

"Because he called me a coward for hiding."

The calm way she said the words chilled Jeff. He gripped her shoulders and held her gaze, hoping, praying he was doing the right thing. "You are one of the bravest people I've ever met, Hannah. You reacted to an out-of-control situation with thought and action. You saved ten children and yourself." When she looked like she might argue, he shook his head, needing her to understand. "I will forever thank God that you had the common sense to lock and barricade that door, that the barricade held and that the bullets he sprayed through the wall didn't hit anyone in your room."

He gathered her back in his arms, feeling her tears wet his shirt, his neck. He didn't know how long he cradled her like that, but when she finally sat up, he read the look of determination on her face and knew she'd made a decision.

"You're going for it, aren't you?" He leaned back, assessing her gaze, the set of her shoulders.

"I have to."

"Why?" Why would she put herself through that?

"Because I won't feel whole again until I face this fear, Jeff. It eats at me. I hide it away and think I'm better, and then it rises up at the worst times, choking me."

"Wouldn't therapy be easier?"

She leaned forward and laid her soft hand atop his arm. "This *is* therapy. My last step. I've come so far, but I need to go the distance, Jeff. Face the dragon."

"I'll buy you a dragon of your own. We can build him a pen in our backyard."

A soft smile chased the shadows for a moment. "*Our* backyard?"

"Hannah, I—"

She put her hand over his mouth and shook her head. "Don't. Please. You have to know the rest, Jeff, that I came totally unglued after the attack. I was hospitalized for a while, and then was treated by a psychiatrist and a therapist for months. I hated myself, I hated my life, I hated the shooters and I wanted to die."

He didn't think his heart could break any further, but it did, seeing the guilt in her face for her very normal reaction to murdering chaos. "Hannah, you crashed afterward. That's normal."

"Nothing I did could be construed as normal," she argued, remembering.

"It was," Jeff insisted. "You're a scientist. You understand the principles of action/reaction. Your emotional *reaction* matched their actions, step-by-step. They attacked your students, your room, your colleague, your job and then your faith. You crashed and burned, then regrouped by coming here. Working here." He hugged her again, feeling the softness of her hair slip beneath his cheek, his hands. "And I'm so glad you did."

"Me, too."

He smiled, feeling her relax in his arms. "So you're going to apply for Jane's job?"

"Yes."

He had no idea if this was a good move or a really stupid one, but he knew one thing: whatever Hannah decided, he'd support her from this day forward. "Okay, then. Where do we start?"

"We?"

He nodded firmly. "I'm a big believer in facing the past. Moving on. Whatever happens, just know I've got your back."

"Really?"

"Absolutely."

"Well, then. Let's start with this." Hannah stood and crossed the room, disappeared for a few seconds, then returned, carrying a box.

Jeff frowned, not understanding.

She held out the box and pointed to the script. "This is from Brian. He was my fiancé at the time of the attack. He's now the vice president of VanDerstraat Communications and a town board member in Big Springs. He didn't have much use for me while I was in the psych wing."

"Hannah."

She waved him off. "In retrospect, he did us both a favor. I wasn't good for anyone or anything at that point. It taught me that true love is required to stand up to the test, that those vows of sickness and health are not just pretty words. They're a solemn pledge."

"So what's in here?"

She made a face and shook her head. "I don't know. I

was tempted to chuck it to the curb when it came, but I realized that was the chicken's way out."

"So you shoved it away…" he teased.

"I wasn't *that* brave," she shot back, a tiny smile curving her mouth. "And notice that I'm opening it with you here, ensuring proper backup."

"Let's do this."

"All right." She tugged the tape free from the sides, then pulled the strip across the box top, the distinct sound leading them to what? More sadness? More sorrow?

Jeff was pretty sure that was humanly impossible.

"Oh."

Jeff leaned forward, his vision obscured by the box flaps, but he needn't have bothered. Hannah withdrew a presidential award for excellence in teaching math and science, her expression soft, her fingers trailing the vellum surface.

"Pretty impressive."

Her bittersweet smile said yes and no.

"May I see?"

She handed it over and withdrew a second one from the box. "Sure. You look at that one and I'll look at this one."

"You won two?"

She nodded. "My Penn projects. I was nominated three times and received the award twice."

"Hannah, that's amazing."

She shrugged the praise away. "It was a wonderful honor for me and the kids. Ah…" She grimaced, pulling out a sheet of folded paper, then sent Jeff a rueful look. "Oh, good. A note."

Jeff leaned over her shoulder, and read out loud. "Hannah, hope all is well. The school asked if I could forward these to you with their apologies. It seems they were lost for a while and the new principal is sorry they weren't sent to you years ago. Best, Brian."

Funny. She'd been worried about what Brian's message might do to her, but sitting here, reading his short words, seeing his script, it meant nothing. Not a thing.

Of course, six feet of wonderful and supportive man sitting alongside her had something to do with that. She crumpled the note into a tight ball and lofted a three-pointer into the small garbage can just inside the kitchen door.

"Sweet shot."

She smiled and flicked a look Jeff's way. "Old news."

"Good."

She lifted the beautiful award, stood and placed it in a position of prominence alongside Nick's family picture. "I'll go see Jane tomorrow."

Jeff stood and crossed the room with the second award. He set it up alongside the family photo, flanking Nick's accomplishments with Hannah's. "And you know I'll help in any way I can, right?"

His promise was worth so much more than he knew. Jeff's faith, his work ethic and his level of commitment were so different from Brian's. How could she have ever thought the two men similar?

"They're beautiful, Hannah." Jeff nodded to the awards, then drew her into his arms, cradling her against his chest, his heart. "And so are you." He dropped his mouth to her hair, her cheek, kissing her gently. "You'll let me know if there's anything you need?"

"Will do."

"Do you want me to go with you tomorrow?"

"Nope."

"All right, then." He paused before he opened the front door. "Call me. Let me know how things go, okay?"

"I will."

He hated to leave after hearing her story. He climbed into his car to return to Wellsville, then paused, chagrined.

Hannah had dealt with more death and destruction in a few short hours than most people face in a lifetime. She'd crashed and burned, then rebuilt her life step-by-step, while he stubbornly refused to move beyond high school anger at his father and half brother. That realization said he had some serious fence-mending of his own to do.

He turned the car around and headed north toward Nunda, unsure where he'd find Matt, but determined to fix things now.

Chapter Fifteen

"Jane?" Hannah tiptoed into Miss Dinsmore's hospital room the next morning. Jane locked relieved, as if she'd been hoping Hannah would come. But then, Hannah had already figured that out. Hannah swallowed a sigh, mustered a smile and stepped in.

"I'm glad you're here."

"Me, too." She sat in the chair by the bed and grasped Jane's hand; the dry skin was lax beneath her fingers. "I had to, but you know that, don't you?"

Jane nodded. She paused long seconds, eyeing the wall, then dragged her gaze back to Hannah's. "Helen and I prayed when we found out I was sick. We asked God to send someone special, someone who could appreciate our children and towns. It's hard to get good teachers in these outlying schools, even with a nice quality of life. We're so far off the beaten path that young people pass us by. And then your application came in for the library position."

Hannah nodded. "I thought God might have had a hand in it," she confessed, then gave Jane a wry smile.

"Now I see that it was just two bossy women engineering things along."

Jane met her gaze with a smile of her own and shook her head as she gripped Hannah's hand. "Except we know He sent you on purpose. There is a time for every purpose under the heaven."

"But three years ago I was a basket case," Hannah said, not trying to soften the skepticism in her tone.

Jane acknowledged the time frame with a slight wince. "You needed healing time. And I had a fight on my hands. But it looks like we've reached the turning point. Will you be my long-term sub, Hannah? Please? I've got my science team preparing for the Christmas break state science games, and we're in the thick of the first semester and you know I don't take that lightly."

"We have that in common."

"So?" Jane studied her face, her expression hopeful but resigned to whatever Hannah might say. She'd obviously put thought and prayer into this petition.

So had Hannah. She leaned forward and grasped Jane's hand. "Yes."

Jane's features softened, a layer of worry removed. She squeezed Hannah's hand, her grip strengthened by hope. "Thank you."

Helen's voice interrupted the moment. "You asked her?"

"She did. I assured her you were both crazy. I'm a librarian now." Hannah gave Jane's hand a reassuring squeeze, letting her in on the joke.

"A librarian with a master's degree in biology and education," Helen retorted as she moved into the room. "Three Ironwood Central School Teacher of the Year awards and three nominations to the President's Award for Academic Excellence in Math and Science, two of which you won." She grasped Hannah's free hand and squeezed, imploring. "I wouldn't ask if the need weren't so great. Will you consider stepping in, taking over Jane's classes? Please?"

"Helen." Jane's deep tone drew Helen's attention.

"Yes?" Helen faced Jane, her concern evident. Jane nodded toward Hannah and smiled. "She's already said yes. Stop annoying her."

"Really?"

"Really."

Hannah met Helen's gaze, amused. "Since seeing Helen beg is a rare occurrence, I'm noting the day and time in my PDA." She paused, all kidding aside, and swept both women a look. "The better question is, *can* I do this?"

"Yes."

"Of course you can." Helen's agreement sounded more vigorous than Jane's for various reasons. First, she'd never had to deal with a room full of hormone-stricken teenagers.

Helen thought everyone was invincible. Hannah had proven that wrong once, did she have what it took to try it again?

"God gifted you with a rare talent, Hannah Moore." Helen drew up a chair alongside Hannah and set her small purse down on the bed. "Don't allow evil to steal that gift or shroud that light under a bushel."

"What do we need to do?"

"The board needs a copy of your application, transcripts and the letters of recommendation you used when applying for the library job. Luckily I already have that."

Hannah wasn't surprised. This was Jeff's grand-mother, after all.

"I've already downloaded your information into the database," Helen went on. "So all you need to do is fill out the forms attached to the email I'm about to send you and we'll proceed from there."

"You've begun the process already?"

Helen didn't even try to act embarrassed. "Weeks ago, when I saw you sparring with my grandson at our initial meeting."

"It's not hard to see where he gets his driven person-ality from," Hannah noted, her wry tone spurring Jane's smile.

A nurse stepped in, gestured to the clock and said, "Five minutes. She needs to rest."

"'Plenty of time for that in the grave,'" Jane barked. Hannah stood and laid a calming hand on her shoulder.

"Benjamin Franklin," she noted. She gave Jane's shoulder a gentle squeeze. "I love that quote. It's one of my favorites."

"Mine, too." Helen rose, walked around the foot of the bed and leaned down to hug her friend. "We'll go straighten out the details. You work on getting better."

"Helen."

"Don't throw in that towel without a fight, Jane."

Jane sighed. "I've been fighting, Helen. Maybe it's time…"

"See what they say in Buffalo, okay?" Helen turned toward Hannah again. "They're sending her up to Ro-swell for an evaluation. If they say there's no hope…" She shifted her gaze back to Jane. "Then we'll talk. But until then, we fight."

"We?"

Helen laughed, hugged her again and shrugged a shoulder toward Hannah. "I helped with this, didn't I?"

Jane yawned and smiled, fatigue weighting her eyes. "You did."

"Well, then."

Hannah studied Helen as Jane's eyes drifted closed. The stark worry was apparent, but when Helen pivoted, her features were calm, business as usual. "How soon do you think you can have that paperwork filled out?"

"This afternoon."

Helen's smile made Hannah feel ten feet tall, but the fear nagging her gut made her wonder what she was doing. She could have said no with no hard feelings on either side. She knew that.

But she *had* to say yes, uncertain if that was conscience or God-willed or a combination of the two. In any case, Hannah Moore was about to retake her place at the front of a classroom, and hopefully wouldn't lose her breakfast doing it.

You'll be fine, you'll be fine, you'll be fine...

Whatever strings Helen pulled to put Hannah in front of the classroom Monday morning were quite impressive, but then this was Helen Walker they were talking about. Hannah approached the school bright and early. Her cell phone rang as she climbed the steps. She saw Jeff's number and answered quickly. "It wouldn't take much to talk me out of this right now, so if that's what you're hoping, now's your chance."

He laughed, which was the best reassurance she could ask for. "Not on your life, I called to encourage you and tell you I'm thinking of you. Got your lunch?"

"Right here."

"And your pencils are all sharpened?"

"Yes, Mom."

He laughed again. "I just wanted you to know I'm praying for you. Thinking of you. Caring about you."

Her heart swelled to impossible proportions. His tender words pushed her to succeed. "Thank you, Jeff. Oops, gotta go. Even teachers aren't supposed to use cell phones in the school."

"A rule that gets broken regularly, I expect. Have a good day, Hannah."

"I will. You, too."

She walked through the doors and nodded to the security guard seated to the left. Hannah wondered what it would have been like to teach a few decades ago, when the idea of school security was a vice principal. Now teams of former sheriffs and police patrolled district schools, and even with all that, assaults happened.

"Hannah?" A woman stepped forward, tall and solid, her short, crisp haircut framing a strong but kindly face. "I'm Laura Henning, the principal."

"Nice to meet you." Hannah accepted Laura's hand and hoped the older woman couldn't feel her thrumming pulse. She looked around. "It's a beautiful school."

"And a little scary right now, I'd expect."

"Downright terrorizing, but I made it this far." Hannah gave the entry a look as they moved to the stairs. "And not to belabor a bad thing, can you give me a mental sketch of security? It helps me preplan a course of action."

"Did you learn that in therapy?" Laura asked as they climbed the wide stairway.

"Nope. In fourth grade during fire safety week. I always scout out my options in the light of day so my brain can kick in as needed."

"That's remarkable."

Hannah sent her a small smile. "It gets the job done. And it helped at Ironwood, because I always have a plan of action in the back of my mind."

Laura nodded, turned left and headed down a hall. "I'll have one emailed to you as soon as I'm back in my office. You have a computer here on your table, a printer alongside, and you're one of only two computer stations with full access to the internet. Most stations have limited access, but Jane was given a reprieve because of the research nature of her methods."

"Wonderful."

She thought she'd hate stepping into the classroom, thought she'd go a little crazy inside, but she loved it. It felt like coming home. The science room was cluttered enough to be user-friendly, the walls covered with great quotes, equations and thoughtful insights Jane commandeered for motivation.

"Give me a call if you need anything." Laura passed along her direct access code to Hannah. "We have security checkpoints on each floor, but there's been little need for them. Still…"

Hannah nodded, understanding. "You never know."

"Exactly. Here is your schedule. I'm having Rose Tomer assist for the first few days. She knows the kids and might be able to defuse any situations that come along."

"A babysitter?" Hannah tipped her head slightly, one brow up, facing Laura directly.

"A facilitator," Laura replied, meeting Hannah's look with frank honesty. "One of these little darlings is going to look you up, see who you are and start asking questions."

Hannah's heart dropped to somewhere in the vicinity of her left foot.

"Rose's presence allows you the option to step away if necessary. And maybe I'm wrong, maybe it won't happen—"

Hannah waved her off as she settled things into her desk. "Oh, it will. I've been working with kids long enough to know that. Having Rose here gives me leverage. Thank you."

Her calm acceptance eased Laura's features. She nodded, then backed toward the door. "Remember, if you need anything…"

Hannah held up the slip of paper with her code. "I'm covered."

"All right."

Once Laura left, Hannah breathed a sigh. The rumble of buses drew her attention to the window, the winding Genesee River a beautiful sight as the sun's rays pinked the hilltops beyond.

Ready or not, here they come.

Jeff's car idled alongside hers when she came out of school at five fifteen. He climbed out and came toward her, his expression wondering until she stepped beneath a parking lot light. He took one look at her face and relaxed into a smile. "It went well."

"Very well." Hannah hunted for words to express her feelings, then settled for a shrug. "I was fine."

"One of us isn't surprised." Jeff pulled her in for a hug. The feeling of being in his arms warmed her despite the cold, bleak afternoon. "Congratulations, Hannah."

She stepped back, trying to remain objective. "It was just one day. I taught long enough to know that's not necessarily indicative of success, but..." She smiled and slanted her gaze up to his. "It felt great."

"Good." He grasped her shoulders and jerked his chin toward their cars. "Can I buy you supper?"

"Don't I wish." She held up her bag as proof. "Lesson planning. I stayed late to get an idea of where Jane was going, but if I'm doing this, I'm doing it right. I'll be lesson planning for this week's classes tonight, then for the month over the weekend."

"But you need to eat."

She nodded. "I ordered a sub from the deli. Tomorrow night, tuna. Wednesday, who knows? But we could get together before the meeting on Thursday. How does that sound?"

He sent her an exaggerated frown. "Like life just got lonelier on me."

She grinned, poked his shoulder and headed for her car. "Presidential science awards come with a price tag, my friend."

"I see that. But you know what else I see?"

Hannah turned, Jeff's warm smile a blanket of comfort in the dull, gray cold. "What?"

"The woman you were born to be." He reached out, tucked a strand of her hair back behind her ear and let his hand linger along the side of her face, his tender smile approving. "And it's wonderful, Hannah."

Hannah glanced around, sighed and smiled, amazed and satisfied, unable to disagree. "It sure is."

"Knock it off, guys," Hannah scolded a group of girls in a first-floor hallway the next day. "Does what Chrissie said to Amelia really matter in the worldwide scheme of things to care about?"

Two of the girls flushed. A third rolled her eyes, her expression saying Hannah was out of touch. Hannah sent the fourth girl a knowing look. "And lose the cell phone. You know you're not supposed to have it out during the day."

"But…"

Hannah arched a brow, glanced at her wrist to show she hated wasting time and tapped her foot.

"Sorry, Miss Moore."

"Thank you, Angie. And for your information, ladies—" she leaned in, inviting their confidence "—I think Chrissie's wrong. Randy Lessman *is* that cute. Totally."

Angie blushed while the other girls laughed. Hannah was glad to see some things never changed. As she rounded the corner to the teacher's lounge, a young man stepped in front of her, angling left while she turned right. She stopped short of bumping into him, then smiled and put a hand on his arm. "Dominic, right?"

"Hey." He nodded, not smiling but looking pleased to meet her. "You work here now, too?"

"I'm Miss Dinsmore's long-term sub. Are you taking science this year?"

"AP Physics."

Hannah paused, surprised. "How old are you?"

"Sixteen."

"That's a hefty load. Do you like physics?"

"Hate it."

She gave him a sympathetic look. "Then why take it?"

He shrugged. "I'm smart. My dad is a physics professor at Alfred University."

"A chip off the old block, huh?"

The vehement shake of his head came quicker than Hannah would have liked. "No."

"Then just be yourself, Dominic," Hannah advised. "If you're good at science, it's an easy A for you, but it's okay to follow your own path."

"You don't know my father."

"True enough. Hey, if you ever want to talk or go over science stuff, I'm here after school." Dominic's lost-puppy demeanor tugged at Hannah's heart. "And the science team is prepping for the Christmas contest. Have you ever thought of joining us?"

"No." He paused, a mix of regret and angst painting his features. "I don't have time for that stuff."

"Well, if you find time, come see me," Hannah told him, remembering the bereft look she'd seen at their first meeting in the candy store. "We're weak in physics and could use your help. Of course, understanding the physical properties driving molecular biology would be a huge help…"

His brightened expression said she'd dangled good bait. "I'm doing a paper on processes for interrupting or diverting proteins to block the spread of cancer."

"Wonderful." Hannah put a gentle hand on his arm. He didn't flinch, a good sign. "Come find me anytime. Maybe we can solve the world's problems together."

She laid the phrase lightly, telling the boy she'd help if she could, but not enough to make him feel targeted.

"Maybe."

"Good enough."

He headed down the hall, head bowed, his hands thrust deep in his pockets, the abject picture of a singular young man.

"Problems?"

Hannah turned and found Laura approaching her. "No. Just a conversation with a kid."

Laura followed the direction of Hannah's gaze, pursed her lips and sighed. "Rough situation. Mother died of a self-inflicted gunshot wound when he was seven. He's brilliant, introverted, hates his stepmother and has been in therapy for as long as I've known the family. They moved here when he was eleven, thought it might help him to be in a new place."

Hannah thought of the interaction she'd witnessed between the stepmother and the boy. A change of setting that didn't address the verbal abuse of a sensitive kid wouldn't accomplish much. "I invited him to sit in on the science team practices."

"So did Jane. He refused."

Hannah shrugged. "Well, the invitation's been issued again. We'll see."

"Everything's going okay?"

Laura's cautious note said she was willing to let Hannah find her way. The fact that she'd found it so easy delighted Hannah. "Wonderful, actually. The *thought* of coming back intimidated me far more than the reality. I'm having the time of my life."

"That's what Rose said." Laura met Hannah's look. "She told me you're a marvel and the kids are eating out of your hand."

Hannah laughed. "Her assessment's a mite generous, but we're having fun and they're learning. It's all good."

"Glad to hear it. And now I must go convince Mr. Bernard to stop haranguing the staff for overuse of paper towels in the ladies' rooms."

"Good luck with that."

Laura smiled. "Thanks. I'll need it. And Hannah?"

"Yes?"

"Good job."

Hannah smiled, the heartfelt praise a blessing. "Thank you."

Chapter Sixteen

Jeff did an internet search for Cavanaugh Construction Thursday morning. Several entries popped up, along with a few current images. Jeff couldn't miss Matt's tough gaze or firm expression, but they were balanced by fairness in his eyes, a welcome new addition. He punched Matt's number into his cell phone, determined. He'd scoured the Nunda area on Friday night, but came up with nothing. One way or another, he needed to see Matt. Talk with him face-to-face. Settle old wrongs.

Matt answered with no preamble. "What's up, Jeff?"

His quick tone tweaked Jeff, but that wasn't Matt's fault. "I need to see you."

"Why?"

"Nothing I can go into over the phone. Where are you?"

Matt didn't answer the question. Instead he said, "Your house. Fifteen minutes."

Jeff stood and headed for the door. "I'm on my way."

He pulled into his driveway and parked alongside Matt's black truck, wondering what to say. As he reached to open his car door, he glanced heavenward. "I could use guidance here. And maybe a clue about when to talk and when to shut up."

He climbed out of the car, motioned Matt to come in and opened the front door, the home's warmth a welcome reprieve from a sharp wind. Matt strode in behind him, eyed the door, then Jeff. "A heavier grade storm door will block that wind and keep the house warmer."

Jeff grimaced. "I actually know that. Just haven't gotten to it yet."

Matt angled him a look and folded his arms. "And you've lived here how long?"

"Eight years."

"Uh-huh." Matt's face said he wasn't surprised. "So. What's so urgent?"

Jeff waved toward the living room. "Come in. Sit down."

"Remembering our past discussions, I probably should stay close to the door," Matt argued, matter-of-fact. "That gives me easier access when you throw me out."

Jeff deserved that. And more. He jerked a thumb toward the comfortable living room. "Come in, sit down and let me get through this, okay?"

Matt studied Jeff's face before obliging him. "All right." He settled into a chair and clasped his hands. "Go for it."

Jeff sat opposite him, praying the right words would come now that he'd forced the issue. "We need to find some kind of common ground if we're both going to live down here."

Matt shrugged. "If by 'we,' you mean 'you,' I couldn't agree more. One of us refuses to fight."

Jeff grimaced, sheepish. "And that just ticked me off even more."

"Listen." Matt hunched forward, his face grim but honest. "I get that you have reason to hate me, that I symbolize all that was bad about our father, but part of making my own way was for me to come back down here. Fix what I can. Make things better."

"Penance?"

"Atonement. I messed up big-time when I was a kid. I've got a lot to make up for, and it would be easier if you didn't try to get in the way."

"The town council."

"Exactly." Matt met his look dead-on. "You almost brought the whole deal down by speaking to them behind the scenes. My lawyer stepped in and cleared things up, but that was a cool three hundred extra I shouldn't have had to pay."

"You're right." Jeff shook his head, chagrined. "I was being a jerk."

Matt didn't disagree.

"But a smart person told me I needed to get over myself and change my attitude."

"Your mother."

Jeff eyed him, surprised. "How would you know that?"

"Because there were only two people who bothered to visit me while I was in juvie. My grandfather. And your mother."

Jeff stared, stunned. "No one else?"

"No."

"Your mother?"

"Busy running with man after man once news of her affair with Neal Brennan came out. She pretty much forgot she had a son. She died during my first tour in Iraq."

"And your father? Don Cavanaugh?"

"Decided that because he wasn't really my father biologically, there was no need to be one physically. He hit the bottle and hasn't stopped yet."

Jeff processed this news, then wondered how Matt could have turned out as normal as he now appeared. Matt answered the question for him.

"Your mother came to see me once a week. She brought me books and cookies. She constantly reminded me that kids make mistakes, but nothing is unfixable. She gave a mother's love to a kid who made her and her family the target of backdoor gossip and never once made me feel guilty or undeserving."

"I guess that was my job." Jeff frowned and scrubbed a hand across the nape of his neck. "And your grandfather?"

"A great man who loved building things. Gentle. Kind. He took me in and helped me see where I went wrong and how to do things right. He died during my second tour."

"So you've got—"

"It's me and God." Matt stood, rolled his shoulders and glanced at his watch. "But I've got things that have to be done so I can close this deal as soon as the bank calls. We're already three weeks behind, and that's a killer for construction this time of year."

Jeff stood and extended his hand. "I want you to accept my apology for being a jerk, for forgetting that you're my brother."

Matt didn't reach out. "Accidental biology. We can leave it at that, Jeff."

"We can't." Jeff stepped forward, determined. "I was wrong. And stupid. First because I was a kid, then because I wasn't smart enough to see things the way they were. You'll get no more trouble from me, Matt. Ever."

"Listen, Jeff, this is nice but unnecessary." Matt met

his gaze and Jeff read the strength there. The sincerity. How had he missed that before? "I'm down here just long enough to finish up Cobbled Creek, make amends, then go on my merry way. I'm not here to stay or infringe on your life."

"Then I'll hope you change your mind." Jeff kept his hand out, refusing to cave. "Because you've got family here and family takes care of one another. I'm just sorry I didn't realize that sooner."

His words touched Matt. He saw it in the softer expression, and when Matt's hand clasped his in a firm handshake, Jeff knew he'd done the right thing, finally. "We'll see."

Jeff nodded and followed Matt out the door. "That's good enough for now," he continued as Matt headed for the truck. "But when you get invited to Thanksgiving dinner at Mom's, just remember, I call dibs on a drumstick."

Matt's slight smile held traces of doubt Jeff hoped to wipe away with time. "Luckily there are two. See ya."

He swung open the cab door, but Jeff caught the edge before he could swing it shut. He thrust his chin toward a bundle stowed behind Matt's seat. "Are you sleeping in this truck?"

Matt's chagrin was answer enough.

"Bunk here," Jeff urged him, waving to the house. "There's plenty of room."

Matt leveled him a look of disbelief. "I don't think we're at the sleepover stage yet." He jerked his chin toward the sleeping bag and pillow. "I gave up my apartment in Nunda because I expected the closing to be done sooner and that forty-minute drive would eat up too much of my workday. Nipping first and last month's rent plus a security deposit out of my bank account right now could ruin the deal, so I'm laying low. Once papers are signed, I'll find a place."

"I'm barely here," Jeff told him, then realized how sad that assertion was. "If you change your mind, the offer's open."

"I appreciate it." Matt gave him a quick nod and swung the door shut.

Jeff watched him go, wishing he'd had the wisdom to do this long ago. As Matt pulled away with a quick wave, Jeff realized something else.

His mother might not have the fast-forward attitude of his grandmother, but she'd showed a strength and wisdom he hadn't fully appreciated. Despite the embarrassment she suffered because of his father, she visited Matt. Ministered to him. Made him feel special and beloved, while Jeff spent two decades harboring grudges.

That realization made him more eager to change things up. With God's help and a humble spirit, he might be able to do just that.

"Hannah Moore. You still live around here?" Jeff joked when he arrived for their weekly fund-raising meeting that evening.

She looked up from sorting papers and laughed. "I do. But thanks to you and your grandmother, I'm pretty much living in the classroom. Luckily Melissa is doing a wonderful job here." She swept the substitute librarian a fond glance.

"And it's going fine?" Jeff studied her face, looking for evidence otherwise.

She nodded. "Wonderful. Almost as if I never left."

"Good."

She handed him a stack of folders. "If you could set these around the table, I'll turn on the coffeemaker."

"Will do."

Callie Burdick walked in as Jeff set up the table. She moved his way, her expression expectant. "I heard you went to bat for us with the town council, Jeff. Thank you."

Jeff took a moment before looking up, choosing his words carefully, wishing he'd never asked the council members to block Matt's building permits, especially with Matt's involvement. "It was worth a try, Callie. But with the property in the bank's hands, there's not much anyone can do."

"I know," she told him, earnest. "But you tried and I have faith that everything will turn out all right."

It couldn't. Not for both parties, anyway, and Jeff knew that. He fumbled for words, then saw Hannah watching them, an eyebrow arched as she read his discomfort. She approached them, gave Callie a quick hug and nodded toward the coffee center. "The regular is brewed and decaf's on its way."

"You read my mind."

Callie headed for the coffee while Hannah turned toward Jeff. "You're playing her."

Jeff shook his head, adamant. "I'm not."

"You know more than you're saying."

He couldn't deny that. Not to Hannah. "Yes."

"Then that's playing her and I thought we had this discussion a long time ago."

"This is different, Hannah."

She sent him a look of quiet disappointment, her gaze shadowed in reality. "It always is, Jeff."

The arrival of other committee members thwarted further conversation, and when Hannah left Melissa to lock up without saying goodbye, Jeff knew they'd back-pedaled. But he'd promised Matt confidentiality and no further interference. He couldn't go back on his word. And he'd told Callie the truth. If the bank approved Matt's application to mortgage the Cobbled Creek subdivision, no one could stand in his way. Nor should they.

But Matt's gain would be Callie's father's loss and Jeff felt the sting of that, wishing he'd never interfered.

A part of Hannah said she shouldn't get hung up on Jeff's actions.

Another part laughed out loud.

Hadn't she traveled this path before? Painted air castles with a man who put the bottom line first and foremost? Hadn't she learned her lesson then?

Obviously not.

She headed into school the next morning, determined to focus on one thing: reestablishing her teaching career. Laura's voice hailed her as she made her way down the entry hall, mentally preparing herself for a day of parent-teacher conferences.

"Hannah, I'm glad I caught you."

Hannah turned. "What's up?"

"I need you to sit in on a couple of conferences today."

"For?"

"Content appraisal," Laura explained. "One of the AP teachers has come down with the flu, and the other one went out on emergency maternity leave yesterday. I need a content teacher on board for two conferences because they were parent requested."

"What time?"

"Two fifteen and six thirty."

Hannah frowned. "The two fifteen is fine, but I've got

a full schedule until six forty-five. Can you reschedule the later one for seven?"

"I'll make it work," Laura assured her. "And I'll send you the info you need on both. And since these are both strong students, there's no major stuff involved, although Mr. Fantigrossi can be tedious. Hopefully we can close them out in the allotted fifteen minutes with no problem."

"Wonderful, because I'm not nearly as diplomatic at 7:00 p.m. as I am at 7:00 a.m."

Laura flashed her a smile as she veered toward the office. "I couldn't agree more."

Dominic was actually Dominic Fantigrossi III.

Mental red flags sprang up the minute his father stalked into Hannah's classroom that evening. She read Laura's look of caution and stepped forward, her hand extended as a young math teacher trailed behind, looking intimidated. "Mr. Fantigrossi, I'm Hannah Moore. Pleased to meet you."

"I'd say the same, except I'm wondering why I'm here at all. In the first place—" one imperative finger was quickly joined by others as he listed his complaints "—my appointment was rearranged with little concern for my schedule. I'm conferencing with a teacher who has no bearing on my son's progress, therefore limiting the efficacy of this conference. And third, I've been kept waiting ten minutes beyond our scheduled time. Already I'm not happy and this meeting hasn't even begun."

"Is Dominic coming?"

"I'm here."

Young Dominic shrugged into the room with reluctance, as if each step grew more difficult. He flicked a possible glance of apology to Hannah, but it was gone too quick to be sure.

"You're late." Dominic Senior's voice cut the kid no slack.

Dominic squirmed, obviously uncomfortable. "I'm sorry."

"I would hope so." His father squared his shoulders, imposing. "Seven o'clock means seven o'clock." He shifted his glare to Laura. "In the real world, that is."

Hannah bit back words of retort, refusing to spar with him. Her last two meetings ran late, but those things happened on a long conference day. She'd learned to accept the missed or late appointments. Obviously, the elder Dominic didn't embrace a similar attitude.

She let Laura steer the meeting and kept her face placid. She'd gone over the boy's grades and the teacher's report, noting the only negative was lack of participation. Dominic's aptitude ranked high and his retention put him at genius levels, all things a parent should embrace with joy.

Not in this case.

While Hannah presented Dominic's science records to his father, she flashed encouraging smiles in the boy's direction, wanting him to jump in. Take part.

He didn't. Chin down, he gazed at his feet, right up until Hannah mentioned the science team. "I've asked him to join because we could use his help, but he's managed to put me off so far." She sent Dominic a friendly grin, trying to draw him in, right before his father's reaction demonstrated her faux pas.

"He refused?"

Too late, Hannah realized her mistake. The senior Dominic wasn't the kind of father that allowed his son to find his own way. Hadn't the boy's words hinted that? And now she'd gone and opened up Pandora's box for the kid, which was the last thing she wanted to do.

"Dominic knows the option is there," Hannah replied smoothly, trying to gloss over the father's reaction. "In the meantime, we can concentrate on his excellent grades, his potential and his work ethic, all of which highlight what a great kid he is."

"And that's fine if you're raising an average kid," countered the senior Fantigrossi. "I'm not. My son has more potential in his little finger than most kids dream of, so don't talk down to me with your edu-speak gibberish about looking at the bright side. Dominic understands that good grades aren't enough to get into the top schools, that he needs to be well-rounded, and since he bombed at sports—" the boy winced, the father's careless words cutting deep "—and he's not gifted musically, utilizing greater potential by joining the science team would help round out his profile. Why didn't you run this by me?" he demanded, confronting his son.

The boy shrugged. "I didn't think it was important."

Dominic's faint words made Hannah's heart cringe. His body language echoed his speech, a slight inward curl hunched his shoulders, his back, his arms, as if ducking blows, but the shots he took were aimed at his mental and emotional well-being, obviously a popular target.

"If it's any help, my invitation stands," Hannah announced.

"I'll think about it." The kid didn't look at her, but his voice said joining the science team ranked last on his list, especially now.

"You'll do it."

"I—"

"Mr. Fantigrossi…"

Dominic's father raised an imperious hand, concluding the meeting and silencing the staff. "This is not open for discussion. You have the room on the team." He pointed toward Hannah, then toward Dominic. "And you have plenty of time. End of story, and this meeting. Let's go."

Dominic stood. Hannah read the anger in his face, in his eyes. She mouthed a quiet apology, but the boy maintained a cool gaze, his demeanor saying what he couldn't verbalize.

What started out as an easy day for her had ended poorly. Hannah longed to call Jeff and seek his opinion, but after last night's interchange with Callie, she realized her romantic instincts might still be unreliable, and that knowledge bit deep.

By the time she crawled into bed, the room bore the distinct odor of dead mouse, the newest victim of the landlord's attic poison, which meant it would only smell worse by morning.

Great.

Chapter Seventeen

Hannah answered the candy store phone the next afternoon. The busy Saturday marked the typical fall upswing in sales. With holidays approaching, people were stocking up or placing orders, keeping them hopping.

"Grandma Mary's Candies, this is Hannah, how can I help you?"

"Why did you tell him about the science team?"

Hannah's heart stopped, the cold, despairing voice setting off her internal warning system. "Dominic?"

"I told you no, didn't I?"

"Yes, but…" With customers moving around the store, Hannah couldn't think straight to direct this conversation. "Dominic, I…"

"No one listens to me," the boy explained, his tone aggrieved but not angry, which only made matters worse. Honest anger provided a release. Bottled misery could ignite in more dangerous ways.

"I'm listening, Dominic."

"No, you're not. You're wondering how to get me off the phone so you can take care of all those customers."

He was watching her.

A chill climbed Hannah's spine. Goose bumps dotted her arms, but she grabbed hold of herself emotionally and kept her voice firm. "If you're close enough to see me—" she raised her gaze and did a visual scan of the street, but didn't catch sight of the boy "—then come over, munch on some caramels and talk to me. I didn't mean to mess things up. I'm new to the school, so your situation with your father took me by surprise. I'm sorry, kiddo, I realized my mistake too late and now you're stuck with me."

"I'm not."

I'm not? Hannah tried to gauge the boy's cryptic response. Was he expressing simple anger? Desperation? Suicidal options? Homicidal tendencies? Teens were notorious for reacting to things too quickly, kind of like that group of girls earlier that week.

Only the girls seemed normal, if a little overzealous. Dominic didn't.

She waved to Megan as her friend finished boxing a large assortment, grabbed a notepad and headed into the kitchen area, pretending she was taking an order. "I'm in the kitchen now, you've got my full attention, so talk. And let me just say, having an overbearing father is tough, but you've got lots of people who care about you, starting with me. So promise me right now you're not going to do something foolish, something we'll both regret."

"Are you going to call the police? Tell them I called you?"

Hannah weighed her words carefully. "If I think you're a threat to yourself or others, then yes. If you're using me as a sounding board, then no. You got caught in a situation I was partially responsible for and I'm sorry, but other than apologizing and making your science team experience fun, I've got nothing. But if giving the science team a try means calming things with your father, why not just do it?"

"It's not that easy."

"Oh, it is," Hannah assured him. "You're making it difficult because you're mad. And caramels are a great stress reliever. All that chewing does wonders for the soul."

"Are you tempting me in so you can call the cops and have me put in the hospital against my will?"

Hannah tried to balance the situation with pre-Ironwood common sense in a post-Ironwood mind, and that was tough, but at least this kid was reaching out.

Father, help him. Comfort him. Sustain him with Your gentle hands, Your loving arms.

"And mess with all that drama? Please, it's Saturday, I turn on my no-drama-zone force field the minute I walk out of the school. Come in here, talk face-to-face and eat candy."

"Really?"

"Yes. Consider it candy store therapy. It works wonders for me."

She walked back out front as he came through the door, his bearing less timid than last night. "Dude."

The one-word greeting made him smile. "Miss Moore."

She held out a small tray of candies and plastic gloves. "Wash your hands, put these on and keep people happy for a few minutes, okay? We're swamped."

He paused, startled, then made a face. "You want me to help you?"

Hannah pointed toward the front. "See all those people? If we feed them, they might not stampede the counter."

A small smile softened his jaw as he surveyed the room. He nodded, washed his hands and donned the gloves. "Will you get in trouble for doing this?"

"Commandeering free help? That's every businessman's dream. Now get going. Time's wasting."

He moved forward, carrying the tray more like a shield, but by the time he'd made a pass through the crowd, he'd relaxed and actually exchanged smiles with a few customers.

And those smiles told Hannah that Dominic Fantigrossi III might be all right with a little tender loving care.

"We need more." he announced a few minutes later as Hannah cashed out a customer.

"The sample trays are in the kitchen. They're marked, and make sure you avoid anything with nuts, okay?"

"Anaphylactic shock being a bad advertising ploy."

Hannah grinned at his joke. "Exactly. Now you're catching on."

And he was. He hung out for the afternoon, handing out samples and bagging orders. He even emptied the garbage cans at closing time. By the time they locked up at eight o'clock, he looked tired but pleased, exactly what Hannah had hoped for.

But was it enough or too little, too late?

She had no idea.

Hannah's cell phone rang just after she arrived home. The Illinois area code listed no name. Hannah hesitated, then grasped the phone, trepidation snaking up her spine. "Hello?"

"Hannah Moore?"

"Yes."

"This is Jill Kantry, Christi Kantry's mother."

Hannah's heart fluttered. Christi had been one of the last students killed in Karen's lab class. "You got my note, Mrs. Kantry?"

"We did." A short pause followed before Jill continued. "I've put you on speaker. Is that okay?"

"Of course. And I just want to say I'm sorry I didn't send that note sooner. I—"

"Miss Moore, this is Jacob Westman."

"And Thomas Kwitchik."

"And Anna Li Phan."

"And…"

Hannah interrupted the litany of voices. "You're all there?"

Jill's voice came through again. "The ones still in this area. If it was possible, we'd have all hopped on a plane to come see you, but this seemed more expedient and affordable. Miss Moore, our consensus is that while your notes of apology were well received, they were unnecessary."

"Totally unnecessary," someone else added.

"But…"

"You offered our children amazing opportunities at Ironwood," Jill interrupted her. "We realize that and felt honored to have our kids work with you. We just want you to know that the unrighteous acts of others can never negate the dedication and devotion our children received from you and Ms. Krenzer. And that's all we wanted to say."

Hannah stopped, searching for words and coming up short. "You're thanking me?"

"And wishing you well," added a strong male voice. "God bless you, Miss Moore. We'll be praying for you."

Praying for her.

They'd buried children. They'd lost their boys and girls, a host of bright minds and inquisitive natures, and yet...

They were praying for her.

Hannah couldn't talk around the lump lodged in her throat, but she tried. "Thank you."

"No, Miss Moore. Thank you," Jill insisted. "And we'll be watching, hoping someday you can do the same things for other kids because you're special. And that's all we wanted to say. You have a good night now, okay?"

"Yes. Okay."

They disconnected the call with a shower of goodbyes, their encouraging voices food for her heart and soul.

"The righteous cry out and the Lord hears them..."

The sweet psalm's truth echoed in that phone call, an upright blessing that strengthened Hannah's determination to do the best she could for her new students, facing forward, no matter what. *For when God is with us, who can stand against us?*

No one, Hannah decided, strength warming her heart. She contemplated the phone, longing to call Jeff, but then decided against it, uncertain. A roomful of grief-stricken parents had just assuaged her soul with warmth and forgiveness. Jeff Brennan could learn a lot from their amazing example.

Hannah found two missed calls the next morning, both from Jeff, with a single cryptic message citing work constraints in place of church.

Hannah sighed, and headed to Holy Name, mixed feelings dogging her steps.

She longed to talk with him. Laugh with him. Spar with him.

But his exchange with Callie reaffirmed what she'd tucked aside. Jeff's romantic side came off as sweet and sincere, but she'd been fooled before.

Never again.

Hannah headed into the church, the grace of the Ironwood parents thrusting her forward.

Jeff Brennan was a player. He put work above all else and disavowed his brother, twin realities that said volumes more than sweet words.

Sure, he was nice to his grandma. And his sense of humor was a treasure she'd miss, that warm, frank smile and quick turn of phrase.

But an unforgiving nature left no foundation for building. Wasn't making amends part of life?

Her cell phone rang and Jane Dinsmore's name came up. "Jane, good morning. How are you?"

"I'm holding my own, dear, and I just wanted to congratulate you on a great beginning." Jane paused for breath, her fatigued voice underscoring her laborious fight. "Laura and Rose filled me in and just knowing you're there makes my physical struggles easier."

Her gentle words pricked Hannah's tears. "You focus on getting well. I'll hold down the fort in the meantime."

"And that's why I called, Hannah." Jane stopped again. Hannah waited, patient, allowing the older woman to catch her breath. "I'm putting in my retirement papers and I wanted you to be the first to know."

"But—"

"No buts. I may beat this thing and I'll be glad of it, but I've decided it's time to make a clean break. God has always appointed the paths in my life, and he's made this detour fairly obvious. I would love for you to stay on and apply for the full-time position, but that, of course, is up to you."

Her strength both humbled and inspired Hannah. "I would love to, Jane. Thank you."

A tiny laugh came through, a laugh that carried the hiccup of a sob before Jane disconnected the call. "No, honey. Thank you."

Hannah closed the phone, decisive. She'd head to the library, clean out her files and let Melissa know the job was about to be posted. Since the library was closed on Sunday, she could get her work done quickly and put things in motion for a new chapter in her life. Remembering Jeff's message, she longed for the whole brass ring, the fairy-tale happy ending, but if nothing else, she felt strong again. Ready to embrace life to the full.

She only wished that could have included Jeff Brennan.

Chapter Eighteen

Jeff watched the technician troubleshoot the factory's robotic application system, a machine crucial to on-time delivery of a current military contract. Quick glances to his watch intensified the loss of time, a day when he'd planned to see Hannah. Talk with her. See if he could set things straight.

"You got somewhere to be?"

The tech looked exaggeratedly at Jeff's watch. Jeff shook his head. "No, sorry, I just had things scheduled for today."

"Don't we all?" The tech resumed his position on the floor while adjustable work lamps flooded his area with light. "If it's shopping, go online. If it's family, I got nothin'."

Trent's foster father had reacted badly to his latest round of chemo. Trent had headed south, leaving Jeff on his own for a weekend that appeared worry free yesterday.

Today?

Jeff squared his shoulders, refusing to sigh, but hating

having things not right with Hannah. Was she avoiding his calls deliberately?

His gut said yes, and that made talking to her imperative, but so was this work obligation. Jeff knew his job, he understood the consequences if supplies got held up in manufacturing. But right now he just wanted a few free hours to see his girl. Convince her he wasn't the conniver she thought him to be.

One look at the tech's face said that wasn't about to happen today.

Creak...

Hannah swung around, unable to identify the sound. She hadn't bothered turning all the library lights on, but foreboding clouds had deepened the gloom in the outer reaches of the library. Tall shelves blocked the little light the window offered, leaving her desk area lit while the rest of the room was dark. She checked the online forecast and sighed at the thought of more rain, but then it was November in the Alleghenies. Rain was a given.

Creeeaaak...

This time the noise drew her up straight, awareness crawling up her spine, tiny hairs rising in protest along her neck.

She saw nothing.

But she *felt* something, and she'd taught science long enough to understand the God-given gift of instinctive fear.

Why hadn't she locked the door? Why hadn't she turned on the lights?

Because this is Jamison, you ninny, her inner voice scolded. *You're letting your imagination run away with you. Turn on the lights, sip your coffee and finish up.*

She stood, crossed to the light panel inside the door and hit the bank of switches.

Dominic.

He stood framed in the back door, his hair messed up by the wind, his face haunted.

Hannah's heart seized. The clutch of surprise coupled with the dark skies, strong wind and the young man's angst transported her back in time to another place, another boy, another dark, stormy day.

Stay calm. Stay connected. Get to your cell phone.

She pulled in a breath, found it impossible to draw in fully with her chest constricted, and then worked to relax her gaze, her shoulders. "How did you get in? And why are you here?"

He came forward slowly, his eyes locked with hers, his look...

She'd seen that look before, she knew it well. Depression. Desolation. Desperation. The last time had preceded an out-of-control situation governed by a power-hungry gang of boys with no conscience, but this time...

Maybe this time she could help.

And then again...

Dominic withdrew a small handgun from the left-hand pocket of his trench coat as Hannah rethought her position. She held his gaze, nodded toward the gun and kept her voice firm with God's help. "Lose the gun, dude."

He shook his head, his jaw trembling.

Guide me, Lord. You wouldn't have brought me all this way, over all this time, without a reason. Give me strength. And wisdom. And please, please, please...keep me safe. Don't let me miss out on this new chance at a life renewed. Please.

She was near the door, but not close enough to escape,

and she had no clue what Dominic intended. Did he want to hurt her? Hurt himself? Seeing the pain in his eyes, his face, she knew she couldn't turn away, but she wasn't willing to take foolish risks either. She thought of Jeff and regret stabbed her heart. Of Caitlyn, her little god-daughter, the niece she hadn't held yet.

But there was something about this boy that encouraged her to take a chance.

A big chance.

Making a decision, she moved toward her desk area and motioned him to come with her. "Sit down and tell me what's going on. But I don't talk to guns. If you want my help, lose the weapon. I mean it."

He stared at her for long ticks of the clock, then slid the gun back into his pocket.

Hannah sent him a disbelieving look. "Really?" She jerked her head toward the DVD drop box. "Put it in there, turn the lock and give me the key. Then we'll talk."

He paused, his indecision hiking her fears, but she absolutely refused to let dread govern this scene. She'd worked long and hard to retake her life, her destiny, and no way was she about to let anything mess that up. Or mess him up for that matter.

Although this kid had been raked over the coals already.

He headed for the lockbox, then darted a look over his shoulder as if expecting her to go for her cell phone or the library phone.

Hannah did neither; her inaction soothed the set of his jaw.

Good.

He put the gun into the box, turned the key and tossed it to her. "You know I can get to it from outside, right?"

She nodded and shrugged. "But I know you won't. You didn't come here to hurt me, but you're thinking of hurting yourself and I won't stand for that in my library. Way too much cleanup. So sit." She motioned him to the chair alongside her and kept her face serene but strong. "And tell me what's going on. What's happened?"

"They're sending me away."

Of course they were. "Where?"

"Kessler Academy."

"Pricey."

He scowled. "Nothing but the best."

"Why?"

"Because they don't let you make choices at Kessler. If you're lagging in any area, they force you to take part, their sole goal being the production of young men of the highest quality, Ivy League–ready candidates."

"So if Penn or Princeton was your goal, you're all set. Tell me, Dominic." She put a hand on his arm after he sat down. "What are your goals?"

He dropped his head into his hands and grimaced. "I don't have goals. I just get by."

"Why?"

He looked up and frowned. "Because it's what I do."

"What you *choose* to do."

His frown deepened. "Well. Maybe."

"So choose differently."

"It's too late."

"Not as long as you're breathing, dude. What do you want out of life right now? As a teenager? And what do you want tomorrow? And next year? What do you see yourself doing, Dominic?"

"Designing."

Hannah paused, surprised.

Dominic pulled a handful of folded papers from his pocket. "I like to design things. My mother was an artist."

"Really?" Hannah opened the sheaf of papers and drew a breath, surprised by the depth and beauty of the commercial designs she held. "You did these? I mean, they're not some building you copied from seeing it online? Because, dude, these are gorgeous."

"You think?"

"Oh, Dominic, I know. Are the designs workable?"

The answer was there in the keen look of his eye, his quick nod. "That's the fun part of doing this, making sure the weight-bearing specs complement the beauty."

"Have you taken Computer-Aided Design?"

He shook his head. "My father won't let me. But Mr. Eschler and Mr. Bernard let me into the CAD lab when no one's around."

"They do, huh?" Hannah would have to rethink her assessment of the gnarly school custodian. It took a good heart to see the brilliant artist inside the angry child's body. "Do they have this option at Kessler?"

"No."

"Well, then." Hannah handed the speculative buildings and bridges back to him. "We need to talk to your father."

"My father doesn't listen. He talks. Then he walks away."

"Did you ever wonder why that is?" Hannah crept into this subject, not wanting to quench the light in Dominic's eyes.

"I know why. I remind him of my mother."

"And yet you look like your father." Hannah let the words dangle, then tapped the papers clutched in Dominic's hand. "Maybe *this* is what reminds him of your mother. Her talent, her artistry. And then you couple that with your anger and depression…" She sat back and let him absorb the idea, the suggestion that his behavior inspired his father's negative reactions. "Maybe your father is scared to death you'll do what your mother did, and doesn't know how to face that. Or change it."

The spark of recognition said her idea intrigued him so she continued. "Perhaps you can take charge of the situation by changing your actions, therefore inspiring different reactions from your father. Maybe you can find a common ground."

"Not with *her* around."

"Variables are a part of scientific exploration," Hannah reminded him. "Every researcher deals with the vagaries of the uncontrollable. But if your father is more content, your stepmother might be happier. Although I don't exactly see her as the happy-go-lucky type. You know that, don't you?"

A tiny smile quirked Dominic's mouth. "I get that."

"So…"

A police bullhorn interrupted their exchange.

Fear replaced Dominic's softened features, and Hannah knew she had two immediate tasks: to reestablish calm with Dominic because she had no idea what else he might have secreted in that coat, and to let the authorities outside know all was well.

He started to stand.

Hannah stopped him. "Stay low." She grabbed her cell phone. "Let me talk to them. I'll explain that we're fine, that all is well."

His stark terror belied her gentle words, but she held his hand while she dialed 911, hoping to stave off a weapons-drawn confrontation.

* * *

Hannah was in trouble. Big trouble.

Jeff raced to his car, Megan's worried voice hounding him. Why had he encouraged her to go back to teaching? Why didn't he put his foot down and condemn the foolish risk of his grandmother's plan? He'd seen the fear in Hannah's eyes, the stark reality of Ironwood imprinted on her face as she told her story.

He'd failed her by not taking her side, and now her well-being lay in the hands of a depressed teen with a gun, according to Megan.

Fear and anguish gripped his heart, his soul. Fear that something would happen before he could get to her, and angst that he didn't have sense enough to protect her. Put her first.

Protect her, God. Yes, I'm angry, we'll discuss that later, but please, please, please. Protect her. Guard her. Uphold her with Your righteousness, cradle her in the palm of Your hand. Please.

A blockade stopped him two blocks short of the library. The rain and wind drove the dark mood of the situation. The police had set up a command center at the convenience store on Route Nineteen. Jeff parked the car, barreled out and headed for the store.

"Hey. You. Back in the car, buddy, and head south. The road's closed."

Jeff raised his arms in the air. "My fiancée is in that library with the kid. I'm not going anywhere, Pete."

Pete Monroe peered closer, recognized Jeff and gave a quick nod. "Come with me."

He took Jeff into the store. What looked like commotion outside was well-organized within, but all Jeff heard was six words.

"We're in position."

"Then let's go."

He grabbed a detective's arm. "You're going in? When she's in there with a kid brandishing a gun? Are you crazy?"

An older man stood off to the side, his hands twining, his expression dark with terror.

The detective met Jeff's gaze with forced calm. "We're not going in, we're just announcing our presence. The blinds are drawn, we've got a tactical team coming so we can snake a camera in from the side vent. But they won't be here for a few minutes, and maybe the kid will negotiate."

"He's my son. He's got a name. It's Dominic," the father spouted from across the aisle. "Dominic Fantigrossi the third."

The detective nodded, his face grave. "I know that, Professor, and we're not trying to be insensitive. It's just a matter of working this out with no one getting hurt. Not Miss Moore." He directed his look to Jeff and Jeff read the concern in his eyes. "Or Dominic."

A part of Jeff wanted to ream out the older man, wondering just what a parent did to a kid to make him react this way, but another part remembered a boy whose father broke every civil and moral law known to mankind twenty years before…

He could have been a Dominic. For whatever reason, he chose to bury himself in work, striving to excel, but he remembered the embarrassment, the pain, the humiliation of being Neal Brennan's son.

Oh, yeah. He could have snapped back then and knowing that was the only thing that kept him on his side of the room, away from the distraught father.

Protect her, please. Watch over her. And the kid. Please.

The detective's face darkened as he listened to whatever was being said through his earpiece, then he glanced Jeff's way, his jaw set. "We've made contact with Miss Moore. She wants to talk to you."

Jeff's heart leaped at this unexpected turn of events. "Have her call my cell."

The detective shook his head. "We've got to use ours for monitoring." He pointed to a communications setup beside the cash register. A cable snaked from the box to a van outside. Jeff moved closer just as the phone rang. He snatched it up, trying to disguise his fear. "Hannah?"

"Jeff. I need your help."

"Anything. You know that."

"Call them off."

Jeff surveyed the room full of cops and winced. "I can't, honey. Tell me your situation."

"I'm having a congenial meeting with a student. End of story."

"He's got a gun, Hannah."

"Not anymore, he doesn't. It's locked up in the DVD return box. And it isn't loaded. Never was. You tell the sheriff that what I've got is a scared kid and a teacher who isn't much better right now, having a normal conversation about teenage choices. If they lose the guns, they're welcome to come inside and see."

"You're okay? Really?"

"Really, truly." The strength in her voice said she was doing all right, considering. "You think I'm going to risk the future of my scarecrow, Jeff? Are you crazy?"

Her reference to the scarecrows sent him a solid message that she was fine, negotiating on her own, unforced.

"Have the police take the gun and stand down, then send one calm guy in and we'll get Dominic home. He's scared, he's been depressed and no matter what happens, I'm not going to let anything happen to this kid, accidentally or self-induced. You got that, Dominic?" She'd obviously redirected her attention to the boy nearby, but kept her voice loud enough for Jeff's benefit. He heard the kid mutter an indistinct "yes."

Jeff gave the detective monitoring the call a thumbs-up.

The detective turned toward the professor. "You had no other guns in the house?"

"None." He shook his head, vehement. "That one was my father's, he left it to me. I don't use guns, I don't have bullets for it, even."

"And it's registered?"

"Yes."

The detective paused, inscrutable, then he contacted the officers surrounding the building. "I'm going in alone once we've secured the weapon. If everything's fine, I'll give the signal."

He didn't reiterate what would happen if everything wasn't all right, if Hannah had been coerced into making that call. But Jeff knew Hannah, her voice. She was mad, not scared. Nervous, not frightened. And frustrated that the situation had gone out of control.

But she was alive and talking, sounding wonderfully normal, and Jeff wanted nothing more than to keep it that way. When he started to follow the detective, a broad-shouldered deputy blocked his way. "Sorry. You've got to stay here."

"But—"

The deputy folded his arms and braced his legs, his face firm. "Let us do our job."

He was right, Jeff knew that, but he hated waiting in the wings.

Pray.

He paused, thought, accepted the cup of coffee the store clerk handed him and closed his eyes. *Keep her safe, Heavenly Father. Please. And, Lord, forgive me for getting her into this, for encouraging her, for letting my grandmother push her into a situation like this. Forgive us for stealing Your role, for messing with Hannah's life, her safety, her security.*

He could only imagine what she must have gone through, the terror, the flashbacks, the pain of reliving Ironwood.

And it was their fault for setting things in motion, encouraging her to get back into the classroom. None of this would have happened if she'd just been Hannah Moore, the Jamison librarian, quietly living her chosen life of obscurity.

Regret shaded his heart and soul. True love didn't take unnecessary risks or embrace harm. And yet he'd done just that, always striving to improve things. His mother, his life, his job, his company.

Was he ever satisfied with the status quo?

He'd have said yes regarding Hannah, but now he realized he'd tried to fix her, too. Right up to the point of endangering her life, her heart, her fragile psyche. What kind of a self-absorbed fool was he?

The worst, he realized as moments ticked on. Instead of trusting God to guide Hannah's path, he'd helped his grandmother direct her back into danger. And whatever price he had to pay for his know-it-all actions, so be it. Just as long as Hannah was all right.

Dear God in Heaven, please let Hannah be all right.

Chapter Nineteen

Hannah was going to go ballistic if someone didn't start listening to her. Dominic's face had paled with the initial police bullhorn announcement, and despite her best efforts to maintain calm, his nervousness was mounting.

She leaned in and held his gaze. "Look me in the eye and tell me you don't have any other weapons."

He shook his head. "Nothing. And I didn't even have bullets for the gun. I don't even know where to get bullets for that old gun."

"Good thing." Hannah paused, dropped her chin and uttered a prayer. "Dear God, we're in a situation here. Help the officers see we're okay, that everything's all right, that no one's going to get hurt. Keep everyone calm. Guide us. Shelter us. Protect us from harm."

Dominic arched a brow when she finished. "I thought teachers couldn't pray around students."

"Dude, do you *see* a school here?"

A little smile softened his face. "Good point."

"That's why I'm the teacher, you're the student. And if you get into trouble over this whole mess, I'll help you. But you've got to get hold of yourself. Depression and anxiety are not good soul mates. Try prayer. God. Church. Helping others. Put yourself out there, Dominic, and put others first. It's amazing how that realigns your perspectives."

"I can't believe you're talking this way when we have a SWAT team aiming guns at us."

Hannah waved that off, pretending nonchalance. "Jeff will set them straight. He knows when I'm doing all right and when I'm not."

"Since Ironwood?"

Hannah shifted a brow up. "You know about that?"

He nodded, sheepish. "I think that's why I came to you, because you'd understand. No one else seemed to. But since the day I saw you in the candy store, I kind of felt like you saw me. Knew me."

Hannah had felt exactly the same way. "We can thank the Holy Spirit for that one."

"You think God wants to help me?"

Hannah met his gaze. "God *is* helping you. He put us together, He gave us a chance to talk, to get to know one another. And He's probably given you other chances, Dominic, but you're too stubborn for your own good."

He didn't deny it. "I am."

"Which is where humility comes in. God blesses us in so many ways. Our job is to embrace and accept those ways. But first we have to recognize them."

"The glass being half-full."

"Exactly." A knock at the door drew Hannah to her feet. "I'm going to go let this officer in. I think you'd be smart to lie down, show them that you have no weapons and no ill intent, okay?"

Her instructions made him look fearful, but then he nodded and did as she asked. "Okay."

Hannah walked to the door and opened it. A lone officer stood outside, wet and bedraggled. She ushered him in, noting how he appraised the situation. Instead of handcuffing Dominic, he reached down and offered the kid a hand up. "Dominic, I'm Detective Parsons of the Allegany sheriff's department. How are you doing?"

Dominic sent a look of surprise from the detective to Hannah. "Okay, I guess. Aren't you going to arrest me?"

"For?"

"Weapon possession?"

The detective gave him a benign look. "I don't see a weapon. Do you?"

"No, sir."

"And did you have ammunition for a weapon on your person today?"

"No, sir."

"And did you secure the unusable antique in a safe spot when asked?"

"Yes, sir."

"Well, then." The detective raised his hands. "I've got to do a pat down."

"Okay."

The detective ascertained that Dominic wasn't carrying anything else on his person, then checked his coat. "All clear." He stepped back and leveled a firm but kind look at Dominic. "Are you suicidal?"

Dominic paused, then shook his head. "No. I was upset, and wondering if the world might be better off without me before, but…" He shrugged and shifted his jaw toward Hannah. "I'm better now."

"And you, Miss Moore?"

"I'm fine. And Dominic knows he did the right thing by seeking help today, and the wrong thing by…"

"Taking my father's gun, loaded or not. I think I just wanted someone to take me seriously."

"You got your wish, kid." The detective passed a hand over his face, glanced up as though seeking divine inspiration, then keyed his mike. "We're good to stand down. Can you send the father and fiancé in here, please? With escort?"

"My father's here?" Dominic looked surprised and afraid, with good reason, Hannah supposed. And since Dominic Senior was married, the fiancé…

She could only hope they meant Jeff.

"Your father alerted us," the detective told Dominic. "He informed us that you and the gun were missing. He explained you were upset and possibly suicidal. When we realized you were here, alone with Miss Moore and she wasn't answering her phone…"

The door swung open. Dominic Senior entered first, his face wet, his color ashen. He grabbed his son in a hug and cradled the boy's head as if he might never let go.

"Hannah."

Hannah turned, overjoyed to hear Jeff's voice, see his face. He moved forward, studying her, his gaze raking her eyes, her cheeks, her mouth. He reached out and hugged her, then backed off and nodded, his voice level. "You're okay."

"Yes. Thank you for intervening for us."

He nodded, his expression unreadable, but she understood that. She'd brushed him off pretty thoroughly, refusing contact, ignoring his calls. No matter what happened, though, she'd always be grateful for his quick support today.

She turned toward the Fantigrossis and waved a hand toward the desk. "Can we talk?"

Dominic's father stared, wide-eyed. "Now?"

"Yes."

"After all this?" His arm indicated the detective, the scene outside, the weapon, his son.

"I think it's best." Hannah didn't dare look at Jeff just then. No way could she manage a professional meeting with a distraught parent and kid and an emotional one with Jeff at the same time.

In typical teacher fashion, she put the kid first and took a seat. Jeff moved off toward the children's section, removing himself from the situation. His cool distance broke her heart, but that had been her option, right? To ease away from his work-first mentality. Right now it felt like the worst choice she could have made, but...

She sat and motioned toward Dominic Senior. "Your son says you're sending him away."

The older man swallowed hard and nodded. "A prep school in Connecticut, yes."

"Because?"

The father frowned, then sighed. "Living with my wife and me is not easy for Dominic."

"Or you," Hannah suggested, keeping her voice easy.

"Any of us," the older man admitted. He met his son's gaze across the short expanse of space. "Your actions confuse me."

Young Dominic snorted. "They always did."

The older man shook his head and laid a hand on his son's arm. "That's not true. When you were little we had a lot of fun. You loved to go places with me, talk with me. But after your mother died—"

"You buried yourself in work and never came home."

The accusation pushed the older man back in his seat. He paused, thoughtful. "I did, yes. I buried myself because I couldn't face you and your grandparents, see the look that said if I'd been a better person, your mother would still be alive."

Young Dominic frowned. "It wasn't your fault. I knew that. Mom was different. Different from anyone."

"But—"

Dominic edged closer to his father. "There are no buts. Even as a kid I realized she was fragile. There were times when she was happy, but they didn't last long, and then she was just gone. And you were gone, and Grandma was so angry and every little thing I did was wrong."

A look of understanding brightened his father's features. "You didn't blame me?"

"No. I thought you stayed away because you blamed me, that I wasn't good enough or smart enough. I mean, what kind of mother prefers death over her kid?" Young Dominic raised his shoulders in question.

"You had nothing to do with it," his father insisted. "She loved you, as much as she was able. It was life she hated. She couldn't handle things that came her way."

"I felt like it was my fault."

"I did, too."

The man and boy eyed one another, pondering the words. Dominic broke the silence first. "I can't go to Kessler. I won't. I'll go to counseling or therapy, and I'll join the science team if Miss Moore will still let me…" He flicked a look to Hannah, expectant.

"No guns?"

He flushed. "No. Sorry. That was stupid."

"No argument there." She glanced toward his pocket where a white corner indicated the sheaf of papers. "Do you have something to show your father, Dominic?"

Dominic sighed, withdrew the papers and handed

them over. His father studied the drawings and the specs, an eyebrow upthrust, nodding as he went through them. "This is your work?"

"Yes."

"This is genius. Pure genius." He stared at his son, lofted the papers and surged forward, gathering Dominic into a hug. "This is amazing work. No one did these for you? These are yours?"

Dominic looked a little embarrassed, but quite pleased with the reaction his work inspired. "All mine. They're just sketches, Dad. Kind of rough at that."

"They're brilliant," his father reiterated, passing a hand across the structural image of a conjoined office complex. "You've combined your mother's talent for art and my head for science into something greater than both, and you don't even realize how special that is."

Young Dominic blushed. "It's not special. It's just me."

"It's beyond special," countered his father. He seized the boy and hugged him. "And you are amazing. I've been foolish to this point, Dominic, but I'm not foolish now. You'll stay home with us, I will go to therapy with you—"

Dominic drew back, surprised. "Really?"

"Yes. We're in this together and I should have realized how you felt long ago, but every time I saw the sadness in your eyes…"

"You thought of Mom."

His father acknowledged that, chagrined. "I did, yes."

Young Dominic pointed toward Hannah. "She told me that."

"Miss Moore." Dominic's father pulled Hannah into a hug. The younger man's surprise said his father wasn't much for spontaneous displays of affection. Dominic Senior stepped back, passed a hand across his face and gave her a watery smile. "Thank you. Thank you so much."

Hannah returned his look, fighting tears, but this time they were tears of joy. "You're welcome. And I do believe Dominic mentioned volunteer work at the church. Or perhaps with a charitable foundation in Wellsville?" She sent the teen an arch look. "There are lots of middle school kids who could use science tutors, as well."

He hugged her. "I will. Promise."

"And science team practice is every day at two thirty, my classroom, ninety minutes. Be there."

"Yes."

He went out the door, the older man's arm slung around his shoulders, a poignant end to a rough day. The detective swept them a look, then faced Hannah. "Will they be okay?"

She nodded. "Yes."

He stuck out a hand. "You're some kind of woman, Miss Moore."

Her smile felt hollow. Jeff stood several feet away, his body language saying too much, and who could blame him? She was like that old cartoon character in the Sunday comics, the one that traipsed around with a dark cloud of doom over his head, a disaster waiting to happen.

Only today's disaster had been averted and she thanked God for that.

She turned to face Jeff as the detective headed for the exit. He studied her, his expression tight. "You're okay? Really?"

Except for the knot in her throat, she was fine. Just fine. "Yes."

"I can take you home."

She lifted her keys. "I've got my car."

"And you're okay to drive?"

"The whole four-minute drive?" She ignored his huff of breath and slipped into her jacket. "Yes."

She wasn't okay to do anything, not with his cool, standoffish approach, but she'd been through this before and survived.

She'd get through it again.

A commotion at the door pulled her attention around. Jeff's brother, Matt, burst through, his worried expression sweeping the scene. "You're both all right?"

Jeff moved forward, reached out and clutched Matt's hand, the action surprising Hannah. "Yes, no thanks to me."

Matt shifted his attention from Jeff to Hannah and back. "Pete said you stayed calm and acted as liaison. I think that's pretty solid for a stuffed-shirt executive."

"That's decent praise from a blue-collar handyman."

Matt grinned and shifted his attention to Hannah. "You're really all right? Megan called Dana and Helen with a family alert."

Jeff grabbed his phone, but Matt stopped him. "I called, told them everything was fine. Of course they'll want to see for themselves so you better stop over there. Let them get a look at the hero."

"I'm no hero." Jeff turned and faced Hannah, determined to have his say, wishing she didn't look so sweet, so endearing. "I should never have encouraged you to go back to teaching. Or let my grandmother push you."

Hannah frowned. "You didn't."

Jeff wasn't about to take the easy way out. "I did, because I thought it would be good for you, but now…" He waved a hand around, indicating the library. "After all this…" He paused, sucked in a breath and shrugged. "I'm sorry, Han. So sorry."

Matt stepped back, his hands up. "Private stuff. I get it." He turned Jeff's way. "If the offer to bunk at your place still holds, I could use a decent night's sleep. The bank emailed me that the closing is tomorrow, and I'd like to have a working brain."

Jeff withdrew his key ring and tossed Matt the house key. "Make yourself at home."

"You've made up?" Hannah eyed both men, then turned her attention to Jeff. "You're being nice to your brother?"

He shrugged, hating to make a big deal out of something he should have done long ago. "Family first, right?"

Hannah's smile bloomed. "Yes. Always."

Matt headed toward the door. "See you guys."

Jeff barely noticed, Hannah's smile drawing him closer. "I called you."

She winced. "I know."

"You were avoiding me."

The wince turned into a grimace. "Yes. When I saw you with Callie, and knew you weren't being honest with her…" Her voice trailed off. She shrugged.

Jeff wanted to move closer, but he needed to say this, clear the air. "You assumed I was guilty and shut me out."

She had, but for good reason, right?

One look at Jeff's face said no. "You were feeding Callie a line. We both know that."

Jeff shook his head. "I was *walking* a thin line, yes, because I promised Matt to keep his deal confidential and I'd almost ruined it once. To make amends to my brother, I needed to honor his wishes."

"His deal?" Hannah frowned, not understanding.

"Matt's about to close on Callie's father's subdivision."
Cobbled Creek.

Hannah sighed, chagrined.

"So when I apologized to Matt and promised to stay out of his way—"

"And offered him a place to bunk..."

"Yes. I couldn't exactly be forthright with Callie because the deal is out of our hands and I didn't want to betray Matt." This time he moved closer, his gaze saying something else. Something more. "But mostly I hated to see that disappointment in your eyes."

And that was exactly how she'd felt that night, as if her knight in shining armor fell way short of his horse. She took a step forward, halving their distance. "I'm sorry. I shouldn't have doubted you."

Jeff closed the last little bit of distance, reached out and tipped her chin up. "Faith, hope and love."

She wrinkled her brow.

"From this moment forward I want you to have faith in me and know it's well deserved."

The thought of trusting him seemed amazingly right. "That sounds doable."

He slipped one arm around her waist, drawing her in. "And I want to inspire hope in you, every single day. Hope for today and hope for tomorrow."

Gentle words. Inspirational words. She tilted her head, wanting more. "And love?"

He smiled down at her, his gaze a promise. "That one's easy. I love you, Hannah, and I'll spend every day showing you that if you'll let me. Be my wife. Have my babies. Deal with the sometimes crazy demands of my job. Can you do that, Han?" He swept her lips a gentle kiss that stretched into something deeper, more meaningful as long seconds ticked by. When he finally broke the kiss, he cradled her face between two strong hands, his gaze sincere. "Can you handle the way my job pulls me sometimes, because it's not likely to change."

She met his gaze, leaned up and kissed him back. "Neither is mine, Jeff, so I'll ask you the same thing. Can you handle knowing that I'll be in that classroom day after day? And that sometimes you'll be on diaper duty because I'm doing test prep or science team practice?"

He laughed and hugged her close. "That's what grandmas are for, honey. Haven't you heard?"

The idea of Dana and Helen helping with their future children didn't sound bad at all. "That sounds like some good strategic planning to me."

"Me, too." Jeff settled one more sweet, long kiss to her mouth, then dropped to one knee. "I believe there's a proper way to finalize this deal."

She smiled through watery eyes.

"Will you marry me? Be my wife? Deal with a stuffed-shirt corporate exec for the rest of your days?"

Nothing on God's green earth could make her happier. "Yes. And soon, please. I want to be your wife, savor every moment God gives us."

Jeff grinned, rose and gave her one last kiss before they headed out the door. The rain had gentled to a cool mist, a welcome respite from the earlier torrent. "Then I suggest we head to my mother's, prove we're fine and make her day by letting her take over the details."

Hannah squeezed his hand. "That's perfect, Jeff."

"Of course it is." He grinned, cocky and delightfully self-assured, but also sincere. "And then the scarecrows can move in together and live happily ever after."

Hannah beamed up at him. "That will make Mrs. Scarecrow very happy."

His answering grin said Mrs. Scarecrow wouldn't be the only one. Hannah blushed and ducked into her car. "I'll follow you, okay?"

He leaned in, gave her one last kiss and stepped back, his smile a blessing. "I couldn't ask for anything more, Hannah."

Epilogue

"We don't have to go," Jeff told Hannah the following Fourth of July, his expression reflecting his concern. Having glimpsed her face in the mirror, she didn't have to ask why, but…

No way was she about to stay home.

"Of course we have to go," she told him, grabbing her bag and breathing slowly, hoping the maneuver worked. Sometimes it did, and sometimes, well… "It's the ribbon-cutting ceremony for the Farmers Free Library, the project that—" she stepped closer to him and swiped a gentle hand across the furrowed lines of his brow "—brought us together. We're not going to let a little thing like morning sickness keep us from it."

"Are you sure?" He cupped her cheek with his palm, his gaze intent. "I could go and send your apologies. Everyone would understand."

"Or I can go and stay far away from anything that smells like cooking meat, which shouldn't be a problem this morning. But the Independence Day Festival later…"

"We'll take a pass on," Jeff announced. "You've got your crackers?"

She patted her bag.

"Ginger ale?"

"In the car."

"All right." He grasped her hand as they headed outside, then gently nudged her as they crossed the broad front porch. "You know people talk about us, don't you?"

"As well they should," she quipped, pretending she didn't understand. "We're young, reasonably good-looking professionals, newly married and expecting our first child before the end of the year. We've given them a lot of things to consider."

"I meant them." Jeff pointed to the porch where a family of scarecrows made a cheerful appearance, their broomstick ends thrust into fresh bales of straw. "Shouldn't we put them away until fall?"

Hannah didn't have to feign surprise. "They're dressed appropriately, Jeff. I've seen to that. And I like seeing them there, all cute and funny in their cutoffs and tank tops. That little red-haired boy scarecrow is adorable, isn't he? Do you have any redheads in your family? Because I don't, but I always thought it would be fun to have a red-haired child."

"People think we're weird because scarecrows are a traditional fall decoration."

"People are silly. Farmers use scarecrows all summer long. Why can't we?"

He could have given a laundry list of reasons, but Jeff had learned the valued lesson of picking battles. With Hannah's morning sickness making these last couple of weeks distinctly uncomfortable, he'd let the scarecrow issue slide. He knew their summer garb only made the straw family seem like a bigger oddity to passersby, but if it made Hannah happy...

He sighed, patted her knee and pulled out of the drive, figuring the straw family could become permanent inhabitants as long as Hannah was happy.

They pulled into the already crowded grass lot several minutes later, the early July sun intense despite the morning hour.

"Over here, you two!" Cindy Pendleton, his grandmother's no-nonsense secretary, directed them to the front of the library where a big red, white and blue ribbon marked the holiday and the ceremonial reopening. "We need to get pictures for the paper and you guys are late." One look at Hannah's face had Cindy shrugging an arm of comfort around Hannah's waist. "It gets better, I promise. Usually," she added with her typical candor. "How far along are you?"

"Sixteen weeks."

Cindy nodded. "It should ease up soon. I can't begin to tell you how excited your grandmother is. She's beside herself. Instead of work specs on her desk, I find baby catalogs. Online receipts for the myriad of things she's already ordered."

"She's adorable."

"Mmm-hmm." Cindy sent Hannah a dubious look. "When all this stuff ends up at your door, remember that. I keep reminding her that babies really need two things—a mother and diapers—but she won't hear a thing I'm saying."

"Then I'm glad we've got a four-bedroom house," Jeff cut in. "And storage over the garage."

Cindy placed them strategically with the rest of the fund-raising committee and the local newspaper photographer snapped several pictures. Then they lined up

Helen, Jeff and Hannah to do the ribbon cutting. "Jeff, you do it," Helen insisted. "Hannah and I will flank you."

"Nope." He put the wide scissors into Hannah's hand and stepped aside. "You two do it together. If I'd had my way I wouldn't have been involved in any of this, and it's only your tenacity—" he sent a direct look to his grandmother "—and your courage—" he switched his gaze to his wife "—that got us here. So, ladies, smile for the camera..." They did, Hannah and Helen grasping the scissors together as a local news crew caught the breaking ribbon on camera. "Let's open the doors so people can examine the fruits of their labors."

Clean red brick had replaced worn vinyl siding. The library had nearly tripled in size, and while still small, it now housed the technology of big-city branches on a more minute scale. They moved inside; the new air-conditioning was a delightful respite from the summer sun. Cool drinks and coffee waited in the social room, a gathering spot in the new wing to the west of the building, the entire room paid for by a significant donation from the Fantigrossi family.

And at that very moment, both Dominics strode into the new facility. The professor pumped a few hands on the way, but young Dominic headed straight for Hannah. "Did you read my applications?"

She nodded. "Of course. They were fine, nothing less than I'd expect. And I like how you used your troubled times as your essay in two of them. It makes you sound real and college boards like kids who don't sound manufactured. I added my recommendation letters to each of them."

He grimaced, then smiled. "I was *too* real for a while, that's for sure. But things are better now."

"And your father's doing okay?"

Dominic nodded. "It's been rough since my step-mother left, but yeah. He's doing all right."

"And you?"

He pumped out a breath, glanced around and gave her a firm nod. "I feel normal. I mean, I *think* I feel normal, but it took so long that I'm not even sure what normal is anymore. But I'm definitely doing better."

Hannah had no trouble relating. "I understand completely."

He smiled and it softened his young features. "I knew you would."

A commotion at the door drew their attention. Hannah moved forward as Trent Michaels wheeled Jane Dinsmore into the foyer. Her look of delight downplayed the gravity of her condition. A wig covered the aftereffects of her latest round of chemo. She beamed as Hannah and Jeff approached, then clasped Hannah's hands in hers in a gesture of respect and honor. "I've heard your good news, and while I'm quite fond of babies in the abstract having raised none of my own, I'm hoping you're modern enough to want to teach *and* have a family." She squeezed Hannah's hands lightly. "The proper response to that is a simple *yes*."

Hannah laughed and kissed the older woman's cheek. "Yes. We've got day care all lined up and since my schedule will coincide with the kids' schedules once they get older, it would be silly to stop doing what I love. As a teacher, I get the best of both worlds. A great profession and time with my kids."

"I'm so glad, Hannah. And I wish I'd been here to see that first-place win in the state science championship," Jane added.

Hannah waved toward young Dominic who was now stuffing his face full of cheese and crackers, looking wonderfully normal for a seventeen-year-old. "Dominic shored up our weak physics link. After that, it was a walk in the park."

Jane's smile said she knew better, but she nodded toward Hannah's midsection. "Do we know if it's a boy or girl yet? And have you picked names?"

"Too early to know," Jeff explained. He slipped an arm around Hannah's waist, letting her take the second question.

"If it's a boy, we're going to name him Jonas, after his great-grandfather."

"Lovely." Jane beamed and nodded. "Helen will be so pleased. And if it's a girl?"

Hannah exchanged a smile with Jeff and bent closer. "We'll call her Jane, after you, and we can only hope she'll grow up to be the kind of woman she's named for. Jane Alice Brennan."

Quick tears filled Jane's eyes. "I don't know what to say. I'm overwhelmed."

"Say you'll keep up the good fight so you can be around to see your namesake," Jeff told her. "If it's a girl, of course."

"I will." She nodded, vigorous, dabbing at her eyes with the tissue Hannah provided. "And if it's a boy, I'll just stay healthy enough until we have a girl."

Hannah crouched to Jane's wheelchair level, her smile forthright. "Your job is to get better and see what happens, because this is one experiment we have no control over."

"So we let go and let God," Jane offered, determined.

Hannah felt the warmth of Jeff's hand on her shoulder,

the grace of new life within and the scope of opportunities she'd embraced by being pushed out of her comfort zone less than a year before. She smiled, her heart full, her soul content. "Amen."

* * * * *

Dear Reader,

My son-in-law did a youth ministry stint in Littleton, Colorado. A local host family took him to see Columbine High School, the scene of a heinous attack. Jon's guide told him, "Most of the teachers that were here have gone." That single sentence sent my brain spinning.

Where did they go? What shadows followed them? How do you deal with a conscienceless act that happens on your watch?

And so began *Mended Hearts*, the story of a survivor who regains her hold on normalcy and the man who reminds her of her past. It's a story of redemptive strength, of gathering scattered pieces and realizing Humpty Dumpty can be fixed. It just takes faith, hope, love and time.

Our family has four wonderful high school teachers. I worked for nine years in a segregated classroom with angry middle school kids. Many bore little conscience. My poverty-stricken youth taught me that good teachers do make a difference. Their impact resounds long after that last bell rings. And true teachers are born to teach, intrinsic to their heart and soul.

I hope you love this story of regaining strength and mustering faith, of bold steps forward in the sweet setting of Allegany County, NY, one of God's prettiest places. I love to hear from readers. Your words bless me. Visit me and "the guys" online at www.menofalleganycounty. com or come play with me at "Ruthy's Place," www. ruthysplace.com, where I shamelessly exploit cute kids, pets and recipes because it's, well…fun. You can email me at loganherne@yahoo.com or snail mail me c/o Love

Inspired Books, Harlequin Enterprises, 195 Broadway, 24th floor, New York, NY 10007. God bless you and keep you!

Ruthy

We hope you enjoyed reading
this special collection.

If you liked reading these stories,
then you will love **Love Inspired®** books!

You believe hearts can heal. **Love Inspired**
stories show that faith, forgiveness and hope
have the power to lift spirits and change
lives—always.

Enjoy six new stories from
Love Inspired every month!

Available wherever books and
ebooks are sold.

**Uplifting romances of faith,
forgiveness and hope.**

STEPLI

Get 2 Free Books,
Plus 2 Free Gifts—
just for trying the Reader Service!

Looking for inspiration in tales
of hope, faith and heartfelt romance?

Check out **Love Inspired**®,
Love Inspired® **Suspense** and
Love Inspired® **Historical** books!

New books available every month!

CONNECT WITH US AT:

www.LoveInspired.com

Harlequin.com/Community

 Facebook.com/LoveInspiredBooks

Twitter.com/LoveInspiredBooks

www.ReaderService.com

Love Inspired®

Inspirational Romance to Warm Your Heart and Soul

Join our social communities to connect with other readers who share your love!

Sign up for the Love Inspired newsletter at **www.LoveInspired.com** to be the first to find out about upcoming titles, special promotions and exclusive content.

CONNECT WITH US AT:

Harlequin.com/Community

 Facebook.com/LoveInspiredBooks

Twitter.com/LoveInspiredBks